THE CAMBRIDGE EDITION OF THE WORKS OF F. SCOTT FITZGERALD

The Commodore Hotel, New York City,
April 29, 1920.

Dear Mr. Perkins:

I am sending herewith eleven stories, with my own selection of the seven best for publication in book form. As you will see from the suggested table of contents, I am also sending six poems, three of which drew quite a bit of notice in the Second Book of Princeton Verse. The other three have never been published. All the stories have been published or will be before June 1st. They average about 8000 words.

Beside the title ~~Shortcake~~ *"Flappers and Philosophers"*, here are several others in the order of my choice: (2) We are Seven. (3) Table D 'hote. (4) A La Carte. (5) Journeys and Journey's End. (6) Bittersweet. *(7) Shortcake*

If you think the book would go better without the poems, with more stories, with different stories, in a different arrangement or under a different title it will be O.K. with me.

Sincerely,

F. Scott Fitzgerald.

P.S. I find I have no copy of "The Four Fists" (June, Scribners)

F. Scott Fitzgerald to Maxwell Perkins, 29 April 1920.
Princeton University Library.

FLAPPERS AND PHILOSOPHERS

* * *

F. SCOTT FITZGERALD

Edited by
JAMES L. W. WEST III

CAMBRIDGE
UNIVERSITY PRESS

CAMBRIDGE UNIVERSITY PRESS
Cambridge, New York, Melbourne, Madrid, Cape Town, Singapore, São Paulo, Delhi, Mexico City

Cambridge University Press
The Edinburgh Building, Cambridge CB2 8RU, UK

Published in the United States of America by Cambridge University Press, New York

www.cambridge.org
Information on this title: www.cambridge.org/9780521170437

First published 2000
Paperback edition 2012

Printed in the United Kingdom at the University Press, Cambridge

A catalogue record for this book is available from the British Library

Library of Congress Cataloguing in Publication data

Fitzgerald, F. Scott (Francis Scott), 1896–1940.
Flappers and philosophers / F. Scott Fitzgerald; edited by James L. W. West III.
p. cm. – (The Cambridge edition of the works of F. Scott Fitzgerald)
ISBN 0 521 40236 0
1. United States – Social life and customs – 20th century – Fiction.
I. West, James L. W. II. Title. III. Series: Fitzgerald, F. Scott (Francis Scott), 1896-1940. Works. 1991.
PS3511.I9F54 1999
813 .52 – dc21 98-33300
CIP

ISBN 978-0-521-40236-1 hardback
ISBN 978-0-521-17043-7 paperback

CONTENTS

ACKNOWLEDGMENTS

I wish to extend sincere thanks to Eleanor Lanahan, to Thomas P. Roche, Jr., and to the late Samuel J. Lanahan, Trustees of the F. Scott Fitzgerald Estate, and to Chris Byrne of Harold Ober Associates, Inc. I also wish to thank Andrew Brown and Anne Sanow of Cambridge University Press, and Lindeth Vasey for her helpful advice.

For their assistance with Fitzgerald's papers at Princeton University Library, I am grateful to William L. Joyce, Don C. Skemer, and AnnaLee Pauls. I am also grateful to Nanci A. Young at the Seeley G. Mudd Manuscript Library, Princeton University, and Patrick Scott and Paul Schultz of the Department of Rare Books and Special Collections, Thomas Cooper Library, University of South Carolina. Anne Skillion of the New York Public Library and Judith Ann Schiff of Yale University Archives were helpful with annotations; thanks also to researchers Ken Benson of New York City and Patricia Hammer of Scandia, Minnesota. For special assistance I wish to mention Bert Fink, the Rodgers and Hammerstein Organization, and Angus Fraser, a friend and fellow book historian.

My colleagues Bryant Mangum of Virginia Commonwealth University and Stanley Weintraub of Pennsylvania State University gave useful assistance. For essential support I thank Susan Welch, Dean of the College of the Liberal Arts, Don Bialostosky, Head of the Department of English, and Robert R. Edwards, Director of the Institute for the Arts and Humanistic Studies, Pennsylvania State University. Sue Reighard, Bonny Farmer, and Carl Blake at the Institute also provided welcome help, as did Sheldon Walcher and Gabriel Welsch. My research assistants LaVerne Kennevan Maginnis, Christopher Weinmann, and Flora M. Buckalew were cheerful and diligent, and I am most grateful to them.

The facsimiles for the frontispiece and Illustration 4 are from originals in the Archives of Charles Scribner's Sons and the Papers of F. Scott Fitzgerald; they are reproduced by courtesy of the Manuscripts

Division, Department of Rare Books and Special Collections, Princeton University Library. The facsimile on the back of the dust jacket is from an original in the Matthew J. and Arlyn Bruccoli Collection of F. Scott Fitzgerald and is published by permission of the Thomas Cooper Library, University of South Carolina. Photographs of the St. Paul ice palace and ice fort first appeared in Fred Anderes and Ann Agranoff, *Ice Palaces* (Abbeville Press, 1983). The first photograph in that volume was credited to C. A. Zimmerman, the second to C. P. Gibson. The sheet music cover for "Home James!" is reproduced courtesy of Columbia University, University Archives and Columbiana Library.

J.L.W.W.III

ILLUSTRATIONS

(*Beginning on page* 381.)

INTRODUCTION

1. BACKGROUND

Flappers and Philosophers was F. Scott Fitzgerald's initial encore. He had made a considerable success with his first novel, *This Side of Paradise*, in the spring of 1920. Now his publisher, Charles Scribner's Sons, wanted to follow with a collection of his short stories for the fall season. This pattern of publishing was customary at Scribners: the firm liked to have its authors issue short-story collections soon after they had published novels. In this way author and firm would capitalize on the visibility that the novels had generated. This pattern—novel/collection/novel/collection—is apparent in the careers of several Scribners authors, including Henry James, Edith Wharton, Richard Harding Davis, Rudyard Kipling, Ernest Hemingway, and Thomas Wolfe. Fitzgerald would exhibit the pattern as well, with *This Side of Paradise* (1920) followed by *Flappers and Philosophers* (1920); *The Beautiful and Damned* (1922) by *Tales of the Jazz Age* (1922); *The Great Gatsby* (1925) by *All the Sad Young Men* (1926); and *Tender Is the Night* (1934) by *Taps at Reveille* (1935).

When he assembled the stories for *Flappers and Philosophers*, Fitzgerald was very much in the spotlight. *This Side of Paradise* was making him famous, and his stories, essays, and reviews were appearing in leading periodicals, from *Scribner's Magazine* to the *Smart Set* to the *Saturday Evening Post*. Fitzgerald was learning the literary game—how to tailor his work for the magazine market, how to recycle his writing, how to keep his name visible, and how to maximize his income. He was also considering several new projects, including a semi-autobiographical novel and a plan to produce plot treatments for the movies.

He had already discovered, however, that his most dependable source of income was going to be the large-circulation magazine market. The stories that he wrote for that market could be produced in short bursts of literary energy, could be based on recently observed experience, could be sold quickly through his agent, and would be paid for immediately. In this way short fiction could finance the fast-paced, expensive style of living that he and his new wife, Zelda Sayre, were beginning to pursue.

There were professional motivations as well: short stories allowed Fitzgerald to try out new characters, themes, and situations that he might later rework for his novels, and they imposed a kind of discipline on him, bringing him regularly to his writing table. The stories also gave Fitzgerald access to his largest audiences, especially when he published in the *Post* and other mass-circulation "slicks"—so called because they were printed on glossy, coated paper. Fitzgerald had things that he wished to say to readers, and he wanted a large hearing. He was an entertainer, but he was also a moralist and chronicler, and he needed a forum, a public platform from which to speak to his constituency. Magazines provided that venue.

Fitzgerald had begun teaching himself to write for the magazine market during the winter and spring of 1919. He had been living in New York, working as a copywriter at an advertising agency and attempting to produce short fiction on the side. Most of his efforts that winter and spring had misfired, earning him a pile of rejection slips, but by trial and error he had learned the mechanics of popular fiction writing. Once *This Side of Paradise* had been accepted by Scribners in the fall of 1919, he had put his new skills to immediate use, placing eleven stories in top magazines and (after paying his agent's commission) collecting nearly $3,000 for his efforts—very good money in 1919 and 1920.[1] Most of these narratives were between 7,000 and 8,000 words in length, loosely organized and structured in scenes. They had chronological plots, amusing dialogue, and sharply rendered passages of observation; many ended with clever twists. These stories had served their initial purpose: now, for *Flappers and Philosophers*, Fitzgerald needed to decide which ones he wished to put between cloth covers. This collection of stories, he

[1] See Appendix 4 for composition and publication dates and earnings from the stories.

knew, would go onto the shelves of libraries and would find its way to the bedside tables of readers who had liked *This Side of Paradise*. These would be the stories for which he would be remembered.

2. STORIES AND TITLE

The surviving correspondence between Fitzgerald and Maxwell Perkins, his editor at Scribners, shows that Fitzgerald was curious early on about the earning potential of a gathering of his short fiction. As early as January 1920, while correcting proofs for *This Side of Paradise*, Fitzgerald asked Perkins in a letter: "There's nothing in collections of short stories is there?" Perkins answered a week later with cautious optimism: "It is generally true that collections of them do not constitute selling books," he wrote, "but there are exceptions." Fitzgerald's stories, Perkins thought, would probably be such an exception: "They have the popular note which would be likely to make them sell in book form," he wrote. A few lines later in the same letter, Perkins added two other important thoughts: "They have great value in making you a reputation," he said, and "they are quite worthwhile in themselves."[2]

In late April 1920, less than a month after formal publication of *This Side of Paradise*, Fitzgerald assembled the materials from which his first collection would be formed. He sent the stories to Perkins with a cover letter in which he suggested several titles for the collection as a whole:

The Commodore Hotel, New York City,
April 29, 1920.

Dear Mr. Perkins:

I am sending herewith eleven stories, with my own selection of the seven best for publication in book form. As you will see from the suggested table of contents, I am also sending six poems, three of which drew quite a bit of

[2]The letters, dated ca. 10 January 1920 and 17 January 1920, are published in *Dear Scott/Dear Max: The Fitzgerald–Perkins Correspondence*, ed. John Kuehl and Jackson R. Bryer (New York: Scribners, 1971): 24–26.

notice in the *Second Book of Princeton Verse*. The other three have never been published. All the stories have been published or will be before June 1st. They average about 8000 words.

Flappers + Philosophers

Beside the title ~~*Short-Cake*~~, here are several others in the order of my choice: (2) We are Seven. (3) Table D 'hote. (4) A La Carte. (5) Journeys and Journey's End. (6) Bittersweet. (7) Short Cake

If you think the book would go better without the poems, with more stories, with different stories, in a different arrangement or under a different title it will be O.K. with me.

Sincerely,
F. Scott Fitzgerald.[3]

P.S. I find I have no copy of "The Four Fists"
(June, Scribners)

The letter is revealing. Perhaps most interesting is the fact that Fitzgerald conceived initially of this collection as a mixture of poetry and prose, perhaps thinking that he might intersperse the six poems between the seven stories he had chosen as his best. Such a mixing of literary forms was logical, since *This Side of Paradise*, though technically a novel, was in fact an experimental book made up of fiction, poetry, and long passages of drama dialogue. At this point in his development, Fitzgerald thought of himself as both a fiction writer and a poet—though, in fact, he would publish little poetry during the rest of his career. Had Fitzgerald followed through on this initial plan, he would have published a book generically akin to Ernest Hemingway's *In Our Time* (1925), with its stories and interchapters. He might also have written more poetry in future years—though one can only speculate about such a matter. In the event, however, no poetry was included in the published volume. Nothing in the correspondence between Fitzgerald and Perkins suggests when or why this decision was made, or who made it. Fitzgerald was in New

[3] As the facsimile in the frontispiece to this volume shows, Fitzgerald's original first choice for a title was *Short-Cake*. He deleted that title from its position in the letter and added "Flappers + Philosophers" in pencil, then moved "Short Cake" to position seven among the possible titles. The postscript was also added by Fitzgerald in pencil.

York frequently during the spring and summer of 1920, and he and Perkins exchanged only a few letters. They saw each other instead at the Scribners offices at 597 Fifth Avenue; perhaps in their talks they decided that the poetry might make the collection look too literary or that the poems were not up to the level of the stories—or perhaps Perkins, ever so kindly, simply said no.

The 29 April letter also gives interesting hints about the selection of a title for the collection as a whole, especially when the original document is viewed in facsimile (see frontispiece). Fitzgerald's original first choice, "Short-Cake," emphasizes the varied contents of the book—like the flour, sugar, butter, salt, and other ingredients of the traditional shortcake. The third and fourth possibilities carry forward the metaphor of food, suggesting a selection of dishes. The sixth, "Bittersweet," indicates a mixture of emotions and styles. All of the possibilities are appropriate for a collection that would show great variety, from clever entertainments such as "The Offshore Pirate" and "Head and Shoulders" to carefully rendered pieces of social observation such as "The Ice Palace" and "Bernice Bobs Her Hair" to didactic stories such as "Dalyrimple Goes Wrong" and "The Four Fists."

The final choice for the title, *Flappers and Philosophers*, added to the letter in Fitzgerald's hand, was apparently suggested to him by Edward L. Burlingame, one of the senior editors at Scribners. The title, taken from an advertising slogan used by the firm for *This Side of Paradise* ("A book about flappers, written for philosophers!") captures the dual nature of Fitzgerald's collection—and indeed of much of his writing then and later. Some of the stories were light tales of youth and love; others were more serious studies of manners and society; the best were blends of the two elements.

The eleven stories that Fitzgerald sent to Perkins included seven that eventually did appear in *Flappers and Philosophers*. These were "The Offshore Pirate," *Saturday Evening Post* 192 (29 May 1920); "The Ice Palace," *Saturday Evening Post* 192 (22 May 1920); "Head and Shoulders," *Saturday Evening Post* 192 (21 February 1920); "The Cut-Glass Bowl," *Scribner's Magazine* 67 (May 1920); "Bernice Bobs Her Hair," *Saturday Evening Post* 192 (1 May 1920); "Benediction," *Smart Set* 61 (February 1920); and "Dalyrimple

Goes Wrong," *Smart Set* 61 (February 1920). "The Four Fists," the eighth and final story in the collection, appeared in *Scribner's Magazine* 67 (June 1920)—as Fitzgerald notes in his postscript.

The other three stories sent to Perkins were probably "Myra Meets His Family," *Saturday Evening Post* 192 (20 March 1920); "The Camel's Back," *Saturday Evening Post* 192 (24 April 1920); and "The Smilers," *Smart Set* 62 (June 1920). "The Camel's Back" was eventually republished in *Tales of the Jazz Age*, Fitzgerald's second short-story collection. "Myra Meets His Family" and "The Smilers" were not collected during his lifetime—but are included in the present edition. The three poems that Fitzgerald mentioned as having appeared in *A Book of Princeton Verse II* (Oxford University Press, 1919) were "Marching Streets," "The Pope at Confession," and "My First Love," all published earlier in the *Nassau Literary Magazine*, the undergraduate literary journal at Princeton.[4] The other three poems have not been identified.

Fitzgerald probably sent Perkins a mixture of tearsheets (printed texts torn from the magazine issues in which they had appeared) and carbon typescripts (for stories that had not yet seen print). No manuscripts or typescripts for the stories in the 1920 *Flappers and Philosophers* are known to survive, but by collating the texts in the Scribners collection against their original serial appearances one can uncover (among other things) the changes that Fitzgerald introduced in the setting copies that he sent to Perkins, and in the proofs that he saw during the first three weeks of June.[5] Such collations disclose that he revised three of the stories fairly heavily ("The Offshore Pirate," "The Ice Palace," and "Head and Shoulders"), that he gave a light polishing to four others ("Bernice Bobs Her Hair," "Benediction," "Dalyrimple Goes Wrong," and "The Four Fists"), and that he made almost no changes in the remaining story ("The Cut-Glass Bowl"). When he was able to do so, Fitzgerald was a

[4]The three published poems are available in *F. Scott Fitzgerald in His Own Time: A Miscellany*, ed. Matthew J. Bruccoli and Jackson R. Bryer (Kent, Ohio: Kent State University Press, 1971).

[5]The letters that document the sending and reading of galley and page proof are in the Scribner Archive at Princeton, dated 18 May, 1 June, and 18 June 1920.

diligent and attentive reviser of his short fiction, nearly always introducing improvements between magazine and book publication. Examination of his changes, as recorded in the textual apparatus of this volume, allows us to observe this process—to look over his shoulder as he revised his stories and made them ready for their second outing.[6]

3. ADDITIONAL WRITINGS

This Cambridge volume includes not only the eight narratives in the original Scribners collection but six other pieces as well—five additional short stories and a one-act play. For this expanded collection one must interpret the term "stories" loosely in order to admit "The Debutante," a play published by Fitzgerald in *Smart Set*, November 1919. In commercial terms "The Debutante," like the stories, was a magazine piece. And Fitzgerald himself would include two drama scripts—"Porcelain and Pink" and "Mr. Icky"—in his next short-fiction collection, *Tales of the Jazz Age*. The mixing of forms in this volume therefore seems justified.

These additional items were all published by Fitzgerald in commercial magazines between the appearance of "Babes in the Woods" (*Smart Set*, September 1919), his first professional publication, and "Two for a Cent" (*Metropolitan Magazine*, April 1922), the last uncollected story to appear before formal publication of *Tales of the Jazz Age* on 22 September 1922. (The other stories published during this period were collected by Fitzgerald in *Tales*.) Thus the reader has in this edition not only the stories that Fitzgerald and Perkins thought worthy of hardbound publication, but also those which for one reason or another they rejected, plus two others omitted from *Tales of the Jazz Age*.

[6] For study of origins and composition, one should know also that "Benediction" derives from an earlier story entitled "The Ordeal," published in the *Nassau Literary Magazine* for June 1915, and collected in *The Apprentice Fiction of F. Scott Fitzgerald, 1907–1917*, ed. John Kuehl (New Brunswick, N.J.: Rutgers University Press, 1965).

Fitzgerald could not have republished "Babes in the Woods" or "The Debutante" in *Flappers and Philosophers* because he had already included versions of them in *This Side of Paradise*.[7] Earlier versions of both had also been published in the *Nassau Lit* in January and May 1917. By changing characters' names, revising the texts, and adding description and dialogue, Fitzgerald had incorporated the two into *This Side of Paradise*. These revisions and augmentations are so extensive as to make all of the separate versions—*Nassau Lit*, *Smart Set*, and *This Side of Paradise*—into distinct works of literature. The *Smart Set* texts are included in the present volume because they are individual literary entities and because they were Fitzgerald's first two professional appearances in print—indeed, the only acceptances that he had during his apprentice period in New York during the winter and spring of 1919.

The remaining additional stories show Fitzgerald as a professional, a writer who made his living with his pen. Some are marred by artificial plotting and surprise endings, but even the least impressive efforts—"The Smilers" (*Smart Set*, June 1920) and "Two for a Cent"—contain passages of excellent prose. "Myra Meets His Family" (*Saturday Evening Post*, 20 March 1920) is a top-caliber magazine story; "The Popular Girl" (*Saturday Evening Post*, in two parts, 11 and 18 February 1922) just misses being a masterpiece.

4. EDITORIAL PRINCIPLES

The texts included in this Cambridge edition can be divided editorially into three groups: the eight stories that appeared in the 1920 Scribners edition of *Flappers and Philosophers*; the two *Smart Set* texts "Babes in the Woods" and "The Debutante"; and the four remaining stories, uncollected during Fitzgerald's lifetime but

[7] The play in the *Smart Set* was entitled "The Débutanté"—(incorrectly, with two acute *e*s). Fitzgerald did not use the acute first *e* when he wrote the word in holograph, probably because, like most Americans, he did not pronounce the word that way. The acute *e* has been omitted in the title of the play for its republication in this volume. The two acute *e*s will not be given whenever the story is referred to in its *Smart Set* incarnation.

republished in posthumous collections. These groups will be dealt with separately in the textual commentary that follows.

Original Stories:

The situation for the eight narratives in the Scribners *Flappers and Philosophers* is straightforward. No manuscript, typescript, or proof for any one of the stories appears to survive. An editor must therefore work with serial versions and with the Scribners texts. The procedure for establishing the texts of these eight stories has been relatively simple. The serial versions have been collated against the collected texts; all variants, substantive and accidental, have been recorded. No copy-text has been declared: the editor has instead followed the principles outlined in G. Thomas Tanselle's "Editing without a Copy-Text" (*Studies in Bibliography*, 47 [1994]: 1–22).[8]

The serial and collected versions are considered to have equal authority—the serial texts because they are closer to Fitzgerald's holograph, the collected texts because they contain Fitzgerald's late revisions and because he saw proof for them, as he often did not for magazine appearances. Where the texts vary, the editor has incorporated the readings judged to be authorial. These choices have been recorded in the apparatus of this volume.

The process of making selections amongst substantives has not been difficult. None of the substantive variants (changes in actual wording) between the serial and book texts appears to result in any way from editorial tampering at Scribners. This is not surprising, since Maxwell Perkins was not an aggressive line editor. In fact he was largely indifferent to such matters, rarely making verbal changes in the writings of his authors and confining himself to general suggestions concerning plot, structure, character, and theme. Nearly all of the substantive changes in the Scribners texts are incorporated into the texts of this Cambridge edition; the readings from the serial

[8] For a more extended discussion of the applicability of Tanselle's thinking to Fitzgerald's texts, see the Cambridge edition of *This Side of Paradise*, ed. James L. W. West III (Cambridge University Press, 1995): xl–xliv.

texts are given in the apparatus. The only exceptions are obvious typos and sophistications: see the entries at 25.29, 168.3, 221.5, and 261.26.

The subsequent history of the Scribners text is quickly told. The first impression of *Flappers and Philosophers* was formally published on 10 September 1920 in a press run of 5,000 copies. The book was priced at $1.75; the dust jacket illustration was by W. E. Hill. The edition was reprinted five times, in September 1920 (3,000 copies), October 1920 (3,025 copies), December 1920 (2,000 copies), December 1921 (1,300 copies), and November 1922 (1,000 copies). Machine collation has uncovered one plate variant: the word "panoply" has been changed to "panorama" at 152.23 of the original edition; Fitzgerald ordered the change in a 12 August 1920 letter to Edward L. Burlingame, a senior editor at Scribners. The reading appeared first in the fourth printing, December 1920. It is accepted for this edition (106.7).

Accidentals for the original eight stories are a more complicated matter. There is little accidental variation between the serial and book texts of the two stories that had appeared in *Scribner's Magazine* ("The Cut-Glass Bowl" and "The Four Fists"), probably because the Scribners house style in capitalization, spelling, and word division had already been imposed by the magazine. But the variation in accidentals between the serial texts from other magazines and the first-edition texts is heavy. It is likely that neither set of accidentals—serial or book—is an accurate reflection of the way Fitzgerald's original holographs read, or of the accidentals in the typescripts that he submitted to magazines. Each magazine imposed its own style of pointing and word division; the Scribners style, for example, in both magazine and book texts, was heavily anglicized. The house styles for the *Saturday Evening Post* and the *Smart Set* were equally distinctive. Further, to judge from the patterns of variation in the six stories that came from those two magazines, the Scribners copy editors and compositors for the book texts seem to have added a further overlay of commas to Fitzgerald's prose.

Fitzgerald's surviving manuscripts of the period—especially the holograph of *This Side of Paradise*—exhibit much more free and open punctuation than any of the systems—serial or book—in the published stories. Fitzgerald usually did not place a comma between two adjectives of equal weight, for example, nor did he customarily use a comma before the last element in a series. In the majority of cases he did not place a comma before the conjunction in a compound sentence, though he was not consistent in this habit. He punctuated by ear—a very fine ear—and not by formal rule. When the texts for the original eight stories vary in punctuation between serial and book, the editor has therefore chosen the reading that appears closer to Fitzgerald's style in his surviving early manuscripts. Sometimes neither choice reflects Fitzgerald's most common practice, but no effort has been made to create an artificial system of pointing typical of Fitzgerald's writing and then to impose it on these texts. To do so would involve heavy repunctuation and would, in fact, only be to impose a new house style on the narratives. All decisions are recorded in the apparatus.

"Babes in the Woods" and "The Debutante":

Editorial problems for "Babes" and "The Debutante" are fairly complex. Neither *Smart Set* text has ever been reprinted, so there are no collations between published versions to perform. But prepublication material survives for both pieces in Fitzgerald's papers at Princeton.

A partial holograph of the *Nassau Lit* "Babes" is extant, as are five typescript sheets of the version of the narrative that Fitzgerald included in "The Romantic Egotist," the ur-version of *This Side of Paradise.*[9] The surviving partial holograph of "Babes" is a draft of the *Nassau Lit* version. This holograph (and the *Nassau Lit* text) are so different from the *Smart Set* version, however, as to be uncollatable. The holograph text, however, does possess the authority of Fitzgerald's hand and has therefore been used as a source to resolve a few questions of accidental texture in the *Smart Set* text. Such cases are noted in the record of variants for the story.

[9] These documents are reproduced in *F. Scott Fitzgerald Manuscripts*, ed. Matthew J. Bruccoli, vol. 1, pt. 1, and vol. 6, pt. 1 (New York: Garland, 1990 and 1991).

The five sheets from the typescript of "The Romantic Egotist" were incorporated into the manuscript of *This Side of Paradise* and preserve—in the *typed* characters—a version of "Babes" that predates the *Smart Set* text. (The remainder of the section in the *This Side of Paradise* manuscript was inscribed in fresh holograph and postdates the *Smart Set* version.) These five typescript sheets—numbered 197–198, 201, 206–207—have been consulted on matters of accidental texture, though their authority is not as strong as that of the incomplete holograph since they were not prepared by Fitzgerald, who could not type.

For "The Debutante" there survives a nearly complete carbon typescript of the setting copy for the *Smart Set* version, this typescript later revised by Fitzgerald and incorporated into the manuscript of *This Side of Paradise* as leaves 389–390, 394, and 395–408.[10] Here the authority for accidentals is stronger, since this carbon preserves the text as it was submitted to the *Smart Set*—minus, of course, any handwritten changes that Fitzgerald might have added to the ribbon copy that he sent to the magazine.[11] Collation of the typed text with the *Smart Set* text reveals significant variation in accidentals; though typed carbons do not carry the authority of holograph drafts, this one is still quite useful. It has served as a source for adjusting the texture of accidentals in the text published here.

Posthumous Reprints:

The remaining four stories in this Cambridge volume were not chosen by Fitzgerald for inclusion in any of the four short-fiction collections that he published during his lifetime. No manuscript or typescript versions of these narratives appear to survive. All were collected posthumously: "The Popular Girl" was republished in *Bits of Paradise: 21 Uncollected Stories by F. Scott and Zelda Fitzgerald*, issued first in London in 1973 by Bodley Head, then reprinted in a

[10] Reproduced in ibid., vol. 1, pt. 2.

[11] In substantive readings this carbon is a near match for the *Smart Set* version, and Fitzgerald's address in New York City for the winter and spring of 1919 is typed on the first leaf, upper left corner.

photo-offset reissue by Scribners in New York in 1974. "Myra Meets His Family," "The Smilers," and "Two for a Cent" were included in *The Price Was High: The Last Uncollected Stories of F. Scott Fitzgerald*, published in New York by Harcourt Brace Jovanovich in 1979.

Textual adjustments in these posthumous collections were minimal. Obvious typos were corrected; some punctuation reflecting Fitzgerald's known preferences was imposed. *Bits of Paradise*, typeset in England, exhibits a modified British system of pointing for "The Popular Girl." The alterations in the serial texts republished in *Bits* were listed in Linda Berry, "The Text of *Bits of Paradise*," *Fitzgerald/Hemingway Annual* 1975: 141–145. No similar record for *The Price Was High* was published, though a copy of the volume with misprints marked in it is in the Fitzgerald Collection at the Thomas Cooper Library, University of South Carolina. None of these misprints occurs in a story collected in the present volume.

One variant, in "Two for a Cent," deserves mention. For the republished text in *The Price Was High*, a passage of forty-one words was cut, likely because of racial overtones in the lines spoken by the character Abercrombie. The excision was acknowledged in an asterisked footnote. The cut passage is restored for the Cambridge text (314.29–32); readers should recognize that the words are uttered by a sour, disillusioned character, not by the author of the story.

British Texts:

Nine of the narratives in this volume appeared in British periodicals during Fitzgerald's lifetime. The British edition of *Smart Set* reprinted "Babes in the Woods" (September 1919), "The Debutante" (November 1919), "Benediction" (February 1920), and "The Smilers" (June 1920). "Head and Shoulders" was republished as "Topsy Turvy" in *Yellow Magazine* (March 1922); "Myra Meets His Family" in *Sovereign* (July 1921); "Bernice Bobs Her Hair" in *20 Story Magazine* (May 1921); "The Offshore Pirate" in *Sovereign* (February 1922); and "Two for a Cent" in *Argosy* (April 1933). Some accidentals in these appearances were changed to reflect British conventions of punctuation, capitalization, and word division; collation reveals no accidental or substantive variants that can be considered authorial.[12]

In fact, Fitzgerald seems to have had virtually no control over some of these British texts. "Bernice Bobs Her Hair," for example, was completely recast as a British story: Bernice becomes a girl from Nottingham visiting her sophisticated cousin in London; U.S. slang ("Splush!") becomes English slang ("Rubbish!"); and the conclusion of the story is changed entirely, with Bernice winning the love of Warren in a saccharine ending concocted by the British editors. Similar wholesale rewriting was done for "The Offshore Pirate" and "Head and Shoulders." No substantive changes were introduced in "Two for a Cent." No readings from these British serial texts, accidental or substantive, have been accepted for the Cambridge text.

The clothbound British edition of *Flappers and Philosophers* was published by W. Collins Sons & Co., Ltd., on 23 March 1922. The same eight stories from the American text appear in the British edition, but in a different order: "The Offshore Pirate," "The Four Fists," "Dalyrimple Goes Wrong," "Head and Shoulders," "The Ice Palace," "The Cut-Glass Bowl," "Bernice Bobs Her Hair," and "Benediction." No letter or other document has been found in the Scribner Archive, or elsewhere, to indicate that Fitzgerald requested this order; likely it was imposed by Collins.

There does survive in the Scribner Archive an unpublished letter from Fitzgerald to Perkins, not dated but written in January 1922. In this letter Fitzgerald suggests a change in the British *Flappers*

[12]The four *Smart Set* stories were reset almost line-for-line by the British compositors, and in a nearly identical typeface, so that to a superficial inspection they appear to have been reprinted from the U.S. typesettings; but they are in fact freshly composed. No substantive changes were introduced in "Babes in the Woods." In "The Debutante," the word "chiffonier," presumably unfamiliar to the British copy editor, was cut or changed to "chest of drawers" (198.22, 214.9, and 217.27 of the Cambridge text); "homely" at 226.6 was altered to "plain." The only substantive change in "Benediction" for the British *Smart Set* was "monkery" (143.9) to "monastery." In "The Smilers," the humorous but obscure reading "as an oil-baron's undershirt affects a cow's husband" (254.12) becomes the more prosaic "as a red flag affects a bull."

and Philosophers, telling Perkins that he wishes to substitute "The Camel's Back" for "The Four Fists." "Suppose I send it to him [Collins] + let him decide," Fitzgerald writes. Then he adds, "I hope to God his copy of *Flappers* had that ghastly error of mine corrected, the 'let it lay' in *The Ice Palace*. Had I better write them?"

Either Fitzgerald did not follow through and communicate with the British publisher, or the editors at Collins decided against the story substitution. "The Camel's Back" was not published in place of "The Four Fists" in the British text, nor was the erroneous "lay" for "lie"—on page 50 of the American text—corrected by the Collins typesetters. (The mistake is mended in the Cambridge text at 37.13.) This evidence, together with the uncertain tone of Fitzgerald's letter, make a weak case for the story substitution; it is therefore not introduced in the Cambridge edition. Practically, one would have difficulty making the switch, since "The Camel's Back" would shortly be included by Fitzgerald in both the American and British editions of *Tales of the Jazz Age*, his next story collection. "The Camel's Back" will accordingly be published in the Cambridge edition of *Tales*.

There were other alterations in the text of the British *Flappers and Philosophers*, however. In addition to accidental restyling, the following substantive changes were made (page and line references are to the Cambridge edition):

56.21	muddled [muffled
56.36	white, of brown and yellow [white, brown, and yellow
62.24|25	clear-|cut [clean|cut
68.9	leaning [looking
106.7	panoply [panorama
168.5	older [elder
178.28	squared off [squared up

Fitzgerald had Scribners send a list of corrections to Collins for the British edition of *This Side of Paradise*.[13] That fact, plus the presence of the "panoply [panorama" variant, which was ordered

[13] See the Cambridge *This Side of Paradise*: xxxvii–viii.

by Fitzgerald in the U.S. text, suggests either that he or Scribners sent that single change to Collins for *Flappers and Philosophers*, or (more likely) that Collins set type from a copy of the Scribners fourth or fifth impression, since both contain the "panorama" reading. The presence of this reading might also suggest that some or all of the other six substantive variants in the Collins edition were sent over by Fitzgerald.

In the editor's judgment, however, none of the six is authorial. The readings at 56.36 and 168.5 are typical of the smoothing work of a copy editor. The word "clean" on page 62 is a typographical error. The word "muffled" on page 56 is wrong for the wild sounds in the echoing hall of ice in "The Ice Palace"; "muffled" is likely a typo for the more appropriate "muddled" in the U.S. text. The change to "looking" on page 68 seems incorrect: it is a "form" that Marcia (in "Head and Shoulders") sees "leaning" over the bannister, not "looking" over, since "forms" do not properly "look" at anything. And the alteration on page 178 is a substituted British usage. All are rejected; the discussion here serves as a record of the decisions; none of the variants is included in the apparatus.

Factual Errors:

It is unwise to attempt to make Fitzgerald's fictional texts conform entirely to reality. Errors in proper names and places have been corrected in this text, and the emendations recorded in the apparatus, but other irregularities have been allowed to stand. An example of the difficulty of attempting to make a story congruent with factual reality occurs in "Head and Shoulders." Horace Tarbox sees Marcia Meadow in a musical play at the Shubert Theatre in New Haven, Connecticut—entirely plausible since Horace is a philosophy student at Yale, and since plays headed for Broadway often received out-of-town tryouts at the Shubert. But the production in which he sees her—"Home James!"—was in fact the 1917 Varsity Show from Columbia University, written by a young Oscar Hammerstein II and his friend Herman Axelrod. Their play had been performed in New York, at the Hotel Astor, in March 1917, where Fitzgerald likely saw it. After the play, Horace and Marcia have a meal at a restaurant that might be in New Haven or might be in New York City (see the explanatory notes at 62.10 and 69.14). It would be impossible to adjust the scene by emendation; in any case such adjustment is not necessary. Fitzgerald was wholly within his rights as a storyteller to amuse himself by scrambling productions, theaters, restaurants, and cities. In fact, the song that Marcia sings in the play is one that Fitzgerald himself wrote and put into his one-act play "Porcelain and Pink" (*Smart Set*, Jan. 1920). See the explanatory note at 62.11.

Cruxes:

In a 12 August 1920 letter to Edward Burlingame, Fitzgerald asked for two changes in the text of *Flappers and Philosophers*. One was the alteration of "panoply" to "panorama" mentioned earlier and introduced in the plates for the fourth impression. The other was a request to change the spelling of a character's name: "Kieth" to "Keith" in "Benediction." Burlingame wrote back to Fitzgerald on 17 August, saying that the first printing was finished, but implying that he would have "panorama" introduced into a later impression. "I don't believe," added Burlingame, "that the spelling of 'Kieth' makes so much difference." He did not add, but could have, that alteration of all occurrences of "Kieth" in the already-cast printing plates would have been troublesome and expensive. Those changes were never made; all printings of *Flappers and Philosophers* read "Kieth" throughout. For the Cambridge edition the change in spelling has been introduced. Fitzgerald was careful about such things: witness the spelling Wolfshiem (not Wolfsheim) in *The Great Gatsby*.[14]

The tearsheets of "Two for a Cent" that Fitzgerald kept in his files, and that are today a part of his papers at Princeton, record

[14] See the Cambridge edition of *The Great Gatsby* (Cambridge University Press, 1991): liv and 148, entry 55.20.

three emendations in his hand—keyed here to the Cambridge text by page and line:

309.4	1910 [nineteen-ten
309.6	dismounted [fell off
323.21	life [life I was just about to enlist in the Army.

When or why Fitzgerald inscribed these three changes is not known, but perhaps he contemplated including "Two for a Cent" in *Tales of the Jazz Age* or reprinting it in some other form. The three changes should therefore be considered for admission into the text of this volume.

The first, however, is a matter of styling: years in the texts of this volume are given in numerals, so the change to "nineteen-ten" is not incorporated. The second revision, from "dismounted" to "fell off," is adopted. The third alteration presents a problem. Fitzgerald apparently wished to introduce the fact that Abercrombie was going to join the army a little earlier in the story, probably to prepare the reader for Abercrombie's presence in the line at the recruiting depot two paragraphs later. But the added sentence—"I was just about to enlist in the Army."—repeats six words of a sentence just a few lines below: "But you see, I was standing in line with a lot of other young fellows down by the Union Depot about to enlist in the army for three years." The repetition is quite noticeable and is uncharacteristic of Fitzgerald. One assumes that he did not remark it when he added the earlier sentence. And this sentence is not necessary for the plot of the story; further, it appears to have been added hastily by Fitzgerald, without adjusting the surrounding punctuation or wording of the rest of the text. For these reasons the added sentence has not been incorporated into the reading text of this edition.

The most interesting crux has been revealed by collating the *Metropolitan Magazine* text of "Two for a Cent" with the reset text of the narrative in *The Best Short Stories of 1922*. This collection, part of an annual series edited by Edward J. O'Brien, was published in 1923 by the Boston firm of Small, Maynard & Co. The accidentals in this story were reworked, probably by a copy editor of schoolmarmish disposition, and have been judged to have no authority. No list of the variants is given in the apparatus, though a record has been put on file at Princeton.

The single substantive variant in the *Best Short Stories* text, however, is of interest. The phrase "The Alabama night," which begins the last paragraph of the story in the *Metropolitan* text—the only geographical reference in the entire narrative—has been changed to "The Georgia night." It is unlikely that a copy editor or the anthologist O'Brien would have made such a change independently. More probably the alteration was requested by Fitzgerald. Because the story pictures the American South as backward and benighted, it might have offended Zelda Sayre, who was a native of Alabama, or might have drawn criticism from a member of her family or social circle in Montgomery, her home city. Fitzgerald could have changed "Alabama" to "Georgia" on the magazine tearsheets that went to O'Brien or might have sent him a message requesting the revision. The likelihood is that the alteration is authorial; it is incorporated into the Cambridge text. Adoption of the reading "Georgia" obscures the origins of the story slightly—Fitzgerald almost certainly drew on his experiences in Montgomery in writing the narrative—but those origins are made clear in this commentary.

The variant is also of interest because it complicates a little Fitzgerald's attitude toward the South. Usually that attitude is romanticized, with "The Ice Palace" cited as convincing evidence. It is worth having "Two for a Cent," now with its Georgia setting, republished in the Cambridge edition with "The Ice Palace." The lesser story serves as a counterweight to the more famous one.

Regularized Features:

Fitzgerald was inconsistent about word division, but analysis of his manuscripts does yield preferences for many compound words ("anybody," for example, or "good-bye" or "worth while"). These usages have been regularized in the text; blanket emendations are given in the apparatus. Fitzgerald normally used U.S. spellings, but he preferred British orthography for a few words: "glamour," "grey," "biasses," and "theatre," for instance. These spellings are accepted for this volume. Variant slang spellings ("floppity"/"floppidy") are retained.

Also made consistent are certain features of typography that Fitzgerald nearly always followed: he reserved italics for emphasis and liked to enclose names of ships, titles of books, and names of other major literary works within quotation marks; he sometimes capitalized words for emphasis ("Oh Yeah!"); he capitalized adjectives such as "Northern" and "Southern" to refer to particular areas of the United States. In the texts of the additional writings, all of which are taken from magazine appearances, breaks indicated by roman numerals are retained. Nonstructural breaks (usually signaled by extra space and a display cap) are removed.

The following features have also been regularized, as they were in the Cambridge *This Side of Paradise* (1995): names of seasons are lowercase; dashes within sentences are one em in length; dashes that end sentences (usually indicating interrupted dialogue) are two ems in length; years are given in arabic numerals; three ellipsis points appear within sentences, four at the ends of sentences; the numbers of avenues in New York City are spelled out, but cross-streets are given in arabic numerals; "Mother" and "Father" as proper names are capitalized.

5. RATIONALE FOR INCLUSIVENESS

Fitzgerald did not wish for his weaker stories to be republished. He culled their texts for good descriptive sentences and phrases, underlining these passages on tearsheets and usually recopying them in his notebooks for possible reuse later in his novels. Then, in his ledger, a professional record of his publications and earnings, he wrote: "*Stripped and permanently buried*" as an epitaph for the story. If he preserved tearsheets in his personal files, he often wrote this legend across the top of the first page: "*Positively not to be republished in any Form!*" An example—the first page of the tearsheets he kept for "The Smilers"—is reproduced as Illustration 4 in this volume.

The directions are unambiguous. Fitzgerald did not want these stories to be reissued. His admonitions in his ledger and on his tearsheets might have been written partly to himself, lest he be tempted to reprint less than his best work, but they seem more probably to have been addressed to future literary executors and editors. It is therefore worth while to state the rationale by which such lesser efforts have been included in this volume, and by which similar stories will be republished in forthcoming volumes of this edition—though always in separate sections or entirely separate volumes, apart from the stories that Fitzgerald chose for his own collections.

The Cambridge Edition of the Works of F. Scott Fitzgerald is a collected edition, an *omnium gatherum*. One of its chief purposes is to make available in one series all of Fitzgerald's published writings. Only in this way can scholars and teachers fully study his career and work; the strongest stories and essays must be seen in company with the others. The result, it should be said, will be to demonstrate that Fitzgerald wrote consistently at a high level and that all of his narratives contain characters, descriptions, and insights that reveal the sharpness of his eye and the penetration of his mind.

Fitzgerald probably thought that republication of some of his stories would harm his reputation; he also did not want to reprint stories containing passages that he had later reused in his novels. (One such passage, recycled in *The Beautiful and Damned*, is marked in Illustration 4.) But such considerations are not as important now as they were during Fitzgerald's lifetime and certainly are outweighed by the great benefit of seeing Fitzgerald's oeuvre whole. His reputation today is solid and enduring; reissuing these stories will not damage it. His writings of this period, from least to most impressive, will be available to readers and scholars in all of their variety, complexity, and range.

FLAPPERS AND PHILOSOPHERS

TO ZELDA

THE OFFSHORE PIRATE

This unlikely story begins on a sea that was a blue dream, as colorful as blue silk stockings, and beneath a sky as blue as the irises of children's eyes. From the western half of the sky the sun was shying little golden disks at the sea—if you gazed intently enough you could see them skip from wave tip to wave tip until they joined a broad collar of golden coin that was collecting half a mile out and would eventually be a dazzling sunset. About halfway between the Florida shore and the golden collar a white steam-yacht, very young and graceful, was riding at anchor and under a blue-and-white awning aft a yellow-haired girl reclined in a wicker settee reading "The Revolt of the Angels," by Anatole France.

She was about nineteen, slender and supple, with a spoiled alluring mouth and quick grey eyes full of a radiant curiosity. Her feet, stockingless, and adorned rather than clad in blue satin slippers which swung nonchalantly from her toes, were perched on the arm of a settee adjoining the one she occupied. And as she read she intermittently regaled herself by a faint application to her tongue of a half-lemon that she held in her hand. The other half, sucked dry, lay on the deck at her feet and rocked very gently to and fro at the almost imperceptible motion of the tide.

The second half-lemon was well-nigh pulpless and the golden collar had grown astonishing in width, when suddenly the drowsy silence which enveloped the yacht was broken by the sound of heavy foot-steps and an elderly man topped with orderly grey hair and clad in a white flannel suit appeared at the head of the companionway. There he paused for a moment until his eyes became accustomed to the sun, and then seeing the girl under the awning he uttered a long even grunt of disapproval.

If he had intended thereby to obtain a rise of any sort he was doomed to disappointment. The girl calmly turned over two pages, turned back one, raised the lemon mechanically to tasting distance, and then very faintly but quite unmistakably yawned.

"Ardita!" said the grey-haired man sternly.

Ardita uttered a small sound indicating nothing.

"Ardita!" he repeated. "Ardita!"

Ardita raised the lemon languidly, allowing three words to slip out before it reached her tongue.

"Oh, shut up."

"Ardita!"

"What?"

"Will you listen to me—or will I have to get a servant to hold you while I talk to you?"

The lemon descended slowly and scornfully.

"Put it in writing."

"Will you have the decency to close that abominable book and discard that damn lemon for two minutes?"

"Oh, can't you lemme alone for a second?"

"Ardita, I have just received a telephone message from the shore——"

"Telephone?" She showed for the first time a faint interest.

"Yes, it was——"

"Do you mean to say," she interrupted wonderingly, "'at they let you run a wire out here?"

"Yes, and just now——"

"Won't other boats bump into it?"

"No. It's run along the bottom. Five min——"

"Well, I'll be darned! Gosh! Science is golden or something—isn't it?"

"Will you let me say what I started to?"

"Shoot!"

"Well, it seems—well, I am up here——" He paused and swallowed several times distractedly. "Oh, yes. Young woman, Colonel Moreland has called up again to ask me to be sure to bring you in to dinner. His son Toby has come all the way from New York to meet you and he's invited several other young people. For the last time, will you——"

"No," said Ardita shortly, "I won't. I came along on this darn cruise with the one idea of going to Palm Beach, and you knew it, and I absolutely refuse to meet any darn old colonel or any darn young Toby or any darn old young people or to set foot in any other darn old town in this crazy state. So you either take me to Palm Beach or else shut up and go away."

"Very well. This is the last straw. In your infatuation for this man—a man who is notorious for his excesses, a man your father would not have allowed to so much as mention your name—you have reflected the demi-monde rather than the circles in which you have presumably grown up. From now on——"

"I know," interrupted Ardita ironically, "from now on you go your way and I go mine. I've heard that story before. You know I'd like nothing better."

"From now on," he announced grandiloquently, "you are no niece of mine. I——"

"O-o-o-oh!" The cry was wrung from Ardita with the agony of a lost soul. "Will you stop boring me! Will you go way! Will you jump overboard and drown! Do you want me to throw this book at you!"

"If you dare do any——"

Smack! "The Revolt of the Angels" sailed through the air, missed its target by the length of a short nose, and bumped cheerfully down the companionway.

The grey-haired man made an instinctive step backward and then two cautious steps forward. Ardita jumped to her five feet four and stared at him defiantly, her grey eyes blazing.

"Keep off!"

"How dare you!" he cried.

"Because I darn please!"

"You've grown unbearable! Your disposition——"

"You've made me that way! No child ever has a bad disposition unless it's her family's fault! Whatever I am, you did it."

Muttering something under his breath her uncle turned and, walking forward, called in a loud voice for the launch. Then he returned to the awning, where Ardita had again seated herself and resumed her attention to the lemon.

"I am going ashore," he said slowly. "I will be out again at nine o'clock tonight. When I return we will start back to New York, where I shall turn you over to your aunt for the rest of your natural, or rather unnatural, life."

He paused and looked at her, and then all at once something in the utter childishness of her beauty seemed to puncture his anger like an inflated tire and render him helpless, uncertain, utterly fatuous.

"Ardita," he said not unkindly, "I'm no fool. I've been round. I know men. And, child, confirmed libertines don't reform until they're tired—and then they're not themselves—they're husks of themselves." He looked at her as if expecting agreement, but receiving no sight or sound of it he continued. "Perhaps the man loves you—that's possible. He's loved many women and he'll love many more. Less than a month ago, one month, Ardita, he was involved in a notorious affair with that red-haired woman, Mimi Merril; promised to give her the diamond bracelet that the Czar of Russia gave his mother. You know—you read the papers."

"Thrilling scandals by an anxious uncle," yawned Ardita. "Have it filmed. Wicked clubman making eyes at virtuous flapper. Virtuous flapper conclusively vamped by his lurid past. Plans to meet him at Palm Beach. Foiled by anxious uncle."

"Will you tell me why the devil you want to marry him?"

"I'm sure I couldn't say," said Ardita shortly. "Maybe because he's the only man I know, good or bad, who has an imagination and the courage of his convictions. Maybe it's to get away from the young fools that spend their vacuous hours pursuing me around the country. But as for the famous Russian bracelet, you can set your mind at rest on that score. He's going to give it to me at Palm Beach—if you'll show a little intelligence."

"How about the—red-haired woman?"

"He hasn't seen her for six months," she said angrily. "Don't you suppose I have enough pride to see to that? Don't you know by this time that I can do any darn thing with any darn man I want to?"

She put her chin in the air like the statue of France Aroused, and then spoiled the pose somewhat by raising the lemon for action.

"Is it the Russian bracelet that fascinates you?"

"No, I'm merely trying to give you the sort of argument that would appeal to your intelligence. And I wish you'd go way," she said, her temper rising again. "You know I never change my mind. You've been boring me for three days until I'm about to go crazy. I won't go ashore! Won't! Do you hear? Won't!"

"Very well," he said, "and you won't go to Palm Beach either. Of all the selfish, spoiled, uncontrolled, disagreeable, impossible girls I have——"

Splush! The half-lemon caught him in the neck. Simultaneously came a hail from over the side.

"The launch is ready, Mr. Farnam."

Too full of words and rage to speak, Mr. Farnam cast one utterly condemning glance at his niece and, turning, ran swiftly down the ladder.

II

Five o'clock rolled down from the sun and plumped soundlessly into the sea. The golden collar widened into a glittering island; and a faint breeze that had been playing with the edges of the awning and swaying one of the dangling blue slippers became suddenly freighted with song. It was a chorus of men in close harmony and in perfect rhythm to an accompanying sound of oars cleaving the blue waters. Ardita lifted her head and listened.

"Carrots and peas,
Beans on their knees,
Pigs in the seas,
  Lucky fellows!
Blow us a breeze,
Blow us a breeze,
Blow us a breeze,
  With your bellows."

Ardita's brow wrinkled in astonishment. Sitting very still she listened eagerly as the chorus took up a second verse.

"Onions and beans,
Marshalls and Deans,
Goldbergs and Greens
  And Costellos.

Blow us a breeze,
Blow us a breeze,
Blow us a breeze,
  With your bellows."

With an exclamation she tossed her book to the deck, where it sprawled at a straddle, and hurried to the rail. Fifty feet away a large rowboat was approaching containing seven men, six of them rowing and one standing up in the stern keeping time to their song with an orchestra leader's baton.

"Oysters and rocks,
Sawdust and socks,
Who could make clocks
  Out of cellos?—"

The leader's eyes suddenly rested on Ardita, who was leaning over the rail spellbound with curiosity. He made a quick movement with his baton and the singing instantly ceased. She saw that he was the only white man in the boat—the six rowers were negroes.

"'Narcissus' ahoy!" he called politely.

"What's the idea of all the discord?" demanded Ardita cheerfully. "Is this the varsity crew from the county nut farm?"

By this time the boat was scraping the side of the yacht and a great hulking negro in the bow turned round and grasped the ladder. Thereupon the leader left his position in the stern and before Ardita had realized his intention he ran up the ladder and stood breathless before her on the deck.

"The women and children will be spared!" he said briskly. "All crying babies will be immediately drowned and all males put in double irons!"

Digging her hands excitedly down into the pockets of her dress Ardita stared at him, speechless with astonishment.

He was a young man with a scornful mouth and the bright blue eyes of a healthy baby set in a dark sensitive face. His hair was pitch black, damp and curly—the hair of a Grecian statue gone brunet. He was trimly built, trimly dressed, and graceful as an agile quarterback.

"Well, I'll be a son of a gun!" she said dazedly.

They eyed each other coolly.

"Do you surrender the ship?"

"Is this an outburst of wit?" demanded Ardita. "Are you an idiot—or just being initiated to some fraternity?"

"I asked you if you surrendered the ship."

"I thought the country was dry," said Ardita disdainfully. "Have you been drinking fingernail enamel? You better get off this yacht!"

"What?" The young man's voice expressed incredulity.

"Get off the yacht! You heard me!"

He looked at her for a moment as if considering what she had said.

"No," said his scornful mouth slowly; "no, I won't get off the yacht. You can get off if you wish."

Going to the rail he gave a curt command and immediately the crew of the rowboat scrambled up the ladder and ranged themselves in line before him, a coal-black and burly darky at one end and a miniature mulatto of four feet nine at the other. They seemed to be uniformly dressed in some sort of blue costume ornamented with dust, mud, and tatters; over the shoulder of each was slung a small, heavy-looking white sack, and under their arms they carried large black cases apparently containing musical instruments.

"'Ten-*shun!*" commanded the young man, snapping his own heels together crisply. "Right *driss!* Front! Step out here, Babe!"

The smallest negro took a quick step forward and saluted.

"Yas-suh!"

"Take command, go down below, catch the crew and tie 'em up—all except the engineer. Bring him up to me. Oh, and pile those bags by the rail there."

"Yas-suh!"

Babe saluted again and wheeling about motioned for the five others to gather about him. Then after a short whispered consultation they all filed noiselessly down the companionway.

"Now," said the young man cheerfully to Ardita, who had witnessed this last scene in withering silence, "if you will swear on your honor as a flapper—which probably isn't worth much—that you'll keep that spoiled little mouth of yours tight shut for forty-eight hours, you can row yourself ashore in our rowboat."

"Otherwise what?"

"Otherwise you're going to sea in a ship."

With a little sigh as for a crisis well passed, the young man sank into the settee Ardita had lately vacated and stretched his arms lazily. The corners of his mouth relaxed appreciatively as he looked round at the rich striped awning, the polished brass and the luxurious fittings of the deck. His eye fell on the book and then on the exhausted lemon.

"Hm," he said, "Stonewall Jackson claimed that lemon juice cleared his head. Your head feel pretty clear?"

Ardita disdained to answer.

"Because inside of five minutes you'll have to make a clear decision whether it's go or stay."

He picked up the book and opened it curiously.

"'The Revolt of the Angels.' Sounds pretty good. French, eh?" He stared at her with new interest. "You French?"

"No."

"What's your name?"

"Farnam."

"Farnam what?"

"Ardita Farnam."

"Well, Ardita, no use standing up there and chewing out the insides of your mouth. You ought to break those nervous habits while you're young. Come over here and sit down."

Ardita took a carved jade case from her pocket, extracted a cigarette and lit it with a conscious coolness, though she knew her hand was trembling a little; then she crossed over with her supple, swinging walk, and sitting down in the other settee blew a mouthful of smoke at the awning.

"You can't get me off this yacht," she said steadily; "and you haven't got very much sense if you think you'll get far with it. My uncle'll have wirelesses zigzagging all over this ocean by half past six."

"Hm."

She looked quickly at his face, caught anxiety stamped there plainly in the faintest depression of the mouth's corners.

"It's all the same to me," she said, shrugging her shoulders. "'Tisn't my yacht. I don't mind going for a coupla hours' cruise. I'll even lend you that book so you'll have something to read on the revenue boat that takes you up to Sing Sing."

He laughed scornfully.

"If that's advice you needn't bother. This is part of a plan arranged before I ever knew this yacht existed. If it hadn't been this one it'd have been the next one we passed anchored along the coast."

"Who are you?" demanded Ardita suddenly. "And what are you?"

"You've decided not to go ashore?"

"I never even faintly considered it."

"We're generally known," he said, "all seven of us, as Curtis Carlyle and his Six Black Buddies, late of the Winter Garden and the Midnight Frolic."

"You're singers?"

"We were until today. At present, due to those white bags you see there, we're fugitives from justice, and if the reward offered for our capture hasn't by this time reached twenty thousand dollars I miss my guess."

"What's in the bags?" asked Ardita curiously.

"Well," he said, "for the present we'll call it—mud—Florida mud."

III

Within ten minutes after Curtis Carlyle's interview with a very frightened engineer the yacht "Narcissus" was under way, steaming south through a balmy tropical twilight. The little mulatto, Babe, who seemed to have Carlyle's implicit confidence, took full command of the situation. Mr. Farnam's valet and the chef, the only members of the crew on board except the engineer, having shown fight, were now reconsidering, strapped securely to their bunks below. Trombone Mose, the biggest negro, was set busy with a can of paint obliterating the name "Narcissus" from the bow, and substituting the name "Hula Hula," and the others congregated aft and became intently involved in a game of craps.

Having given orders for a meal to be prepared and served on deck at seven-thirty, Carlyle rejoined Ardita and, sinking back into his settee, half-closed his eyes and fell into a state of profound abstraction.

Ardita scrutinized him carefully—and classed him immediately as a romantic figure. He gave the effect of towering self-confidence erected on a slight foundation—just under the surface of each of his decisions she discerned a hesitancy that was in decided contrast to the arrogant curl of his lips.

"He's not like me," she thought. "There's a difference somewhere."

Being a supreme egotist Ardita frequently thought about herself; never having had her egotism disputed she did it entirely naturally and with no detraction from her unquestioned charm. Though she was nineteen she gave the effect of a high-spirited precocious child, and in the present glow of her youth and beauty all the men and women she had known were but driftwood on the ripples of her temperament. She had met other egotists—in fact she found that selfish people bored her rather less than unselfish people—but as yet there had not been one she had not eventually defeated and brought to her feet.

But though she recognized an egotist in the settee next to her, she felt none of that usual shutting of doors in her mind which meant clearing ship for action; on the contrary her instinct told her that this man was somehow completely pregnable and quite defenseless. When Ardita defied convention—and of late it had been her chief amusement—it was from an intense desire to be herself, and she felt that this man, on the contrary, was preoccupied with his own defiance.

She was much more interested in him than she was in her own situation, which affected her as the prospect of a matinée might affect a ten-year-old child. She had implicit confidence in her ability to take care of herself under any and all circumstances.

The night deepened. A pale new moon smiled misty-eyed upon the sea, and as the shore faded dimly out and dark clouds were blown like leaves along the far horizon a great haze of moonshine suddenly bathed the yacht and spread an avenue of glittering mail in her swift path. From time to time there was the bright flare of a match as one of them lighted a cigarette, but except for the low undertone of the throbbing engines and the even wash of the waves about the stern the yacht was quiet as a dream boat star-bound through the heavens. Round them flowed the smell of the night sea, bringing with it an infinite languor.

Carlyle broke the silence at last.

"Lucky girl," he sighed, "I've always wanted to be rich—and buy all this beauty."

Ardita yawned.

"I'd rather be you," she said frankly.

"You would—for about a day. But you do seem to possess a lot of nerve for a flapper."

"I wish you wouldn't call me that."

"Beg your pardon."

"As to nerve," she continued slowly, "it's my one redeeming feature. I'm not afraid of anything in heaven or earth."

"Hm, I am."

"To be afraid," said Ardita, "a person has either to be very great and strong—or else a coward. I'm neither." She paused for a moment, and eagerness crept into her tone. "But I want to talk about you. What on earth have you done—and how did you do it?"

"Why?" he demanded cynically. "Going to write a movie about me?"

"Go on," she urged. "Lie to me by the moonlight. Do a fabulous story."

A negro appeared, switched on a string of small lights under the awning and began setting the wicker table for supper. And while they ate cold sliced chicken, salad, artichokes and strawberry jam from the plentiful larder below, Carlyle began to talk, hesitatingly at first, but eagerly as he saw she was interested. Ardita scarcely touched her food as she watched his dark young face—handsome, ironic, faintly ineffectual.

He began life as a poor kid in a Tennessee town, he said, so poor that his people were the only white family in their street. He never remembered any white children—but there were inevitably a dozen pickaninnies streaming in his trail, passionate admirers whom he kept in tow by the vividness of his imagination and the amount of trouble he was always getting them in and out of. And it seemed that this association diverted a rather unusual musical gift into a strange channel.

There had been a colored woman named Belle Pope Calhoun who played the piano at parties given for white children—nice white children that would have passed Curtis Carlyle with a sniff. But the ragged little "poh white" used to sit beside her piano by the hour and try to get in an alto with one of those kazoos that boys hum through. Before he was thirteen he was picking up a living teasing ragtime out of a battered violin in little cafés round Nashville. Eight years later the ragtime craze hit the country and he took six darkies on the Orpheum circuit. Five of them were boys he had grown up with; the other was the little mulatto, Babe Divine, who was a wharf nigger round New York, and long before that a plantation hand in Bermuda, until he stuck an eight-inch stiletto in his master's back. Almost before Carlyle realized his good fortune he was on Broadway, with offers of engagements on all sides, and more money than he had ever dreamed of.

It was about then that a change began in his whole attitude, a rather curious, embittering change. It was when he realized that he was spending the golden years of his life gibbering round a stage with a lot of black men. His act was good of its kind—three trombones, three saxophones and Carlyle's flute—and it was his own peculiar sense of rhythm that made all the difference; but he began to grow strangely sensitive about it, began to hate the thought of appearing, dreaded it from day to day.

They were making money—each contract he signed called for more—but when he went to managers and told them that he wanted to separate from his sextet and go on as a regular pianist, they laughed at him and told him he was crazy—it would be an artistic suicide. He used to laugh afterward at the phrase "artistic suicide." They all used it.

Half a dozen times they played at private dances at three thousand dollars a night, and it seemed as if these crystallized all his distaste for his mode of livelihood. They took place in clubs and houses that he couldn't have gone into in the daytime. After all, he was merely playing the rôle of the eternal monkey, a sort of sublimated chorus man. He was sick of the very smell of the theatre, of powder and rouge and the chatter of the greenroom and the patronizing approval of the boxes. He couldn't put his heart into it anymore. The idea of a slow approach to the luxury of leisure drove him wild. He was, of course, progressing toward it but, like a child, eating his ice cream so slowly that he couldn't taste it at all.

He wanted to have a lot of money and time, and opportunity to read and play, and the sort of men and women round him that he could never have—the kind who, if they thought of him at all, would have considered him rather contemptible; in short he wanted all those things which he was beginning to lump under the general head of aristocracy, an aristocracy which it seemed almost any money could buy except money made as he was making it. He was twenty-five then, without family or education or any promise that he would succeed in a business career. He began speculating wildly, and within three weeks he had lost every cent he had saved.

Then the war came. He went to Plattsburg, and even there his profession followed him. A brigadier general called him up to headquarters and told him he could serve the country better as a band leader—so he spent the war entertaining celebrities behind the line with a headquarters band. It was not so bad—except that when the infantry came limping back from the trenches he wanted to be one of them. The sweat and mud they wore seemed only one of those ineffable symbols of aristocracy that were forever eluding him.

"It was the private dances that did it. After I came back from the war the old routine started. We had an offer from a syndicate of Florida hotels. It was only a question of time then."

He broke off and Ardita looked at him expectantly, but he shook his head.

"No," he said, "I'm not going to tell you about it. I'm enjoying it too much, and I'm afraid I'd lose a little of that enjoyment if I shared it with anyone else. I want to hang on to those few breathless, heroic moments when I stood out before them all and let them know I was more than a damn bobbing, squawking clown."

From up forward came suddenly the low sound of singing. The negroes had gathered together on the deck and their voices rose together in a haunting melody that soared in poignant harmonics toward the moon. And Ardita listened in enchantment.

"Oh down—
  Oh down,
Mammy wanna take me downa milky way,
Oh down—
  Oh down,

Pappy say to-morra-a-a-ah!
But mammy say today,
Yes—mammy say today!"

Carlyle sighed and was silent for a moment, looking up at the gathered host of stars blinking like arc-lights in the warm sky. The negroes' song had died away to a plaintive humming and it seemed as if minute by minute the brightness and the great silence were increasing until he could almost hear the midnight toilet of the mermaids as they combed their silver dripping curls under the moon and gossiped to each other of the fine wrecks they lived in on the green opalescent avenues below.

"You see," said Carlyle softly, "this is the beauty I want. Beauty has got to be astonishing, astounding—it's got to burst in on you like a dream, like the exquisite eyes of a girl."

He turned to her, but she was silent.

"You see, don't you, Anita—I mean, Ardita?"

Again she made no answer. She had been sound asleep for some time.

IV

In the dense sun-flooded noon of next day a spot in the sea before them resolved casually into a green-and-grey islet, apparently composed of a great granite cliff at its northern end which slanted south through a mile of vivid coppice and grass to a sandy beach melting lazily into the surf. When Ardita, reading in her favorite seat, came to the last page of "The Revolt of the Angels," and slamming the book shut looked up and saw it, she gave a little cry of delight and called to Carlyle, who was standing moodily by the rail.

"Is this it? Is this where you're going?"

Carlyle shrugged his shoulders carelessly.

"You've got me." He raised his voice and called up to the acting skipper: "Oh, Babe, is this your island?"

The mulatto's miniature head appeared from round the corner of the deckhouse.

"Yas-suh! This yeah's it."

Carlyle joined Ardita.

"Looks sort of sporting, doesn't it?"

"Yes," she agreed; "but it doesn't look big enough to be much of a hiding place."

"You still putting your faith in those wirelesses your uncle was going to have zigzagging round?"

"No," said Ardita frankly. "I'm all for you. I'd really like to see you make a get-away."

He laughed.

"You're our Lady Luck. Guess we'll have to keep you with us as a mascot—for the present anyway."

"You couldn't very well ask me to swim back," she said coolly. "If you do I'm going to start writing dime novels founded on that interminable history of your life you gave me last night."

He flushed and stiffened slightly.

"I'm very sorry I bored you."

"Oh, you didn't—until just at the end with some story about how furious you were because you couldn't dance with the ladies you played music for."

He rose angrily.

"You have got a darn mean little tongue."

"Excuse me," she said, melting into laughter, "but I'm not used to having men regale me with the story of their life ambitions—especially if they've lived such deathly platonic lives."

"Why? What do men usually regale you with?"

"Oh, they talk about me," she yawned. "They tell me I'm the spirit of youth and beauty."

"What do you tell them?"

"Oh, I agree quietly."

"Does every man you meet tell you he loves you?"

Ardita nodded.

"Why shouldn't he? All life is just a progression toward, and then a recession from, one phrase—'I love you.'"

Carlyle laughed and sat down.

"That's very true. That's—that's not bad. Did you make that up?"

"Yes—or rather I found it out. It doesn't mean anything especially. It's just clever."

"It's the sort of remark," he said gravely, "that's typical of your class."

"Oh," she interrupted impatiently, "don't start that lecture on aristocracy again! I distrust people who can be intense at this hour in the morning. It's a mild form of insanity—a sort of breakfast-food jag. Morning's the time to sleep, swim and be careless."

Ten minutes later they had swung round in a wide circle as if to approach the island from the north.

"There's a trick somewhere," commented Ardita thoughtfully. "He can't mean just to anchor up against this cliff."

They were heading straight in now toward the solid rock, which must have been well over a hundred feet tall, and not until they were within fifty yards of it did Ardita see their objective. Then she clapped her hands in delight. There was a break in the cliff entirely hidden by a curious overlapping of rock, and through this break the yacht entered and very slowly traversed a narrow channel of crystal-clear water between high grey walls. Then they were riding at anchor in a miniature world of green and gold, a gilded bay smooth as glass and set round with tiny palms, the whole resembling the mirror lakes and twig trees that children set up in sand piles.

"Not so darned bad!" cried Carlyle excitedly. "I guess that little coon knows his way round this corner of the Atlantic."

His exuberance was contagious and Ardita became quite jubilant.

"It's an absolutely sure-fire hiding place!"

"Lordy, yes! It's the sort of island you read about."

The rowboat was lowered into the golden lake and they pulled ashore.

"Come on," said Carlyle as they landed in the slushy sand, "we'll go exploring."

The fringe of palms was in turn ringed in by a round mile of flat sandy country. They followed it south and brushing through a farther rim of tropical vegetation came out on a pearl-grey virgin beach where Ardita kicked off her brown golf shoes—she seemed to have permanently abandoned stockings—and went wading. Then they sauntered back to the yacht, where the indefatigable Babe had luncheon ready for them. He had posted a lookout on the high cliff to the north to watch the sea on both sides, though he doubted if the entrance to the cliff was generally known—he had never even seen a map on which the island was marked.

"What's its name," asked Ardita—"the island, I mean?"

"No name 'tall," chuckled Babe. "Reckin she jus' island, 'at's all."

In the late afternoon they sat with their backs against great boulders on the highest part of the cliff and Carlyle sketched for her his vague plans. He was sure they were hot after him by this time. The total proceeds of the coup he had pulled off, and concerning which he still refused to enlighten her, he estimated as just under a million dollars. He counted on lying up here several weeks and then setting off southward, keeping well outside the usual channels of travel, rounding the Horn and heading for Callao, in Peru. The details of coaling and provisioning he was leaving entirely to Babe, who, it seemed, had sailed these seas in every capacity from cabin boy aboard a coffee trader to virtual first mate on a Brazilian pirate craft, whose skipper had long since been hanged.

"If he'd been white he'd have been king of South America long ago," said Carlyle emphatically. "When it comes to intelligence he makes Booker T. Washington look like a moron. He's got the guile of every race and nationality whose blood is in his veins, and that's half a dozen or I'm a liar. He worships me because I'm the only man in the world who can play better ragtime than he can. We used to sit together on the wharfs down on the New York waterfront, he with a bassoon and me with an oboe, and we'd blend minor keys in African harmonics a thousand years old until the rats would crawl up the posts and sit round groaning and squeaking like dogs will in front of a phonograph."

Ardita roared.

"How you can tell 'em!"

Carlyle grinned.

"I swear that's the gos——"

"What you going to do when you get to Callao?" she interrupted.

"Take ship for India. I want to be a rajah. I mean it. My idea is to go up into Afghanistan somewhere, buy up a palace and a reputation, and then after about five years appear in England with a foreign accent and a mysterious past. But India first. Do you know, they say that all the gold in the world drifts very gradually back to

India. Something fascinating about that to me. And I want leisure to read—an immense amount."

"How about after that?"

"Then," he answered defiantly, "comes aristocracy. Laugh if you want to—but at least you'll have to admit that I know what I want—which I imagine is more than you do."

"On the contrary," contradicted Ardita, reaching in her pocket for her cigarette case, "when I met you I was in the midst of a great uproar of all my friends and relatives because I did know what I wanted."

"What was it?"

"A man."

He started.

"You mean you were engaged?"

"After a fashion. If you hadn't come aboard I had every intention of slipping ashore yesterday evening—how long ago it seems—and meeting him in Palm Beach. He's waiting there for me with a bracelet that once belonged to Catharine of Russia. Now don't mutter anything about aristocracy," she put in quickly. "I liked him simply because he had had an imagination and the utter courage of his convictions."

"But your family disapproved, eh?"

"What there is of it—only a silly uncle and a sillier aunt. It seems he got into some scandal with a red-haired woman named Mimi something—it was frightfully exaggerated, he said, and men don't lie to me—and anyway I didn't care what he'd done; it was the future that counted. And I'd see to that. When a man's in love with me he doesn't care for other amusements. I told him to drop her like a hot cake, and he did."

"I feel rather jealous," said Carlyle, frowning—and then he laughed. "I guess I'll just keep you along with us until we get to Callao. Then I'll lend you enough money to get back to the States. By that time you'll have had a chance to think that gentleman over a little more."

"Don't talk to me like that!" fired up Ardita. "I won't tolerate the parental attitude from anybody! Do you understand me?"

He chuckled and then stopped, rather abashed, as her cold anger seemed to fold him about and chill him.

"I'm sorry," he offered uncertainly.

'Oh, don't apologize! I can't stand men who say 'I'm sorry' in that manly, reserved tone. Just shut up!"

A pause ensued, a pause which Carlyle found rather awkward, but which Ardita seemed not to notice at all as she sat contentedly enjoying her cigarette and gazing out at the shining sea. After a minute she crawled out on the rock and lay with her face over the edge looking down. Carlyle, watching her, reflected how it seemed impossible for her to assume an ungraceful attitude.

"Oh, look!" she cried. "There's a lot of sort of ledges down there. Wide ones of all different heights."

He joined her and together they gazed down the dizzy height.

"We'll go swimming tonight!" she said excitedly. "By moonlight."

"Wouldn't you rather go in at the beach on the other end?"

"Not a chance. I like to dive. You can use my uncle's bathing suit, only it'll fit you like a gunny sack, because he's a very flabby man. I've got a one-piece affair that's shocked the natives all along the Atlantic coast from Biddeford Pool to St. Augustine."

"I suppose you're a shark."

"Yes, I'm pretty good. And I look cute too. A sculptor up at Rye last summer told me my calves were worth five hundred dollars."

There didn't seem to be any answer to this, so Carlyle was silent, permitting himself only a discreet interior smile.

V

When the night crept down in shadowy blue and silver they threaded the shimmering channel in the rowboat and, tying it to a jutting rock, began climbing the cliff together. The first shelf was ten feet up, wide, and furnishing a natural diving platform. There they sat down in the bright moonlight and watched the faint incessant surge of the waters, almost stilled now as the tide set seaward.

"Are you happy?" he asked suddenly.

She nodded.

"Always happy near the sea. You know," she went on, "I've been thinking all day that you and I are somewhat alike. We're both rebels—only for different reasons. Two years ago, when I was just eighteen, and you were——"

"Twenty-five."

"—well, we were both conventional successes. I was an utterly devastating debutante and you were a prosperous musician just commissioned in the army——"

"Gentleman by act of Congress," he put in ironically.

"Well, at any rate, we both fitted. If our corners were not rubbed off they were at least pulled in. But deep in us both was something that made us require more for happiness. I didn't know what I wanted. I went from man to man, restless, impatient, month by month getting less acquiescent and more dissatisfied. I used to sit sometimes chewing at the insides of my mouth and thinking I was going crazy—I had a frightful sense of transiency. I wanted things now—now—now! Here I was—beautiful—I am, aren't I?"

"Yes," agreed Carlyle tentatively.

Ardita rose suddenly.

"Wait a second. I want to try this delightful-looking sea."

She walked to the end of the ledge and shot out over the sea, doubling up in midair and then straightening out and entering the water straight as a blade in a perfect jackknife dive.

In a minute her voice floated up to him.

"You see, I used to read all day and most of the night. I began to resent society——"

"Come on up here," he interrupted. "What on earth are you doing?"

"Just floating round on my back. I'll be up in a minute. Let me tell you. The only thing I enjoyed was shocking people; wearing something quite impossible and quite charming to a fancy-dress party, going round with the fastest men in New York and getting into some of the most hellish scrapes imaginable."

The sounds of splashing mingled with her words, and then he heard her hurried breathing as she began climbing up the side to the ledge.

"Go on in!" she called.

Obediently he rose and dived. When he emerged, dripping, and made the climb he found that she was no longer on the ledge, but after a frightened second he heard her light laughter from another shelf ten feet up. There he joined her and they both sat quietly for a moment, their arms clasped round their knees, panting a little from the climb.

"The family were wild," she said suddenly. "They tried to marry me off. And then when I'd begun to feel that after all life was scarcely worth living I found something"—her eyes went skyward exultantly—"I found something!"

Carlyle waited and her words came with a rush.

"Courage—just that; courage as a rule of life and something to cling to always. I began to build up this enormous faith in myself. I began to see that in all my idols in the past some manifestation of courage had unconsciously been the thing that attracted me. I began separating courage from the other things of life. All sorts of courage—the beaten, bloody prizefighter coming up for more—I used to make men take me to prizefights; the déclassé woman sailing through a nest of cats and looking at them as if they were mud under her feet; the liking what you like always; the utter disregard for other people's opinions—just to live as I liked always and to die in my own way—— Did you bring up the cigarettes?"

He handed one over and held a match for her silently.

"Still," Ardita continued, "the men kept gathering—old men and young men, my mental and physical inferiors, most of them, but all intensely desiring to have me—to own this rather magnificent proud tradition I'd built up round me. Do you see?"

"Sort of. You never were beaten and you never apologized."

"Never!"

She sprang to the edge, poised for a moment like a crucified figure against the sky; then describing a dark parabola plunked without a splash between two silver ripples twenty feet below.

Her voice floated up to him again.

"And courage to me meant plowing through that dull grey mist that comes down on life—not only overriding people and circumstances but overriding the bleakness of living. A sort of insistence on the value of life and the worth of transient things."

She was climbing up now, and at her last words her head, with the damp yellow hair slicked symmetrically back, appeared on his level.

"All very well," objected Carlyle. "You can call it courage, but your courage is really built, after all, on a pride of birth. You were bred to that defiant attitude. On my grey days even courage is one of the things that's grey and lifeless."

She was sitting near the edge, hugging her knees and gazing abstractedly at the white moon; he was farther back, crammed like a grotesque god into a niche in the rock.

"I don't want to sound like Pollyanna," she began, "but you haven't grasped me yet. My courage is faith—faith in the eternal resilience of me—that joy'll come back, and hope and spontaneity. And I feel that till it does I've got to keep my lips shut and my chin high and my eyes wide—not necessarily any silly smiling. Oh, I've been through hell without a whine quite often—and the female hell is deadlier than the male."

"But supposing," suggested Carlyle, "that before joy and hope and all that came back the curtain was drawn on you for good?"

Ardita rose, and going to the wall climbed with some difficulty to the next ledge, another ten or fifteen feet above.

"Why," she called back, "then I'd have won!"

He edged out till he could see her.

"Better not dive from there! You'll break your back," he said quickly.

She laughed.

"Not I!"

Slowly she spread her arms and stood there swan-like, radiating a pride in her young perfection that lit a warm glow in Carlyle's heart.

"We're going through the black air with our arms wide," she called, "and our feet straight out behind like a dolphin's tail, and we're going to think we'll never hit the silver down there till suddenly it'll be all warm round us and full of little kissing, caressing waves."

Then she was in the air and Carlyle involuntarily held his breath. He had not realized that the dive was nearly forty feet. It seemed an eternity before he heard the swift compact sound as she reached the sea.

And it was with his glad sigh of relief when her light watery laughter curled up the side of the cliff and into his anxious ears that he knew he loved her.

VI

Time, having no ax to grind, showered down upon them three days of afternoons. When the sun cleared the porthole of Ardita's cabin an hour after dawn she rose cheerily, donned her bathing suit and went up on deck. The negroes would leave their work when they saw her, and crowd, chuckling and chattering, to the rail as she floated, an agile minnow, on and under the surface of the clear water. Again in the cool of the afternoon she would swim—and loll and smoke with Carlyle upon the cliff; or else they would lie on their sides in the sands of the southern beach, talking little, but watching the day fade colorfully and tragically into the infinite languor of a tropical evening.

And with the long sunny hours Ardita's idea of the episode as incidental, madcap, a sprig of romance in a desert of reality, gradually left her. She dreaded the time when he would strike off southward; she dreaded all the eventualities that presented themselves to her; thoughts were suddenly troublesome and decisions odious. Had prayers found place in the pagan rituals of her soul she would have asked of life only to be unmolested for awhile, lazily acquiescent to the ready, naïf flow of Carlyle's ideas, his vivid boyish imagination and the vein of monomania that seemed to run crosswise through his temperament and colored his every action.

But this is not a story of two on an island nor concerned primarily with love bred of isolation. It is merely the presentation of two personalities, and its idyllic setting among the palms of the Gulf Stream is quite incidental. Most of us are content to exist and breed and fight for the right to do both; and the dominant idea, the foredoomed attempt to control one's destiny, is reserved for the fortunate or unfortunate few. To me the interesting thing about Ardita is the courage that will tarnish with her beauty and youth.

"Take me with you," she said late one night as they sat lazily in the grass under the shadowy spreading palms. The negroes had brought ashore their musical instruments and the sound of weird ragtime was drifting softly over on the warm breath of the night. "I'd love to reappear in ten years as a fabulously wealthy high-caste Indian lady," she continued.

Carlyle looked at her quickly.

"You can, you know."

She laughed.

"Is it a proposal of marriage? Extra! Ardita Farnam becomes pirate's bride. Society girl kidnapped by ragtime bank robber."

"It wasn't a bank."

"What was it? Why won't you tell me?"

"I don't want to break down your illusions."

"My dear man, I have no illusions about you."

"I mean your illusions about yourself."

She looked up in surprise.

"About myself! What on earth have I got to do with whatever stray felonies you've committed?"

"That remains to be seen."

She reached over and patted his hand.

"Dear Mr. Curtis Carlyle," she said softly, "are you in love with me?"

"As if it mattered."

"But it does—because I think I'm in love with you."

He looked at her ironically.

"Thus swelling your January total to half a dozen," he suggested. "Suppose I call your bluff and ask you to come to India with me?"

"Shall I?"

He shrugged his shoulders.

"We can get married in Callao."

"What sort of life can you offer me? I don't mean that unkindly, but seriously; what would become of me if the people who want that twenty-thousand-dollar reward ever catch up with you?"

"I thought you weren't afraid."

"I never am—but I won't throw my life away just to show one man I'm not."

"I wish you'd been poor. Just a little poor girl dreaming over a fence in a warm cow country."

"Wouldn't it have been nice?"

"I'd have enjoyed astonishing you—watching your eyes open on things. If you only wanted things! Don't you see?"

"I know—like girls who stare into the windows of jewelry stores."

"Yes—and want the big oblong watch that's platinum and has diamonds all round the edge. Only you'd decide it was too expensive and choose one of white gold for a hundred dollars. Then I'd say: 'Expensive? I should say not!' And we'd go into the store and pretty soon the platinum one would be gleaming on your wrist."

"That sounds so nice and vulgar—and fun, doesn't it?" murmured Ardita.

"Doesn't it? Can't you see us traveling round and spending money right and left and being worshipped by bell-boys and waiters? Oh, blessed are the simple rich, for they inherit the earth!"

"I honestly wish we were that way."

"I love you, Ardita," he said gently.

Her face lost its childish look for a moment and became oddly grave.

"I love to be with you," she said, "more than with any man I've ever met. And I like your looks and your dark old hair and the way you go over the side of the rail when we come ashore. In fact, Curtis Carlyle, I like all the things you do when you're perfectly natural. I think you've got nerve, and you know how I feel about that. Sometimes when you're round I've been tempted to kiss you suddenly and tell you that you were just an idealistic boy with a lot of caste nonsense in his head. Perhaps if I were just a little bit older and a little more bored I'd go with you. As it is, I think I'll go back and marry—that other man."

Over across the silver lake the figures of the negroes writhed and squirmed in the moonlight, like acrobats who, having been too long inactive, must go through their tricks from sheer surplus energy. In single file they marched, weaving in concentric circles, now with their heads thrown back, now bent over their instruments like piping fauns. And from trombone and saxophone ceaselessly whined a blended melody, sometimes riotous and jubilant, sometimes haunting and plaintive as a death dance from the Congo's heart.

"Let's dance!" cried Ardita. "I can't sit still with that perfect jazz going on."

Taking her hand he led her out into a broad stretch of hard sandy soil that the moon flooded with great splendor. They floated out like drifting moths under the rich hazy light, and as the fantastic symphony wept and exulted and wavered and despaired Ardita's last sense of reality dropped away, and she abandoned her imagination to the dreamy summer scents of tropical flowers and the infinite starry spaces overhead, feeling that if she opened her eyes it would be to find herself dancing with a ghost in a land created by her own fancy.

"This is what I should call an exclusive private dance," he whispered.

"I feel quite mad—but delightfully mad!"

"We're enchanted. The shades of unnumbered generations of cannibals are watching us from high up on the side of the cliff there."

"And I'll bet the cannibal women are saying that we dance too close, and that it was immodest of me to come without my nose ring."

They both laughed softly—and then their laughter died as over across the lake they heard the trombones stop in the middle of a bar, and the saxophones give a startled moan and fade out.

"What's the matter?" called Carlyle.

After a moment's silence they made out the dark figure of a man rounding the silver lake at a run. As he came closer they saw it was Babe in a state of unusual excitement. He drew up before them and gasped out his news in a breath.

"Ship stan'in' off sho' 'bout half a mile, suh. Mose, he uz on watch, he say look's if she's done ancho'd."

"A ship—what kind of a ship?" demanded Carlyle anxiously.

Dismay was in his voice and Ardita's heart gave a sudden wrench as she saw his whole face suddenly droop.

"He say he don't know, suh."

"Are they landing a boat?"

"No, suh."

"We'll go up," said Carlyle.

They ascended the hill in silence, Ardita's hand still resting in Carlyle's as it had when they finished dancing. She felt it clench nervously from time to time as though he were unaware of the contact, but though he hurt her she made no attempt to remove it. It seemed an hour's climb before they reached the top and crept cautiously across the silhouetted plateau to the edge of the cliff. After one short look Carlyle involuntarily gave a little cry. It was a revenue boat with six-inch guns mounted fore and aft.

"They know!" he said with a short intake of breath. "They know! They picked up the trail somewhere."

"Are you sure they know about the channel? They may be only standing by to take a look at the island in the morning. From where they are they couldn't see the opening in the cliff."

"They could with field glasses," he said hopelessly. He looked at his wrist watch. "It's nearly two now. They won't do anything until dawn, that's certain. Of course there's always the faint possibility that they're waiting for some other ship to join; or for a coaler."

"I suppose we may as well stay right here."

The hours passed and they lay there side by side, very silently, their chins in their hands like dreaming children. In back of them squatted the negroes, patient, resigned, acquiescent, announcing now and then with sonorous snores that not even the presence of danger could subdue their unconquerable African craving for sleep.

Just before five o'clock Babe approached Carlyle. There were half a dozen rifles aboard the "Narcissus" he said. Had it been decided to offer no resistance? A pretty good fight might be made, he thought, if they worked out some plan.

Carlyle laughed and shook his head.

"That isn't a Spic army out there, Babe. That's a revenue boat. It'd be like a bow and arrow trying to fight a machine-gun. If you want to bury those bags somewhere and take a chance on recovering them later, go on and do it. But it won't work—they'd dig this island over from one end to the other. It's a lost battle all round, Babe."

Babe inclined his head silently and turned away, and Carlyle's voice was husky as he turned to Ardita.

"There's the best friend I ever had. He'd die for me, and be proud to, if I'd let him."

"You've given up?"

"I've no choice. Of course there's always one way out—the sure way—but that can wait. I wouldn't miss my trial for anything—it'll be an interesting experiment in notoriety. 'Miss Farnam testifies that the pirate's attitude to her was at all times that of a gentleman.'"

"Don't!" she said. "I'm awfully sorry."

When the color faded from the sky and lusterless blue changed to leaden grey a commotion was visible on the ship's deck, and they made out a group of officers clad in white duck, gathered near the rail. They had field glasses in their hands and were attentively examining the islet.

"It's all up," said Carlyle grimly.

"Damn!" whispered Ardita. She felt tears gathering in her eyes.

"We'll go back to the yacht," he said. "I prefer that to being hunted out up here like a 'possum."

Leaving the plateau they descended the hill, and reaching the lake were rowed out to the yacht by the silent negroes. Then, pale and weary, they sank into the settees and waited.

Half an hour later in the dim grey light the nose of the revenue boat appeared in the channel and stopped, evidently fearing that the bay might be too shallow. From the peaceful look of the yacht, the man and the girl in the settees and the negroes lounging curiously against the rail, they evidently judged that there would be no resistance, for two boats were lowered casually over the side, one containing an officer and six bluejackets, and the other, four rowers and in the stern two grey-haired men in yachting flannels. Ardita and Carlyle stood up and half-unconsciously started toward each other. Then he paused and putting his hand suddenly into his pocket he pulled out a round glittering object and held it out to her.

"What is it?" she asked wonderingly.

"I'm not positive, but I think from the Russian inscription inside that it's your promised bracelet."

"Where—where on earth——"

"It came out of one of those bags. You see, Curtis Carlyle and his Six Black Buddies, in the middle of their performance in the tea room of the hotel at Palm Beach, suddenly changed their instruments for automatics and held up the crowd. I took this bracelet from a pretty, overrouged woman with red hair."

Ardita frowned and then smiled.

"So that's what you did! You *have* got nerve!"

He bowed.

"A well-known bourgeois quality," he said.

And then dawn slanted dynamically across the deck and flung the shadows reeling into grey corners. The dew rose and turned to golden mist, thin as a dream, enveloping them until they seemed gossamer relics of the late night, infinitely transient and already fading. For a moment sea and sky were breathless and dawn held a pink hand over the young mouth of life—then from out in the lake came the complaint of a rowboat and the swish of oars.

Suddenly against the golden furnace low in the east their two graceful figures melted into one and he was kissing her spoiled young mouth.

"It's a sort of glory," he murmured after a second.

She smiled up at him.

"Happy, are you?"

Her sigh was a benediction—an ecstatic surety that she was youth and beauty now as much as she would ever know. For another instant life was radiant and time a phantom and their strength eternal—then there was a bumping, scraping sound as the rowboat scraped alongside.

Up the ladder scrambled the two grey-haired men, the officer and two of the sailors with their hands on their revolvers. Mr. Farnam folded his arms and stood looking at his niece.

"So," he said, nodding his head slowly.

With a sigh her arms unwound from Carlyle's neck, and her eyes, transfigured and far away, fell upon the boarding party. Her uncle saw her upper lip slowly swell into that arrogant pout he knew so well.

"So," he repeated savagely. "So this is your idea of—of romance. A runaway affair, with a high-seas pirate."

Ardita glanced at him carelessly.

"What an old fool you are!" she said quietly.

"Is that the best you can say for yourself?"

"No," she said as if considering. "No, there's something else. There's that well-known phrase with which I have ended most of our conversations for the past few years—'Shut up!'"

And with that she turned, included the two old men, the officer, and the two sailors in a curt glance of contempt, and walked proudly down the companionway.

But had she waited an instant longer she would have heard a sound from her uncle quite unfamiliar in most of their interviews. He gave vent to a whole-hearted amused chuckle, in which the second old man joined.

The latter turned briskly to Carlyle, who had been regarding this scene with an air of cryptic amusement.

"Well, Toby," he said genially, "you incurable, harebrained, romantic chaser of rainbows, did you find that she was the person you wanted?"

Carlyle smiled confidently.

"Why—naturally," he said. "I've been perfectly sure ever since I first heard tell of her wild career. That's why I had Babe send up the rocket last night."

"I'm glad you did," said Colonel Moreland gravely. "We've been keeping pretty close to you in case you should have trouble with those six strange niggers. And we hoped we'd find you two in some such compromising position," he sighed. "Well, set a crank to catch a crank!"

"Your father and I sat up all night hoping for the best—or perhaps it's the worst. Lord knows you're welcome to her, my boy. She's run me crazy. Did you give her the Russian bracelet my detective got from that Mimi woman?"

Carlyle nodded.

"Sh!" he said. "She's coming on deck."

Ardita appeared at the head of the companionway and gave a quick involuntary glance at Carlyle's wrists. A puzzled look passed across her face. Back aft the negroes had begun to sing, and the cool lake, fresh with dawn, echoed serenely to their low voices.

"Ardita," said Carlyle unsteadily.

She swayed a step toward him.

"Ardita," he repeated breathlessly, "I've got to tell you the—the truth. It was all a plant, Ardita. My name isn't Carlyle. It's Moreland, Toby Moreland. The story was invented, Ardita, invented out of thin Florida air."

She stared at him, bewildered amazement, disbelief and anger flowing in quick waves across her face. The three men held their breaths. Moreland, Senior, took a step toward her; Mr. Farnam's mouth dropped a little open as he waited, panic-stricken, for the expected crash.

But it did not come. Ardita's face became suddenly radiant, and with a little laugh she went swiftly to young Moreland and looked up at him without a trace of wrath in her grey eyes.

"Will you swear," she said quietly, "that it was entirely a product of your own brain?"

"I swear," said young Moreland eagerly.

She drew his head down and kissed him gently.

"What an imagination!" she said softly and almost enviously. "I want you to lie to me just as sweetly as you know how for the rest of my life."

The negroes' voices floated drowsily back, mingled in an air that she had heard them sing before.

> "Time is a thief;
> Gladness and grief
> Cling to the leaf
> As it yellows——"

"What was in the bags?" she asked softly.

"Florida mud," he answered. "That was one of the two true things I told you."

"Perhaps I can guess the other one," she said; and reaching up on her tiptoes she kissed him softly in the illustration.

THE ICE PALACE

The sunlight dripped over the house like golden paint over an art jar, and the freckling shadows here and there only intensified the rigor of the bath of light. The Butterworth and Larkin houses flanking were intrenched behind great stodgy trees; only the Happer house took the full sun and all day long faced the dusty road-street with a tolerant kindly patience. This was the city of Tarleton in southernmost Georgia—September afternoon.

Up in her bedroom window Sally Carrol Happer rested her nineteen-year-old chin on a fifty-two-year-old sill and watched Clark Darrow's ancient Ford turn the corner. The car was hot—being partly metallic it retained all the heat it absorbed or evolved—and Clark Darrow sitting bolt upright at the wheel wore a pained, strained expression as though he considered himself a spare part and rather likely to break. He laboriously crossed two dust ruts, the wheels squeaking indignantly at the encounter, and then with a terrifying expression he gave the steering-gear a final wrench and deposited self and car approximately in front of the Happer steps. There was a plaintive heaving sound, a death-rattle, followed by a short silence; and then the air was rent by a startling whistle.

Sally Carrol gazed down sleepily. She started to yawn, but finding this quite impossible unless she raised her chin from the window-sill, changed her mind and continued silently to regard the car, whose owner sat brilliantly if perfunctorily at attention as he waited for an answer to his signal. After a moment the whistle once more split the dusty air.

"Good mawnin'."

With difficulty Clark twisted his tall body round and bent a distorted glance on the window.

"'Tain't mawnin', Sally Carrol."

"Isn't it, sure enough?"

"What you doin'?"

"Eatin' 'n apple."

"Come on go swimmin'—want to?"

"Reckon so."

"How 'bout hurryin' up?"

"Sure enough."

Sally Carrol sighed voluminously and raised herself with profound inertia from the floor, where she had been occupied in alternately destroying parts of a green apple and painting paper dolls for her younger sister. She approached a mirror, regarded her expression with a pleased and pleasant languor, dabbed two spots of rouge on her lips and a grain of powder on her nose and covered her bobbed corn-colored hair with a rose-littered sunbonnet. Then she kicked over the painting water, said, "Oh, damn!"—but let it lie—and left the room.

"How you, Clark?" she inquired a minute later as she slipped nimbly over the side of the car.

"Mighty fine, Sally Carrol."

"Where we go swimmin'?"

"Out to Walley's Pool. Told Marylyn we'd call by an' get her an' Joe Ewing."

Clark was dark and lean and when on foot was rather inclined to stoop. His eyes were ominous and his expression somewhat petulant except when startlingly illuminated by one of his frequent smiles. Clark had "a income"—just enough to keep himself in ease and his car in gasoline—and he had spent the two years since he graduated from Georgia Tech in dozing round the lazy streets of his home town, discussing how he could best invest his capital for an immediate fortune.

Hanging round he found not at all difficult; a crowd of little girls had grown up beautifully, the amazing Sally Carrol foremost among them; and they enjoyed being swum with and danced with and made love to in the flower-filled summery evenings—and they all liked Clark immensely. When feminine company palled there were half a dozen other youths who were always just about to do something, and meanwhile were quite willing to join him in a few holes of golf, or a game of billiards, or the consumption of a quart of "hard yella licker." Every once in awhile one of these contemporaries made a farewell round of calls before going up to New York or Philadelphia or Pittsburgh to go into business, but mostly they just stayed round in this languid paradise of dreamy skies and firefly evenings and noisy niggery street fairs—and especially of gracious soft-voiced girls, who were brought up on memories instead of money.

The Ford having been excited into a sort of restless resentful life Clark and Sally Carrol rolled and rattled down Valley Avenue into Jefferson Street, where the dust road became a pavement; along opiate Millicent Place, where there were half a dozen prosperous substantial mansions; and on into the downtown section. Driving was perilous here, for it was shopping time; the population idled casually across the streets and a drove of low-moaning oxen were being urged along in front of a placid street-car; even the shops seemed only yawning their doors and blinking their windows in the sunshine before retiring into a state of utter and finite coma.

"Sally Carrol," said Clark suddenly, "it a fact that you're engaged?"

She looked at him quickly.

"Where'd you hear that?"

"Sure enough, you engaged?"

"'At's a nice question!"

"Girl told me you were engaged to a Yankee you met up in Asheville last summer."

Sally Carrol sighed.

"Never saw such an old town for rumors."

"Don't marry a Yankee, Sally Carrol. We need you round here."

Sally Carrol was silent a moment.

"Clark," she demanded suddenly, "who on earth shall I marry?"

"I offer my services."

"Honey, you couldn't support a wife," she answered cheerfully. "Anyway, I know you too well to fall in love with you."

"'At doesn't mean you ought to marry a Yankee," he persisted.

"S'pose I love him?"

He shook his head.

"You couldn't. He'd be a lot different from us, every way."

He broke off as he halted the car in front of a rambling, dilapidated house. Marylyn Wade and Joe Ewing appeared in the doorway.

"'Lo, Sally Carrol."

"Hi!"

"How you-all?"

"Sally Carrol," demanded Marylyn as they started off again, "you engaged?"

"Lawdy, where'd all this start? Can't I look at a man 'thout everybody in town engagin' me to him?"

Clark stared straight in front of him at a bolt on the clattering windshield.

"Sally Carrol," he said with a curious intensity, "don't you like us?"

"What?"

"Us down here?"

"Why, Clark, you know I do. I adore all you boys."

"Then why you gettin' engaged to a Yankee?"

"Clark, I don't know. I'm not sure what I'll do, but—well, I want to go places and see people. I want my mind to grow. I want to live where things happen on a big scale."

"What you mean?"

"Oh, Clark, I love you, and I love Joe here, and Ben Arrot, and you-all, but you'll—you'll——"

"We'll all be failures?"

"Yes. I don't mean only money failures, but just sort of—of ineffectual and sad, and—oh, how can I tell you?"

"You mean because we stay here in Tarleton?"

"Yes, Clark; and because you like it and never want to change things or think or go ahead."

He nodded and she reached over and pressed his hand.

"Clark," she said softly, "I wouldn't change you for the world. You're sweet the way you are. The things that'll make you fail I'll love always—the living in the past, the lazy days and nights you have, and all your carelessness and generosity."

"But you're goin' away?"

"Yes—because I couldn't ever marry you. You've a place in my heart no one else ever could have, but tied down here I'd get restless. I'd feel I was—wastin' myself. There's two sides to me, you see. There's the sleepy old side you love; an' there's a sort of energy—the feelin' that makes me do wild things. That's the part of me that may be useful somewhere, that'll last when I'm not beautiful anymore."

She broke off with characteristic suddenness and sighed, "Oh, sweet cooky!" as her mood changed.

Half-closing her eyes and tipping back her head till it rested on the seat-back she let the savory breeze fan her eyes and ripple the fluffy curls of her bobbed hair. They were in the country now, hurrying between tangled growths of bright-green coppice and grass and tall trees that sent sprays of foliage to hang a cool welcome over the road. Here and there they passed a battered negro cabin, its oldest white-haired inhabitant smoking a corncob pipe beside the door and half a dozen scantily clothed pickaninnies parading tattered dolls on the wild-grown grass in front. Farther out were lazy cotton fields, where even the workers seemed intangible shadows lent by the sun to the earth not for toil but to while away some age-old tradition in the golden September fields. And round the drowsy picturesqueness, over the trees and shacks and muddy rivers, flowed the heat, never hostile, only comforting like a great warm nourishing bosom for the infant earth.

"Sally Carrol, we're here!"

"Poor chile's soun' asleep."

"Honey, you dead at last outa sheer laziness?"

"Water, Sally Carrol! Cool water waitin' for you!"

Her eyes opened sleepily.

"Hi!" she murmured, smiling.

II

In November Harry Bellamy, tall, broad and brisk, came down from his Northern city to spend four days. His intention was to settle a matter that had been hanging fire since he and Sally Carrol had met in Asheville, North Carolina, in midsummer. The settlement took only a quiet afternoon and an evening in front of a glowing open fire, for Harry Bellamy had everything she wanted; and, besides, she loved him—loved him with that side of her she kept especially for loving. Sally Carrol had several rather clearly defined sides.

On his last afternoon they walked, and she found their steps tending half-unconsciously toward one of her favorite haunts, the cemetery. When it came in sight, grey-white and golden-green under the cheerful late sun, she paused irresolute by the iron gate.

"Are you mournful by nature, Harry?" she asked with a faint smile.

"Mournful? Not I."

"Then let's go in here. It depresses some folks, but I like it."

They passed through the gateway and followed a path that led through a wavy valley of graves—dusty-grey and moldy for the fifties; quaintly carved with flowers and jars for the seventies; ornate and hideous for the nineties, with fat marble cherubs lying in sodden sleep on stone pillows, and great impossible growths of nameless granite flowers. Occasionally they saw a kneeling figure with tributary flowers, but over most of the graves lay silence and withered leaves with only the fragrance that their own shadowy memories could waken in living minds.

They reached the top of a hill where they were fronted by a tall, round headstone, freckled with dark spots of damp and half grown over with vines.

"Margery Lee," she read; "1844–1873. Wasn't she nice? She died when she was twenty-nine. Dear Margery Lee," she added softly. "Can't you see her, Harry?"

"Yes, Sally Carrol."

He felt a little hand insert itself into his.

"She was dark, I think; and she always wore her hair with a ribbon in it, and gorgeous hoop-skirts of alice blue and old rose."

"Yes."

"Oh, she was sweet, Harry! And she was the sort of girl born to stand on a wide pillared porch and welcome folks in. I think perhaps a lot of men went away to war meanin' to come back to her; but maybe none of 'em ever did."

He stooped down close to the stone, hunting for any record of marriage.

"There's nothing here to show."

"Of course not. How could there be anything there better than just 'Margery Lee,' and that eloquent date?"

She drew close to him and an unexpected lump came into his throat as her yellow hair brushed his cheek.

"You see how she was, don't you, Harry?"

"I see," he agreed gently. "I see through your precious eyes. You're beautiful now, so I know she must have been."

Silent and close they stood, and he could feel her shoulders trembling a little. An ambling breeze swept up the hill and stirred the brim of her floppidy hat.

"Let's go down there!"

She was pointing to a flat stretch on the other side of the hill where along the green turf were a thousand greyish-white crosses stretching in endless ordered rows like the stacked arms of a battalion.

"Those are the Confederate dead," said Sally Carrol simply.

They walked along and read the inscriptions, always only a name and a date, sometimes quite indecipherable.

"The last row is the saddest—see, 'way over there. Every cross has just a date on it and the word 'Unknown.'"

She looked at him and her eyes brimmed with tears.

"I can't tell you how real it is to me, darling—if you don't know."

"How you feel about it is beautiful to me."

"No, no, it's not me, it's them—that old time that I've tried to have live in me. These were just men, unimportant evidently or they wouldn't have been 'unknown'; but they died for the most beautiful thing in the world—the dead South. You see," she continued, her voice still husky, her eyes glistening with tears, "people have these dreams they fasten onto things, and I've always grown up with that dream. It was so easy because it was all dead and there weren't any disillusions comin' to me. I've tried in a way to live up to those past standards of noblesse oblige—there's just the last remnants of it, you know, like the roses of an old garden dying all round us—streaks of strange courtliness and chivalry in some of these boys an' stories I used to hear from a Confederate soldier who lived next door, and a few old darkies. Oh, Harry, there was something, there was something! I couldn't ever make you understand, but it was there."

"I understand," he assured her again quietly.

Sally Carrol smiled and dried her eyes on the tip of a handkerchief protruding from his breast pocket.

"You don't feel depressed, do you, lover? Even when I cry I'm happy here, and I get a sort of strength from it."

Hand in hand they turned and walked slowly away. Finding soft grass she drew him down to a seat beside her with their backs against the remnants of a low broken wall.

"Wish those three old women would clear out," he complained. "I want to kiss you, Sally Carrol."

"Me, too."

They waited impatiently for the three bent figures to move off, and then she kissed him until the sky seemed to fade out and all her smiles and tears to vanish in an ecstasy of eternal seconds.

Afterward they walked slowly back together, while on the corners twilight played at somnolent black-and-white checkers with the end of day.

"You'll be up about mid-January," he said, "and you've got to stay a month at least. It'll be slick. There's a winter carnival on, and if you've never really seen snow it'll be like fairyland to you. There'll be skating and skiing and tobogganing and sleigh-riding and all sorts of torchlight parades on snow-shoes. They haven't had one for years, so they're going to make it a knock-out."

"Will I be cold, Harry?" she asked suddenly.

"You certainly won't. You may freeze your nose, but you won't be shivery cold. It's hard and dry, you know."

"I guess I'm a summer child. I don't like any cold I've ever seen." She broke off and they were both silent for a minute.

"Sally Carrol," he said very slowly, "what do you say to—March?"

"I say I love you."

"March?"

"March, Harry."

III

All night in the Pullman it was very cold. She rang for the porter to ask for another blanket, and when he couldn't give her one she tried vainly, by squeezing down into the bottom of her berth and doubling back the bedclothes, to snatch a few hours' sleep. She wanted to look her best in the morning.

She rose at six and sliding uncomfortably into her clothes stumbled up to the diner for a cup of coffee. The snow had filtered into the vestibules and covered the floor with a slippery coating. It was intriguing, this cold, it crept in everywhere. Her breath was quite visible and she blew into the air with a naïve enjoyment. Seated in the diner she stared out the window at white hills and valleys and scattered pines whose every branch was a green platter for a cold feast of snow. Sometimes a solitary farmhouse would fly by, ugly and bleak and lone on the white waste; and with each one she had an instant of chill compassion for the souls shut in there waiting for spring.

As she left the diner and swayed back into the Pullman she experienced a surging rush of energy and wondered if she was feeling the bracing air of which Harry had spoken. This was the North, the North—her land now!

> "Then blow, ye winds, heigho!
> A-roving I will go,"

she chanted exultantly to herself.

"What's 'at?" inquired the porter politely.

"I said: 'Brush me off.'"

The long wires of the telegraph poles doubled; two tracks ran up beside the train—three—four; came a succession of white-roofed houses, a glimpse of a trolley car with frosted windows, streets—more streets—the city.

She stood for a dazed moment in the frosty station before she saw three fur-bundled figures descending upon her.

"There she is!"

"Oh, Sally Carrol!"

Sally Carrol dropped her bag.

"Hi!"

A faintly familiar icy-cold face kissed her, and then she was in a group of faces all apparently emitting great clouds of heavy smoke; she was shaking hands. There were Gordon, a short, eager man of thirty who looked like an amateur knocked-about model for Harry, and his wife, Myra, a listless lady with flaxen hair under a fur automobile cap. Almost immediately Sally Carrol thought of her as vaguely Scandinavian. A cheerful chauffeur adopted her bag, and amid ricochets of half-phrases, exclamations, and perfunctory listless "my dears" from Myra, they swept each other from the station.

Then they were in a sedan bound through a crooked succession of snowy streets where dozens of little boys were hitching sleds behind grocery wagons and automobiles.

"Oh," cried Sally Carrol, "I want to do that! Can we, Harry?"

"That's for kids. But we might——"

"It looks like such a circus!" she said regretfully.

Home was a rambling frame house set on a white lap of snow, and there she met a big, grey-haired man of whom she approved, and a lady who was like an egg and who kissed her—these were Harry's parents. There was a breathless indescribable hour crammed full of half-sentences, hot water, bacon and eggs and confusion; and after that she was alone with Harry in the library, asking him if she dared smoke.

It was a large room with a Madonna over the fireplace and rows upon rows of books in covers of light gold and dark gold and shiny red. All the chairs had little lace squares where one's head should rest, the couch was just comfortable, the books looked as if they had been read—some—and Sally Carrol had an instantaneous vision of the battered old library at home with her father's huge medical books and the oil paintings of her three great-uncles and the old couch that had been mended up for forty-five years and was still luxurious to dream in. This room struck her as being neither attractive nor particularly otherwise. It was simply a room with a lot of fairly expensive things in it that all looked about fifteen years old.

"What do you think of it up here?" demanded Harry eagerly. "Does it surprise you? Is it what you expected, I mean?"

"You are, Harry," she said quietly, and reached out her arms to him.

But after a brief kiss he seemed anxious to extort enthusiasm from her.

"The town, I mean. Do you like it? Can you feel the pep in the air?"

"Oh, Harry," she laughed, "you'll have to give me time. You can't just fling questions at me."

She puffed at her cigarette with a sigh of contentment.

"One thing I want to ask you," he began rather apologetically; "you Southerners put quite an emphasis on family and all that—not that it isn't quite all right, but you'll find it a little different here. I mean—you'll notice a lot of things that'll seem to you sort of vulgar display at first, Sally Carrol; but just remember that this is a three-generation town. Everybody has a father and about half of us have grandfathers. Back of that we don't go."

"Of course," she murmured.

"Our grandfathers, you see, founded the place, and a lot of them had to take some pretty queer jobs while they were doing the founding. For instance, there's one woman who at present is about the social model for the town; well, her father was the first public ash man—things like that."

"Why," said Sally Carrol, puzzled, "did you s'pose I was goin' to make remarks about people?"

"Not at all," interrupted Harry; "and I'm not apologizing for anyone either. It's just that—well, a Southern girl came up here last summer and said some unfortunate things, and—oh, I just thought I'd tell you."

Sally Carrol felt suddenly indignant—as though she had been unjustly spanked—but Harry evidently considered the subject closed, for he went on with a great surge of enthusiasm.

"It's carnival time, you know. First in ten years. And there's an ice palace they're building now that's the first they've had since eighty-five. Built out of blocks of the clearest ice they could find—on a tremendous scale."

She rose and walking to the window pushed aside the heavy Turkish portières and looked out.

"Oh!" she cried suddenly. "There's two little boys makin' a snow-man! Harry, do you reckon I can go out an' help 'em?"

"You dream! Come here and kiss me."

She left the window rather reluctantly.

"I don't guess this is a very kissable climate, is it? I mean, it makes you so you don't want to sit round, doesn't it?"

"We're not going to. I've got a vacation for the first week you're here, and there's a dinner-dance tonight."

"Oh, Harry," she confessed, subsiding in a heap, half in his lap, half in the pillows, "I sure do feel confused. I haven't got an idea whether I'll like it or not, an' I don't know what people expect or anythin'. You'll have to tell me, honey."

"I'll tell you," he said softly, "if you'll just tell me you're glad to be here."

"Glad—just awful glad!" she whispered, insinuating herself into his arms in her own peculiar way. "Where you are is home for me, Harry."

And as she said this she had the feeling for almost the first time in her life that she was acting a part.

That night, amid the gleaming candles of a dinner party where the men seemed to do most of the talking while the girls sat in a haughty and expensive aloofness, even Harry's presence on her left failed to make her feel at home.

"They're a good-looking crowd, don't you think?" he demanded. "Just look round. There's Spud Hubbard, tackle at Princeton last year, and Junie Morton—he and the red-haired fellow next to him were both Yale hockey captains; Junie was in my class. Why, the best athletes in the world come from these states round here. This is a man's country, I tell you. Look at John J. Fishburn!"

"Who's he?" asked Sally Carrol innocently.

"Don't you know?"

"I've heard the name."

"Greatest wheat man in the Northwest, and one of the greatest financiers in the country."

She turned suddenly to a voice on her right.

"I guess they forgot to introduce us. My name's Roger Patton."

"My name is Sally Carrol Happer," she said graciously.

"Yes, I know. Harry told me you were coming."

"You a relative?"

"No, I'm a professor."

"Oh," she laughed.

"At the university. You're from the South, aren't you?"

"Yes; Tarleton, Georgia."

She liked him immediately—a reddish-brown mustache under watery blue eyes that had something in them that these other eyes lacked, some quality of appreciation. They exchanged stray sentences through dinner and she made up her mind to see him again.

After coffee she was introduced to numerous good-looking young men who danced with conscious precision and seemed to take it for granted that she wanted to talk about nothing except Harry.

"Heavens," she thought, "they talk as if my being engaged made me older than they are—as if I'd tell their mothers on them!"

In the South an engaged girl, even a young married woman, expected the same amount of half-affectionate badinage and flattery that would be accorded a debutante, but here all that seemed banned. One young man, after getting well started on the subject of Sally Carrol's eyes and how they had allured him ever since she entered the room, went into a violent confusion when he found she was visiting the Bellamys—was Harry's fiancée. He seemed to feel as though he had made some risqué and inexcusable blunder, became immediately formal and left her at the first opportunity.

She was rather glad when Roger Patton cut in on her and suggested that they sit out awhile.

"Well," he inquired, blinking cheerily, "how's Carmen from the South?"

"Mighty fine. How's—how's Dangerous Dan McGrew? Sorry, but he's the only Northerner I know much about."

He seemed to enjoy that.

"Of course," he confessed, "as a professor of literature I'm not supposed to have read Dangerous Dan McGrew."

"Are you a native?"

"No, I'm a Philadelphian. Imported from Harvard to teach French. But I've been here ten years."

"Nine years, three hundred an' sixty-four days longer than me."

"Like it here?"

"Uh-huh. Sure do!"

"Really?"

"Well, why not? Don't I look as if I were havin' a good time?"

"I saw you look out the window a minute ago—and shiver."

"Just my imagination," laughed Sally Carrol. "I'm used to havin' everythin' quiet outside, an' sometimes I look out an' see a flurry of snow, an' it's just as if somethin' dead was movin'."

He nodded appreciatively.

"Ever been North before?"

"Spent two Julys in Asheville, North Carolina."

"Nice-looking crowd, aren't they?" suggested Patton, indicating the swirling floor.

Sally Carrol started. This had been Harry's remark.

"Sure are! They're—canine."

"What?"

She flushed.

"I'm sorry; that sounded worse than I meant it. You see I always think of people as feline or canine, irrespective of sex."

"Which are you?"

"I'm feline. So are you. So are most Southern men an' most of these girls here."

"What's Harry?"

"Harry's canine distinctly. All the men I've met tonight seem to be canine."

"What does 'canine' imply? A certain conscious masculinity as opposed to subtlety?"

"Reckon so. I never analyzed it—only I just look at people an' say 'canine' or 'feline' right off. It's right absurd, I guess."

"Not at all. I'm interested. I used to have a theory about these people. I think they're freezing up."

"What?"

"I think they're growing like Swedes—Ibsenesque, you know. Very gradually getting gloomy and melancholy. It's these long winters. Ever read any Ibsen?"

She shook her head.

"Well, you find in his characters a certain brooding rigidity. They're righteous, narrow and cheerless, without infinite possibilities for great sorrow or joy."

"Without smiles or tears?"

"Exactly. That's my theory. You see there are thousands of Swedes up here. They come, I imagine, because the climate is very much like their own, and there's been a gradual mingling. There're probably not half a dozen here tonight, but—we've had four Swedish governors. Am I boring you?"

"I'm mighty interested."

"Your future sister-in-law is half Swedish. Personally I like her, but my theory is that Swedes react rather badly on us as a whole. Scandinavians, you know, have the largest suicide rate in the world."

"Why do you live here if it's so depressing?"

"Oh, it doesn't get me. I'm pretty well cloistered, and I suppose books mean more than people to me anyway."

"But writers all speak about the South being tragic. You know—Spanish señoritas, black hair and daggers an' haunting music."

He shook his head.

"No, the Northern races are the tragic races—they don't indulge in the cheering luxury of tears."

Sally Carrol thought of her graveyard. She supposed that that was vaguely what she had meant when she said it didn't depress her.

"The Italians are about the gayest people in the world—but it's a dull subject," he broke off. "Anyway, I want to tell you you're marrying a pretty fine man."

Sally Carrol was moved by an impulse of confidence.

"I know. I'm the sort of person who wants to be taken care of after a certain point, and I feel sure I will be."

"Shall we dance? You know," he continued as they rose, "it's encouraging to find a girl who knows what she's marrying for. Nine-tenths of them think of it as a sort of walking into a moving-picture sunset."

She laughed, and liked him immensely.

Two hours later on the way home she nestled near Harry in the back seat.

"Oh, Harry," she whispered, "it's so co-old!"

"But it's warm in here, darling girl."

"But outside it's cold; and oh, that howling wind!"

She buried her face deep in his fur coat and trembled involuntarily as his cold lips kissed the tip of her ear.

IV

The first week of her visit passed in a whirl. She had her promised toboggan ride at the back of an automobile through a chill January twilight. Swathed in furs she put in a morning tobogganing on the country-club hill; even tried skiing, to sail through the air for a glorious moment and then land in a tangled laughing bundle on a soft snowdrift. She liked all the winter sports, except an afternoon spent snow-shoeing over a glaring plain under pale yellow sunshine, but she soon realized that these things were for children—that she was being humored and that the enjoyment round her was only a reflection of her own.

At first the Bellamy family puzzled her. The men were reliable and she liked them; to Mr. Bellamy especially, with his iron-grey hair and energetic dignity, she took an immediate fancy, once she found that he was born in Kentucky; this made of him a link between the old life and the new. But toward the women she felt a definite hostility. Myra, her future sister-in-law, seemed the essence of spiritless conventionality. Her conversation was so utterly devoid of personality that Sally Carrol, who came from a country where a certain amount of charm and assurance could be taken for granted in the women, was inclined to despise her.

"If those women aren't beautiful," she thought, "they're nothing. They just fade out when you look at them. They're glorified domestics. Men are the center of every mixed group."

Lastly there was Mrs. Bellamy, whom Sally Carrol detested. The first day's impression of an egg had been confirmed—an egg with a cracked, veiny voice and such an ungracious dumpiness of carriage that Sally Carrol felt that if she once fell she would surely scramble. In addition, Mrs. Bellamy seemed to typify the town in being innately hostile to strangers. She called Sally Carrol "Sally," and could not be persuaded that the double name was anything more than a tedious ridiculous nickname. To Sally Carrol this shortening of her name was like presenting her to the public half-clothed. She loved "Sally Carrol"; she loathed "Sally." She knew also that Harry's mother disapproved of her bobbed hair; and she had never dared smoke downstairs after that first day when Mrs. Bellamy had come into the library sniffing violently.

Of all the men she met she preferred Roger Patton, who was a frequent visitor at the house. He never again alluded to the Ibsenesque tendency of the populace, but when he came in one day and found her curled upon the sofa bent over "Peer Gynt" he laughed and told her to forget what he'd said—that it was all rot.

And then one afternoon in her second week she and Harry hovered on the edge of a dangerously steep quarrel. She considered that he precipitated it entirely, though the Serbia in the case was an unknown man who had not had his trousers pressed.

They had been walking homeward between mounds of high-piled snow and under a sun which Sally Carrol scarcely recognized. They passed a little girl done up in grey wool until she resembled a small Teddy bear, and Sally Carrol could not resist a gasp of maternal appreciation.

"Look! Harry!"

"What?"

"That little girl—did you see her face?"

"Yes, why?"

"It was red as a little strawberry. Oh, she was cute!"

"Why, your own face is almost as red as that already! Everybody's healthy here. We're out in the cold as soon as we're old enough to walk. Wonderful climate!"

She looked at him and had to agree. He was mighty healthy-looking; so was his brother. And she had noticed the new red in her own cheeks that very morning.

Suddenly their glances were caught and held and they stared for a moment at the street corner ahead of them. A man was standing there, his knees bent, his eyes gazing upward with a tense expression as though he were about to make a leap toward the chilly sky. And then they both exploded into a shout of laughter, for coming closer they discovered it had been a ludicrous momentary illusion produced by the extreme bagginess of the man's trousers.

"Reckon that's one on us," she laughed.

"He must be a Southerner, judging by those trousers," suggested Harry mischievously.

"Why, Harry!"

Her surprised look must have irritated him.

"Those damn Southerners!"

Sally Carrol's eyes flashed.

"Don't call 'em that!"

"I'm sorry, dear," said Harry, malignantly apologetic, "but you know what I think of them. They're sort of—sort of degenerates—

not at all like the old Southerners. They've lived so long down there with all the colored people that they've gotten lazy and shiftless."

"Hush your mouth, Harry!" she cried angrily. "They're not! They may be lazy—anybody would be in that climate—but they're my best friends, an' I don't want to hear 'em criticized in any such sweepin' way. Some of 'em are the finest men in the world."

"Oh, I know. They're all right when they come North to college, but of all the hangdog, ill-dressed, slovenly lot I ever saw, a bunch of small-town Southerners are the worst!"

Sally Carrol was clenching her gloved hands and biting her lip furiously.

"Why," continued Harry, "there was one in my class at New Haven and we all thought that at last we'd found the true type of Southern aristocrat, but it turned out that he wasn't an aristocrat at all—just the son of a Northern carpetbagger who owned about all the cotton round Mobile."

"A Southerner wouldn't talk the way you're talking now," she said evenly.

"They haven't the energy!"

"Or the somethin' else."

"I'm sorry, Sally Carrol, but I've heard you say yourself that you'd never marry——"

"That's quite different. I told you I wouldn't want to tie my life to any of the boys that are round Tarleton now, but I never made any sweepin' generalities."

They walked along in silence.

"I probably spread it on a bit thick, Sally Carrol. I'm sorry."

She nodded but made no answer. Five minutes later as they stood in the hallway she suddenly threw her arms round him.

"Oh, Harry," she cried, her eyes brimming with tears, "let's get married next week. I'm afraid of having fusses like that. I'm afraid, Harry. It wouldn't be that way if we were married."

But Harry, being in the wrong, was still irritated.

"That'd be idiotic. We decided on March."

The tears in Sally Carrol's eyes faded; her expression hardened slightly.

"Very well—I suppose I shouldn't have said that."

Harry melted.

"Dear little nut!" he cried. "Come and kiss me and let's forget."

That very night at the end of a vaudeville performance the orchestra played "Dixie" and Sally Carrol felt something stronger and more enduring than her tears and smiles of the day brim up inside her. She leaned forward gripping the arms of her chair until her face grew crimson.

"Sort of get you, dear?" whispered Harry.

But she did not hear him. To the spirited throb of the violins and the inspiring beat of the kettledrums her own old ghosts were marching by and on into the darkness, and as fifes whistled and sighed in the low encore they seemed so nearly out of sight that she could have waved good-bye.

"Away, Away,
  Away down South in Dixie!
Away, away,
  Away down South in Dixie!"

V

It was a particularly cold night. A sudden thaw had nearly cleared the streets the day before, but now they were traversed again with a powdery wraith of loose snow that traveled in wavy lines before the feet of the wind and filled the lower air with a fine-particled mist. There was no sky—only a dark, ominous tent that draped in the tops of the streets and was in reality a vast approaching army of snowflakes—while over it all, chilling away the comfort from the brown-and-green glow of lighted windows and muffling the steady trot of the horse pulling their sleigh, interminably washed the north wind. It was a dismal town after all, she thought—dismal.

Sometimes at night it had seemed to her as though no one lived here—they had all gone long ago—leaving lighted houses to be covered in time by tombing heaps of sleet. Oh, if there should be snow on her grave! To be beneath great piles of it all winter long, where even her headstone would be a light shadow against light shadows.

Her grave—a grave that should be flower-strewn and washed with sun and rain.

She thought again of those isolated country houses that her train had passed, and of the life there the long winter through—the ceaseless glare through the windows, the crust forming on the soft drifts of snow, finally the slow, cheerless melting and the harsh spring of which Roger Patton had told her. Her spring—to lose it forever—with its lilacs and the lazy sweetness it stirred in her heart. She was laying away that spring—afterward she would lay away that sweetness.

With a gradual insistence the storm broke. Sally Carrol felt a film of flakes melt quickly on her eyelashes and Harry reached over a furry arm and drew down her complicated flannel cap. Then the small flakes came in skirmish line and the horse bent his neck patiently as a transparency of white appeared momentarily on his coat.

"Oh, he's cold, Harry," she said quickly.

"Who? The horse? Oh, no, he isn't. He likes it!"

After another ten minutes they turned a corner and came in sight of their destination. On a tall hill outlined in vivid glaring green against the wintry sky stood the ice palace. It was three stories in the air, with battlements and embrasures and narrow icicled windows, and the innumerable electric lights inside made a gorgeous transparency of the great central hall. Sally Carrol clutched Harry's hand under the fur robe.

"It's beautiful!" he cried excitedly. "My golly, it's beautiful, isn't it! They haven't had one here since eighty-five!"

Somehow the notion of there not having been one since eighty-five oppressed her. Ice was a ghost, and this mansion of it was surely peopled by those shades of the eighties, with pale faces and blurred snow-filled hair.

"Come on, dear," said Harry.

She followed him out of the sleigh and waited while he hitched the horse. A party of four—Gordon, Myra, Roger Patton and another girl—drew up beside them with a mighty jingle of bells. There was quite a crowd already, bundled in fur or sheepskin, shouting and calling to each other as they moved through the snow, which was now so thick that people could scarcely be distinguished a few yards away.

"It's a hundred and seventy feet tall," Harry was saying to a muffled figure beside him as they trudged toward the entrance; "covers six thousand square yards."

She caught snatches of conversation: "One main hall"—"walls twenty to forty inches thick"—"and the ice cave has almost a mile of—"—"this Canuck who built it——"

They found their way inside, and dazed by the magic of the great crystal walls Sally Carrol found herself repeating over and over two lines from "Kubla Khan":

> "It was a miracle of rare device,
> A sunny pleasure-dome with caves of ice!"

In the great glittering cavern with the dark shut out she took a seat on a wooden bench, and the evening's oppression lifted. Harry was right—it was beautiful; and her gaze traveled the smooth surface of the walls, the blocks for which had been selected for their purity and clearness to obtain this opalescent, translucent effect.

"Look! Here we go—oh, boy!" cried Harry.

A band in a far corner struck up "Hail, Hail, the Gang's All Here!" which echoed over to them in wild muddled acoustics, and then the lights suddenly went out; silence seemed to flow down the icy sides and sweep over them. Sally Carrol could still see her white breath in the darkness, and a dim row of pale faces over on the other side.

The music eased to a sighing complaint, and from outside drifted in the full-throated resonant chant of the marching clubs. It grew louder like some pæan of a viking tribe traversing an ancient wild; it swelled—they were coming nearer; then a row of torches appeared, and another and another, and keeping time with their moccasined feet a long column of grey-mackinawed figures swept in, snow-shoes slung at their shoulders, torches soaring and flickering as their voices rose along the great walls.

The grey column ended and another followed, the light streaming luridly this time over red toboggan caps and flaming crimson mackinaws, and as they entered they took up the refrain; then came a long platoon of blue and white, of green, of white, of brown and yellow.

"Those white ones are the Wacouta Club," whispered Harry eagerly. "Those are the men you've met round at dances."

The volume of the voices grew; the great cavern was a phantasmagoria of torches waving in great banks of fire, of colors and the rhythm of soft-leather steps. The leading column turned and halted, platoon deployed in front of platoon until the whole procession made a solid flag of flame, and then from thousands of voices burst a mighty shout that filled the air like a crash of thunder and sent the torches wavering. It was magnificent, it was tremendous! To Sally Carrol it was the North offering sacrifice on some mighty altar to the grey pagan God of Snow. As the shout died the band struck up again and there came more singing, and then long reverberating cheers by each club. She sat very quiet listening while the staccato cries rent the stillness; and then she started, for there was a volley of explosion, and great clouds of smoke went up here and there through the cavern—the flashlight photographers at work—and the council was over. With the band at their head the clubs formed in column once more, took up their chant and began to march out.

"Come on!" shouted Harry. "We want to see the labyrinths downstairs before they turn the lights off!"

They all rose and started toward the chute—Harry and Sally Carrol in the lead, her little mitten buried in his big fur gauntlet. At the bottom of the chute was a long empty room of ice with the ceiling so low that they had to stoop—and their hands were parted. Before she realized what he intended Harry had darted down one of the half-dozen glittering passages that opened into the room and was only a vague receding blot against the green shimmer.

"Harry!" she called.

"Come on!" he cried back.

She looked round the empty chamber; the rest of the party had evidently decided to go home, were already outside somewhere in the blundering snow. She hesitated and then darted in after Harry.

"Harry!" she shouted.

She had reached a turning point thirty feet down; she heard a faint muffled answer far to the left, and with a touch of panic fled toward it. She passed another turning, two more yawning alleys.

"Harry!"

No answer. She started to run straight forward, and then turned like lightning and sped back the way she had come, enveloped in a sudden icy terror.

She reached a turn—was it here?—took the left and came to what should have been the outlet into the long low room, but it was only another glittering passage with darkness at the end. She called again, but the walls gave back a flat lifeless echo with no reverberations. Retracing her steps she turned another corner, this time following a wide passage. It was like the green lane between the parted waters of the Red Sea, like a damp vault connecting empty tombs.

She slipped a little now as she walked, for ice had formed on the bottom of her overshoes; she had to run her gloves along the half-slippery, half-sticky walls to keep her balance.

"Harry!"

Still no answer. The sound she made bounced mockingly down to the end of the passage.

Then on an instant the lights went out and she was in complete darkness. She gave a small frightened cry and sank down into a cold little heap on the ice. She felt her left knee do something as she fell, but she scarcely noticed it as some deep terror far greater than any fear of being lost settled upon her. She was alone with this presence that came out of the North, the dreary loneliness that rose from ice-bound whalers in the Arctic seas, from smokeless trackless wastes where were strewn the whitened bones of adventure. It was an icy breath of death; it was rolling down low across the land to clutch at her.

With a furious despairing energy she rose again and started blindly down the darkness. She must get out. She might be lost in here for days, freeze to death and lie embedded in the ice like corpses she had read of, kept perfectly preserved until the melting of a glacier. Harry probably thought she had left with the others—he had gone by now; no one would know until late next day. She reached pitifully for the wall. Forty inches thick, they had said—forty inches thick!

"Oh!"

On both sides of her along the walls she felt things creeping, damp souls that haunted this palace, this town, this North.

"Oh, send somebody—send somebody!" she cried aloud.

Clark Darrow—he would understand; or Joe Ewing; she couldn't be left here to wander forever—to be frozen, heart, body and soul. This her—this Sally Carrol! Why, she was a happy thing. She was a happy little girl. She liked warmth and summer and Dixie. These things were foreign—foreign.

"You're not crying," something said aloud. "You'll never cry any more. Your tears would just freeze; all tears freeze up here!"

She sprawled full length on the ice.

"Oh, God!" she faltered.

A long single file of minutes went by, and with a great weariness she felt her eyes closing. Then someone seemed to sit down near her and take her face in warm, soft hands. She looked up gratefully.

"Why, it's Margery Lee," she crooned softly to herself. "I knew you'd come." It really was Margery Lee, and she was just as Sally Carrol had known she would be, with a young white brow and wide welcoming eyes and a hoop-skirt of some soft material that was quite comforting to rest on.

"Margery Lee."

It was getting darker now and darker—all those tombstones ought to be repainted, sure enough, only that would spoil 'em, of course. Still, you ought to be able to see 'em.

Then after a succession of moments that went fast and then slow, but seemed to be ultimately resolving themselves into a multitude of blurred rays converging toward a pale yellow sun, she heard a great cracking noise break her new-found stillness.

It was the sun, it was a light; a torch, and a torch beyond that, and another one, and voices; a face took flesh below the torch, heavy arms raised her and she felt something on her cheek—it felt wet. Someone had seized her and was rubbing her face with snow. How ridiculous—with snow!

"Sally Carrol! Sally Carrol!"

It was Dangerous Dan McGrew; and two other faces she didn't know.

"Child, child! We've been looking for you two hours! Harry's half-crazy!"

Things came rushing back into place—the singing, the torches, the great shout of the marching clubs. She squirmed in Patton's arms and gave a long low cry.

"Oh, I want to get out of here! I'm going back home. Take me home"—her voice rose to a scream that sent a chill to Harry's heart as he came racing down the next passage—"tomorrow!" she cried with delirious, unrestrained passion—"Tomorrow! Tomorrow! Tomorrow!"

VI

The wealth of golden sunlight poured a quite enervating yet oddly comforting heat over the house where day-long it faced the dusty stretch of road. Two birds were making a great to-do in a cool spot found among the branches of a tree next door, and down the street a colored woman was announcing herself melodiously as a purveyor of strawberries. It was April afternoon.

Sally Carrol Happer, resting her chin on her arm and her arm on an old window seat, gazed sleepily down over the spangled dust whence the heat waves were rising for the first time this spring. She was watching a very ancient Ford turn a perilous corner and rattle and groan to a jolting stop at the end of the walk. She made no sound, and in a minute a strident familiar whistle rent the air. Sally Carrol smiled and blinked.

"Good mawnin'."

A head appeared tortuously from under the car top below.

"'Tain't mawnin', Sally Carrol."

"Sure enough!" she said in affected surprise. "I guess maybe not."

"What you doin'?"

"Eatin' green peach. 'Spect to die any minute."

Clark twisted himself a last impossible notch to get a view of her face.

"Water's warm as a kettla steam, Sally Carrol. Wanta go swimmin'?"

"Hate to move," sighed Sally Carrol lazily, "but I reckon so."

HEAD AND SHOULDERS

In 1915 Horace Tarbox was thirteen years old. In that year he took the examinations for entrance to Princeton University and received the Grade A—excellent—in Cæsar, Cicero, Vergil, Xenophon, Homer, Algebra, Plane Geometry, Solid Geometry and Chemistry.

Two years later, while George M. Cohan was composing "Over There," Horace was leading the sophomore class by several lengths and digging out theses on "The Syllogism as an Obsolete Scholastic Form," and during the battle of Château-Thierry he was sitting at his desk deciding whether or not to wait until his seventeenth birthday before beginning his series of essays on "The Pragmatic Bias of the New Realists."

After a while some newsboy told him that the war was over, and he was glad, because it meant that Peat Brothers, publishers, would get out their new edition of "Spinoza's Improvement of the Understanding." Wars were all very well in their way, made young men self-reliant or something, but Horace felt that he could never forgive the President for allowing a brass band to play under his window on the night of the false armistice, causing him to leave three important sentences out of his thesis on "German Idealism."

The next year he went up to Yale to take his degree as Master of Arts.

He was seventeen then, tall and slender, with near-sighted grey eyes and an air of keeping himself utterly detached from the mere words he let drop.

"I never feel as though I'm talking to him," expostulated Professor Dillinger to a sympathetic colleague. "He makes me feel as though I were talking to his representative. I always expect him to say: 'Well, I'll ask myself and find out.'"

And then, just as nonchalantly as though Horace Tarbox had been Mr. Beef the butcher or Mr. Hat the haberdasher, life reached in, seized him, handled him, stretched him and unrolled him like a piece of Irish lace on a Saturday-afternoon bargain counter.

To move in the literary fashion I should say that this was all because when way back in colonial days the hardy pioneers had come to a bald place in Connecticut and asked of each other, "Now, what shall we build here?" the hardiest one among 'em had answered: "Let's build a town where theatrical managers can try out musical comedies!" How afterward they founded Yale College there, to try the musical comedies on, is a story everyone knows. At any rate one December, "Home James!" opened at the Shubert and all the students encored Marcia Meadow, who sang a song about the Blundering Blimp in the first act and did a shaky, shivery, celebrated dance in the last.

Marcia was nineteen. She didn't have wings, but audiences agreed generally that she didn't need them. She was a blonde by natural pigment, and she wore no paint on the streets at high noon. Outside of that she was no better than most women.

It was Charlie Moon who promised her five thousand Pall Malls if she would pay a call on Horace Tarbox, prodigy extraordinary. Charlie was a senior in Sheffield and he and Horace were first cousins. They liked and pitied each other.

Horace had been particularly busy that night. The failure of the Frenchman Laurier to appreciate the significance of the new realists was preying on his mind. In fact, his only reaction to a low, clear-cut rap at his study was to make him speculate as to whether any rap would have actual existence without an ear there to hear it. He fancied he was verging more and more toward pragmatism. But at that moment, though he did not know it, he was verging with astounding rapidity toward something quite different.

The rap sounded—three seconds leaked by—the rap sounded.

"Come in," muttered Horace automatically.

He heard the door open and then close, but, bent over his book in the big armchair before the fire, he did not look up.

"Leave it on the bed in the other room," he said absently.

"Leave what on the bed in the other room?"

Marcia Meadow had to talk her songs, but her speaking voice was like byplay on a harp.

"The laundry."

"I can't."

Horace stirred impatiently in his chair.

"Why can't you?"

"Why, because I haven't got it."

"Hm!" he replied testily. "Suppose you go back and get it."

Across the fire from Horace was another easy chair. He was accustomed to change to it in the course of an evening by way of exercise and variety. One chair he called Berkeley, the other he called Hume. He suddenly heard a sound as of a rustling, diaphanous form sinking into Hume. He glanced up.

"Well," said Marcia with the sweet smile she used in Act Two ("Oh, so the Duke liked my dancing!"), "Well, Omar Khayyam, here I am beside you singing in the wilderness."

Horace stared at her dazedly. The momentary suspicion came to him that she existed there only as a phantom of his imagination. Women didn't come into men's rooms and sink into men's Humes. Women brought laundry and took your seat in the streetcar and married you later on when you were old enough to know fetters.

This woman had clearly materialized out of Hume. The very froth of her brown gauzy dress was an emanation from Hume's leather arm there! If he looked long enough he would see Hume right through her and then he would be alone again in the room. He passed his fist across his eyes. He really must take up those trapeze exercises again.

"For Pete's sake, don't look so critical!" objected the emanation pleasantly. "I feel as if you were going to wish me away with that patent dome of yours. And then there wouldn't be anything left of me except my shadow in your eyes."

Horace coughed. Coughing was one of his two gestures. When he talked you forgot he had a body at all. It was like hearing a phonograph record by a singer who had been dead a long time.

"What do you want?" he asked.

"I want them letters," whined Marcia melodramatically—"them letters of mine you bought from my grandsire in 1881."

Horace considered.

"I haven't got your letters," he said evenly. "I am only seventeen years old. My father was not born until March 3, 1879. You evidently have me confused with someone else."

"You're only seventeen?" repeated Marcia suspiciously.

"Only seventeen."

"I knew a girl," said Marcia reminiscently, "who went on the ten-twenty-thirty when she was sixteen. She was so stuck on herself that she could never say 'sixteen' without putting the 'only' before it. We got to calling her 'Only Jessie.' And she's just where she was when she started—only worse. 'Only' is a bad habit, Omar—it sounds like an alibi."

"My name is not Omar."

"I know," agreed Marcia, nodding—"your name's Horace. I just call you Omar because you remind me of a smoked cigarette."

"And I haven't your letters. I doubt if I've ever met your grandfather. In fact, I think it very improbable that you yourself were alive in 1881."

Marcia stared at him in wonder.

"Me—1881? Why sure! I was second-line stuff when the Florodora Sextette was still in the convent. I was the original nurse to Mrs. Sol Smith's Juliet. Why, Omar, I was a canteen singer during the War of 1812."

Horace's mind made a sudden successful leap and he grinned.

"Did Charlie Moon put you up to this?"

Marcia regarded him inscrutably.

"Who's Charlie Moon?"

"Small—wide nostrils—big ears."

She grew several inches and sniffed.

"I'm not in the habit of noticing my friends' nostrils."

"Then it was Charlie?"

Marcia bit her lip—and then yawned.

"Oh, let's change the subject, Omar. I'll pull a snore in this chair in a minute."

"Yes," replied Horace gravely, "Hume has often been considered soporific."

"Who's your friend—and will he die?"

Then of a sudden Horace Tarbox rose slenderly and began to pace the room with his hands in his pockets. This was his other gesture.

"I don't care for this," he said as if he were talking to himself—"at all. Not that I mind your being here—I don't. You're quite a pretty little thing, but I don't like Charlie Moon's sending you up here. Am I a laboratory experiment on which the janitors as well as the chemists can make experiments? Is my intellectual development humorous in any way? Do I look like the pictures of the little Boston boy in the comic magazines? Has that callow ass, Moon, with his eternal tales about his week in Paris, any right to——"

"No," interrupted Marcia emphatically. "And you're a sweet boy. Come here and kiss me."

Horace stopped quickly in front of her.

"Why do you want me to kiss you?" he asked intently. "Do you just go round kissing people?"

"Why, yes," admitted Marcia, unruffled. "'At's all life is. Just going round kissing people."

"Well," replied Horace emphatically, "I must say your ideas are horribly garbled! In the first place life isn't just that, and in the second place I won't kiss you. It might get to be a habit and I can't get rid of habits. This year I've got in the habit of lolling in bed until seven-thirty."

Marcia nodded understandingly.

"Do you ever have any fun?" she asked.

"What do you mean by fun?"

"See here," said Marcia sternly, "I like you, Omar, but I wish you'd talk as if you had a line on what you were saying. You sound as if you were gargling a lot of words in your mouth and lost a bet every time you spilled a few. I asked you if you ever had any fun."

Horace shook his head.

"Later, perhaps," he answered. "You see I'm a plan. I'm an experiment. I don't say that I don't get tired of it sometimes—I do. Yet—oh, I can't explain! But what you and Charlie Moon call fun wouldn't be fun to me."

"Please explain."

Horace stared at her, started to speak and then, changing his mind, resumed his walk. After an unsuccessful attempt to determine whether or not he was looking at her Marcia smiled at him.

"Please explain."

Horace turned.

"If I do, will you promise to tell Charlie Moon that I wasn't in?"

"Uh-uh."

"Very well, then. Here's my history: I was a 'why' child. I wanted to see the wheels go round. My father was a young economics professor at Princeton. He brought me up on the system of answering every question I asked him to the best of his ability. My response to that gave him the idea of making an experiment in precocity. To aid in the massacre I had ear trouble—seven operations between the ages of nine and twelve. Of course this kept me apart from other boys and made me ripe for forcing. Anyway, while my generation was laboring through Uncle Remus I was honestly enjoying Catullus in the original.

"I passed off my college examinations when I was thirteen because I couldn't help it. My chief associates were professors and I took a tremendous pride in knowing that I had a fine intelligence, for though I was unusually gifted I was not abnormal in other ways. When I was sixteen I got tired of being a freak; I decided that someone had made a bad mistake. Still as I'd gone that far I concluded to finish it up by taking my degree of Master of Arts. My chief interest in life is the study of modern philosophy. I am a realist of the School of Anton Laurier—with Bergsonian trimmings—and I'll be eighteen years old in two months. That's all."

"Whew!" exclaimed Marcia. "That's enough! You do a neat job with the parts of speech."

"Satisfied?"

"No, you haven't kissed me."

"It's not in my program," demurred Horace. "Understand that I don't pretend to be above physical things. They have their place, but——"

"Oh, don't be so darned reasonable!"

"I can't help it."

"I hate these slot-machine people."

"I assure you I——" began Horace.

"Oh, shut up!"

"My own rationality——"

"I didn't say anything about your nationality. You're an Amuricun, ar'n't you?"

"Yes."

"Well, that's O.K. with me. I got a notion I want to see you do something that isn't in your highbrow program. I want to see if a what-ch-call-em with Brazilian trimmings—that thing you said you were—can be a little human."

Horace shook his head again.

"I won't kiss you."

"My life is blighted," muttered Marcia tragically. "I'm a beaten woman. I'll go through life without ever having a kiss with Brazilian trimmings." She sighed. "Anyways, Omar, will you come and see my show?"

"What show?"

"I'm a wicked actress from 'Home James!'"

"Light opera?"

"Yes—at a stretch. One of the characters is a Brazilian rice planter. That might interest you."

"I saw 'The Bohemian Girl' once," reflected Horace aloud. "I enjoyed it—to some extent."

"Then you'll come?"

"Well, I'm—I'm——"

"Oh, I know—you've got to run down to Brazil for the week-end."

"Not at all. I'd be delighted to come."

Marcia clapped her hands.

"Goodyforyou! I'll mail you a ticket—Thursday night?"

"Why, I——"

"Good! Thursday night it is."

She stood up and walking close to him laid both hands on his shoulders.

"I like you, Omar. I'm sorry I tried to kid you. I thought you'd be sort of frozen, but you're a nice boy."

He eyed her sardonically.

"I'm several thousand generations older than you are."

"You carry your age well."

They shook hands gravely.

"My name's Marcia Meadow," she said emphatically. "'Member it—Marcia Meadow. And I won't tell Charlie Moon you were in."

An instant later as she was skimming down the last flight of stairs three at a time she heard a voice call over the upper banister: "Oh, say——"

She stopped and looked up—made out a vague form leaning over.

"Oh, say!" called the prodigy again. "Can you hear me?"

"Here's your connection, Omar."

"I hope I haven't given you the impression that I consider kissing intrinsically irrational."

"Impression? Why, you didn't even give me the kiss! Never fret—so long."

Two doors near her opened curiously at the sound of a feminine voice. A tentative cough sounded from above. Gathering her skirts, Marcia dived wildly down the last flight and was swallowed up in the murky Connecticut air outside.

Upstairs Horace paced the floor of his study. From time to time he glanced toward Berkeley waiting there in suave dark-red respectability, an open book lying suggestively on his cushions. And then he found that his circuit of the floor was bringing him each time nearer to Hume. There was something about Hume that was strangely and inexpressibly different. The diaphanous form still seemed hovering near, and had Horace sat there he would have felt as if he were sitting on a lady's lap. And though Horace couldn't have named the quality of difference, there was such a quality—quite intangible to the speculative mind, but real nevertheless. Hume was radiating something that in all the two hundred years of his influence he had never radiated before.

Hume was radiating attar of roses.

II

On Thursday night Horace Tarbox sat in an aisle seat in the fifth row and witnessed "Home James!" Oddly enough he found that he was enjoying himself. The cynical students near him were annoyed at his audible appreciation of time-honored jokes in the Hammerstein tradition. But Horace was waiting with anxiety for Marcia Meadow singing her song about a Jazz-bound Blundering Blimp. When she did appear, radiant under a floppity flower-faced hat, a warm glow settled over him, and when the song was over he did not join in the storm of applause. He felt somewhat numb.

In the intermission after the second act an usher materialized beside him, demanded to know if he were Mr. Tarbox, and then handed him a note written in a round adolescent hand. Horace read it in some confusion, while the usher lingered with withering patience in the aisle.

"DEAR OMAR: After the show I always grow an awful hunger. If you want to satisfy it for me in the Taft Grill just communicate your answer to the big-timber guide that brought this and oblige.

Your friend,
MARCIA MEADOW."

"Tell her"—he coughed—"tell her that it will be quite all right. I'll meet her in front of the theatre."

The big-timber guide smiled arrogantly.

"I giss she meant for you to come roun' t' the stage door."

"Where—where is it?"

"Ou'side. Tunayulef. Down ee alley."

"What?"

"Ou'side. Turn to y' left! Down ee alley!"

The arrogant person withdrew. A freshman behind Horace snickered.

Then half an hour later, sitting in the Taft Grill opposite the hair that was yellow by natural pigment, the prodigy was saying an odd thing.

"Do you have to do that dance in the last act?" he was asking earnestly—"I mean, would they dismiss you if you refused to do it?"

Marcia grinned.

"It's fun to do it. I like to do it."

And then Horace came out with a *faux pas*.

"I should think you'd detest it," he remarked succinctly. "The people behind me were making remarks about your bosom."

Marcia blushed fiery red.

"I can't help that," she said quickly. "The dance to me is only a sort of acrobatic stunt. Lord, it's hard enough to do! I rub liniment into my shoulders for an hour every night."

"Do you have—fun while you're on the stage?"

"Uh-huh—sure! I got in the habit of having people look at me, Omar, and I like it."

"Hm!" Horace sank into a brownish study.

"How's the Brazilian trimmings?"

"Hm!" repeated Horace, and then after a pause: "Where does the play go from here?"

"New York."

"For how long?"

"All depends. Winter—maybe."

"Oh!"

"Coming up to lay eyes on me, Omar, or aren't you int'rested? Not as nice here, is it, as it was up in your room? I wish we was there now."

"I feel idiotic in this place," confessed Horace, looking round him nervously.

"Too bad! We got along pretty well."

At this he looked suddenly so melancholy that she changed her tone, and reaching over patted his hand.

"Ever take an actress out to supper before?"

"No," said Horace miserably, "and I never will again. I don't know why I came tonight. Here under all these lights and with all these people laughing and chattering I feel completely out of my sphere. I don't know what to talk to you about."

"We'll talk about me. We talked about you last time."

"Very well."

"Well, my name really is Meadow, but my first name isn't Marcia—it's Veronica. I'm nineteen. Question—how did the girl make her leap to the footlights? Answer—she was born in Passaic, New Jersey, and up to a year ago she got the right to breathe by pushing Nabiscos in Marcel's tea room in Trenton. She started going with a guy named Robbins, a singer in the Trent House cabaret, and he got her to try a song and dance with him one evening. In a month we were filling the supper room every night. Then we went to New York with meet-my-friend letters thick as a pile of napkins.

"In two days we'd landed a job at Divinerries' and I learned to shimmy from a kid at the Palais Royal. We stayed at Divinerries' six months until one night Peter Boyce Wendell, the columnist, ate his milk toast there. Next morning a poem about Marvelous Marcia came out in his newspaper and within two days I had three vaudeville offers and a chance at the Midnight Frolic. I wrote Wendell a thank-you letter and he printed it in his column—said that the style was like Carlyle's, only more rugged, and that I ought to quit dancing and do North American literature. This got me a coupla more vaudeville offers and a chance as an ingénue in a regular show. I took it—and here I am, Omar."

When she finished they sat for a moment in silence, she draping the last skeins of a Welsh rabbit on her fork and waiting for him to speak.

"Let's get out of here," he said suddenly.

Marcia's eyes hardened.

"What's the idea? Am I making you sick?"

"No, but I don't like it here. I don't like to be sitting here with you."

Without another word Marcia signaled for the waiter.

"What's the check?" she demanded briskly. "My part—the rabbit and the ginger ale."

Horace watched blankly as the waiter figured it.

"See here," he began, "I intended to pay for yours too. You're my guest."

With a half-sigh Marcia rose from the table and walked from the room. Horace, his face a document in bewilderment, laid a bill down and followed her out, up the stairs and into the lobby. He overtook her in front of the elevator and they faced each other.

"See here," he repeated, "you're my guest. Have I said something to offend you?"

After an instant of wonder Marcia's eyes softened.

"You're a rude fella," she said slowly. "Don't you know you're rude?"

"I can't help it," said Horace with a directness she found quite disarming. "You know I like you."

"You said you didn't like being with me."

"I didn't like it."

"Why not?"

Fire blazed suddenly from the grey forests of his eyes.

"Because I didn't. I've formed the habit of liking you. I've been thinking of nothing much else for two days."

"Well, if you——"

"Wait a minute," he interrupted. "I've got something to say. It's this: in six weeks I'll be eighteen years old. When I'm eighteen years old I'm coming up to New York to see you. Is there some place in New York where we can go and not have a lot of people in the room?"

"Sure!" smiled Marcia. "You can come up to my 'partment. Sleep on the couch if you want to."

"I can't sleep on couches," he said shortly. "But I want to talk to you."

"Why, sure," repeated Marcia—"in my 'partment."

In his excitement Horace put his hands in his pockets.

"All right—just so I can see you alone. I want to talk to you as we talked up in my room."

"Honey boy," cried Marcia laughing, "is it that you want to kiss me?"

"Yes," Horace almost shouted. "I'll kiss you if you want me to."

The elevator man was looking at them reproachfully. Marcia edged toward the grated door.

"I'll drop you a post card," she said.

Horace's eyes were quite wild.

"Send me a post card! I'll come up any time after January first. I'll be eighteen then."

And as she stepped into the elevator he coughed enigmatically, yet with a vague challenge, at the ceiling, and walked quickly away.

III

He was there again. She saw him when she took her first glance at the restless Manhattan audience—down in the front row with his head bent a bit forward and his grey eyes fixed on her. And she knew that to him they were alone together in a world where the high-rouged row of ballet faces and the massed whines of the violins were as imperceivable as powder on a marble Venus. An instinctive defiance rose within her.

"Silly boy!" she said to herself hurriedly and she didn't take her encore.

"What do they expect for a hundred a week—perpetual motion?" she grumbled to herself in the wings.

"What's the trouble, Marcia?"

"Guy I don't like down in front."

During the last act as she waited for her specialty she had an odd attack of stage fright. She had never sent Horace the promised post card. Last night she had pretended not to see him—had hurried from the theatre immediately after her dance to pass a sleepless night in her apartment, thinking—as she had so often in the last month—of his pale, rather intent face, his slim, boyish figure, the merciless, unworldly abstraction that made him charming to her.

And now that he had come she felt vaguely sorry—as though an unwonted responsibility was being forced on her.

"Infant prodigy!" she said aloud.

"What?" demanded the negro comedian standing beside her.

"Nothing—just talking about myself."

On the stage she felt better. This was her dance—and she always felt that the way she did it wasn't suggestive any more than to some men every pretty girl is suggestive. She made it a stunt.

> "Uptown, downtown, jelly on a spoon,
> After sundown shiver by the moon."

He was not watching her now. She saw that clearly. He was looking very deliberately at a castle on the back drop, wearing that expression he had worn in the Taft Grill. A wave of exasperation swept over her—he was criticizing her.

> "That's the vibration that thr-ills me,
> Funny how affection fi-lls me,
> Uptown, downtown——"

Unconquerable revulsion seized her. She was suddenly and horribly conscious of her audience as she had never been since her first appearance. Was that a leer on a pallid face in the front row, a droop of disgust on one young girl's mouth? These shoulders of hers—these shoulders shaking—were they hers? Were they real? Surely shoulders weren't made for this!

> "Then—you'll see at a glance
> I'll need some funeral ushers with St. Vitus dance
> At the end of the world I'll——"

The bassoon and two cellos crashed into a final chord. She paused and poised a moment on her toes with every muscle tense, her young face looking out dully at the audience in what one young girl afterward called "such a curious, puzzled look," and then without bowing rushed from the stage. Into the dressing room she sped, kicked out of one dress and into another and caught a taxi outside.

Her apartment was very warm—small, it was, with a row of professional pictures and sets of Kipling and O. Henry which she had bought once from a blue-eyed agent and read occasionally. And there were several chairs which matched, but were none of them comfortable, and a pink-shaded lamp with blackbirds painted on it and an atmosphere of rather stifled pink throughout. There were nice things in it—nice things unrelentingly hostile to each other, offsprings of a vicarious, impatient taste acting in stray moments. The worst was typified by a great picture framed in oak bark of Passaic as seen from the Erie Railroad—altogether a frantic, oddly extravagant, oddly penurious attempt to make a cheerful room. Marcia knew it was a failure.

Into this room came the prodigy and took her two hands awkwardly.

"I followed you this time," he said.

"Oh!"

"I want you to marry me," he said.

Her arms went out to him. She kissed his mouth with a sort of passionate wholesomeness.

"There!"

"I love you," he said.

She kissed him again and then with a little sigh flung herself into an armchair and half lay there, shaken with absurd laughter.

"Why, you infant prodigy!" she cried.

"Very well, call me that if you want to. I once told you that I was ten thousand years older than you—I am."

She laughed again.

"I don't like to be disapproved of."

"No one's ever going to disapprove of you again."

"Omar," she asked, "why do you want to marry me?"

The prodigy rose and put his hands in his pockets.

"Because I love you, Marcia Meadow."

And then she stopped calling him Omar.

"Dear boy," she said, "you know I sort of love you. There's something about you—I can't tell what—that just puts my heart through the wringer every time I'm round you. But, honey——" She paused.

"But what?"

"But lots of things. But you're only just eighteen, and I'm nearly twenty."

"Nonsense!" he interrupted. "Put it this way—that I'm in my nineteenth year and you're nineteen. That makes us pretty close—without counting that other ten thousand years I mentioned."

Marcia laughed.

"But there are some more 'buts.' Your people——"

"My people!" exclaimed the prodigy ferociously. "My people tried to make a monstrosity out of me." His face grew quite crimson at the enormity of what he was going to say. "My people can go way back and sit down!"

"My heavens!" cried Marcia in alarm. "All that? On tacks, I suppose."

"Tacks—yes," he agreed wildly—"on anything. The more I think of how they allowed me to become a little dried-up mummy——"

"What makes you think you're that?" asked Marcia quietly—"me?"

"Yes. Every person I've met on the streets since I met you has made me jealous because they knew what love was before I did. I used to call it the 'sex impulse.' Heavens!"

"There's more 'buts,'" said Marcia.

"What are they?"

"How could we live?"

"I'll make a living."

"You're in college."

"Do you think I care anything about taking a Master of Arts degree?"

"You want to be Master of Me, hey?"

"Yes! What? I mean, no!"

Marcia laughed, and crossing swiftly over sat in his lap. He put his arm round her wildly and implanted the vestige of a kiss somewhere near her neck.

"There's something white about you," mused Marcia, "but it doesn't sound very logical."

"Oh, don't be so darned reasonable!"

"I can't help it," said Marcia.

"I hate these slot-machine people!"

"But we——"

"Oh, shut up!"

And as Marcia couldn't talk through her ears she had to.

IV

Horace and Marcia were married early in February. The sensation in academic circles both at Yale and Princeton was tremendous. Horace Tarbox, who at fourteen had been played up in the Sunday magazine sections of metropolitan newspapers, was throwing over his career, his chance of being a world authority on American philosophy, by marrying a chorus girl—they made Marcia a chorus girl. But like all modern stories it was a four-and-a-half-day wonder.

They took a flat in Harlem. After two weeks' search, during which his idea of the value of academic knowledge faded unmercifully, Horace took a position as clerk with a South American export company—someone had told him that exporting was the coming thing. Marcia was to stay in her show for a few months—anyway until he got on his feet. He was getting a hundred and twenty-five to start with, and though of course they told him it was only a question of months until he would be earning double that, Marcia refused even to consider giving up the hundred and fifty a week that she was getting at the time.

"We'll call ourselves Head and Shoulders, dear," she said softly, "and the shoulders'll have to keep shaking a little longer until the old head gets started."

"I hate it," he objected gloomily.

"Well," she replied emphatically, "your salary wouldn't keep us in a tenement. Don't think I want to be public—I don't. I want to be yours. But I'd be a half-wit to sit in one room and count the sunflowers on the wallpaper while I waited for you. When you pull down three hundred a month I'll quit."

And much as it hurt his pride, Horace had to admit that hers was the wiser course.

March mellowed into April. May read a gorgeous riot act to the parks and waters of Manhattan and they were very happy. Horace, who had no habits whatsoever—he had never had time to form any—proved the most adaptable of husbands, and as Marcia entirely lacked opinions on the subjects that engrossed him there were very few joltings and bumpings. Their minds moved in different spheres. Marcia acted as practical factotum and Horace lived either in his old world of abstract ideas or in a sort of triumphantly earthy worship and adoration of his wife. She was a continual source of astonishment to him—the freshness and originality of her mind, her dynamic, clear-headed energy and her unfailing good humor.

And Marcia's coworkers in the nine-o'clock show, whither she had transferred her talents, were impressed with her tremendous pride in her husband's mental powers. Horace they knew only as a very slim, tight-lipped and immature-looking young man who waited every night to take her home.

"Horace," said Marcia one evening when she met him as usual at eleven, "you looked like a ghost standing there against the street lights. You losing weight?"

He shook his head vaguely.

"I don't know. They raised me to a hundred and thirty-five dollars today and——"

"I don't care," said Marcia severely. "You're killing yourself working at night. You read those big books on economy——"

"Economics," corrected Horace.

"Well, you read 'em every night long after I'm asleep. And you're getting all stooped over like you were before we were married."

"But, Marcia, I've got to——"

"No, you haven't, dear. I guess I'm running this shop for the present, and I won't let my fella ruin his health and eyes. You got to get some exercise."

"I do. Every morning I——"

"Oh, I know! But those dumb-bells of yours wouldn't give a consumptive two degrees of fever. I mean real exercise. You've got to join a gymnasium. 'Member you told me you were such a trick gymnast once that they tried to get you out for the team in college and they couldn't because you had a standing date with Herb Spencer?"

"I used to enjoy it," mused Horace, "but it would take up too much time now."

"All right," said Marcia. "I'll make a bargain with you. You join a gym and I'll read one of those books from the brown row of 'em."

"'Pepys' Diary'? Why, that ought to be enjoyable. He's very light."

"Not for me—he isn't. It'll be like digesting plate glass. But you been telling me how much it'd broaden my lookout. Well, you go to a gym three nights a week and I'll take one big dose of Sammy."

Horace hesitated.

"Well——"

"Come on, now! You do some giant swings for me and I'll chase some culture for you."

So Horace finally consented, and all through a baking summer he spent three and sometimes four evenings a week experimenting on the trapeze in Skipper's Gymnasium. And in August he admitted to Marcia that it made him capable of more mental work during the day.

"*Mens sana in corpore sano*," he said.

"Don't believe in it," replied Marcia. "I tried one of those patent medicines once and they're all bunk. You stick to gymnastics."

One night in early September while he was going through one of his contortions on the rings in the nearly deserted room he was addressed by a meditative fat man whom he had noticed watching him for several nights.

"Say, lad, do that stunt you were doin' last night."

Horace grinned at him from his perch.

"I invented it," he said. "I got the idea from the fourth proposition of Euclid."

"What circus he with?"

"He's dead."

"Well, he must of broke his neck doin' that stunt. I set here last night thinkin' sure you was goin' to break yours."

"Like this!" said Horace, and swinging onto the trapeze he did his stunt.

"Don't it kill your neck an' shoulder muscles?"

"It did at first, but inside of a week I wrote the *quod erat demonstrandum* on it."

"Hm!"

Horace swung idly on the trapeze.

"Ever think of takin' it up professionally?" asked the fat man.

"Not I."

"Good money in it if you're willin' to do stunts like 'at an' can get away with it."

"Here's another," chirped Horace eagerly, and the fat man's mouth dropped suddenly agape as he watched this pink-jerseyed Prometheus again defy the gods and Isaac Newton.

The night following this encounter Horace got home from work to find a rather pale Marcia stretched out on the sofa waiting for him.

"I fainted twice today," she began without preliminaries.

"What?"

"Yep. You see baby's due in four months now. Doctor says I ought to have quit dancing two weeks ago."

Horace sat down and thought it over.

"I'm glad, of course," he said pensively—"I mean glad that we're going to have a baby. But this means a lot of expense."

"I've got two hundred and fifty in the bank," said Marcia hopefully, "and two weeks' pay coming."

Horace computed quickly.

"Including my salary, that'll give us nearly fourteen hundred for the next six months."

Marcia looked blue.

"That all? Course I can get a job singing somewhere this month. And I can go to work again in March."

"Of course nothing!" said Horace gruffly. "You'll stay right here. Let's see now—there'll be doctor's bills and a nurse, besides the maid. We've got to have some more money."

"Well," said Marcia wearily, "I don't know where it's coming from. It's up to the old head now. Shoulders is out of business."

Horace rose and pulled on his coat.

"Where are you going?"

"I've got an idea," he answered. "I'll be right back."

Ten minutes later as he headed down the street toward Skipper's Gymnasium he felt a placid wonder, quite unmixed with humor, at what he was going to do. How he would have gaped at himself a year before! How everyone would have gaped! But when you opened your door at the rap of life you let in many things.

The gymnasium was brightly lit and when his eyes became accustomed to the glare he found the meditative fat man seated on a pile of canvas mats smoking a big cigar.

"Say," began Horace directly, "were you in earnest last night when you said I could make money on my trapeze stunts?"

"Why, yes," said the fat man in surprise.

"Well, I've been thinking it over and I believe I'd like to try it. I could work at night and on Saturday afternoons—and regularly if the pay is high enough."

The fat man looked at his watch.

"Well," he said, "Charlie Paulson's the man to see. He'll book you inside of four days, once he sees you work out. He won't be in now, but I'll get hold of him for tomorrow night."

The fat man was as good as his word. Charlie Paulson arrived next night and put in a wondrous hour watching the prodigy swoop through the air in amazing parabolas, and on the night following he brought two large men with him who looked as though they had been born smoking black cigars and talking about money in low passionate voices. Then on the succeeding Saturday Horace

Tarbox's torso made its first professional appearance in a gymnastic exhibition at the Coleman Street Gardens. But though the audience numbered nearly five thousand people, Horace felt no nervousness. From his childhood he had read papers to audiences—learned that trick of detaching himself.

"Marcia," he said cheerfully later that same night, "I think we're out of the woods. Paulson thinks he can get me an opening at the Hippodrome, and that means an all-winter engagement. The Hippodrome, you know, is a big——"

"Yes, I believe I've heard of it," interrupted Marcia, "but I want to know about this stunt you're doing. It isn't any spectacular suicide, is it?"

"It's nothing," said Horace quietly. "But if you can think of any nicer way of a man killing himself than taking a risk for you, why that's the way I want to die."

Marcia reached up and wound both arms tightly round his neck.

"Kiss me," she whispered, "and call me 'dear heart.' I love to hear you say 'dear heart.' And bring me a book to read tomorrow. No more Sam Pepys, but something trick and trashy. I've been wild for something to do all day. I felt like writing letters, but I didn't have anybody to write to."

"Write to me," said Horace. "I'll read them."

"I wish I could," breathed Marcia. "If I knew words enough I could write you the longest love letter in the world—and never get tired."

But after two more months Marcia grew very tired indeed, and for a row of nights it was a very anxious, weary-looking young athlete who walked out before the Hippodrome crowd. Then there were two days when his place was taken by a young man who wore pale blue instead of white and got very little applause. But after the two days Horace appeared again, and those who sat close to the stage remarked an expression of beatific happiness on that young acrobat's face, even when he was twisting breathlessly in the air in the middle of his amazing and original shoulder swing. After that performance he laughed at the elevator man and dashed up the stairs to the flat five steps at a time—and then tiptoed very carefully into a quiet room.

"Marcia," he whispered.

"Hello!" She smiled up at him wanly. "Horace, there's something I want you to do. Look in my top bureau drawer and you'll find a big stack of paper. It's a book—sort of—Horace. I wrote it down in these last three months while I've been laid up. I wish you'd take it to that Peter Boyce Wendell who put my letter in his paper. He could tell you whether it'd be a good book. I wrote it just the way I talk, just the way I wrote that letter to him. It's just a story about a lot of things that happened to me. Will you take it to him, Horace?"

"Yes, darling."

He leaned over the bed until his head was beside her on the pillow and began stroking back her yellow hair.

"Dearest Marcia," he said softly.

"No," she murmured, "call me what I told you to call me."

"Dear heart," he whispered passionately—"dearest, dearest heart."

"What'll we call her?"

They rested a minute in happy drowsy content, while Horace considered.

"We'll call her Marcia Hume Tarbox," he said at length.

"Why the Hume?"

"Because he's the fellow who first introduced us."

"That so?" she murmured, sleepily surprised. "I thought his name was Moon."

Her eyes closed and after a moment the slow, lengthening surge of the bedclothes over her breast showed that she was asleep.

Horace tiptoed over to the bureau and opening the top drawer found a heap of closely scrawled, lead-smeared pages. He looked at the first sheet:

SANDRA PEPYS, SYNCOPATED

BY MARCIA TARBOX

He smiled. So Samuel Pepys had made an impression on her after all. He turned a page and began to read. His smile deepened—he read on. Half an hour passed and he became aware that Marcia had waked and was watching him from the bed.

"Honey," came in a whisper.

"What, Marcia?"

"Do you like it?"

Horace coughed.

"I seem to be reading on. It's bright."

"Take it to Peter Boyce Wendell. Tell him you got the highest marks in Princeton once and that you ought to know when a book's good. Tell him this one's a world beater."

"All right, Marcia," said Horace gently.

Her eyes closed again and Horace crossing over kissed her forehead—stood there for a moment with a look of tender pity. Then he left the room.

All that night the sprawly writing on the pages, the constant mistakes in spelling and grammar and the weird punctuation danced before his eyes. He woke several times in the night, each time full of a welling chaotic sympathy for this desire of Marcia's soul to express itself in words. To him there was something infinitely pathetic about it, and for the first time in months he began to turn over in his mind his own half-forgotten dreams.

He had meant to write a series of books, to popularize the new realism as Schopenhauer had popularized pessimism and William James pragmatism.

But life hadn't come that way. Life took hold of people and forced them into flying rings. He laughed to think of that rap at his door, the diaphanous shadow in Hume, Marcia's threatened kiss.

"And it's still me," he said aloud in wonder as he lay awake in the darkness. "I'm the man who sat in Berkeley with temerity to wonder if that rap would have had actual existence had my ear not been there to hear it. I'm still that man. I could be electrocuted for the crimes he committed.

"Poor gauzy souls trying to express ourselves in something tangible. Marcia with her written book; I with my unwritten ones. Trying to choose our mediums and then taking what we get—and being glad."

V

"Sandra Pepys, Syncopated," with an introduction by Peter Boyce Wendell, the columnist, appeared serially in "Jordan's Magazine," and came out in book form in March. From its first published installment it attracted attention far and wide. A trite enough subject—a girl from a small New Jersey town coming to New York to go on the stage—treated simply, with a peculiar vividness of phrasing and a haunting undertone of sadness in the very inadequacy of its vocabulary, it made an irresistible appeal.

Peter Boyce Wendell, who happened at that time to be advocating the enrichment of the American language by the immediate adoption of expressive vernacular words, stood as its sponsor and thundered his indorsement over the placid bromides of the conventional reviewers.

Marcia received three hundred dollars an installment for the serial publication, which came at an opportune time, for though Horace's monthly salary at the Hippodrome was now more than Marcia's had ever been, young Marcia was emitting shrill cries which they interpreted as a demand for country air. So early April found them installed in a bungalow in Westchester County with a place for a lawn, a place for a garage, and a place for everything, including a sound-proof impregnable study in which Marcia faithfully promised Mr. Jordan she would shut herself up when her daughter's demands began to be abated and compose immortally illiterate literature.

"It's not half bad," thought Horace one night as he was on his way from the station to his house. He was considering several prospects that had opened up, a four months' vaudeville offer in five figures, a chance to go back to Princeton in charge of all gymnasium work. Odd! He had once intended to go back there in charge of all philosophic work, and now he had not even been stirred by the arrival in New York of Anton Laurier, his old idol.

The gravel crunched raucously under his heel. He saw the lights of his sitting room gleaming and noticed a big car standing in the drive. Probably Mr. Jordan again, come to persuade Marcia to settle down to work.

She had heard the sound of his approach and her form was silhouetted against the lighted door as she came out to meet him.

"There's some Frenchman here," she whispered nervously. "I can't pronounce his name, but he sounds awful deep. You'll have to jaw with him."

"What Frenchman?"

"You can't prove it by me. He drove up an hour ago with Mr. Jordan and said he wanted to meet Sandra Pepys, and all that sort of thing."

Two men rose from chairs as they went inside.

"Hello, Tarbox," said Jordan. "I've just been bringing together two celebrities. I've brought M'sieur Laurier out with me. M'sieur Laurier, let me present Mr. Tarbox, Mrs. Tarbox's husband."

"Not Anton Laurier!" exclaimed Horace.

"But, yes. I must come. I have to come. I have read the book of Madame and I have been charmed"—he fumbled in his pocket—"ah, I have read of you too. In this newspaper which I read today it has your name."

He finally produced a clipping from a magazine.

"Read it!" he said eagerly. "It has about you too."

Horace's eye skipped down the page.

"A distinct contribution to American dialect literature," it said. "No attempt at literary tone; the book derives its very quality from this fact, as did 'Huckleberry Finn.'"

Horace's eyes caught a passage lower down; he became suddenly aghast—read on hurriedly:

"Marcia Tarbox's connection with the stage is not only as a spectator but as the wife of a performer. She was married last year to Horace Tarbox, who every evening delights the children at the Hippodrome with his wondrous flying-ring performance. It is said that the young couple have dubbed themselves Head and Shoulders, referring doubtless to the fact that Mrs. Tarbox supplies the literary and mental qualities while the supple and agile shoulders of her husband contribute their share to the family fortunes.

"Mrs. Tarbox seems to merit that much-abused title—'prodigy.' Only twenty——"

Horace stopped reading and with a very odd expression in his eyes gazed intently at Anton Laurier.

"I want to advise you——" he began hoarsely.

"What?"

"About raps. Don't answer them! Let them alone—have a padded door."

THE CUT-GLASS BOWL

There was a rough stone age and a smooth stone age and a bronze age and many years afterward a cut-glass age. In the cut-glass age, when young ladies had persuaded young men with long, curly mustaches to marry them, they sat down several months afterward and wrote thank-you notes for all sorts of cut-glass presents—punch-bowls, finger-bowls, dinner-glasses, wine-glasses, ice-cream dishes, bonbon dishes, decanters, and vases—for, though cut glass was nothing new in the nineties, it was then especially busy reflecting the dazzling light of fashion from the Back Bay to the fastnesses of the Middle West.

After the wedding the punch-bowls were arranged on the sideboard with the big bowl in the center; the glasses were set up in the china-closet; the candlesticks were put at both ends of things—and then the struggle for existence began. The bonbon dish lost its little handle and became a pin-tray upstairs; a promenading cat knocked the little bowl off the sideboard, and the hired girl chipped the middle-sized one with the sugar-dish; then the wine-glasses succumbed to leg fractures, and even the dinner-glasses disappeared one by one like the ten little niggers, the last one ending up, scarred and maimed, as a toothbrush holder among other shabby genteels on the bathroom shelf. But by the time all this had happened the cut-glass age was over, anyway.

It was well past its first glory on the day the curious Mrs. Roger Fairboalt came to see the beautiful Mrs. Harold Piper.

"My *dear*," said the curious Mrs. Roger Fairboalt, "I *love* your house. I think it's *quite* artistic."

"I'm *so* glad," said the beautiful Mrs. Harold Piper, lights appearing in her young, dark eyes; "and you *must* come often. I'm almost *always* alone in the afternoon."

Mrs. Fairboalt would have liked to remark that she didn't believe this at all and couldn't see how she'd be expected to—it was all over town that Mr. Freddy Gedney had been dropping in on Mrs. Piper five afternoons a week for the past six months. Mrs. Fairboalt was at that ripe age where she distrusted all beautiful women——

"I love the dining room *most,*" she said, "all that *marvellous* china, and that *huge* cut-glass bowl."

Mrs. Piper laughed, so prettily that Mrs. Fairboalt's lingering reservations about the Freddy Gedney story quite vanished.

"Oh, that big bowl !" Mrs. Piper's mouth forming the words was a vivid rose petal. "There's a story about that bowl——"

"Oh——"

"You remember young Carleton Canby? Well, he was very attentive at one time, and the night I told him I was going to marry Harold, seven years ago, in ninety-two, he drew himself way up and said: 'Evylyn, I'm going to give a present that's as hard as you are and as beautiful and as empty and as easy to see through.' He frightened me a little—his eyes were so black. I thought he was going to deed me a haunted house or something that would explode when you opened it. That bowl came, and of course it's beautiful. Its diameter or circumference or something is two and a half feet—or perhaps it's three and a half. Anyway, the sideboard is really too small for it; it sticks way out."

"My *dear*, wasn't that *odd!* And he left town about then, didn't he?" Mrs. Fairboalt was scribbling italicized notes on her memory—"hard, beautiful, empty, and easy to see through."

"Yes, he went West—or South—or somewhere," answered Mrs. Piper, radiating that divine vagueness that helps to lift beauty out of time.

Mrs. Fairboalt drew on her gloves, approving the effect of largeness given by the open sweep from the spacious music room through the library, disclosing a part of the dining room beyond. It was really the nicest smaller house in town, and Mrs. Piper had talked of moving to a larger one on Devereaux Avenue. Harold Piper must be *coining* money.

As she turned into the sidewalk under the gathering autumn dusk she assumed that disapproving, faintly unpleasant expression that almost all successful women of forty wear on the street.

If *I* were Harold Piper, she thought, I'd spend a *little* less time on business and a *little* more time at home. Some *friend* should speak to him.

But if Mrs. Fairboalt had considered it a successful afternoon she would have named it a triumph had she waited two minutes longer. For while she was still a black receding figure a hundred yards down the street, a very good-looking distraught young man turned up the walk to the Piper house. Mrs. Piper answered the doorbell herself, and with a rather dismayed expression led him quickly into the library.

"I had to see you," he began wildly; "your note played the devil with me. Did Harold frighten you into this?"

She shook her head.

"I'm through, Fred," she said slowly, and her lips had never looked to him so much like tearings from a rose. "He came home last night sick with it. Jessie Piper's sense of duty was too much for her, so she went down to his office and told him. He was hurt and—oh, I can't help seeing it his way, Fred. He says we've been club gossip all summer and he didn't know it, and now he understands snatches of conversation he's caught and veiled hints people have dropped about me. He's mighty angry, Fred, and he loves me and I love him—rather."

Gedney nodded slowly and half closed his eyes.

"Yes," he said, "yes, my trouble's like yours. I can see other people's points of view too plainly." His grey eyes met her dark ones frankly. "The blessed thing's over. My God, Evylyn, I've been sitting down at the office all day looking at the outside of your letter, and looking at it and looking at it——"

"You've got to go, Fred," she said steadily, and the slight emphasis of hurry in her voice was a new thrust for him. "I gave him my word of honor I wouldn't see you. I know just how far I can go with Harold, and being here with you this evening is one of the things I can't do."

They were still standing, and as she spoke she made a little movement toward the door. Gedney looked at her miserably, trying, here at the end, to treasure up a last picture of her—and then suddenly both of them were stiffened into marble at the sound of steps on the walk outside. Instantly her arm reached out grasping the lapel of his coat—half-urged, half-swung him through the big door into the dark dining room.

"I'll make him go upstairs," she whispered close to his ear; "don't move till you hear him on the stairs. Then go out the front way."

Then he was alone listening as she greeted her husband in the hall.

Harold Piper was thirty-six, nine years older than his wife. He was handsome—with marginal notes: these being eyes that were too close together, and a certain woodenness when his face was in repose. His attitude toward this Gedney matter was typical of all his attitudes. He had told Evylyn that he considered the subject closed and would never reproach her nor allude to it in any form; and he told himself that this was rather a big way of looking at it—that she was not a little impressed. Yet, like all men who are preoccupied with their own broadness, he was exceptionally narrow.

He greeted Evylyn with emphasized cordiality this evening.

"You'll have to hurry and dress, Harold," she said eagerly; "we're going to the Bronsons'."

He nodded.

"It doesn't take me long to dress, dear," and, his words trailing off, he walked on into the library. Evylyn's heart clattered loudly.

"Harold——" she began, with a little catch in her voice, and followed him in. He was lighting a cigarette. "You'll have to hurry, Harold," she finished, standing in the doorway.

"Why?" he asked, a trifle impatiently; "you're not dressed yourself yet, Evie."

He stretched out in a Morris chair and unfolded a newspaper. With a sinking sensation Evylyn saw that this meant at least ten minutes—and Gedney was standing breathless in the next room. Supposing Harold decided that before he went upstairs he wanted a drink from the decanter on the sideboard. Then it occurred to her to forestall this contingency by bringing him the decanter and a glass. She dreaded calling his attention to the dining room in any way, but she couldn't risk the other chance.

But at the same moment Harold rose and, throwing his paper down, came toward her.

"Evie, dear," he said, bending and putting his arms about her, "I hope you're not thinking about last night——" She moved close to him, trembling. "I know," he continued, "it was just an imprudent friendship on your part. We all make mistakes."

Evylyn hardly heard him. She was wondering if by sheer clinging to him she could draw him out and up the stairs. She thought of playing sick, asking to be carried up—unfortunately, she knew he would lay her on the couch and bring her whiskey.

Suddenly her nervous tension moved up a last impossible notch. She had heard a very faint but quite unmistakable creak from the floor of the dining room. Fred was trying to get out the back way.

Then her heart took a flying leap as a hollow ringing note like a gong echoed and re-echoed through the house. Gedney's arm had struck the big cut-glass bowl.

"What's that!" cried Harold. "Who's there?"

She clung to him but he broke away, and the room seemed to crash about her ears. She heard the pantry-door swing open, a scuffle, the rattle of a tin pan, and in wild despair she rushed into the kitchen and pulled up the gas. Her husband's arm slowly unwound from Gedney's neck, and he stood there very still, first in amazement, then with pain dawning in his face.

"My golly!" he said in bewilderment, and then repeated: "My *golly!*"

He turned as if to jump again at Gedney, stopped, his muscles visibly relaxed, and he gave a bitter little laugh.

"You people—you people——" Evylyn's arms were around him and her eyes were pleading with him frantically, but he pushed her away and sank dazed into a kitchen chair, his face like porcelain. "You've been doing things to me, Evylyn. Why, you little devil! You little *devil!*"

She had never felt so sorry for him; she had never loved him so much.

"It wasn't her fault," said Gedney rather humbly. "I just came." But Piper shook his head, and his expression when he stared up was as if some physical accident had jarred his mind into a temporary inability to function. His eyes, grown suddenly pitiful, struck a deep, unsounded chord in Evylyn—and simultaneously a furious anger surged in her. She felt her eyelids burning; she stamped her foot violently; her hands scurried nervously over the table as if searching for a weapon, and then she flung herself wildly at Gedney.

"Get out!" she screamed, dark eyes blazing, little fists beating helplessly on his outstretched arm. "You did this! Get out of here—get out—get *out! Get out!*"

II

Concerning Mrs. Harold Piper at thirty-five, opinion was divided—women said she was still handsome; men said she was pretty no longer. And this was probably because the qualities in her beauty that women had feared and men had followed had vanished. Her eyes were still as large and as dark and as sad, but the mystery had departed; their sadness was no longer eternal, only human, and she had developed a habit, when she was startled or annoyed, of twitching her brows together and blinking several times. Her mouth also had lost: the red had receded and the faint down-turning of its corners when she smiled, that had added to the sadness of the eyes and been vaguely mocking and beautiful, was quite gone. When she smiled now the corners of her lips turned up. Back in the days when she revelled in her own beauty Evylyn had enjoyed that smile of hers—she had accentuated it. When she stopped accentuating it, it faded out and the last of her mystery with it.

Evylyn had ceased accentuating her smile within a month after the Freddy Gedney affair. Externally things had gone on very much as they had before. But in those few minutes during which she had discovered how much she loved her husband Evylyn had realized how indelibly she had hurt him. For a month she struggled against aching silences, wild reproaches and accusations—she pled with him, made quiet, pitiful little love to him, and he laughed at her bitterly—and then she, too, slipped gradually into silence and a shadowy, unpenetrable barrier dropped between them. The surge of love that had risen in her she lavished on Donald, her little boy, realizing him almost wonderingly as a part of her life.

The next year a piling up of mutual interests and responsibilities and some stray flicker from the past brought husband and wife together again—but after a rather pathetic flood of passion Evylyn realized that her great opportunity was gone. There simply wasn't anything left. She might have been youth and love for both—but that time of silence had slowly dried up the springs of affection and her own desire to drink again of them was dead.

She began for the first time to seek women friends, to prefer books she had read before, to sew a little where she could watch her two children to whom she was devoted. She worried about little things—if she saw crumbs on the dinner table her mind drifted off the conversation: she was receding gradually into middle age.

Her thirty-fifth birthday had been an exceptionally busy one, for they were entertaining on short notice that night, and as she stood in her bedroom window in the late afternoon she discovered that she was quite tired. Ten years before she would have lain down and slept, but now she had a feeling that things needed watching: maids were cleaning downstairs, bric-à-brac was all over the floor, and there were sure to be grocery men that had to be talked to imperatively—and then there was a letter to write Donald, who was fourteen and in his first year away at school.

She had nearly decided to lie down, nevertheless, when she heard a sudden familiar signal from little Julie downstairs. She compressed her lips, her brows twitched together, and she blinked.

"Julie!" she called.

"Ah-h-h-ow!" prolonged Julie plaintively. Then the voice of Hilda, the second maid, floated up the stairs.

"She cut herself a little, Mis' Piper."

Evylyn flew to her sewing-basket, rummaged until she found a torn handkerchief, and hurried downstairs. In a moment Julie was crying in her arms as she searched for the cut, faint, disparaging evidences of which appeared on Julie's dress!

"My *thu*-umb!" explained Julie. "Oh-h-h-h, t'urts."

"It was the bowl here, the he one," said Hilda apologetically. "It was waitin' on the floor while I polished the sideboard, and Julie come along an' went to foolin' with it. She yust scratch herself."

Evylyn frowned heavily at Hilda and, twisting Julie decisively in her lap, began tearing strips off the handkerchief.

"Now—let's see it, dear."

Julie held it up and Evylyn pounced.

"There!"

Julie surveyed her swathed thumb doubtfully. She crooked it; it waggled. A pleased, interested look appeared in her tear-stained face. She sniffled and waggled it again.

"You *precious!*" cried Evylyn and kissed her, but before she left the room she levelled another frown at Hilda. Careless! Servants all that way nowadays. If she could get a good Irishwoman—but you couldn't anymore—and these Swedes——

At five o'clock Harold arrived and, coming up to her room, threatened in a suspiciously jovial tone to kiss her thirty-five times for her birthday. Evylyn resisted.

"You've been drinking," she said shortly, and then added qualitatively, "a little. You know I loathe the smell of it."

"Evie," he said, after a pause, seating himself in a chair by the window, "I can tell you something now. I guess you've known things haven't been going quite right downtown."

She was standing at the window combing her hair, but at these words she turned and looked at him.

"How do you mean? You've always said there was room for more than one wholesale hardware house in town." Her voice expressed some alarm.

"There *was*," said Harold significantly, "but this Clarence Ahearn is a smart man."

"I was surprised when you said he was coming to dinner."

"Evie," he went on, with another slap at his knee, "after January first 'The Clarence Ahearn Company' becomes 'The Ahearn, Piper Company'—and 'Piper Brothers' as a company ceases to exist."

Evylyn was startled. The sound of his name in second place was somehow hostile to her; still he appeared jubilant.

"I don't understand, Harold."

"Well, Evie, Ahearn has been fooling around with Marx. If those two had combined we'd have been the little fellow, struggling along, picking up smaller orders, hanging back on risks. It's a question of capital, Evie, and 'Ahearn and Marx' would have had the business just like 'Ahearn and Piper' is going to now." He paused and coughed and a little cloud of whiskey floated up to her nostrils. "Tell you the truth, Evie, I've suspected that Ahearn's wife had something to do with it. Ambitious little lady, I'm told. Guess she knew the Marxes couldn't help her much here."

"Is she—common?" asked Evie.

"Never met her, I'm sure—but I don't doubt it. Clarence Ahearn's name's been up at the country club five months—no action taken." He waved his hand disparagingly. "Ahearn and I had lunch together today and just about clinched it, so I thought it'd be nice to have him and his wife up tonight—just have nine, mostly family. After all, it's a big thing for me, and of course we'll have to see something of them, Evie."

"Yes," said Evie thoughtfully, "I suppose we will."

Evylyn was not disturbed over the social end of it—but the idea of "Piper Brothers" becoming "The Ahearn, Piper Company" startled her. It seemed like going down in the world.

Half an hour later, as she began to dress for dinner, she heard his voice from downstairs.

"Oh, Evie, come down!"

She went out into the hall and called over the banister:

"What is it?"

"I want you to help me make some of that punch before dinner."

Hurriedly rehooking her dress, she descended the stairs and found him grouping the essentials on the dining-room table. She went to the sideboard and, lifting one of the bowls, carried it over.

"Oh, no," he protested, "let's use the big one. There'll be Ahearn and his wife and you and I and Milton, that's five, and Tom and Jessie, that's seven, and your sister and Joe Ambler, that's nine. You don't know how quick that stuff goes when *you* make it."

"We'll use this bowl," she insisted. "It'll hold plenty. You know how Tom is."

Tom Lowrie, husband to Jessie, Harold's first cousin, was rather inclined to finish anything in a liquid way that he began.

Harold shook his head.

"Don't be foolish. That one holds only about three quarts and there's nine of us, and the servants'll want some—and it isn't strong punch. It's so much more cheerful to have a lot, Evie; we don't have to drink all of it."

"I say the small one."

Again he shook his head obstinately.

"No; be reasonable."

"I *am* reasonable," she said shortly. "I don't want any drunken men in the house."

"Who said you did?"

"Then use the small bowl."

"Now, Evie——"

He grasped the smaller bowl to lift it back. Instantly her hands were on it, holding it down. There was a momentary struggle, and then, with a little exasperated grunt, he raised his side, slipped it from her fingers, and carried it to the sideboard.

She looked at him and tried to make her expression contemptuous, but he only laughed. Acknowledging her defeat but disclaiming all future interest in the punch, she left the room.

III

At seven-thirty, her cheeks glowing and her high-piled hair gleaming with a suspicion of brilliantine, Evylyn descended the stairs. Mrs. Ahearn, a little woman concealing a slight nervousness under red hair and an extreme Empire gown, greeted her volubly. Evylyn disliked her on the spot, but the husband she rather approved of. He had keen blue eyes and a natural gift of pleasing people that might have made him, socially, had he not so obviously committed the blunder of marrying too early in his career.

"I'm glad to know Piper's wife," he said simply. "It looks as though your husband and I are going to see a lot of each other in the future."

She bowed, smiled graciously, and turned to greet the others: Milton Piper, Harold's quiet, unassertive younger brother; the two

Lowries, Jessie and Tom; Irene, her own unmarried sister; and finally Joe Ambler, a confirmed bachelor and Irene's perennial beau.

Harold led the way into dinner.

"We're having a punch evening," he announced jovially—Evylyn saw that he had already sampled his concoction—"so there won't be any cocktails except the punch. It's m' wife's greatest achievement, Mrs. Ahearn; she'll give you the recipe if you want it; but owing to a slight"—he caught his wife's eye and paused—"to a slight indisposition, I'm responsible for this batch. Here's how!"

All through dinner there was punch, and Evylyn, noticing that Ahearn and Milton Piper and all the women were shaking their heads negatively at the maid, knew she had been right about the bowl; it was still half-full. She resolved to caution Harold directly afterward, but when the women left the table Mrs. Ahearn cornered her, and she found herself talking cities and dressmakers with a polite show of interest.

"We've moved around a lot," chattered Mrs. Ahearn, her red head nodding violently. "Oh, yes, we've never stayed so long in a town before—but I do hope we're here for good. I like it here; don't you?"

"Well, you see, I've always lived here, so, naturally——"

"Oh, that's true," said Mrs. Ahearn and laughed. "Clarence always used to tell me he had to have a wife he could come home to and say: 'Well, we're going to Chicago tomorrow to live, so pack up.' I got so I never expected to live *any*where." She laughed her little laugh again; Evylyn suspected that it was her society laugh.

"Your husband is a very able man, I imagine."

"Oh, yes," Mrs. Ahearn assured her eagerly. "He's brainy, Clarence is. Ideas and enthusiasm, you know. Finds out what he wants and then goes and gets it."

Evylyn nodded. She was wondering if the men were still drinking punch back in the dining room. Mrs. Ahearn's history kept unfolding jerkily, but Evylyn had ceased to listen. The first odor of massed cigars began to drift in. It wasn't really a large house, she reflected; on an evening like this the library sometimes grew blue with smoke, and next day one had to leave the windows open for hours to air the heavy staleness out of the curtains. Perhaps this partnership might . . . she began to speculate on a new house. . . .

Mrs. Ahearn's voice drifted in on her:

"I really would like the recipe if you have it written down somewhere——"

Then there was a sound of chairs in the dining room and the men strolled in. Evylyn saw at once that her worst fears were realized. Harold's face was flushed and his words ran together at the ends of sentences, while Tom Lowrie lurched when he walked and narrowly missed Irene's lap when he tried to sink onto the couch beside her. He sat there blinking dazedly at the company. Evylyn found herself blinking back at him, but she saw no humor in it. Joe Ambler was smiling contentedly and purring on his cigar. Only Ahearn and Milton Piper seemed unaffected.

"It's a pretty fine town, Ahearn," said Ambler, "you'll find that."

"I've found it so," said Ahearn pleasantly.

"You find it more, Ahearn," said Harold, nodding emphatically, "'f I've an'thin' do 'th it."

He soared into a eulogy of the city, and Evylyn wondered uncomfortably if it bored everyone as it bored her. Apparently not. They were all listening attentively. Evylyn broke in at the first gap.

"Where've you been living, Mr. Ahearn?" she asked interestedly. Then she remembered that Mrs. Ahearn had told her, but it didn't matter. Harold mustn't talk so much. He was such an *ass* when he'd been drinking. But he plopped directly back in.

"Tell you, Ahearn. Firs' you wanna get a house up here on the hill. Get Stearne house or Ridgeway house. Wanna have it so people say: 'There's Ahearn house.' Solid, you know, tha's effec' it gives."

Evylyn flushed. This didn't sound right at all. Still Ahearn didn't seem to notice anything amiss, only nodded gravely.

"Have you been looking——" But her words trailed off unheard as Harold's voice boomed on.

"Get house—tha's start. Then you get know people. Snobbish town first toward outsider, but not long—not after know you. People like you"—he indicated Ahearn and his wife with a sweeping gesture—"all right. Cordial as an'thin' once get by first barrer-bar-barrer——" He swallowed, and then said "barrier," repeated it masterfully.

Evylyn looked appealingly at her brother-in-law, but before he could intercede a thick mumble had come crowding out of Tom Lowrie, hindered by the dead cigar which he gripped firmly with his teeth.

"Huma uma ho huma ahdy um——"

"What?" demanded Harold earnestly.

Resignedly and with difficulty Tom removed the cigar—that is, he removed part of it, and then blew the remainder with a *whut* sound across the room, where it landed liquidly and limply in Mrs. Ahearn's lap.

"Beg pardon," he mumbled, and rose with the vague intention of going after it. Milton's hand on his coat collapsed him in time, and Mrs. Ahearn not ungracefully flounced the tobacco from her skirt to the floor, never once looking at it.

"I was sayin'," continued Tom thickly, "'fore 'at happened"—he waved his hand apologetically toward Mrs. Ahearn—"I was sayin' I heard all truth that country club matter."

Milton leaned and whispered something to him.

"Lemme 'lone," he said petulantly; "know what I'm doin'. 'At's what they came for."

Evylyn sat there in a panic, trying to make her mouth form words. She saw her sister's sardonic expression and Mrs. Ahearn's face turning a vivid red. Ahearn was looking down at his watchchain, fingering it.

"I heard who's been keepin' y' out, an' he's not a bit better'n you. I can fix whole damn thing up. Would've before, but I didn't know you. Harol' tol' me you felt bad about the thing——"

Milton Piper rose suddenly and awkwardly to his feet. In a second everyone was standing tensely and Milton was saying something very hurriedly about having to go early, and the Ahearns were listening with eager intentness. Then Mrs. Ahearn swallowed and turned with a forced smile toward Jessie. Evylyn saw Tom lurch forward and put his hand on Ahearn's shoulder—and suddenly she was listening to a new, anxious voice at her elbow, and, turning, found Hilda, the second maid.

"Please, Mis' Piper, I tank Yulie got her hand poisoned. It's all swole up and her cheeks is hot and she's moanin' an' groanin'——"

"Julie is?" Evylyn asked sharply. The party suddenly receded. She turned quickly, sought with her eyes for Mrs. Ahearn, slipped toward her.

"If you'll excuse me, Mrs.——" She had momentarily forgotten the name, but she went right on: "My little girl's been taken sick. I'll be down when I can." She turned and ran quickly up the stairs, retaining a confused picture of rays of cigar smoke and a loud discussion in the center of the room that seemed to be developing into an argument.

Switching on the light in the nursery, she found Julie tossing feverishly and giving out odd little cries. She put her hand against the cheeks. They were burning. With an exclamation she followed the arm down under the cover until she found the hand. Hilda was right. The whole thumb was swollen to the wrist and in the center was a little inflamed sore. Blood-poisoning! her mind cried in terror. The bandage had come off the cut and she'd gotten something in it. She'd cut it at three o'clock—it was now nearly eleven. Eight hours. Blood-poisoning couldn't possibly develop so soon. She rushed to the phone.

Doctor Martin across the street was out. Doctor Foulke, their family physician, didn't answer. She racked her brains and in desperation called her throat specialist, and bit her lip furiously while he looked up the numbers of two physicians. During that interminable moment she thought she heard loud voices downstairs—but she seemed to be in another world now. After fifteen minutes she located a physician who sounded angry and sulky at being called out of bed. She ran back to the nursery and, looking at the hand, found it was somewhat more swollen.

"Oh, God!" she cried, and kneeling beside the bed began smoothing back Julie's hair over and over. With a vague idea of getting some hot water, she rose and started toward the door, but the lace of her dress caught in the bed-rail and she fell forward on her hands and knees. She struggled up and jerked frantically at the lace. The bed moved and Julie groaned. Then more quietly but with suddenly fumbling fingers she found the pleat in front, tore the whole pannier completely off, and rushed from the room.

Out in the hall she heard a single loud, insistent voice, but as she reached the head of the stairs it ceased and an outer door banged.

The music room came into view. Only Harold and Milton were there, the former leaning against a chair, his face very pale, his collar open, and his mouth moving loosely.

"What's the matter?"

Milton looked at her anxiously.

"There was a little trouble——"

Then Harold saw her and, straightening up with an effort, began to speak.

"'Sult m'own cousin m'own house. God damn common nouveau rish. 'Sult m'own cousin——"

"Tom had trouble with Ahearn and Harold interfered," said Milton.

"My Lord, Milton," cried Evylyn, "couldn't you have done something?"

"I tried; I——"

"Julie's sick," she interrupted; "she's poisoned herself. Get him to bed if you can."

Harold looked up.

"Julie sick?"

Paying no attention, Evylyn brushed by through the dining room, catching sight, with a burst of horror, of the big punch-bowl still on the table, the liquid from melted ice in its bottom. She heard steps on the front stairs—it was Milton helping Harold up—and then a mumble: "Why, Julie's a'righ'."

"Don't let him go into the nursery!" she shouted.

The hours blurred into a nightmare. The doctor arrived just before midnight and within a half-hour had lanced the wound. He left at two after giving her the addresses of two nurses to call up and promising to return at half past six. It was blood-poisoning.

At four, leaving Hilda by the bedside, she went to her room and, slipping with a shudder out of her evening dress, kicked it into a corner. She put on a house dress and returned to the nursery while Hilda went to make coffee.

Not until noon could she bring herself to look into Harold's room, but when she did it was to find him awake and staring very miserably at the ceiling. He turned blood-shot hollow eyes upon her. For a minute she hated him, couldn't speak. A husky voice came from the bed.

"What time is it?"

"Noon."

"I made a damn fool——"

"It doesn't matter," she said sharply. "Julie's got blood-poisoning. They may"—she choked over the words—"they think she'll have to lose her hand."

"What?"

"She cut herself on that—that bowl."

"Last night?"

"Oh, what does it matter?" she cried; "she's got blood-poisoning. Can't you hear?"

He looked at her bewildered—sat halfway up in bed.

"I'll get dressed," he said.

Her anger subsided and a great wave of weariness and pity for him rolled over her. After all, it was his trouble, too.

"Yes," she answered listlessly, "I suppose you'd better."

IV

If Evylyn's beauty had hesitated in her early thirties it came to an abrupt decision just afterward and completely left her. A tentative outlay of wrinkles on her face suddenly deepened and flesh collected rapidly on her legs and hips and arms. Her mannerism of drawing her brows together had become an expression—it was habitual when she was reading or speaking and even while she slept. She was forty-six.

As in most families whose fortunes have gone down rather than up, she and Harold had drifted into a colorless antagonism. In repose they looked at each other with the toleration they might have felt for broken old chairs; Evylyn worried a little when he was sick and did her best to be cheerful under the wearying depression of living with a disappointed man.

Family bridge was over for the evening and she sighed with relief. She had made more mistakes than usual this evening and she didn't care. Irene shouldn't have made that remark about the infantry being particularly dangerous. There had been no letter for three weeks now, and, while this was nothing out of the ordinary, it never failed to make her nervous; naturally she hadn't known how many clubs were out.

Harold had gone upstairs, so she stepped out on the porch for a breath of fresh air. There was a bright glamour of moonlight diffusing on the sidewalks and lawns, and with a little half-yawn, half-laugh, she remembered one long moonlight affair of her youth. It was astonishing to think that life had once been the sum of her current love affairs. It was now the sum of her current problems.

There was the problem of Julie—Julie was thirteen, and lately she was growing more and more sensitive about her deformity and preferred to stay always in her room reading. A few years before she had been frightened at the idea of going to school, and Evylyn could not bring herself to send her, so she grew up in her mother's shadow, a pitiful little figure with the artificial hand that she made no attempt to use but kept forlornly in her pocket. Lately she had been taking lessons in using it because Evylyn had feared she would cease to lift the arm altogether, but after the lessons, unless she made a move with it in listless obedience to her mother, the little hand would creep back to the pocket of her dress. For a while her dresses were made without pockets, but Julie had moped around the house so miserably at a loss all one month that Evylyn weakened and never tried the experiment again.

The problem of Donald had been different from the start. She had attempted vainly to keep him near her as she had tried to teach Julie to lean less on her—lately the problem of Donald had been snatched out of her hands; his division had been abroad for three months.

She yawned again—life was a thing for youth. What a happy youth she must have had! She remembered her pony, Bijou, and the trip to Europe with her mother when she was eighteen——

"Very, very complicated," she said aloud and severely to the moon, and, stepping inside, was about to close the door when she heard a noise in the library and started.

It was Martha, the middle-aged servant: they kept only one now.

"Why, Martha!" she said in surprise.

Martha turned quickly.

"Oh, I thought you was upstairs. I was jist——"

"Is anything the matter?"

Martha hesitated.

"No; I——" She stood there fidgeting. "It was a letter, Mrs. Piper, that I put somewhere."

"A letter? Your own letter?" asked Evylyn, switching on the light.

"No, it was to you. 'Twas this afternoon, Mrs. Piper, in the last mail. The postman give it to me and then the back doorbell rang. I had it in my hand, so I must have stuck it somewhere. I thought I'd just slip in now and find it."

"What sort of a letter? From Mr. Donald?"

"No, it was an advertisement, maybe, or a business letter. It was a long, narrow one, I remember."

They began a search through the music room, looking on trays and mantelpieces, and then through the library, feeling on the tops of rows of books. Martha paused in despair.

"I can't think where. I went straight to the kitchen. The dining room, maybe." She started hopefully for the dining room, but turned suddenly at the sound of a gasp behind her. Evylyn had sat down heavily in a Morris chair, her brows drawn very close together, eyes blinking furiously.

"Are you sick?"

For a minute there was no answer. Evylyn sat there very still and Martha could see the very quick rise and fall of her bosom.

"Are you sick?" she repeated.

"No," said Evylyn slowly, "but I know where the letter is. Go 'way, Martha. I know."

Wonderingly, Martha withdrew, and still Evylyn sat there, only the muscles around her eyes moving—contracting and relaxing and contracting again. She knew now where the letter was—she knew as well as if she had put it there herself. And she felt instinctively and unquestionably what the letter was. It was long and narrow like an advertisement, but up in the corner in large letters it said "War Department" and, in smaller letters below, "Official Business." She knew it lay there in the big bowl with her name in ink on the outside and her soul's death within.

Rising uncertainly, she walked toward the dining room, feeling her way along the bookcases and through the doorway. After a moment she found the light and switched it on.

There was the bowl, reflecting the electric light in crimson squares edged with black-and-yellow squares edged with blue, ponderous and glittering, grotesquely and triumphantly ominous. She took a step forward and paused again; another step and she would see over the top and into the inside—another step and she would see an edge of white—another step—her hands fell on the rough, cold surface——

In a moment she was tearing it open, fumbling with an obstinate fold, holding it before her while the typewritten page glared out and struck at her. Then it fluttered like a bird to the floor. The house that had seemed whirring, buzzing a moment since, was suddenly very quiet; a breath of air crept in through the open front door carrying the noise of a passing motor; she heard faint sounds from upstairs and then a grinding racket in the pipe behind the bookcases—her husband turning off a water-tap——

And in that instant it was as if this were not, after all, Donald's hour except in so far as he was a marker in the insidious contest that had gone on in sudden surges and long, listless interludes between Evylyn and this cold, malignant thing of beauty, a gift of enmity from a man whose face she had long since forgotten. With its massive, brooding passivity it lay there in the center of her house as it had lain for years, throwing out the ice-like beams of a thousand eyes, perverse glitterings merging each into each, never aging, never changing.

Evylyn sat down on the edge of the table and stared at it fascinated. It seemed to be smiling now, a very cruel smile, as if to say:

"You see, this time I didn't have to hurt you directly. I didn't bother. You know it was I who took your son away. You know how cold I am and how hard and how beautiful, because once you were just as cold and hard and beautiful."

The bowl seemed suddenly to turn itself over and then to distend and swell until it became a great canopy that glittered and trembled over the room, over the house, and, as the walls melted slowly into mist, Evylyn saw that it was still moving out, out and far away from her, shutting off far horizons and suns and moons and stars except as inky blots seen faintly through it. And under it walked all the people, and the light that came through to them was refracted and twisted until shadow seemed light and light seemed shadow—until the whole panorama of the world became changed and distorted under the twinkling heaven of the bowl.

Then there came a far-away, booming voice like a low, clear bell. It came from the center of the bowl and down the great sides to the ground and then bounced toward her eagerly.

"You see, I am fate," it shouted, "and stronger than your puny plans; and I am how-things-turn-out and I am different from your little dreams, and I am the flight of time and the end of beauty and unfulfilled desire; all the accidents and imperceptions and the little minutes that shape the crucial hours are mine. I am the exception that proves no rules, the limits of your control, the condiment in the dish of life."

The booming sound stopped; the echoes rolled away over the wide land to the edge of the bowl that bounded the world and up the great sides and back to the center where they hummed for a moment and died. Then the great walls began slowly to bear down upon her, growing smaller and smaller, coming closer and closer as if to crush her; and as she clenched her hands and waited for the swift bruise of the cold glass, the bowl gave a sudden wrench and turned over—and lay there on the side board, shining and inscrutable, reflecting in a hundred prisms, myriad, many-colored glints and gleams and crossings and interlacings of light.

The cold wind blew in again through the front door, and with a desperate, frantic energy Evylyn stretched both her arms around the bowl. She must be quick—she must be strong. She tightened her arms until they ached, tauted the thin strips of muscle under her soft flesh, and with a mighty effort raised it and held it. She felt the wind blow cold on her back where her dress had come apart from the strain of her effort, and as she felt it she turned toward it and staggered under the great weight out through the library and on toward the front door. She must be quick—she must be strong. The blood in her arms throbbed dully and her knees kept giving way under her, but the feel of the cool glass was good.

Out the front door she tottered and over to the stone steps, and there, summoning every fibre of her soul and body for a last effort, swung herself half around—for a second, as she tried to loose her hold, her numb fingers clung to the rough surface, and in that second she slipped and, losing balance, toppled forward with a despairing cry, her arms still around the bowl . . . down. . . .

Over the way lights went on; far down the block the crash was heard, and pedestrians rushed up wonderingly; upstairs a tired man awoke from the edge of sleep and a little girl whimpered in a haunted doze. And all over the moonlit sidewalk around the still, black form, hundreds of prisms and cubes and splinters of glass reflected the light in little gleams of blue, and black edged with yellow, and yellow, and crimson edged with black.

BERNICE BOBS HER HAIR

After dark on Saturday night one could stand on the first tee of the golf course and see the country club windows as a yellow expanse over a very black and wavy ocean. The waves of this ocean, so to speak, were the heads of many curious caddies, a few of the more ingenious chauffeurs, the golf professional's deaf sister—and there were usually several stray, diffident waves who might have rolled inside had they so desired. This was the gallery.

The balcony was inside. It consisted of the circle of wicker chairs that lined the wall of the combination clubroom and ballroom. At these Saturday-night dances it was largely feminine; a great babel of middle-aged ladies with sharp eyes and icy hearts behind lorgnettes and large bosoms. The main function of the balcony was critical. It occasionally showed grudging admiration, but never approval, for it is well known among ladies over thirty-five that when the younger set dance in the summer time it is with the very worst intentions in the world, and if they are not bombarded with stony eyes stray couples will dance weird barbaric interludes in the corners, and the more popular, more dangerous girls will sometimes be kissed in the parked limousines of unsuspecting dowagers.

But after all, this critical circle is not close enough to the stage to see the actors' faces and catch the subtler byplay. It can only frown and lean, ask questions and make satisfactory deductions from its set of postulates, such as the one which states that every young man with a large income leads the life of a hunted partridge. It never really appreciates the drama of the shifting, semicruel world of adolescence. No; boxes, orchestra-circle, principals, and chorus are represented by the medley of faces and voices that sway to the plaintive African rhythm of Dyer's dance orchestra.

From sixteen-year-old Otis Ormonde, who has two more years at Hill School, to G. Reece Stoddard, over whose bureau at home hangs a Harvard law diploma; from little Madeleine Hogue, whose hair still feels strange and uncomfortable on top of her head, to Bessie MacRae, who has been the life of the party a little too long—more than ten years—the medley is not only the center of the stage but contains the only people capable of getting an unobstructed view of it.

With a flourish and a bang the music stops. The couples exchange artificial, effortless smiles, facetiously repeat "*la*-de-*da-da* dum-*dum*," and then the clatter of young feminine voices soars over the burst of clapping.

A few disappointed stags caught in midfloor as they had been about to cut in subsided listlessly back to the walls, because this was not like the riotous Christmas dances—these summer hops were considered just pleasantly warm and exciting, where even the younger marrieds rose and performed ancient waltzes and terrifying fox-trots to the tolerant amusement of their younger brothers and sisters.

Warren McIntyre, who casually attended Yale, being one of the unfortunate stags, felt in his dinner-coat pocket for a cigarette and strolled out onto the wide, semidark veranda, where couples were scattered at tables, filling the lantern-hung night with vague words and hazy laughter. He nodded here and there at the less absorbed and as he passed each couple some half-forgotten fragment of a story played in his mind, for it was not a large city and everyone was Who's Who to everyone else's past. There, for example, were Jim Strain and Ethel Demorest, who had been privately engaged for three years. Everyone knew that as soon as Jim managed to hold a job for more than two months she would marry him. Yet how bored they both looked and how wearily Ethel regarded Jim sometimes, as if she wondered why she had trained the vines of her affection on such a wind-shaken poplar.

Warren was nineteen and rather pitying with those of his friends who hadn't gone East to college. But, like most boys, he bragged tremendously about the girls of his city when he was away from it. There was Genevieve Ormonde, who regularly made the rounds of dances, house-parties and football games at Princeton, Yale, Williams and Cornell; there was black-eyed Roberta Dillon, who was quite as famous to her own generation as Hiram Johnson or Ty Cobb; and, of course, there was Marjorie Harvey, who besides having a fairylike face and a dazzling, bewildering tongue was already justly celebrated for having turned five cart-wheels in succession during the last pump-and-slipper dance at New Haven.

Warren, who had grown up across the street from Marjorie, had long been "crazy about her." Sometimes she seemed to reciprocate his feeling with a faint gratitude, but she had tried him by her infallible test and informed him gravely that she did not love him. Her test was that when she was away from him she forgot him and had affairs with other boys. Warren found this discouraging, especially as Marjorie had been making little trips all summer, and for the first two or three days after each arrival home he saw great heaps of mail on the Harveys' hall table addressed to her in various masculine handwritings. To make matters worse, all during the month of August she had been visited by her cousin Bernice from Eau Claire, and it seemed impossible to see her alone. It was always necessary to hunt round and find someone to take care of Bernice. As August waned this was becoming more and more difficult.

Much as Warren worshipped Marjorie, he had to admit that Cousin Bernice was sorta dopeless. She was pretty, with dark hair and high color, but she was no fun on a party. Every Saturday night he danced a long arduous duty dance with her to please Marjorie, but he had never been anything but bored in her company.

"Warren"—a soft voice at his elbow broke in upon his thoughts, and he turned to see Marjorie, flushed and radiant as usual. She laid a hand on his shoulder and a glow settled almost imperceptibly over him.

"Warren," she whispered, "do something for me—dance with Bernice. She's been stuck with little Otis Ormonde for almost an hour."

Warren's glow faded.

"Why—sure," he answered half-heartedly.

"You don't mind, do you? I'll see that you don't get stuck."

"'Sall right."

Marjorie smiled—that smile that was thanks enough.

"You're an angel, and I'm obliged loads."

With a sigh the angel glanced round the veranda, but Bernice and Otis were not in sight. He wandered back inside, and there in front of the women's dressing room he found Otis in the center of a group of young men who were convulsed with laughter. Otis was brandishing a piece of timber he had picked up, and discoursing volubly.

"She's gone in to fix her hair," he announced wildly. "I'm waiting to dance another hour with her."

Their laughter was renewed.

"Why don't some of you cut in?" cried Otis resentfully. "She likes more variety."

"Why, Otis," suggested a friend, "you've just barely got used to her."

"Why the two-by-four, Otis?" inquired Warren, smiling.

"The two-by-four? Oh, this? This is a club. When she comes out I'll hit her on the head and knock her in again."

Warren collapsed on a settee and howled with glee.

"Never mind, Otis," he articulated finally. "I'm relieving you this time."

Otis simulated a sudden fainting attack and handed the stick to Warren.

"If you need it, old man," he said hoarsely.

No matter how beautiful or brilliant a girl may be, the reputation of not being frequently cut in on makes her position at a dance unfortunate. Perhaps boys prefer her company to that of the butterflies with whom they dance a dozen times an evening, but youth in this jazz-nourished generation is temperamentally restless, and the idea of fox-trotting more than one full fox-trot with the same girl is distasteful, not to say odious. When it comes to several dances and the intermissions between she can be quite sure that a young man, once relieved, will never tread on her wayward toes again.

Warren danced the next full dance with Bernice, and finally, thankful for the intermission, he led her to a table on the veranda. There was a moment's silence while she did unimpressive things with her fan.

"It's hotter here than in Eau Claire," she said.

Warren stifled a sigh and nodded. It might be for all he knew or cared. He wondered idly whether she was a poor conversationalist because she got no attention or got no attention because she was a poor conversationalist.

"You going to be here much longer?" he asked, and then turned rather red. She might suspect his reasons for asking.

"Another week," she answered, and stared at him as if to lunge at his next remark when it left his lips.

Warren fidgeted. Then with a sudden charitable impulse he decided to try part of his line on her. He turned and looked at her eyes.

"You've got an awfully kissable mouth," he began quietly.

This was a remark that he sometimes made to girls at college proms when they were talking in just such half-dark as this. Bernice distinctly jumped. She turned an ungraceful red and became clumsy with her fan. No one had ever made such a remark to her before.

"Fresh!"—the word had slipped out before she realized it, and she bit her lip. Too late she decided to be amused, and offered him a flustered smile.

Warren was annoyed. Though not accustomed to have that remark taken seriously, still it usually provoked a laugh or a paragraph of sentimental banter. And he hated to be called fresh, except in a joking way. His charitable impulse died and he switched the topic.

"Jim Strain and Ethel Demorest sitting out as usual," he commented.

This was more in Bernice's line, but a faint regret mingled with her relief as the subject changed. Men did not talk to her about kissable mouths, but she knew that they talked in some such way to other girls.

"Oh, yes," she said, and laughed. "I hear they've been mooning round for years without a red penny. Isn't it silly?"

Warren's disgust increased. Jim Strain was a close friend of his brother's, and anyway he considered it bad form to sneer at people for not having money. But Bernice had had no intention of sneering. She was merely nervous.

II

When Marjorie and Bernice reached home at half after midnight they said good-night at the top of the stairs. Though cousins, they were not intimates. As a matter of fact Marjorie had no female intimates—she considered girls stupid. Bernice on the contrary all through this parent-arranged visit had rather longed to exchange those confidences flavored with giggles and tears that she considered an indispensable factor in all feminine intercourse. But in this respect she found Marjorie rather cold; felt somehow the same difficulty in talking to her that she had in talking to men. Marjorie never giggled, was never frightened, seldom embarrassed, and in fact had very few of the qualities which Bernice considered appropriately and blessedly feminine.

As Bernice busied herself with toothbrush and paste this night she wondered for the hundredth time why she never had any attention when she was away from home. That her family were the wealthiest in Eau Claire; that her mother entertained tremendously, gave little dinners for her daughter before all dances and bought her a car of her own to drive round in, never occurred to her as factors in her home-town social success. Like most girls she had been brought up on the warm milk prepared by Annie Fellows Johnston and on novels in which the female was beloved because of certain mysterious womanly qualities, always mentioned but never displayed.

Bernice felt a vague pain that she was not at present engaged in being popular. She did not know that had it not been for Marjorie's campaigning she would have danced the entire evening with one man; but she knew that even in Eau Claire other girls with less position and less pulchritude were given a much bigger rush. She attributed this to something subtly unscrupulous in those girls. It had never worried her, and if it had her mother would have assured her that the other girls cheapened themselves and that men really respected girls like Bernice.

She turned out the light in her bathroom, and on an impulse decided to go in and chat for a moment with her aunt Josephine, whose light was still on. Her soft slippers bore her noiselessly down the carpeted hall, but hearing voices inside she stopped near the partly opened door. Then she caught her own name, and without any definite intention of eavesdropping lingered—and the thread of the conversation going on inside pierced her consciousness sharply, as if it had been drawn through with a needle.

"She's absolutely hopeless!" It was Marjorie's voice. "Oh, I know what you're going to say! So many people have told you how pretty and sweet she is, and how she can cook! What of it? She has a bum time. Men don't like her."

"What's a little cheap popularity?"

Mrs. Harvey sounded annoyed.

"It's everything when you're eighteen," said Marjorie emphatically. "I've done my best. I've been polite and I've made men dance with her, but they just won't stand being bored. When I think of that gorgeous coloring wasted on such a ninny, and think what Martha Carey could do with it—oh!"

"There's no courtesy these days."

Mrs. Harvey's voice implied that modern situations were too much for her. When she was a girl all young ladies who belonged to nice families had glorious times.

"Well," said Marjorie, "no girl can permanently bolster up a lame-duck visitor, because these days it's every girl for herself. I've even tried to drop her hints about clothes and things, and she's been furious—given me the funniest looks. She's sensitive enough to know she's not getting away with much, but I'll bet she consoles herself by thinking that she's very virtuous and that I'm too gay and fickle and will come to a bad end. All unpopular girls think that way. Sour grapes! Sarah Hopkins refers to Genevieve and Roberta and me as gardenia girls! I'll bet she'd give ten years of her life and her European education to be a gardenia girl and have three or four men in love with her and be cut in on every few feet at dances."

"It seems to me," interrupted Mrs. Harvey rather wearily, "that you ought to be able to do something for Bernice. I know she's not very vivacious."

Marjorie groaned.

"Vivacious! Good grief! I've never heard her say anything to a boy except that it's hot or the floor's crowded or that she's going to school in New York next year. Sometimes she asks them what kind of car they have and tells them the kind she has. Thrilling!"

There was a short silence, and then Mrs. Harvey took up her refrain:

"All I know is that other girls not half so sweet and attractive get partners. Martha Carey, for instance, is stout and loud, and her mother is distinctly common. Roberta Dillon is so thin this year that she looks as though Arizona were the place for her. She's dancing herself to death."

"But, Mother," objected Marjorie impatiently, "Martha is cheerful and awfully witty and an awfully slick girl, and Roberta's a marvelous dancer. She's been popular for ages!"

Mrs. Harvey yawned.

"I think it's that crazy Indian blood in Bernice," continued Marjorie. "Maybe she's a reversion to type. Indian women all just sat round and never said anything."

"Go to bed, you silly child," laughed Mrs. Harvey. "I wouldn't have told you that if I'd thought you were going to remember it. And I think most of your ideas are perfectly idiotic," she finshed sleepily.

There was another silence, while Marjorie considered whether or not convincing her mother was worth the trouble. People over forty can seldom be permanently convinced of anything. At eighteen our convictions are hills from which we look; at forty-five they are caves in which we hide.

Having decided this, Marjorie said good-night. When she came out into the hall it was quite empty.

III

While Marjorie was breakfasting late next day Bernice came into the room with a rather formal good-morning, sat down opposite, stared intently over and slightly moistened her lips.

"What's on your mind?" inquired Marjorie, rather puzzled.

Bernice paused before she threw her hand grenade.

"I heard what you said about me to your mother last night."

Marjorie was startled, but she showed only a faintly heightened color and her voice was quite even when she spoke.

"Where were you?"

"In the hall. I didn't mean to listen—at first."

After an involuntary look of contempt Marjorie dropped her eyes and became very interested in balancing a stray corn flake on her finger.

"I guess I'd better go back to Eau Claire—if I'm such a nuisance." Bernice's lower lip was trembling violently and she continued on a wavering note: "I've tried to be nice, and—and I've been first neglected and then insulted. No one ever visited me and got such treatment."

Marjorie was silent.

"But I'm in the way, I see. I'm a drag on you. Your friends don't like me." She paused, and then remembered another one of her grievances. "Of course I was furious last week when you tried to hint to me that that dress was unbecoming. Don't you think I know how to dress myself?"

"No," murmured Marjorie less than half-aloud.

"What?"

"I didn't hint anything," said Marjorie succinctly. "I said, as I remember, that it was better to wear a becoming dress three times straight than to alternate it with two frights."

"Do you think that was a very nice thing to say?"

"I wasn't trying to be nice." Then after a pause: "When do you want to go?"

Bernice drew in her breath sharply.

"Oh!" It was a little half-cry.

Marjorie looked up in surprise.

"Didn't you say you were going?"

"Yes, but——"

"Oh, you were only bluffing!"

They stared at each other across the breakfast table for a moment. Misty waves were passing before Bernice's eyes, while Marjorie's face wore that rather hard expression that she used when slightly intoxicated undergraduates were making love to her.

"So you were bluffing," she repeated as if it were what she might have expected.

Bernice admitted it by bursting into tears. Marjorie's eyes showed boredom.

"You're my cousin," sobbed Bernice. "I'm v-v-visiting you. I was to stay a month, and if I go home my mother will know and she'll wah-wonder——"

Marjorie waited until the shower of broken words collapsed into little sniffles.

"I'll give you my month's allowance," she said coldly, "and you can spend this last week anywhere you want. There's a very nice hotel——"

Bernice's sobs rose to a flute note, and rising of a sudden she fled from the room.

An hour later, while Marjorie was in the library absorbed in composing one of those noncommittal, marvelously elusive letters that only a young girl can write, Bernice reappeared, very red-eyed and consciously calm. She cast no glance at Marjorie but took a book at random from the shelf and sat down as if to read. Marjorie seemed absorbed in her letter and continued writing. When the clock showed noon Bernice closed her book with a snap.

"I suppose I'd better get my railroad ticket."

This was not the beginning of the speech she had rehearsed upstairs, but as Marjorie was not getting her cues—wasn't urging her to be reasonable; it's all a mistake—it was the best opening she could muster.

"Just wait till I finish this letter," said Marjorie without looking round. "I want to get it off in the next mail."

After another minute, during which her pen scratched busily, she turned round and relaxed with an air of "at your service." Again Bernice had to speak.

"Do you want me to go home?"

"Well," said Marjorie, considering, "I suppose if you're not having a good time you'd better go. No use being miserable."

"Don't you think common kindness——"

"Oh, please don't quote 'Little Women'!" cried Marjorie impatiently. "That's out of style."

"You think so?"

"Heavens, yes! What modern girl could live like those inane females?"

"They were the models for our mothers."

Marjorie laughed.

"Yes, they were—not! Besides, our mothers were all very well in their way, but they know very little about their daughters' problems."

Bernice drew herself up.

"Please don't talk about my mother."

Marjorie laughed.

"I don't think I mentioned her."

Bernice felt that she was being led away from her subject.

"Do you think you've treated me very well?"

"I've done my best. You're rather hard material to work with."

The lids of Bernice's eyes reddened.

"I think you're hard and selfish, and you haven't a feminine quality in you."

"Oh, my Lord!" cried Marjorie in desperation. "You little nut! Girls like you are responsible for all the tiresome colorless marriages; all those ghastly inefficiencies that pass as feminine qualities. What a blow it must be when a man with imagination marries the beautiful bundle of clothes that he's been building ideals round, and finds that she's just a weak, whining, cowardly mass of affectations!"

Bernice's mouth had slipped half open.

"The womanly woman!" continued Marjorie. "Her whole early life is occupied in whining criticisms of girls like me who really do have a good time."

Bernice's jaw descended farther as Marjorie's voice rose.

"There's some excuse for an ugly girl whining. If I'd been irretrievably ugly I'd never have forgiven my parents for bringing me into the world. But you're starting life without any handicap——" Marjorie's little fist clenched. "If you expect me to weep with you you'll be disappointed. Go or stay, just as you like." And picking up her letters she left the room.

Bernice claimed a headache and failed to appear at luncheon. They had a matinée date for the afternoon, but the headache persisting, Marjorie made explanation to a not very downcast boy. But when she returned late in the afternoon she found Bernice with a strangely set face waiting for her in her bedroom.

"I've decided," began Bernice without preliminaries, "that maybe you're right about things—possibly not. But if you'll tell me why your friends aren't—aren't interested in me I'll see if I can do what you want me to."

Marjorie was at the mirror shaking down her hair.

"Do you mean it?"

"Yes."

"Without reservations? Will you do exactly what I say?"

"Well, I——"

"Well nothing! Will you do exactly as I say?"

"If they're sensible things."

"They're not! You're no case for sensible things."

"Are you going to make—to recommend——"

"Yes, everything. If I tell you to take boxing lessons you'll have to do it. Write home and tell your mother you're going to stay another two weeks."

"If you'll tell me——"

"All right—I'll just give you a few examples now. First, you have no ease of manner. Why? Because you're never sure about your personal appearance. When a girl feels that she's perfectly groomed and dressed she can forget that part of her. That's charm. The more parts of yourself you can afford to forget the more charm you have."

"Don't I look all right?"

"No; for instance, you never take care of your eyebrows. They're black and lustrous, but by leaving them straggly they're a blemish. They'd be beautiful if you'd take care of them in one-tenth the time you take doing nothing. You're going to brush them so that they'll grow straight."

Bernice raised the brows in question.

"Do you mean to say that men notice eyebrows?"

"Yes—subconsciously. And when you go home you ought to have your teeth straightened a little. It's almost imperceptible, still——"

"But I thought," interrupted Bernice in bewilderment, "that you despised little dainty feminine things like that."

"I hate dainty minds," answered Marjorie. "But a girl has to be dainty in person. If she looks like a million dollars she can talk about Russia, ping-pong, or the League of Nations and get away with it."

"What else?"

"Oh, I'm just beginning! There's your dancing."

"Don't I dance all right?"

"No, you don't—you lean on a man; yes, you do—ever so slightly. I noticed it when we were dancing together yesterday. And you dance standing up straight instead of bending over a little. Probably some old lady on the side-line once told you that you looked so dignified that way. But except with a very small girl it's much harder on the man, and he's the one that counts."

"Go on." Bernice's brain was reeling.

"Well, you've got to learn to be nice to men who are sad birds. You look as if you'd been insulted whenever you're thrown with any except the most popular boys. Why, Bernice, I'm cut in on every few feet—and who does most of it? Why, those very sad birds. No girl can afford to neglect them. They're the big part of any crowd. Young boys too shy to talk are the very best conversational practice. Clumsy boys are the best dancing practice. If you can follow them and yet look graceful you can follow a baby tank across a barb-wire skyscraper."

Bernice sighed profoundly, but Marjorie was not through.

"If you go to a dance and really amuse, say, three sad birds that dance with you; if you talk so well to them that they forget they're stuck with you, you've done something. They'll come back next time, and gradually so many sad birds will dance with you that the attractive boys will see there's no danger of being stuck—then they'll dance with you."

"Yes," agreed Bernice faintly. "I think I begin to see."

"And finally," concluded Marjorie, "poise and charm will just come. You'll wake up some morning knowing you've attained it, and men will know it too."

Bernice rose.

"It's been awfully kind of you—but nobody's ever talked to me like this before, and I feel sort of startled."

Marjorie made no answer but gazed pensively at her own image in the mirror.

"You're a peach to help me," continued Bernice.

Still Marjorie did not answer, and Bernice thought she had seemed too grateful.

"I know you don't like sentiment," she said timidly.

Marjorie turned to her quickly.

"Oh, I wasn't thinking about that. I was considering whether we hadn't better bob your hair."

Bernice collapsed backward upon the bed.

IV

On the following Wednesday evening there was a dinner-dance at the country club. When the guests strolled in Bernice found her place-card with a slight feeling of irritation. Though at her right sat G. Reece Stoddard, a most desirable and distinguished young bachelor, the all-important left held only Charley Paulson. Charley lacked height, beauty and social shrewdness, and in her new enlightenment Bernice decided that his only qualification to be her partner was that he had never been stuck with her. But this feeling of irritation left with the last of the soup plates, and Marjorie's specific instruction came to her. Swallowing her pride she turned to Charley Paulson and plunged.

"Do you think I ought to bob my hair, Mr. Charley Paulson?"

Charley looked up in surprise.

"Why?"

"Because I'm considering it. It's such a sure and easy way of attracting attention."

Charley smiled pleasantly. He could not know this had been rehearsed. He replied that he didn't know much about bobbed hair. But Bernice was there to tell him.

"I want to be a society vampire, you see," she announced coolly, and went on to inform him that bobbed hair was the necessary prelude. She added that she wanted to ask his advice, because she had heard he was so critical about girls.

Charley, who knew as much about the psychology of women as he did of the mental states of Buddhist contemplatives, felt vaguely flattered.

"So I've decided," she continued, her voice rising slightly, "that early next week I'm going down to the Sevier Hotel barber shop, sit in the first chair and get my hair bobbed." She faltered, noticing that the people near her had paused in their conversation and were listening; but after a confused second Marjorie's coaching told, and she finished her paragraph to the vicinity at large. "Of course I'm charging admission, but if you'll all come down and encourage me I'll issue passes for the inside seats."

There was a ripple of appreciative laughter, and under cover of it G. Reece Stoddard leaned over quickly and said close to her ear: "I'll take a box right now."

She met his eyes and smiled as if he had said something surpassingly brilliant.

"Do you believe in bobbed hair?" asked G. Reece in the same undertone.

"I think it's unmoral," affirmed Bernice gravely. "But, of course, you've either got to amuse people or feed 'em or shock 'em." Marjorie had culled this from Oscar Wilde. It was greeted with a ripple of laughter from the men and a series of quick, intent looks from the girls. And then as though she had said nothing of wit or moment Bernice turned again to Charley and spoke confidentially in his ear.

"I want to ask you your opinion of several people. I imagine you're a wonderful judge of character."

Charley thrilled faintly—paid her a subtle compliment by overturning her water.

Two hours later, while Warren McIntyre was standing passively in the stag line abstractedly watching the dancers and wondering whither and with whom Marjorie had disappeared, an unrelated perception began to creep slowly upon him—a perception that Bernice, cousin to Marjorie, had been cut in on several times in the past five minutes. He closed his eyes, opened them and looked again. Several minutes back she had been dancing with a visiting boy, a matter easily accounted for; a visiting boy would know no better. But now she was dancing with someone else, and there was Charley Paulson headed for her with enthusiastic determination in his eye. Funny—Charley seldom danced with more than three girls an evening.

Warren was distinctly surprised when—the exchange having been effected—the man relieved proved to be none other than G. Reece Stoddard himself. And G. Reece seemed not at all jubilant at being relieved. Next time Bernice danced near, Warren regarded her intently. Yes, she was pretty, distinctly pretty; and tonight her face seemed really vivacious. She had that look that no woman, however histrionically proficient, can successfully counterfeit—she looked as if she were having a good time. He liked the way she had her hair arranged, wondered if it was brilliantine that made it glisten so. And that dress was becoming—a dark red that set off her shadowy eyes and high coloring. He remembered that he had thought her pretty when she first came to town, before he had realized that she was dull. Too bad she was dull—dull girls unbearable—certainly pretty though.

His thoughts zigzagged back to Marjorie. This disappearance would be like other disappearances. When she reappeared he would demand where she had been—would be told emphatically that it was none of his business. What a pity she was so sure of him! She basked in the knowledge that no other girl in town interested him; she defied him to fall in love with Genevieve or Roberta.

Warren sighed. The way to Marjorie's affections was a labyrinth indeed. He looked up. Bernice was again dancing with the visiting boy. Half-unconsciously he took a step out from the stag line in her direction, and hesitated. Then he said to himself that it was charity. He walked toward her—collided suddenly with G. Reece Stoddard.

"Pardon me," said Warren.

But G. Reece had not stopped to apologize. He had again cut in on Bernice.

That night at one o'clock Marjorie, with one hand on the electric-light switch in the hall, turned to take a last look at Bernice's sparkling eyes.

"So it worked?"

"Oh, Marjorie, yes!" cried Bernice.

"I saw you were having a gay time."

"I did! The only trouble was that about midnight I ran short of talk. I had to repeat myself—with different men of course. I hope they won't compare notes."

"Men don't," said Marjorie, yawning, "and it wouldn't matter if they did—they'd think you were even trickier."

She snapped out the light, and as they started up the stairs Bernice grasped the banister thankfully. For the first time in her life she had been danced tired.

"You see," said Marjorie at the top of the stairs, "one man sees another man cut in and he thinks there must be something there. Well, we'll fix up some new stuff tomorrow. Good-night."

"Good-night."

As Bernice took down her hair she passed the evening before her in review. She had followed instructions exactly. Even when Charley Paulson cut in for the eighth time she had simulated delight and had apparently been both interested and flattered. She had not talked about the weather or Eau Claire or automobiles or her school, but had confined her conversation to me, you, and us.

But a few minutes before she fell asleep a rebellious thought was churning drowsily in her brain—after all, it was she who had done it. Marjorie, to be sure, had given her her conversation, but then Marjorie got much of her conversation out of things she read. Bernice had bought the red dress, though she had never valued it highly before Marjorie dug it out of her trunk—and her own voice had said the words, her own lips had smiled, her own feet had danced. Marjorie nice girl—vain, though—nice evening—nice boys—like Warren—Warren—Warren—what's-his-name—Warren——

She fell asleep.

V

To Bernice the next week was a revelation. With the feeling that people really enjoyed looking at her and listening to her came the foundation of self-confidence. Of course there were numerous mistakes at first. She did not know, for instance, that Draycott Deyo was studying for the ministry; she was unaware that he had cut in on her because he thought she was a quiet, reserved girl. Had she known these things she would not have treated him to the line which began "Hello, Shell Shock!" and continued with the bathtub story—"It takes a frightful lot of energy to fix my hair in the summer—there's so much of it—so I always fix it first and powder my face and put on my hat; then I get into the bathtub, and dress afterward. Don't you think that's the best plan?"

Though Draycott Deyo was in the throes of difficulties concerning baptism by immersion and might possibly have seen a connection, it must be admitted that he did not. He considered feminine bathing an immoral subject, and gave her some of his ideas on the depravity of modern society.

But to offset that unfortunate occurrence Bernice had several signal successes to her credit. Little Otis Ormonde pleaded off from a trip East and elected instead to follow her with a puppylike devotion, to the amusement of his crowd and to the irritation of G. Reece Stoddard, several of whose afternoon calls Otis completely ruined by the disgusting tenderness of the glances he bent on Bernice. He even told her the story of the two-by-four and the dressing room to show her how frightfully mistaken he and everyone else had been in their first judgment of her. Bernice laughed off that incident with a slight sinking sensation.

Of all Bernice's conversation perhaps the best-known and most universally approved was the line about the bobbing of her hair.

"Oh, Bernice, when you goin' to get the hair bobbed?"

"Day after tomorrow maybe," she would reply, laughing. "Will you come and see me? Because I'm counting on you, you know."

"Will we? You know! But you better hurry up."

Bernice, whose tonsorial intentions were strictly dishonorable, would laugh again.

"Pretty soon now. You'd be surprised."

But perhaps the most significant symbol of her success was the grey car of the hypercritical Warren McIntyre, parked daily in front of the Harvey house. At first the parlor maid was distinctly startled when he asked for Bernice instead of Marjorie; after a week of it she told the cook that Miss Bernice had gotta holda Miss Marjorie's best fella.

And Miss Bernice had. Perhaps it began with Warren's desire to rouse jealousy in Marjorie; perhaps it was the familiar though unrecognized strain of Marjorie in Bernice's conversation; perhaps it was both of these and something of sincere attraction besides. But somehow the collective mind of the younger set knew within a week that Marjorie's most reliable beau had made an amazing face-about and was giving an indisputable rush to Marjorie's guest. The question of the moment was how Marjorie would take it. Warren called Bernice on the phone twice a day, sent her notes, and they were frequently seen together in his roadster, obviously engrossed in one of those tense, significant conversations as to whether or not he was sincere.

Marjorie on being twitted only laughed. She said she was mighty glad that Warren had at last found someone who appreciated him. So the younger set laughed, too, and guessed that Marjorie didn't care and let it go at that.

One afternoon when there were only three days left of her visit Bernice was waiting in the hall for Warren, with whom she was going to a bridge party. She was in rather a blissful mood, and when Marjorie—also bound for the party—appeared beside her and began casually to adjust her hat in the mirror, Bernice was utterly unprepared for anything in the nature of a clash. Marjorie did her work very coldly and succinctly in three sentences.

"You may as well get Warren out of your head," she said coldly.

"What?" Bernice was utterly astounded.

"You may as well stop making a fool of yourself over Warren McIntyre. He doesn't care a snap of his fingers about you."

For a tense moment they regarded each other—Marjorie scornful, aloof; Bernice astounded, half-angry, half-afraid. Then two cars drove up in front of the house and there was a riotous honking. Both of them gasped faintly, turned, and side by side hurried out.

All through the bridge party Bernice strove in vain to master a rising uneasiness. She had offended Marjorie, the sphinx of sphinxes. With the most wholesome and innocent intentions in the world she had stolen Marjorie's property. She felt suddenly and horribly guilty. After the bridge game, when they sat in an informal circle and the conversation became general, the storm gradually broke. Little Otis Ormonde inadvertently precipitated it.

"When you going back to kindergarten, Otis?" someone had asked.

"Me? Day Bernice gets her hair bobbed."

"Then your education's over," said Marjorie quickly. "That's only a bluff of hers. I should think you'd have realized."

"That a fact?" demanded Otis, giving Bernice a reproachful glance.

Bernice's ears burned as she tried to think up an effectual comeback. In the face of this direct attack her imagination was paralyzed.

"There's a lot of bluffs in the world," continued Marjorie quite pleasantly. "I should think you'd be young enough to know that, Otis."

"Well," said Otis, "maybe so. But gee! With a line like Bernice's——"

"Really?" yawned Marjorie. "What's her latest bon mot?"

No one seemed to know. In fact, Bernice, having trifled with her muse's beau, had said nothing memorable of late.

"Was that really all a line?" asked Roberta curiously.

Bernice hesitated. She felt that wit in some form was demanded of her, but under her cousin's suddenly frigid eyes she was completely incapacitated.

"I don't know," she stalled.

"Splush!" said Marjorie. "Admit it!"

Bernice saw that Warren's eyes had left a ukulele he had been tinkering with and were fixed on her questioningly.

"Oh, I don't know!" she repeated steadily. Her cheeks were glowing.

"Splush!" remarked Marjorie again.

"Come through, Bernice," urged Otis. "Tell her where to get off."

Bernice looked round again—she seemed unable to get away from Warren's eyes.

"I like bobbed hair," she said hurriedly, as if he had asked her a question, "and I intend to bob mine."

"When?" demanded Marjorie.

"Any time."

"No time like the present," suggested Roberta.

Otis jumped to his feet.

"Good stuff!" he cried. "We'll have a summer bobbing party. Sevier Hotel barber shop, I think you said."

In an instant all were on their feet. Bernice's heart throbbed violently.

"What?" she gasped.

Out of the group came Marjorie's voice, very clear and contemptuous.

"Don't worry—she'll back out!"

"Come on, Bernice!" cried Otis, starting toward the door.

Four eyes—Warren's and Marjorie's—stared at her, challenged her, defied her. For another second she wavered wildly.

"All right," she said swiftly, "I don't care if I do."

An eternity of minutes later, riding downtown through the late afternoon beside Warren, the others following in Roberta's car close behind, Bernice had all the sensations of Marie Antoinette bound for the guillotine in a tumbrel. Vaguely she wondered why she did not cry out that it was all a mistake. It was all she could do to keep from clutching her hair with both hands to protect it from the suddenly hostile world. Yet she did neither. Even the thought of her mother was no deterrent now. This was the test supreme of her sportsmanship; her right to walk unchallenged in the starry heaven of popular girls.

Warren was moodily silent, and when they came to the hotel he drew up at the curb and nodded to Bernice to precede him out. Roberta's car emptied a laughing crowd into the shop, which presented two bold plate-glass windows to the street.

Bernice stood on the curb and looked at the sign, Sevier Barber Shop. It was a guillotine indeed, and the hangman was the first barber, who, attired in a white coat and smoking a cigarette, leaned nonchalantly against the first chair. He must have heard of her; he must have been waiting all week, smoking eternal cigarettes beside that portentous, too-often-mentioned first chair. Would they blindfold her? No, but they would tie a white cloth round her neck lest any of her blood—nonsense, hair—should get on her clothes.

"All right, Bernice," said Warren quickly.

With her chin in the air she crossed the sidewalk, pushed open the swinging screen door, and giving not a glance to the uproarious, riotous row that occupied the waiting bench, went up to the first barber.

"I want you to bob my hair."

The first barber's mouth slid somewhat open. His cigarette dropped to the floor.

"Huh?"

"My hair—bob it!"

Refusing further preliminaries, Bernice took her seat on high. A man in the chair next to her turned on his side and gave her a glance, half-lather, half-amazement. One barber started and spoiled little Willy Schuneman's monthly haircut. Mr. O'Reilly in the last chair grunted and swore musically in ancient Gaelic as a razor bit into his cheek. Two bootblacks became wide-eyed and rushed for her feet. No, Bernice didn't care for a shine.

Outside a passer-by stopped and stared; a couple joined him; half a dozen small boys' noses sprang into life, flattened against the glass; and snatches of conversation borne on the summer breeze drifted in through the screen door.

"Lookada long hair on a kid!"

"Where'd yuh get 'at stuff? 'At's a bearded lady he just finished shavin'."

But Bernice saw nothing, heard nothing. Her only living sense told her that this man in the white coat had removed one tortoise-shell comb and then another; that his fingers were fumbling clumsily with unfamiliar hairpins; that this hair, this wonderful hair of hers, was going—she would never again feel its long voluptuous pull as it hung in a dark-brown glory down her back. For a second she was near breaking down, and then the picture before her swam mechanically into her vision—Marjorie's mouth curling in a faint ironic smile as if to say:

"Give up and get down! You tried to buck me and I called your bluff. You see you haven't got a prayer."

And some last energy rose up in Bernice, for she clenched her hands under the white cloth, and there was a curious narrowing of her eyes that Marjorie remarked on to someone long afterward.

Twenty minutes later the barber swung her round to face the mirror, and she flinched at the full extent of the damage that had been wrought. Her hair was not curly, and now it lay in lank lifeless blocks on both sides of her suddenly pale face. It was ugly as sin—she had known it would be ugly as sin. Her face's chief charm had been a Madonna-like simplicity. Now that was gone and she was—well, frightfully mediocre—not stagy; only ridiculous, like a Greenwich Villager who had left her spectacles at home.

As she climbed down from the chair she tried to smile—failed miserably. She saw two of the girls exchange glances; noticed Marjorie's mouth curved in attenuated mockery—and that Warren's eyes were suddenly very cold.

"You see"—her words fell into an awkward pause—"I've done it."

"Yes, you've—done it," admitted Warren.

"Do you like it?"

There was a half-hearted "Sure" from two or three voices, another awkward pause, and then Marjorie turned swiftly and with serpentlike intensity to Warren.

"Would you mind running me down to the cleaners?" she asked. "I've simply got to get a dress there before supper. Roberta's driving right home and she can take the others."

Warren stared abstractedly at some infinite speck out the window. Then for an instant his eyes rested coldly on Bernice before they turned to Marjorie.

"Be glad to," he said slowly.

VI

Bernice did not fully realize the outrageous trap that had been set for her until she met her aunt's amazed glance just before dinner.

"Why, Bernice!"

"I've bobbed it, Aunt Josephine."

"Why, child!"

"Do you like it?"

"Why, Ber-nice!"

"I suppose I've shocked you."

"No, but what'll Mrs. Deyo think tomorrow night? Bernice, you should have waited until after the Deyos' dance—you should have waited if you wanted to do that."

"It was sudden, Aunt Josephine. Anyway, why does it matter to Mrs. Deyo particularly?"

"Why, child," cried Mrs. Harvey, "in her paper on 'The Foibles of the Younger Generation' that she read at the last meeting of the Thursday Club she devoted fifteen minutes to bobbed hair. It's her pet abomination. And the dance is for you and Marjorie!"

"I'm sorry."

"Oh, Bernice, what'll your mother say? She'll think I let you do it."

"I'm sorry."

Dinner was an agony. She had made a hasty attempt with a curling-iron, and burned her finger and much hair. She could see that her aunt was both worried and grieved, and her uncle kept saying, "Well, I'll be darned!" over and over in a hurt and faintly hostile tone. And Marjorie sat very quietly, intrenched behind a faint smile, a faintly mocking smile.

Somehow she got through the evening. Three boys called; Marjorie disappeared with one of them, and Bernice made a listless unsuccessful attempt to entertain the two others—sighed thankfully as she climbed the stairs to her room at half-past ten. What a day!

When she had undressed for the night the door opened and Marjorie came in.

"Bernice," she said, "I'm awfully sorry about the Deyo dance. I'll give you my word of honor I'd forgotten all about it."

"'Sall right," said Bernice shortly. Standing before the mirror she passed her comb slowly through her short hair.

"I'll take you downtown tomorrow," continued Marjorie, "and the hairdresser'll fix it so you'll look slick. I didn't imagine you'd go through with it. I'm really mighty sorry."

"Oh, 'sall right!"

"Still it's your last night, so I suppose it won't matter much."

Then Bernice winced as Marjorie tossed her own hair over her shoulders and began to twist it slowly into two long blond braids until in her cream-colored negligée she looked like a delicate painting of some Saxon princess. Fascinated, Bernice watched the braids grow. Heavy and luxurious they were, moving under the supple fingers like restive snakes—and to Bernice remained this relic and the curling-iron and a tomorrow full of eyes. She could see G. Reece Stoddard, who liked her, assuming his Harvard manner and telling his dinner partner that Bernice shouldn't have been allowed to go to the movies so much; she could see Draycott Deyo exchanging glances with his mother and then being conscientiously charitable to her. But then perhaps by tomorrow Mrs. Deyo would have heard the news; would send round an icy little note requesting that she fail to appear—and behind her back they would all laugh and know that Marjorie had made a fool of her; that her chance at beauty had been sacrificed to the jealous whim of a selfish girl. She sat down suddenly before the mirror, biting the inside of her cheek.

"I like it," she said with an effort. "I think it'll be becoming."

Marjorie smiled.

"It looks all right. For heaven's sake, don't let it worry you!"

"I won't."

"Good night, Bernice."

But as the door closed something snapped within Bernice. She sprang dynamically to her feet, clenching her hands, then swiftly and noiselessly crossed over to her bed and from underneath it dragged out her suitcase. Into it she tossed toilet articles and a change of clothing. Then she turned to her trunk and quickly dumped in two drawerfuls of lingerie and summer dresses. She moved quietly, but with deadly efficiency, and in three-quarters of an hour her trunk was locked and strapped and she was fully dressed in a becoming new traveling suit that Marjorie had helped her pick out.

Sitting down at her desk she wrote a short note to Mrs. Harvey, in which she briefly outlined her reasons for going. She sealed it, addressed it and laid it on her pillow. She glanced at her watch. The train left at one, and she knew that if she walked down to the Marborough Hotel two blocks away she could easily get a taxi-cab.

Suddenly she drew in her breath sharply and an expression flashed into her eyes that a practiced character reader might have connected vaguely with the set look she had worn in the barber's chair—somehow a development of it. It was quite a new look for Bernice—and it carried consequences.

She went stealthily to the bureau, picked up an article that lay there, and turning out all the lights stood quietly until her eyes became accustomed to the darkness. Softly she pushed open the door to Marjorie's room. She heard the quiet, even breathing of an untroubled conscience asleep.

She was by the bedside now, very deliberate and calm. She acted swiftly. Bending over she found one of the braids of Marjorie's hair, followed it up with her hand to the point nearest the head, and then holding it a little slack so that the sleeper would feel no pull, she reached down with the shears and severed it. With the pigtail in her hand she held her breath. Marjorie had muttered something in her sleep. Bernice deftly amputated the other braid, paused for an instant, and then flitted swiftly and silently back to her own room.

Downstairs she opened the big front door, closed it carefully behind her, and feeling oddly happy and exuberant stepped off the porch into the moonlight, swinging her heavy grip like a shopping bag. After a minute's brisk walk she discovered that her left hand still held the two blonde braids. She laughed unexpectedly—had to shut her mouth hard to keep from emitting an absolute peal. She was passing Warren's house now, and on the impulse she set down her baggage, and swinging the braids like pieces of rope flung them at the wooden porch, where they landed with a slight thud. She laughed again, no longer restraining herself.

"Huh!" she giggled wildly. "Scalp the selfish thing!"

Then picking up her suitcase she set off at a half-run down the moonlit street.

BENEDICTION

The Baltimore Station was hot and crowded, so Lois was forced to stand by the telegraph desk for interminable, sticky seconds while a clerk with big front teeth counted and recounted a large lady's day message, to determine whether it contained the innocuous forty-nine words or the fatal fifty-one.

Lois, waiting, decided she wasn't quite sure of the address, so she took the letter out of her bag and ran over it again.

"Darling": *it began*—"I understand and I'm happier than life ever meant me to be. If I could give you the things you've always been in tune with—but I can't, Lois; we can't marry and we can't lose each other and let all this glorious love end in nothing.

"Until your letter came, dear, I'd been sitting here in the half-dark thinking and thinking where I could go and ever forget you; abroad, perhaps, to drift through Italy or Spain and dream away the pain of having lost you where the crumbling ruins of older, mellower civilizations would mirror only the desolation of my heart—and then your letter came.

"Sweetest, bravest girl, if you'll wire me I'll meet you in Wilmington—till then I'll be here just waiting and hoping for every long dream of you to come true.

"HOWARD."

She had read the letter so many times that she knew it word by word, yet it still startled her. In it she found many faint reflections of the man who wrote it—the mingled sweetness and sadness in his dark eyes, the furtive, restless excitement she felt sometimes when he talked to her, his dreamy sensuousness that lulled her mind to sleep. Lois was nineteen and very romantic and curious and courageous.

The large lady and the clerk having compromised on fifty words, Lois took a blank and wrote her telegram. And there were no overtones to the finality of her decision.

It's just destiny—she thought—it's just the way things work out in this damn world. If cowardice is all that's been holding me back there won't be any more holding back. So we'll just let things take their course, and never be sorry.

The clerk scanned her telegram:

"*Arrived Baltimore today spend day with my brother meet me Wilmington three P.M. Wednesday Love*

"Lois."

"Fifty-four cents," said the clerk admiringly.

And never be sorry—thought Lois—and never be sorry——

II

Trees filtering light onto dappled grass. Trees like tall, languid ladies with feather fans coquetting airily with the ugly roof of the monastery. Trees like butlers, bending courteously over placid walks and paths. Trees, trees over the hills on either side and scattering out in clumps and lines and woods all through eastern Maryland, delicate lace on the hems of many yellow fields, dark opaque backgrounds for flowered bushes or wild climbing gardens.

Some of the trees were very gay and young, but the monastery trees were older than the monastery which, by true monastic standards, wasn't very old at all. And, as a matter of fact, it wasn't technically called a monastery, but only a seminary; nevertheless it shall be a monastery here despite its Victorian architecture or its Edward VII additions, or even its Woodrow Wilsonian, patented, last-a-century roofing.

Out behind was the farm where half a dozen lay brothers were sweating lustily as they moved with deadly efficiency around the vegetable gardens. To the left, behind a row of elms, was an informal baseball diamond where three novices were being batted out by a fourth, amid great chasings and puffings and blowings. And in front, as a great mellow bell boomed the half-hour, a swarm of black, human leaves were blown over the checker-board of paths under the courteous trees.

Some of these black leaves were very old with cheeks furrowed like the first ripples of a splashed pool. Then there was a scattering of middle-aged leaves whose forms when viewed in profile in their revealing gowns were beginning to be faintly unsymmetrical. These carried thick volumes of Thomas Aquinas and Henry James and Cardinal Mercier and Immanuel Kant and many bulging notebooks filled with lecture data.

But most numerous were the young leaves; blond boys of nineteen with very stern, conscientious expressions; men in the late twenties with a keen self-assurance from having taught out in the world for five years—several hundreds of them, from city and town and country in Maryland and Pennsylvania and Virginia and West Virginia and Delaware.

There were many Americans and some Irish and some tough Irish and a few French, and several Italians and Poles, and they walked informally arm in arm with each other in twos and threes or in long rows, almost universally distinguished by the straight mouth and the considerable chin—for this was the Society of Jesus, founded in Spain five hundred years before by a tough-minded soldier who trained men to hold a breach or a salon, preach a sermon or write a treaty, and do it and not argue....

Lois got out of a bus into the sunshine down by the outer gate. She was nineteen with yellow hair and eyes that people were tactful enough not to call green. When men of talent saw her in a street-car they often furtively produced little stub-pencils and backs of envelopes and tried to sum up that profile or the thing that the eyebrows did to her eyes. Later they looked at their results and usually tore them up with wondering sighs.

Though Lois was very jauntily attired in an expensively appropriate traveling affair, she did not linger to pat out the dust which covered her clothes, but started up the central walk with curious glances at either side. Her face was very eager and expectant, yet she hadn't at all that glorified expression that girls wear when they arrive for a Senior Prom at Princeton or New Haven; still, as there were no senior proms here, perhaps it didn't matter.

She was wondering what he would look like, whether she'd possibly know him from his picture. In the picture, which hung over her mother's bureau at home, he seemed very young and hollow-cheeked and rather pitiful, with only a well-developed mouth and an ill-fitting probationer's gown to show that he had already made a momentous decision about his life. Of course he had been only nineteen then and now he was thirty-six—didn't look like that at all; in recent snapshots he was much broader and his hair had grown a little thin—but the impression of her brother she had always retained was that of the big picture. And so she had always been a little sorry for him. What a life for a man! Seventeen years of preparation and he wasn't even a priest yet—wouldn't be for another year.

Lois had an idea that this was all going to be rather solemn if she let it be. But she was going to give her very best imitation of undiluted sunshine, the imitation she could give even when her head was splitting or when her mother had a nervous breakdown or when she was particularly romantic and curious and courageous. This brother of hers undoubtedly needed cheering up, and he was going to be cheered up, whether he liked it or not.

As she drew near the great, homely front door she saw a man break suddenly away from a group and, pulling up the skirts of his gown, run toward her. He was smiling, she noticed, and he looked very big and—and reliable. She stopped and waited, knew that her heart was beating unusually fast.

"Lois!" he cried, and in a second she was in his arms. She was suddenly trembling.

"Lois!" he cried again, "why, this is wonderful! I can't tell you, Lois, how *much* I've looked forward to this. Why, Lois, you're beautiful!"

Lois gasped.

His voice, though restrained, was vibrant with energy and that odd sort of enveloping personality she had thought that she only of the family possessed.

"I'm mighty glad, too—Keith."

She flushed, but not unhappily, at this first use of his name.

"Lois—Lois—Lois," he repeated in wonder. "Child, we'll go in here a minute, because I want you to meet the rector and then we'll walk around. I have a thousand things to talk to you about."

His voice became graver. "How's Mother?"

She looked at him for a moment and then said something that she had not intended to say at all, the very sort of thing she had resolved to avoid.

"Oh, Keith—she's—she's getting worse all the time, every way."

He nodded slowly as if he understood.

"Nervous, well—you can tell me about that later. Now——"

She was in a small study with a large desk, saying something to a little, jovial, white-haired priest who retained her hand for some seconds.

"So this is Lois!"

He said it as if he had heard of her for years.

He entreated her to sit down.

Two other priests arrived enthusiastically and shook hands with her and addressed her as "Keith's little sister," which she found she didn't mind a bit.

How assured they seemed; she had expected a certain shyness, reserve at least. There were several jokes unintelligible to her, which seemed to delight everyone, and the little Father Rector referred to the trio of them as "dim old monks," which she appreciated, because of course they weren't monks at all. She had a lightning impression that they were especially fond of Keith—the Father Rector had called him "Keith" and one of the others had kept a hand on his shoulder all through the conversation. Then she was shaking hands again and promising to come back a little later for some ice cream, and smiling and smiling and being rather absurdly happy . . . she told herself that it was because Keith was so delighted in showing her off.

Then she and Keith were strolling along a path, arm in arm, and he was informing her what an absolute jewel the Father Rector was.

"Lois," he broke off suddenly, "I want to tell you before we go any farther how much it means to me to have you come up here. I think it was—mighty sweet of you. I know what a gay time you've been having."

Lois gasped. She was not prepared for this. At first when she had conceived the plan of taking the hot journey down to Baltimore, staying the night with a friend and then coming out to see her brother, she had felt rather consciously virtuous, hoped he wouldn't be priggish or resentful about her not having come before—but walking here with him under the trees seemed such a little thing, and surprisingly a happy thing.

"Why, Keith," she said quickly, "you know I couldn't have waited a day longer. I saw you when I was five, but of course I didn't remember, and how could I have gone on without practically ever having seen my only brother?"

"It was mighty sweet of you, Lois," he repeated.

Lois blushed—he *did* have personality.

"I want you to tell me all about yourself," he said after a pause. "Of course I have a general idea what you and Mother did in Europe those fourteen years, and then we were all so worried, Lois, when you had pneumonia and couldn't come down with Mother—let's see, that was two years ago—and then, well, I've seen your name in the papers, but it's all been so unsatisfactory. I haven't known you, Lois."

She found herself analyzing his personality as she analyzed the personality of every man she met. She wondered if the effect of—of intimacy that he gave was bred by his constant repetition of her name. He said it as if he loved the word, as if it had an inherent meaning to him.

"Then you were at school," he continued.

"Yes, at Farmington. Mother wanted me to go to a convent—but I didn't want to."

She cast a side glance at him to see if he would resent this.

But he only nodded slowly.

"Had enough convents abroad, eh?"

"Yes—and Keith, convents are different there anyway. Here even in the nicest ones there are so many *common* girls."

He nodded again.

"Yes," he agreed, "I suppose there are, and I know how you feel about it. It grated on me here, at first, Lois, though I wouldn't say that to anyone but you; we're rather sensitive, you and I, to things like this."

"You mean the men here?"

"Yes, some of them of course were fine, the sort of men I'd always been thrown with, but there were others; a man named Regan, for instance—I hated the fellow, and now he's about the best friend I have. A wonderful character, Lois; you'll meet him later. Sort of man you'd like to have with you in a fight."

Lois was thinking that Keith was the sort of man she'd like to have with *her* in a fight.

"How did you—how did you first happen to do it?" she asked, rather shyly, "to come here, I mean. Of course Mother told me the story about the Pullman car."

"Oh, that——" He looked rather annoyed.

"Tell me that. I'd like to hear you tell it."

"Oh, it's nothing, except what you probably know. It was evening and I'd been riding all day and thinking about—about a hundred things, Lois, and then suddenly I had a sense that someone was sitting across from me, felt that he'd been there for some time, and had a vague idea that he was another traveler. All at once he leaned over toward me and I heard a voice say: 'I want you to be a priest, that's what I want.' Well, I jumped up and cried out, 'Oh, my God, not that!'—made an idiot of myself before about twenty people; you see there wasn't anyone sitting there at all. A week after that I went to the Jesuit College in Philadelphia and crawled up the last flight of stairs to the rector's office on my hands and knees."

There was another silence and Lois saw that her brother's eyes wore a far-away look, that he was staring unseeingly out over the sunny fields. She was stirred by the modulations of his voice and the sudden silence that seemed to flow about him when he finished speaking.

She noticed now that his eyes were of the same fibre as hers, with the green left out, and that his mouth was much gentler, really, than in the picture—or was it that the face had grown up to it lately? He was getting a little bald just on top of his head. She wondered if that was from wearing a hat so much. It seemed awful for a man to grow bald and no one to care about it.

"Were you—pious when you were young, Keith?" she asked. "You know what I mean. Were you religious? If you don't mind these personal questions."

"Yes," he said with his eyes still far away—and she felt that his intense abstraction was as much a part of his personality as his attention. "Yes, I suppose I was, when I was—sober."

Lois thrilled slightly.

"Did you drink?"

He nodded.

"I was on the way to making a bad hash of things." He smiled and, turning his grey eyes on her, changed the subject.

"Child, tell me about Mother. I know it's been awfully hard for you there, lately. I know you've had to sacrifice a lot and put up with a great deal, and I want you to know how fine of you I think it is. I feel, Lois, that you're sort of taking the place of both of us there."

Lois thought quickly how little she had sacrificed; how lately she had constantly avoided her nervous, half-invalid mother.

"Youth shouldn't be sacrificed to age, Keith," she said steadily.

"I know," he sighed, "and you oughtn't to have the weight on your shoulders, child. I wish I were there to help you."

She saw how quickly he had turned her remark and instantly she knew what this quality was that he gave off. He was *sweet*. Her thoughts went off on a side-track and then she broke the silence with an odd remark.

"Sweetness is hard," she said suddenly.

"What?"

"Nothing," she denied in confusion. "I didn't mean to speak aloud. I was thinking of something—of a conversation with a man named Freddy Kebble."

"Maury Kebble's brother?"

"Yes," she said, rather surprised to think of him having known Maury Kebble. Still there was nothing strange about it. "Well, he and I were talking about sweetness a few weeks ago. Oh, I don't know—I said that a man named Howard—that a man I knew was sweet, and he didn't agree with me, and we began talking about what sweetness in a man was. He kept telling me I meant a sort of soppy softness, but I knew I didn't—yet I didn't know exactly how to put it. I see now. I meant just the opposite. I suppose real sweetness is a sort of hardness—and strength."

Keith nodded.

"I see what you mean. I've known old priests who had it."

"I'm talking about young men," she said, rather defiantly.

"Oh!"

They had reached the now deserted baseball diamond and, pointing her to a wooden bench, he sprawled full length on the grass.

"Are these *young* men happy here, Keith?"

"Don't they look happy, Lois?"

"I suppose so, but those *young* ones, those two we just passed—have they—are they——"

"Are they signed up?" he laughed. "No, but they will be next month."

"Permanently?"

"Yes—unless they break down mentally or physically. Of course in a discipline like ours a lot drop out."

"But those *boys*. Are they giving up fine chances outside—like you did?"

He nodded. "Some of them."

"But, Keith, they don't know what they're doing. They haven't had any experience of what they're missing."

"No, I suppose not."

"It doesn't seem fair. Life has just sort of scared them at first. Do they all come in so *young*?"

"No, some of them have knocked around, led pretty wild lives—Regan, for instance."

"I should think that sort would be better," she said meditatively, "men that had *seen* life."

"No," said Keith earnestly, "I'm not sure that knocking about gives a man the sort of experience he can communicate to others. Some of the broadest men I've known have been absolutely rigid about themselves. And reformed libertines are a notoriously intolerant class. Don't you think so, Lois?"

She nodded, still meditative, and he continued:

"It seems to me that when one weak person goes to another, it isn't help they want; it's a sort of companionship in guilt, Lois. After you were born, when Mother began to get nervous she used to go and weep with a certain Mrs. Comstock. Lord, it used to make me shiver.

She said it comforted her, poor old Mother. No, I don't think that to help others you've got to show yourself at all. Real help comes from a stronger person whom you respect. And their sympathy is all the bigger because it's impersonal."

"But people want human sympathy," objected Lois. "They want to feel the other person's been tempted."

"Lois, in their hearts they want to feel that the other person's been weak. That's what they mean by human.

"Here in this old monkery, Lois," he continued with a smile, "they try to get all that self-pity and pride in our own wills out of us right at the first. They put us to scrubbing floors—and other things. It's like that idea of saving your life by losing it. You see we sort of feel that the less human a man is, in your sense of human, the better servant he can be to humanity. We carry it out to the end, too. When one of us dies his family can't even have him then. He's buried here under a plain wooden cross with a thousand others."

His tone changed suddenly and he looked at her with a great brightness in his grey eyes.

"But way back in a man's heart there are some things he can't get rid of—and one of them is that I'm awfully in love with my little sister."

With a sudden impulse she knelt beside him in the grass and, leaning over, kissed his forehead.

"You're hard, Keith," she said, "and I love you for it—and you're sweet."

III

Back in the reception room Lois met a half-dozen more of Keith's particular friends; there was a young man named Jarvis, rather pale and delicate-looking, who, she knew, must be a grandson of old Mrs. Jarvis at home, and she mentally compared this ascetic with a brace of his riotous uncles.

And there was Regan with a scarred face and piercing intent eyes that followed her about the room and often rested on Keith with something very like worship. She knew then what Keith had meant about "a good man to have with you in a fight."

He's the missionary type—she thought vaguely—China or something.

"I want Keith's sister to show us what the shimmy is," demanded one young man with a broad grin.

Lois laughed.

"I'm afraid the Father Rector would send me shimmying out the gate. Besides, I'm not an expert."

"I'm sure it wouldn't be best for Jimmy's soul anyway," said Keith solemnly. "He's inclined to brood about things like shimmys. They were just starting to do the—maxixe, wasn't it, Jimmy?—when he became a monk, and it haunted him his whole first year. You'd see him when he was peeling potatoes, putting his arm around the bucket and making irreligious motions with his feet."

There was a general laugh in which Lois joined.

"An old lady who comes here to Mass sent Keith this ice cream," whispered Jarvis under cover of the laugh, "because she'd heard you were coming. It's pretty good, isn't it?"

There were tears trembling in Lois' eyes.

IV

Then half an hour later over in the chapel things suddenly went all wrong. It was several years since Lois had been at Benediction and at first she was thrilled by the gleaming monstrance with its central spot of white, the air rich and heavy with incense, and the sun shining through the stained-glass window of St. Francis Xavier overhead and falling in warm red tracery on the cassock of the man in front of her, but at the first notes of the *O Salutaris Hostia* a heavy weight seemed to descend upon her soul. Keith was on her right and young Jarvis on her left, and she stole uneasy glances at both of them.

What's the matter with me? she thought impatiently.

She looked again. Was there a certain coldness in both their profiles that she had not noticed before—a pallor about the mouth and a curious set expression in their eyes? She shivered slightly: they were like dead men.

She felt her soul recede suddenly from Keith's. This was her brother —this, this unnatural person. She caught herself in the act of a little laugh.

"What is the matter with me?"

She passed her hand over her eyes and the weight increased. The incense sickened her and a stray, ragged note from one of the tenors in the choir grated on her ear like the shriek of a slate-pencil. She fidgeted and raising her hand to her hair touched her forehead, found moisture on it.

"It's hot in here, hot as the deuce."

Again she repressed a faint laugh, and then in an instant the weight upon her heart suddenly diffused into cold fear. . . . It was that candle on the altar. It was all wrong—wrong. Why didn't somebody see it? There was something *in* it. There was something coming out of it, taking form and shape above it.

She tried to fight down her rising panic, told herself it was the wick. If the wick wasn't straight, candles did something—but they didn't do this! With incalculable rapidity a force was gathering within her, a tremendous, assimilative force, drawing from every sense, every corner of her brain, and as it surged up inside her she felt an enormous, terrified repulsion. She drew her arms in close to her side, away from Keith and Jarvis.

Something in that candle . . . she was leaning forward—in another moment she felt she would go forward toward it—didn't anyone see it? . . . anyone?

"Ugh!"

She felt a space beside her and something told her that Jarvis had gasped and sat down very suddenly . . . then she was kneeling and as the flaming monstrance slowly left the altar in the hands of the priest, she heard a great rushing noise in her ears—the crash of the bells was like hammer blows . . . and then in a moment that seemed eternal a great torrent rolled over her heart—there was a shouting there and a lashing as of waves . . .

. . . She was calling, felt herself calling for Keith, her lips mouthing the words that would not come:

"Keith! Oh, my God! *Keith!*"

Suddenly she became aware of a new presence, something external, in front of her, consummated and expressed in warm red tracery.

Then she knew. It was the window of St. Francis Xavier. Her mind gripped at it, clung to it finally, and she felt herself calling again endlessly, impotently—Keith—Keith!

Then out of a great stillness came a voice:

"*Blessed be God.*"

With a gradual rumble sounded the response rolling heavily through the chapel:

"Blessed be God."

The words sang instantly in her heart; the incense lay mystically and sweetly peaceful upon the air, and *the candle on the altar went out.*

"Blessed be His Holy Name."

"Blessed be His Holy Name."

Everything blurred into a swinging mist. With a sound half-gasp, half-cry she rocked on her feet and reeled backward into Keith's suddenly outstretched arms.

V

"Lie still, child."

She closed her eyes again. She was on the grass outside, pillowed on Keith's arm, and Regan was dabbing her head with a cold towel.

"I'm all right," she said quietly.

"I know, but just lie still a minute longer. It was too hot in there. Jarvis felt it, too."

She laughed as Regan again touched her gingerly with the towel. "I'm all right," she repeated.

But though a warm peace was filling her mind and heart she felt oddly broken and chastened, as if someone had held her stripped soul up and laughed.

VI

Half an hour later she walked leaning on Keith's arm down the long central path toward the gate.

"It's been such a short afternoon," he sighed, "and I'm so sorry you were sick, Lois."

"Keith, I'm feeling fine now, really; I wish you wouldn't worry."

"Poor old child. I didn't realize that Benediction'd be a long service for you after your hot trip out here and all."

She laughed cheerfully.

"I guess the truth is I'm not much used to Benediction. Mass is the limit of my religious exertions."

She paused and then continued quickly:

"I don't want to shock you, Keith, but I can't tell you how—how *inconvenient* being a Catholic is. It really doesn't seem to apply anymore. As far as morals go, some of the wildest boys I know are Catholics. And the brightest boys—I mean the ones who think and read a lot, don't seem to believe in much of anything anymore."

"Tell me about it. The bus won't be here for another half-hour."

They sat down on a bench by the path.

"For instance, Gerald Carter, he's published a novel. He absolutely roars when people mention immortality. And then Howa—well, another man I've known well, lately, who was Phi Beta Kappa at Harvard, says that no intelligent person can believe in Supernatural Christianity. He says Christ was a great socialist, though. Am I shocking you?"

She broke off suddenly.

Keith smiled.

"You can't shock a monk. He's a professional shock-absorber."

"Well," she continued, "that's about all. It seems so—so *narrow*. Church schools, for instance. There's more freedom about things that Catholic people can't see—like birth control."

Keith winced, almost imperceptibly, but Lois saw it.

"Oh," she said quickly, "everybody talks about everything now."

"It's probably better that way."

"Oh, yes, much better. Well, that's all, Keith. I just wanted to tell you why I'm a little—lukewarm, at present."

"I'm not shocked, Lois. I understand better than you think. We all go through those times. But I know it'll come out all right, child. There's that gift of faith that we have, you and I, that'll carry us past the bad spots."

He rose as he spoke and they started again down the path.

"I want you to pray for me sometimes, Lois. I think your prayers would be about what I need. Because we've come very close in these few hours, I think."

Her eyes were suddenly shining.

"Oh, we have, we have!" she cried. "I feel closer to you now than to anyone in the world."

He stopped suddenly and indicated the side of the path.

"We might—just a minute——"

It was a pietà, a life-size statue of the Blessed Virgin set within a semicircle of rocks.

Feeling a little self-conscious she dropped on her knees beside him and made an unsuccessful attempt at prayer.

She was only half through when he rose. He took her arm again.

"I wanted to thank Her for letting us have this day together," he said simply.

Lois felt a sudden lump in her throat and she wanted to say something that would tell him how much it had meant to her, too. But she found no words.

"I'll always remember this," he continued, his voice trembling a little—"this summer day with you. It's been just what I expected. You're just what I expected, Lois."

"I'm awfully glad, Keith."

"You see, when you were little they kept sending me snapshots of you, first as a baby and then as a child in socks playing on the beach with a pail and shovel, and then suddenly as a wistful little girl with wondering, pure eyes—and I used to build dreams about you. A man has to have something living to cling to. I think, Lois, it was your little white soul I tried to keep near me—even when life was at its loudest and every intellectual idea of God seemed the sheerest mockery, and desire and love and a million things came up to me and said: 'Look here at me! See, I'm Life. You're turning your back on it!' All the way through that shadow, Lois, I could always see your baby soul flitting on ahead of me, very frail and clear and wonderful."

Lois was crying softly. They had reached the gate and she rested her elbow on it and dabbed furiously at her eyes.

"And then later, child, when you were sick I knelt all one night and asked God to spare you for me—for I knew then that I wanted more; He had taught me to want more. I wanted to know you moved and breathed in the same world with me. I saw you growing up, that white innocence of yours changing to a flame and burning to give light to other weaker souls. And then I wanted someday to take your children on my knee and hear them call the crabbed old monk Uncle Keith."

He seemed to be laughing now as he talked.

"Oh, Lois, Lois, I was asking God for more then. I wanted the letters you'd write me and the place I'd have at your table. I wanted an awful lot, Lois, dear."

"You've got me, Keith," she sobbed, "you know it, say you know it. Oh, I'm acting like a baby but I didn't think you'd be this way, and I—oh, Keith—Keith——"

He took her hand and patted it softly.

"Here's the bus. You'll come again, won't you?"

She put her hands on his cheeks, and drawing his head down, pressed her tear-wet face against his.

"Oh, Keith, brother, someday I'll tell you something——"

He helped her in, saw her take down her handkerchief and smile bravely at him, as the driver flicked his whip and the bus rolled off. Then a thick cloud of dust rose around it and she was gone.

For a few minutes he stood there on the road, his hand on the gate-post, his lips half-parted in a smile.

"Lois," he said aloud in a sort of wonder, "Lois, Lois."

Later, some probationers passing noticed him kneeling before the pietà, and coming back after a time found him still there. And he was there until twilight came down and the courteous trees grew garrulous overhead and the crickets took up their burden of song in the dusky grass.

VII

The first clerk in the telegraph booth in the Baltimore Station whistled through his buck teeth at the second clerk:

"S'matter?"

"See that girl—no, the pretty one with the big black dots on her veil. Too late—she's gone. You missed somep'n."

"What about her?"

"Nothing. 'Cept she's damn good-looking. Came in here yesterday and sent a wire to some guy to meet her somewhere. Then a minute ago she came in with a telegram all written out and was standin' there goin' to give it to me when she changed her mind or somep'n and all of a sudden tore it up."

"Hm."

The first clerk came around the counter and picking up the two pieces of paper from the floor put them together idly. The second clerk read them over his shoulder and subconsciously counted the words as he read. There were just thirteen.

"*This is in the way of a permanent good-bye. I should suggest Italy.*

"Lois."

"Tore it up, eh?" said the second clerk.

DALYRIMPLE GOES WRONG

In the millennium an educational genius will write a book to be given to every young man on the date of his disillusion. This work will have the flavor of Montaigne's essays and Samuel Butler's notebooks—and a little of Tolstoi and Marcus Aurelius. It will be neither cheerful nor pleasant but will contain numerous passages of striking humor. Since first-class minds never believe anything very strongly until they've experienced it, its value will be purely relative . . . all people over thirty will refer to it as "depressing."

This prelude belongs to the story of a young man who lived, as you and I do, before the book.

II

The generation which numbered Bryan Dalyrimple drifted out of adolescence to a mighty fanfare of trumpets. Bryan played the star in an affair which included a Lewis gun and a nine-day romp behind the retreating German lines, so luck triumphant or sentiment rampant awarded him a row of medals and on his arrival in the States he was told that he was second in importance only to General Pershing and Sergeant York. This was a lot of fun. The governor of his state, a stray congressman and a citizens' committee gave him enormous smiles and "By God, Sirs" on the dock at Hoboken; there were newspaper reporters and photographers who said "would you mind" and "if you could just"; and back in his home town there were old ladies, the rims of whose eyes grew red as they talked to him, and girls who hadn't remembered him so well since his father's business went blah! in nineteen-twelve.

But when the shouting died he realized that for a month he had been the house-guest of the mayor, that he had only fourteen dollars in the world, and that "the name that will live forever in the annals and legends of this state" was already living there very quietly and obscurely.

One morning he lay late in bed and just outside his door he heard the upstairs maid talking to the cook. The upstairs maid said that Mrs. Hawkins, the mayor's wife, had been trying for a week to hint Dalyrimple out of the house. He left at eleven o'clock in intolerable confusion, asking that his trunk be sent to Mrs. Beebe's boarding house.

Dalyrimple was twenty-three and he had never worked. His father had given him two years at the state university and passed away about the time of his son's nine-day romp, leaving behind him some mid-Victorian furniture and a thin packet of folded papers that turned out to be grocery bills. Young Dalyrimple had very keen grey eyes, a mind that delighted the army psychological examiners, a trick of having read it—whatever it was—sometime before, and a cool hand in a hot situation. But these things did not save him a final, unresigned sigh when he realized that he had to go to work—right away.

It was early afternoon when he walked into the office of Theron G. Macy, who owned the largest wholesale grocery house in town. Plump, prosperous, wearing a pleasant but quite unhumorous smile, Theron G. Macy greeted him warmly.

"Well—How do, Bryan. What's on your mind?"

To Dalyrimple, straining with his admission, his own words, when they came, sounded like an Arab beggar's whine for alms.

"Why—this question of a job." ("This question of a job" seemed somehow more clothed than just "a job.")

"A job?" An almost imperceptible breeze blew across Mr. Macy's expression.

"You see, Mr. Macy," continued Dalyrimple, "I feel I'm wasting time. I want to get started at something. I had several chances about a month ago but they all seem to have—gone——"

"Let's see," interrupted Mr. Macy. "What were they?"

"Well, just at the first the governor said something about a vacancy on his staff. I was sort of counting on that for awhile but I hear he's given it to Allen Gregg, you know, son of G. P. Gregg. He sort of forgot what he said to me—just talking I guess."

"You ought to push those things."

"Then there was that engineering expedition, but they decided they'd have to have a man who knew hydraulics, so they couldn't use me unless I paid my own way."

"You had just a year at the university?"

"Two. But I didn't take any science or mathematics. Well, the day the battalion paraded, Mr. Peter Jordan said something about a vacancy in his store. I went around there today and I found he meant a sort of floor-walker—and then you said something one day"—he paused and waited for the older man to take him up, but noting only a minute wince continued—"about a position, so I thought I'd come and see you."

"There was a position," confessed Mr. Macy reluctantly, "but since then we've filled it." He cleared his throat again. "You've waited quite awhile."

"Yes, I suppose I did. Everybody told me there was no hurry—and I'd had these various offers."

Mr. Macy delivered a paragraph on present-day opportunities which Dalyrimple's mind completely skipped.

"Have you had any business experience?"

"I worked on a ranch two summers as a rider."

"Oh, well," Mr. Macy disparaged this neatly, and then continued: "What do you think you're worth?"

"I don't know."

"Well, Bryan, I tell you, I'm willing to strain a point and give you a chance."

Dalyrimple nodded.

"Your salary won't be much. You'll start by learning the stock. Then you'll come in the office for awhile. Then you'll go on the road. When could you begin?"

"How about tomorrow?"

"All right. Report to Mr. Hanson in the stock room. He'll start you off."

He continued to regard Dalyrimple steadily until the latter, realizing that the interview was over, rose awkwardly.

"Well, Mr. Macy, I'm certainly much obliged."

"That's all right. Glad to help you, Bryan."

After an irresolute moment, Dalyrimple found himself in the hall. His forehead was covered with perspiration, and the room had not been hot.

"Why the devil did I thank the son of a gun?" he muttered.

III

Next morning Mr. Hanson informed him coldly of the necessity of punching the time-clock at seven every morning and delivered him for instruction into the hands of a fellow worker, one Charley Moore.

Charley was twenty-six, with that faint musk of weakness hanging about him that is often mistaken for the scent of evil. It took no psychological examiner to decide that he had drifted into indulgence and laziness as casually as he had drifted into life, and was to drift out. He was pale and his clothes stank of smoke; he enjoyed burlesque shows, billiards and Robert Service, and was always looking back upon his last intrigue or forward to his next one. In his youth his taste had run to loud ties but now it seemed to have faded, like his vitality, and was expressed in pale lilac four-in-hands and indeterminate grey collars. Charley was listlessly struggling that losing struggle against mental, moral and physical anemia that takes place ceaselessly on the lower fringe of the middle classes.

The first morning he stretched himself on a row of cereal cartons and carefully went over the limitations of the Theron G. Macy Company.

"It's a piker organization. My Gosh! Lookit what they give me. I'm quittin' in a coupla months. Hell! Me stay with this bunch!"

The Charley Moores are always going to change jobs next month. They do, once or twice in their careers, after which they sit around comparing their last job with the present one, to the infinite disparagement of the latter.

"What do you get?" asked Dalyrimple curiously.

"Me? I get sixty." This rather defiantly.

"Did you start at sixty?"

"Me? No, I started at thirty-five. He told me he'd put me on the road after I learned the stock. That's what he tells 'em all."

"How long've you been here?" asked Dalyrimple with a sinking sensation.

"Me? Four years. My last year, too, you bet your boots."

Dalyrimple rather resented the presence of the store detective as he resented the time-clock, and he came into contact with him almost immediately through the rule against smoking. This rule was a thorn in his side. He was accustomed to his three or four cigarettes in a morning and after three days without it, he followed Charley Moore by a circuitous route up a flight of back stairs to a little balcony where they indulged in peace. But this was not for long. One day in his second week the detective met him in a nook of the stairs, on his descent, and told him sternly that next time he'd be reported to Mr. Macy. Dalyrimple felt like an errant schoolboy.

Unpleasant facts came to his knowledge. There were "cave-dwellers" in the basement who had worked there for ten or fifteen years at sixty dollars a month, rolling barrels and carrying boxes through damp, cement-walled corridors, lost in that echoing half-darkness between seven and five-thirty and, like himself, compelled several times a month to work until nine at night.

At the end of a month he stood in line and received forty dollars. He pawned a cigarette case and a pair of field glasses and managed to live—to eat, sleep and smoke. It was, however, a narrow scrape; as the ways and means of economy were a closed book to him and the second month brought no increase, he voiced his alarm.

"If you've got a drag with old Macy, maybe he'll raise you," was Charley's disheartening reply. "But he didn't raise *me* till I'd been here nearly two years."

"I've got to live," said Dalyrimple simply. "I could get more pay as a laborer on the railroad but, Golly, I want to feel I'm where there's a chance to get ahead."

Charles shook his head skeptically and Mr. Macy's answer next day was equally unsatisfactory.

Dalyrimple had gone to the office just before closing time.

"Mr. Macy, I'd like to speak to you."

"Why—yes." The unhumorous smile appeared. The voice was faintly resentful.

"I want to speak to you in regard to more salary."

Mr. Macy nodded.

"Well," he said doubtfully, "I don't know exactly what you're doing. I'll speak to Mr. Hanson."

He knew exactly what Dalyrimple was doing, and Dalyrimple knew he knew.

"I'm in the stock room—and, sir, while I'm here I'd like to ask you how much longer I'll have to stay there."

"Why—I'm not sure exactly. Of course it takes some time to learn the stock."

"You told me two months when I started."

"Yes. Well, I'll speak to Mr. Hanson."

Dalyrimple paused irresolute.

"Thank you, sir."

Two days later he again appeared in the office with the result of a count that had been asked for by Mr. Hesse, the bookkeeper. Mr. Hesse was engaged and Dalyrimple, waiting, began idly fingering a ledger on the stenographer's desk.

Half-unconsciously he turned a page—he caught sight of his name—it was a salary list:

Dalyrimple
Demming
Donahoe
Everett

His eyes stopped——

Everett..................................$60

So Tom Everett, Macy's weak-chinned nephew, had started at sixty—and in three weeks he had been out of the packing room and into the office.

So that was it! He was to sit and see man after man pushed over him: sons, cousins, sons of friends, irrespective of their capabilities, while *he* was cast for a pawn, with "going on the road" dangled before his eyes—put off with the stock remark: "I'll see; I'll look into it." At forty, perhaps, he would be a bookkeeper like old Hesse, tired, listless Hesse with dull routine for his stint and a dull background of boarding house conversation.

This was a moment when a genie should have pressed into his hand the book for disillusioned young men. But the book has not been written.

A great protest swelling into revolt surged up in him. Ideas half-forgotten, chaotically perceived and assimilated, filled his mind. Get on—that was the rule of life—and that was all. How he did it, didn't matter—but to be Hesse or Charley Moore.

"I won't!" he cried aloud.

The bookkeeper and the stenographers looked up in surprise.

"What?"

For a second Dalyrimple stared—then walked up to the desk.

"Here's that data," he said brusquely. "I can't wait any longer."

Mr. Hesse's face expressed surprise.

It didn't matter what he did—just so he got out of this rut. In a dream he stepped from the elevator into the stock room, and walking to an unused aisle, sat down on a box, covering his face with his hands.

His brain was whirring with the frightful jar of discovering a platitude for himself.

"I've got to get out of this," he said aloud and then repeated, "I've got to get out"—and he didn't mean only out of Macy's wholesale house.

When he left at five-thirty it was pouring rain but he struck off in the opposite direction from his boarding house, feeling, in the first cool moisture that oozed soggily through his old suit, an odd exultation and freshness. He wanted a world that was like walking through rain, even though he could not see far ahead of him, but fate had put him in the world of Mr. Macy's fetid store rooms and corridors. At first merely the overwhelming need of change took him, then half-plans began to formulate in his imagination.

"I'll go East—to a big city—meet people—bigger people—people who'll help me. Interesting work somewhere. My God, there *must* be."

With sickening truth it occurred to him that his facility for meeting people was limited. Of all places it was here in his own town that he should be known, was known—famous—before the waters of oblivion had rolled over him.

You had to cut corners, that was all. Pull—relationship—wealthy marriages——

For several miles the continued reiteration of this preoccupied him and then he perceived that the rain had become thicker and more opaque in the heavy grey of twilight and that the houses were falling away. The district of full blocks, then of big houses, then of scattering little ones, passed and great sweeps of misty country opened out on both sides. It was hard walking here. The sidewalk had given place to a dirt road, streaked with furious brown rivulets that splashed and squashed around his shoes.

Cutting corners—the words began to fall apart, forming curious phrasings—little illuminated pieces of themselves. They resolved into sentences, each of which had a strangely familiar ring.

Cutting corners meant rejecting the old childhood principles that success came from faithfulness to duty, that evil was necessarily punished or virtue necessarily rewarded—that honest poverty was happier than corrupt riches.

It meant being hard.

This phrase appealed to him and he repeated it over and over. It had to do somehow with Mr. Macy and Charley Moore—the attitudes, the methods of each of them.

He stopped and felt his clothes. He was drenched to the skin. He looked about him and, selecting a place in the fence where a tree sheltered it, perched himself there.

In my credulous years—he thought—they told me that evil was a sort of dirty hue, just as definite as a soiled collar, but it seems to me that evil is only a manner of hard luck, or heredity-and-environment, or "being found out." It hides in the vacillations of dubs like Charley Moore as certainly as it does in the intolerance of Macy, and if it ever gets much more tangible it becomes merely an arbitrary label to paste on the unpleasant things in other people's lives.

In fact—he concluded—it isn't worth worrying over what's evil and what isn't. Good and evil aren't any standard to me—and they can be a devil of a bad hindrance when I want something. When I want something bad enough, common sense tells me to go and take it—and not get caught.

And then suddenly Dalyrimple knew what he wanted first. He wanted fifteen dollars to pay his overdue board bill.

With a furious energy he jumped from the fence, whipped off his coat and from its black lining cut with his knife a piece about five inches square. He made two holes near its edge and then fixed it on his face, pulling his hat down to hold it in place. It flapped grotesquely and then dampened and clung to his forehead and cheeks.

Now. . . . The twilight had merged to dripping dusk . . . black as pitch. He began to walk quickly back toward town, not waiting to remove the mask but watching the road with difficulty through the jagged eye-holes. He was not conscious of any nervousness . . . the only tension was caused by a desire to do the thing as soon as possible.

He reached the first sidewalk, continued on until he saw a hedge far from any lamp-post and turned in behind it. Within a minute he heard several series of foot-steps—he waited—it was a woman and he held his breath until she passed . . . and then a man, a laborer. The next passer, he felt, would be what he wanted . . . the laborer's foot-falls died far up the drenched street . . . other steps grew near, grew suddenly louder.

Dalyrimple braced himself.

"Put up your hands!"

The man stopped, uttered an absurd little grunt and thrust pudgy arms skyward.

Dalyrimple went through the waistcoat.

"Now, you shrimp," he said, setting his hand suggestively to his own hip pocket, "you run, and stamp—loud! If I hear your feet stop I'll put a shot after you!"

Then he stood there in sudden uncontrollable laughter as audibly frightened foot-steps scurried away into the night.

After a moment he thrust the roll of bills into his pocket, snatched off his mask, and running quickly across the street, darted down an alley.

IV

Yet, however Dalyrimple justified himself intellectually, he had many bad moments in the weeks immediately following his decision. The tremendous pressure of sentiment and inherited tradition kept raising riot with his attitude. He felt morally lonely.

The noon after his first venture he ate in a little lunch room with Charley Moore and, watching him unspread the paper, waited for a remark about the hold-up of the day before. But either the hold-up was not mentioned or Charley wasn't interested. He turned listlessly to the sporting sheet, read Doctor Crane's crop of seasoned bromides, took in an editorial on ambition with his mouth slightly ajar, and then skipped to Mutt and Jeff.

Poor Charley—with his faint aura of evil and his mind that refused to focus, playing a lifeless solitaire with cast-off mischief.

Yet Charley belonged on the other side of the fence. In him could be stirred up all the flamings and denunciations of righteousness; he would weep at a stage heroine's lost virtue, he could become lofty and contemptuous at the idea of dishonor.

On my side, thought Dalyrimple, there aren't any resting places; a man who's a strong criminal is after the weak criminals as well, so it's all guerilla warfare over here.

What will it all do to me? he thought, with a persistent weariness. Will it take the color out of life with the honor? Will it scatter my courage and dull my mind?—despiritualize me completely?—does it mean eventual barrenness, eventual remorse, failure?

With a great surge of anger, he would fling his mind upon the barrier—and stand there with the flashing bayonet of his pride. Other men who broke the laws of justice and charity lied to all the world. He at any rate would not lie to himself. He was more than Byronic now: not the spiritual rebel, Don Juan; not the philosophical rebel, Faust; but a new psychological rebel of his own century—defying the sentimental a priori forms of his own mind——

Happiness was what he wanted—a slowly rising scale of gratifications of the normal appetites—and he had a strong conviction that the materials, if not the inspiration of happiness, could be bought with money.

V

The night came that drew him out upon his second venture, and as he walked the dark street he felt in himself a great resemblance to a cat—a certain supple, swinging litheness. His muscles were rippling smoothly and sleekly under his spare, healthy flesh—he had an absurd desire to bound along the street, to run dodging among trees, to turn "cart-wheels" over soft grass.

It was not crisp, but in the air lay a faint suggestion of acerbity, inspirational rather than chilling.

"*The moon is down—I have not heard the clock!*"

He laughed in delight at the line which an early memory had endowed with a hushed, awesome beauty.

He passed a man, and then another a quarter of a mile afterward.

He was on Philmore Street now and it was very dark. He blessed the city council for not having put in new lamp-posts as a recent budget had recommended. Here was the red-brick Sterner residence which marked the beginning of the avenue; here was the Jordon house, the Eisenhaurs', the Dents', the Markhams', the Frasers'; the Hawkins', where he had been a guest; the Willoughbys', the Everetts', colonial and ornate; the little cottage where lived the Watts old maids between the imposing fronts of the Macys' and the Krupstadts'; the Craigs'——

Ah ... *there!* He paused, wavered violently—far up the street was a blot, a man walking, possibly a policeman. After an eternal second he found himself following the vague, ragged shadow of a lamp-post across a lawn, running bent very low. Then he was standing tense, without breath or need of it, in the shadow of his limestone prey.

Interminably he listened—a mile off a cat howled, a hundred yards away another took up the hymn in a demoniacal snarl, and he felt his heart dip and swoop, acting as shock-absorber for his mind. There were other sounds; the faintest fragment of song far away; strident, gossiping laughter from a back porch diagonally across the alley; and crickets, crickets singing in the patched, patterned, moonlit grass of the yard. Within the house there seemed to lie an ominous silence. He was glad he did not know who lived here.

His slight shiver hardened to steel; the steel softened and his nerves became pliable as leather; gripping his hands he gratefully found them supple, and taking out knife and pliers he went to work on the screen.

So sure was he that he was unobserved that, from the dining room where in a minute he found himself, he leaned out and carefully pulled the screen up into position, balancing it so it would neither fall by chance nor be a serious obstacle to a sudden exit.

Then he put the open knife in his coat pocket, took out his pocket-flash and tiptoed around the room.

There was nothing here he could use—the dining room had never been included in his plans, for the town was too small to permit disposing of silver.

As a matter of fact his plans were of the vaguest. He had found that with a mind like his, lucrative in intelligence, intuition and lightning decision, it was best to have but the skeleton of a campaign. The machine-gun episode had taught him that. And he was afraid that a method preconceived would give him two points of view in a crisis—and two points of view meant wavering.

He stumbled slightly on a chair, held his breath, listened, went on, found the hall, found the stairs, started up; the seventh stair creaked at his step, the ninth, the fourteenth. He was counting them automatically. At the third creak he paused again for over a minute—and in that minute he felt more alone than he had ever felt before. Between the lines on patrol, even when alone, he had had behind him the moral support of half a billion people; now he was alone, pitted against that same moral pressure—a bandit. He had never felt this fear, yet he had never felt this exultation.

The stairs came to an end, a doorway approached; he went in and listened to regular breathing. His feet were economical of steps and his body swayed sometimes at stretching as he felt over the bureau, pocketing all articles which held promise—he could not have enumerated them ten seconds afterwards. He felt on a chair for possible trousers, found soft garments, women's lingerie. The corners of his mouth smiled mechanically.

Another room ... the same breathing, enlivened by one ghastly snort that sent his heart again on its tour of his breast. Round object—watch; chain; roll of bills; stick-pins; two rings—he remembered that he had got rings from the other bureau. He started out, winced as a faint glow flashed in front of him, facing him. God!—it was the glow of his own wrist watch on his outstretched arm.

Down the stairs. He skipped two creaking steps but found another. He was all right now, practically safe; as he neared the bottom he felt a slight boredom. He reached the dining room—considered the silver—again decided against it.

Back in his room at the boarding house he examined the additions to his personal property:

Sixty-five dollars in bills.

A platinum ring with three medium diamonds, worth, probably, about seven hundred dollars. Diamonds were going up.

A cheap gold-plated ring with the initials O.S. and the date inside —'03—probably a class ring from school. Worth a few dollars. Unsalable.

A red cloth case containing a set of false teeth.

A silver watch.

A gold chain worth more than the watch.

An empty ring-box.

A little ivory Chinese god—probably a desk ornament.

A dollar and sixty-two cents in small change.

He put the money under his pillow and the other things in the toe of an infantry boot, stuffing a stocking in on top of them. Then for two hours his mind raced like a high-power engine here and there through his life, past and future, through fear and laughter. With a vague, inopportune wish that he were married, he fell into a deep sleep about half past five.

VI

Though the newspaper account of the burglary failed to mention the false teeth, they worried him considerably. The picture of a human waking in the cool dawn and groping for them in vain, of a soft, toothless breakfast, of a strange, hollow, lisping voice calling the police station, of weary, dispirited visits to the dentist, roused a great fatherly pity in him.

Trying to ascertain whether they belonged to a man or a woman, he took them carefully out of the case and held them up near his mouth. He moved his own jaws experimentally; he measured with his fingers; but he failed to decide: they might belong either to a large-mouthed woman or a small-mouthed man.

On a warm impulse he wrapped them in brown paper from the bottom of his army trunk, and printed FALSE TEETH on the package in clumsy pencil letters. Then, the next night, he walked down Philmore Street, and shied the package onto the lawn so that it would be near the door. Next day the paper announced that the police had a clue—they knew that the burglar was in town. However, they didn't mention what the clue was.

VII

At the end of a month "Burglar Bill of the Silver District" was the nurse-girl's standby for frightening children. Five burglaries were attributed to him, but though Dalyrimple had only committed three, he considered that majority had it and appropriated the title to himself. He had once been seen—"a large bloated creature with the meanest face you ever laid eyes on." Mrs. Henry Coleman, awaking at two o'clock at the beam of an electric torch flashed in her eye, could not have been expected to recognize Bryan Dalyrimple at whom she had waved flags last Fourth of July, and whom she had described as "not at all the daredevil type, do you think?"

When Dalyrimple kept his imagination at white heat he managed to glorify his own attitude, his emancipation from petty scruples and remorses—but let him once allow his thought to rove unarmored, great unexpected horrors and depressions would overtake him. Then for reassurance he had to go back to think out the whole thing over again. He found that it was on the whole better to give up considering himself as a rebel. It was more consoling to think of everyone else as a fool.

His attitude toward Mr. Macy underwent a change. He no longer felt a dim animosity and inferiority in his presence. As his fourth month in the store ended he found himself regarding his employer in a manner that was almost fraternal. He had a vague but very assured conviction that Mr. Macy's innermost soul would have abetted and approved. He no longer worried about his future. He had the intention of accumulating several thousand dollars and then clearing out—going east, back to France, down to South America. Half a dozen times in the last two months he had been about to stop work, but a fear of attracting attention to his being in funds prevented him. So he worked on, no longer in listlessness, but with contemptuous amusement.

VIII

Then with astounding suddenness something happened that changed his plans and put an end to his burglaries.

Mr. Macy sent for him one afternoon and with a great show of jovial mystery asked him if he had an engagement that night. If he hadn't, would he please call on Mr. Alfred J. Fraser at eight o'clock. Dalyrimple's wonder was mingled with uncertainty. He debated with himself whether it were not his cue to take the first train out of town. But an hour's consideration decided him that his fears were unfounded and at eight o'clock he arrived at the big Fraser house in Philmore Avenue.

Mr. Fraser was commonly supposed to be the biggest political influence in the city. His brother was Senator Fraser, his son-in-law was Congressman Demming, and his influence, though not wielded in such a way as to make him an objectionable boss, was strong nevertheless.

He had a great, huge face, deep-set eyes and a barn-door of an upper lip, the melange approaching a worthy climax in a long professional jaw.

During his conversation with Dalyrimple his expression kept starting toward a smile, reached a cheerful optimism and then receded back to imperturbability.

"How do you do, sir," he said, holding out his hand. "Sit down. I suppose you're wondering why I wanted you. Sit down."

Dalyrimple sat down.

"Mr. Dalyrimple, how old are you?"

"I'm twenty-three."

"You're young. But that doesn't mean you're foolish. Mr. Dalyrimple, what I've got to say won't take long. I'm going to make you a proposition. To begin at the beginning, I've been watching you ever since last Fourth of July when you made that speech in response to the loving cup."

Dalyrimple murmured disparagingly, but Fraser waved him to silence.

"It was a speech I've remembered. It was a brainy speech, straight from the shoulder, and it got to everybody in that crowd. I know. I've watched crowds for years." He cleared his throat, as if tempted to digress on his knowledge of crowds—then continued. "But, Mr. Dalyrimple, I've seen too many young men who promised brilliantly go to pieces, fail through want of steadiness, too many high-power ideas, and not enough willingness to work. So I waited. I wanted to see what you'd do. I wanted to see if you'd go to work, and if you'd stick to what you started."

Dalyrimple felt a glow settle over him.

"So," continued Fraser, "when Theron Macy told me you'd started down at his place, I kept watching you, and I followed your record through him. The first month I was afraid for awhile. He told me you were getting restless, too good for your job, hinting around for a raise——"

Dalyrimple started.

"—but he said after that you evidently made up your mind to shut up and stick to it. That's the stuff I like in a young man! That's the stuff that wins out. And don't think I don't understand. I know how much harder it was for you, after all that silly flattery a lot of old women had been giving you. I know what a fight it must have been——"

Dalyrimple's face was burning brightly. He felt young and strangely ingenuous.

"Dalyrimple, you've got brains and you've got the stuff in you—and that's what I want. I'm going to put you into the State Senate."

"The *what?*"

"The State Senate. We want a young man who has got brains, but is solid and not a loafer. And when I say State Senate I don't stop there. We're up against it here, Dalyrimple. We've got to get some young men into politics—you know the old blood that's been running on the party ticket year in and year out."

Dalyrimple licked his lips.

"You'll run me for the State Senate?"

"I'll *put* you in the State Senate."

Mr. Fraser's expression had now reached the point nearest a smile and Dalyrimple in a happy frivolity felt himself urging it mentally on—but it stopped, locked, and slid from him. The barn-door and the jaw were separated by a line straight as a nail. Dalyrimple remembered with an effort that it was a mouth, and talked to it.

"But I'm through," he said. "My notoriety's dead. People are fed up with me."

"Those things," answered Mr. Fraser, "are mechanical. Linotype is a resuscitator of reputations. Wait till you see the "Herald," beginning next week—that is if you're with us—that is," and his voice hardened slightly, "if you haven't got too many ideas yourself about how things ought to be run."

"No," said Dalyrimple, looking him frankly in the eyes. "You'll have to give me a lot of advice at first."

"Very well. I'll take care of your reputation then. Just keep yourself on the right side of the fence."

Dalyrimple started at this repetition of a phrase he had thought of so much lately. There was a sudden ring at the doorbell.

"That's Macy now," observed Fraser, rising. "I'll go let him in. The servants have gone to bed."

He left Dalyrimple there in a dream. The world was opening up suddenly—— The State Senate, the United States Senate—so life was this after all—cutting corners—cutting corners—common sense, that was the rule. No more foolish risks now unless necessity called—but it was being hard that counted—— Never to let remorse or self-reproach lose him a night's sleep—let his life be a sword of courage—there was no payment—all that was drivel—drivel. He sprang to his feet with clenched hands in a sort of triumph.

"Well, Bryan," said Mr. Macy stepping through the portières.

The two older men smiled their half-smiles at him.

"Well, Bryan," said Mr. Macy again.

Dalyrimple smiled also.

"How do, Mr. Macy?"

He wondered if some telepathy between them had made this new appreciation possible—some invisible realization. . . .

Mr. Macy held out his hand.

"I'm glad we're to be associated in this scheme—I've been for you all along—especially lately. I'm glad we're to be on the same side of the fence."

"I want to thank you, sir," said Dalyrimple simply. He felt a whimsical moisture gathering back of his eyes.

THE FOUR FISTS

At the present time no one I know has the slightest desire to hit Samuel Meredith; possibly this is because a man over fifty is liable to be rather severely cracked at the impact of a hostile fist, but, for my part, I am inclined to think that all his hitable qualities have quite vanished. But it is certain that at various times in his life hitable qualities were in his face, as surely as kissable qualities have ever lurked in a girl's lips.

I'm sure everyone has met a man like that, been casually introduced, even made a friend of him, yet felt he was the sort who aroused passionate dislike—expressed by some in the involuntary clenching of fists, and in others by mutterings about "takin' a poke" and "landin' a swift smash in ee eye." In the juxtaposition of Samuel Meredith's features this quality was so strong that it influenced his entire life.

What was it? Not the shape, certainly, for he was a pleasant-looking man from earliest youth: broad-browed, with grey eyes that were frank and friendly. Yet I've heard him tell a room full of reporters angling for a "success" story that he'd be ashamed to tell them the truth, that they wouldn't believe it, that it wasn't one story but four, that the public would not want to read about a man who had been walloped into prominence.

It all started at Phillips Andover Academy when he was fourteen. He had been brought up on a diet of caviar and bell-boys' legs in half the capitals of Europe, and it was pure luck that his mother had nervous prostration and had to delegate his education to less tender, less biased hands.

At Andover he was given a roommate named Gilly Hood. Gilly was thirteen, undersized, and rather the school pet. From the September day when Mr. Meredith's valet stowed Samuel's clothing in the best bureau and asked, on departing, "hif there was hanything helse, Master Samuel?" Gilly cried out that the faculty had played him false. He felt like an irate frog in whose bowl has been put a goldfish.

"Good gosh!" he complained to his sympathetic contemporaries, "he's a damn stuck-up Willie. He said, 'Are the crowd here gentlemen?' and I said, 'No, they're boys,' and he said age didn't matter, and I said, 'Who said it did?' Let him get fresh with me, the ole pieface!"

For three weeks Gilly endured in silence young Samuel's comments on the clothes and habits of Gilly's personal friends, endured French phrases in conversation, endured a hundred half-feminine meannesses that show what a nervous mother can do to a boy, if she keeps close enough to him—then a storm broke in the aquarium.

Samuel was out. A crowd had gathered to hear Gilly be wrathful about his roommate's latest sins.

"He said, 'Oh, I don't like the windows open at night,' he said, 'except only a little bit,'" complained Gilly.

"Don't let him boss you."

"Boss me? You bet he won't. I open those windows, I guess, but the darn fool won't take turns shuttin' 'em in the morning."

"Make him, Gilly, why don't you?"

"I'm going to." Gilly nodded his head in fierce agreement. "Don't you worry. He needn't think I'm any ole butler."

"Le's see you make him."

At this point the darn fool entered in person and included the crowd in one of his irritating smiles. Two boys said, "'Lo, Mer'dith"; the others gave him a chilly glance and went on talking to Gilly. But Samuel seemed unsatisfied.

"Would you mind not sitting on my bed?" he suggested politely to two of Gilly's particulars who were perched very much at ease.

"Huh?"

"My bed. Can't you understand English?"

This was adding insult to injury. There were several comments on the bed's sanitary condition and the evidence within it of animal life.

"S'matter with your old bed?" demanded Gilly truculently.

"The bed's all right, but——"

Gilly interrupted this sentence by rising and walking up to Samuel. He paused several inches away and eyed him fiercely.

"You an' your crazy ole bed," he began. "You an' your crazy——"

"Go to it, Gilly," murmured someone.

"Show the darn fool——"

Samuel returned the gaze coolly.

"Well," he said finally, "it's my bed——"

He got no further, for Gilly hauled off and hit him succinctly in the nose.

"Yea! Gilly!'

"Show the big bully!"

"Just let him touch you—he'll see!"

The group closed in on them and for the first time in his life Samuel realized the insuperable inconvenience of being passionately detested. He gazed around helplessly at the glowering, violently hostile faces. He towered a head taller than his roommate, so if he hit back he'd be called a bully and have half a dozen more fights on his hands within five minutes; yet if he didn't he was a coward. For a moment he stood there facing Gilly's blazing eyes, and then, with a sudden choking sound, he forced his way through the ring and rushed from the room.

The month following bracketed the thirty most miserable days of his life. Every waking moment he was under the lashing tongues of his contemporaries; his habits and mannerisms became butts for intolerable witticisms and, of course, the sensitiveness of adolescence was a further thorn. He considered that he was a natural pariah; that the unpopularity at school would follow him through life. When he went home for the Christmas holidays he was so despondent that his father sent him to a nerve specialist. When he returned to Andover he arranged to arrive late so that he could be alone in the bus during the drive from station to school.

Of course when he had learned to keep his mouth shut everyone promptly forgot all about him. The next autumn, with his realization that consideration for others was the discreet attitude, he made good use of the clean start given him by the shortness of boyhood memory. By the beginning of his senior year Samuel Meredith was one of the best-liked boys of his class—and no one was any stronger for him than his first friend and constant companion, Gilly Hood.

II

Samuel became the sort of college student who in the early nineties drove tandems and coaches and tallyhos between Princeton and Yale and New York City to show that they appreciated the social importance of football games. He believed passionately in good form—his choosing of gloves, his tying of ties, his holding of reins were imitated by impressionable freshmen. Outside of his own set he was considered rather a snob, but as his set was *the* set, it never worried him. He played football in the autumn, drank highballs in the winter, and rowed in the spring. Samuel despised all those who were merely sportsmen without being gentlemen, or merely gentlemen without being sportsmen.

He lived in New York and often brought home several of his friends for the week-end. Those were the days of the horse-car and in case of a crush it was, of course, the proper thing for anyone of Samuel's set to rise and deliver his seat to a standing lady with a formal bow. One night in Samuel's junior year he boarded a car with two of his intimates. There were three vacant seats. When Samuel sat down he noticed a heavy-eyed laboring man sitting next to him who smelt objectionably of garlic, sagged slightly against Samuel and, spreading a little as a tired man will, took up quite too much room.

The car had gone several blocks when it stopped for a quartet of young girls, and, of course, the three men of the world sprang to their feet and proffered their seats with due observance of form. Unfortunately, the laborer, being unacquainted with the code of neckties and tallyhos, failed to follow their example, and one young lady was left at an embarrassed stance. Fourteen eyes glared reproachfully at the barbarian; seven lips curled slightly; but the object of scorn stared stolidly into the foreground in sturdy unconsciousness of his despicable conduct. Samuel was the most violently affected. He was humiliated that any male should so conduct himself. He spoke aloud.

"There's a lady standing," he said sternly.

That should have been quite enough, but the object of scorn only looked up blankly. The standing girl tittered and exchanged nervous glances with her companions. But Samuel was aroused.

"There's a lady standing," he repeated, rather raspingly. The man seemed to comprehend.

"I pay my fare," he said quietly.

Samuel turned red and his hands clenched, but the conductor was looking their way, so at a warning nod from his friends he subsided into sullen gloom.

They reached their destination and left the car, but so did the laborer, who followed them, swinging his little pail. Seeing his chance, Samuel no longer resisted his aristocratic inclination. He turned around and, launching a full-featured, dime-novel sneer, made a loud remark about the right of the lower animals to ride with human beings.

In a half-second the workman had dropped his pail and let fly at him. Unprepared, Samuel took the blow neatly on the jaw and sprawled full-length into the cobblestone gutter.

"Don't laugh at me!" cried his assailant. "I been workin' all day. I'm tired as hell!"

As he spoke the sudden anger died out of his eyes and the mask of weariness dropped again over his face. He turned and picked up his pail. Samuel's friends took a quick step in his direction.

"Wait!" Samuel had risen slowly and was motioning them back. Sometime, somewhere, he had been struck like that before. Then he remembered—Gilly Hood. In the silence, as he dusted himself off, the whole scene in the room at Andover was before his eyes—and he knew intuitively that he had been wrong again. This man's strength, his rest, was the protection of his family. He had more use for his seat in the street-car than any young girl.

"It's all right," said Samuel gruffly. "Don't touch him. I've been a damn fool."

Of course it took more than an hour, or a week, for Samuel to rearrange his ideas on the essential importance of good form. At first he simply admitted that his wrongness had made him powerless—as it had made him powerless against Gilly—but eventually his mistake about the workman influenced his entire attitude. Snobbishness is, after all, merely good breeding grown dictatorial; so Samuel's code remained, but the necessity of imposing it upon others had faded out in a certain gutter. Within that year his class had somehow stopped referring to him as a snob.

III

After a few years Samuel's university decided that it had shone long enough in the reflected glory of his neckties, so they declaimed to him in Latin, charged him ten dollars for the paper which proved him irretrievably educated and sent him into the turmoil with much self-confidence, a few friends, and the proper assortment of harmless bad habits.

His family had by that time started back to shirt-sleeves, through a sudden decline in the sugar-market, and it had already unbuttoned its vest, so to speak, when Samuel went to work. His mind was that exquisite *tabula rasa* that a university education sometimes leaves, but he had both energy and influence, so he used his former ability as a dodging half-back in twisting through Wall Street crowds as runner for a bank.

His diversion was—women. There were half a dozen: two or three debutantes, an actress (in a minor way), a grass-widow, and one sentimental little brunette who was married and lived in a little house in Jersey City.

They had met on a ferry-boat. Samuel was crossing from New York on business (he had been working several years by this time) and he helped her look for a package that she had dropped in the crush.

"Do you come over often?" he inquired casually.

"Just to shop," she said shyly. She had great brown eyes and the pathetic kind of little mouth. "I've only been married three months, and we find it cheaper to live over here."

"Does he—does your husband like your being alone like this?"

She laughed, a cheery young laugh.

"Oh, dear me, no. We were to meet for dinner but I must have misunderstood the place. He'll be awfully worried."

"Well," said Samuel disapprovingly, "he ought to be. If you'll allow me I'll see you home."

She accepted his offer thankfully, so they took the cable-car together. When they walked up the path to her little house they saw a light there; her husband had arrived before her.

"He's frightfully jealous," she announced, laughingly apologetic.

"Very well," answered Samuel, rather stiffly. "I'd better leave you here."

She thanked him and, waving a good-night, he left her.

That would have been quite all if they hadn't met on Fifth Avenue one morning a week later. She started and blushed and seemed so glad to see him that they chatted like old friends. She was going to her dressmaker's, eat lunch alone at Taine's, shop all afternoon, and meet her husband on the ferry at five. Samuel told her that her husband was a very lucky man. She blushed again and scurried off.

Samuel whistled all the way back to his office, but about twelve o'clock he began to see that pathetic, appealing little mouth everywhere—and those brown eyes. He fidgeted when he looked at the clock; he thought of the grill downstairs where he lunched and the heavy male conversation thereof, and opposed to that picture appeared another: a little table at Taine's with the brown eyes and the mouth a few feet away. A few minutes before twelve-thirty he dashed on his hat and rushed for the cable-car.

She was quite surprised to see him.

"Why—hello," she said. Samuel could tell that she was just pleasantly frightened.

"I thought we might lunch together. It's so dull eating with a lot of men."

She hesitated.

"Why, I suppose there's no harm in it. How could there be!"

It occurred to her that her husband should have taken lunch with her—but he was generally so hurried at noon. She told Samuel all about him: he was a little smaller than Samuel, but, oh, *much* better-looking. He was a bookkeeper and not making a lot of money, but they were very happy and expected to be rich within three or four years.

Samuel's grass-widow had been in a quarrelsome mood for three or four weeks, and, through contrast, he took an accentuated pleasure in this meeting; so fresh was she, and earnest, and faintly adventurous. Her name was Marjorie.

They made another engagement; in fact, for a month they lunched together two or three times a week. When she was sure that her husband would work late Samuel took her over to New Jersey on the ferry, leaving her always on the tiny front porch, after she had gone in and lit the gas to use the security of his masculine presence outside. This grew to be a ceremony—and it annoyed him. Whenever the comfortable glow fell out through the front windows, that was his *congé*; yet he never suggested coming in and Marjorie didn't invite him.

Then, when Samuel and Marjorie had reached a stage in which they sometimes touched each other's arms gently, just to show that they were very good friends, Marjorie and her husband had one of those ultra-sensitive, super-critical quarrels that couples never indulge in unless they care a great deal about each other. It started with a cold mutton-chop or a leak in the gas-jet—and one day Samuel found her in Taine's, with dark shadows under her brown eyes and a terrifying pout.

By this time Samuel thought he was in love with Marjorie—so he played up the quarrel for all it was worth. He was her best friend and patted her hand—and leaned down close to her brown curls while she whispered in little sobs what her husband had said that morning; and he was a little more than her best friend when he took her over to the ferry in a hansom.

"Marjorie," he said gently, when he left her, as usual, on the porch, "if at any time you want to call on me, remember that I am always waiting, always waiting."

She nodded gravely and put both her hands in his.

"I know," she said. "I know you're my friend, my best friend."

Then she ran into the house and he watched there until the gas went on.

For the next week Samuel was in a nervous turmoil. Some persistently rational strain warned him that at bottom he and Marjorie had little in common, but in such cases there is usually so much mud in the water that one can seldom see to the bottom. Every dream and desire told him that he loved Marjorie, wanted her, had to have her.

The quarrel developed. Marjorie's husband took to staying in New York until late at night, came home several times disagreeably overstimulated, and made her generally miserable. They must have had too much pride to talk it out—for Marjorie's husband was, after all, pretty decent—so it drifted on from one misunderstanding to another. Marjorie kept coming more and more to Samuel; when a woman can accept masculine sympathy it is much more satisfactory to her than crying to another girl. But Marjorie didn't realize how much she had begun to rely on him, how much he was part of her little cosmos.

One night, instead of turning away when Marjorie went in and lit the gas, Samuel went in, too, and they sat together on the sofa in the little parlor. He was very happy. He envied their home, and he felt that the man who neglected such a possession out of stubborn pride was a fool and unworthy of his wife. But when he kissed Marjorie for the first time she cried softly and told him to go. He sailed home on the wings of desperate excitement, quite resolved to fan this spark of romance, no matter how big the blaze or who was burned. At the time he considered that his thoughts were unselfishly of her; in a later perspective he knew that she had meant no more than the white screen in a motion picure: it was just Samuel—blind, desirous.

Next day at Taine's, when they met for lunch, Samuel dropped all pretense and made frank love to her. He had no plans, no definite intentions, except to kiss her lips again, to hold her in his arms and feel that she was very little and pathetic and lovable.... He took her home, and this time they kissed until both their hearts beat high—words and phrases formed on his lips.

And then suddenly there were steps on the porch—a hand tried the outside door. Marjorie turned dead-white.

"Wait!" she whispered to Samuel, in a frightened voice, but in angry impatience at the interruption he walked to the front door and threw it open.

Everyone has seen such scenes on the stage—seen them so often that when they actually happen people behave very much like actors. Samuel felt that he was playing a part and the lines came quite naturally: he announced that all had a right to lead their own lives and looked at Marjorie's husband menacingly, as if daring him to doubt it. Marjorie's husband spoke of the sanctity of the home, forgetting that it hadn't seemed very holy to him lately; Samuel continued along the line of "the right to happiness"; Marjorie's husband mentioned firearms and the divorce court. Then suddenly he stopped and scrutinized both of them—Marjorie in pitiful collapse on the sofa, Samuel haranguing the furniture in a consciously heroic pose.

"Go upstairs, Marjorie," he said, in a different tone.

"Stay where you are!" Samuel countered quickly.

Marjorie rose, wavered, and sat down, rose again and moved hesitatingly toward the stairs.

"Come outside," said her husband to Samuel. "I want to talk to you."

Samuel glanced at Marjorie, tried to get some message from her eyes; then he shut his lips and went out.

There was a bright moon and when Marjorie's husband came down the steps Samuel could see plainly that he was suffering—but he felt no pity for him.

They stood and looked at each other, a few feet apart, and the husband cleared his throat as though it were a bit husky.

"That's my wife," he said quietly, and then a wild anger surged up inside him. "Damn you!" he cried—and hit Samuel in the face with all his strength.

In that second, as Samuel slumped to the ground, it flashed to him that he had been hit like that twice before, and simultaneously the incident altered like a dream—he felt suddenly awake. Mechanically he sprang to his feet and squared off. The other man was waiting, fists up, a yard away, but Samuel knew that though physically he had him by several inches and many pounds, he wouldn't hit him. The situation had miraculously and entirely changed—a moment before Samuel had seemed to himself heroic; now he seemed the cad, the outsider, and Marjorie's husband, silhouetted against the lights of the little house, the eternal heroic figure, the defender of his home.

There was a pause and then Samuel turned quickly away and went down the path for the last time.

IV

Of course, after the third blow Samuel put in several weeks at conscientious introspection. The blow years before at Andover had landed on his personal unpleasantness; the workman of his college days had jarred the snobbishness out of his system, and Marjorie's husband had given a severe jolt to his greedy selfishness. It threw women out of his ken until a year later, when he met his future wife; for the only sort of woman worth while seemed to be the one who could be protected as Marjorie's husband had protected her. Samuel could not imagine his grass-widow, Mrs. De Ferriac, causing any very righteous blows on her own account.

His early thirties found him well on his feet. He was associated with old Peter Carhart, who was in those days a national figure. Carhart's physique was like a rough model for a statue of Hercules, and his record was just as solid—a pile made for the pure joy of it, without cheap extortion or shady scandal. He had been a great friend of Samuel's father, but he watched the son for six years before taking him into his own office. Heaven knows how many things he controlled at that time—mines, railroads, banks, whole cities. Samuel was very close to him, knew his likes and dislikes, his prejudices, weaknesses and many strengths.

One day Carhart sent for Samuel and, closing the door of his inner office, offered him a chair and a cigar.

"Everything O.K., Samuel?" he asked.

"Why, yes."

"I've been afraid you're getting a bit stale."

"Stale?" Samuel was puzzled.

"You've done no work outside the office for nearly ten years?"

"But I've had vacations, in the Adiron——"

Carhart waved this aside.

"I mean outside work. Seeing the things move that we've always pulled the strings of here."

"No," admitted Samuel; "I haven't."

"So," he said abruptly, "I'm going to give you an outside job that'll take about a month."

Samuel didn't argue. He rather liked the idea and he made up his mind that, whatever it was, he would put it through just as Carhart wanted it. That was his employer's greatest hobby, and the men around him were as dumb under direct orders as infantry subalterns.

"You'll go to San Antonio and see Hamil," continued Carhart. "He's got a job on hand and he wants a man to take charge."

Hamil was in charge of the Carhart interests in the Southwest, a man who had grown up in the shadow of his employer, and with whom, though they had never met, Samuel had had much official correspondence.

"When do I leave?"

"You'd better go tomorrow," answered Carhart, glancing at the calendar. "That's the first of May. I'll expect your report here on the first of June."

Next morning Samuel left for Chicago, and two days later he was facing Hamil across a table in the office of the Merchants' Trust in San Antonio. It didn't take long to get the gist of the thing. It was a big deal in oil which concerned the buying up of seventeen huge adjoining ranches. This buying up had to be done in one week, and it was a pure squeeze. Forces had been set in motion that put the seventeen owners between the devil and the deep sea, and Samuel's part was simply to "handle" the matter from a little village near Pueblo. With tact and efficiency the right man could bring it off without any friction, for it was merely a question of sitting at the wheel and keeping a firm hold. Hamil, with an astuteness many times valuable to his chief, had arranged a situation that would give a much greater clear gain than any dealing in the open market. Samuel shook hands with Hamil, arranged to return in two weeks, and left for San Felipe, New Mexico.

It occurred to him, of course, that Carhart was trying him out. Hamil's report on his handling of this might be a factor in something big for him, but even without that he would have done his best to put the thing through. Ten years in New York hadn't made him sentimental, and he was quite accustomed to finish everything he began—and a little bit more.

All went well at first. There was no enthusiasm, but each one of the seventeen ranchers concerned knew Samuel's business, knew what he had behind him, and that they had as little chance of holding out as flies on a window pane. Some of them were resigned—some of them cared like the devil, but they'd talked it over, argued it with lawyers and couldn't see any possible loophole. Five of the ranches had oil, the other twelve were part of the chance, but quite as necessary to Hamil's purpose, in any event.

Samuel soon saw that the real leader was an early settler named McIntyre, a man of perhaps fifty, grey-haired, clean-shaven, bronzed by forty New Mexico summers, and with those clear, steady eyes that Texas and New Mexico weather are apt to give. His ranch had not as yet shown oil, but it was in the pool, and if any man hated to lose his land McIntyre did. Everyone had rather looked to him at first to avert the big calamity, and he had hunted all over the territory for the legal means with which to do it, but he had failed, and he knew it. He avoided Samuel assiduously, but Samuel was sure that when the day came for the signatures he would appear.

It came—a baking May day, with hot waves rising off the parched land as far as eyes could see, and as Samuel sat stewing in his little improvised office—a few chairs, a bench, and a wooden table—he was glad the thing was almost over. He wanted to get back East the worst way, and join his wife and children for a week at the seashore.

The meeting was set for four o'clock, and he was rather surprised at three-thirty when the door opened and McIntyre came in. Samuel could not help respecting the man's attitude, and feeling a bit sorry for him. McIntyre seemed closely related to the prairies, and Samuel had the little flicker of envy that city people feel toward men who live in the open.

"Afternoon," said McIntyre, standing in the open doorway, with his feet apart and his hands on his hips.

"Hello, Mr. McIntyre." Samuel rose, but omitted the formality of offering his hand. He imagined the rancher cordially loathed him, and he hardly blamed him. McIntyre came in and sat down leisurely.

"You got us," he said suddenly.

This didn't seem to require any answer.

"When I heard Carhart was back of this," he continued, "I gave up."

"Mr. Carhart is——" began Samuel, but McIntyre waved him silent.

"Don't talk about the dirty sneak-thief!"

"Mr. McIntyre," said Samuel briskly, "if this half-hour is to be devoted to that sort of talk——"

"Oh, dry up, young man," McIntyre interrupted, "you can't abuse a man who'd do a thing like this."

Samuel made no answer.

"It's simply a dirty filch. There just *are* skunks like him too big to handle."

"You're being paid liberally," offered Samuel.

"Shut up!" roared McIntyre suddenly. "I want the privilege of talking." He walked to the door and looked out across the land, the sunny, steaming pasturage that began almost at his feet and ended with the grey-green of the distant mountains. When he turned around his mouth was trembling.

"Do you fellows love Wall Street?" he said hoarsely, "or wherever you do your dirty scheming——" He paused. "I suppose you do. No critter gets so low that he doesn't sort of love the place he's worked, where he's sweated out the best he's had in him."

Samuel watched him awkwardly. McIntyre wiped his forehead with a huge blue handkerchief, and continued:

"I reckon this rotten old devil had to have another million. I reckon we're just a few of the poor beggars he's blotted out to buy a couple more carriages or something." He waved his hand toward the door. "I built a house out there when I was seventeen, with these two hands. I took a wife there at twenty-one, added two wings, and with four mangy steers I started out. Forty summers I've saw the sun come up over those mountains and drop down red as blood in the evening, before the heat drifted off and the stars came out. I been happy in that house. My boy was born there and he died there, late one spring, in the hottest part of an afternoon like this. Then the wife and I lived there alone like we'd lived before, and sort of tried to have a home, after all, not a real home but nigh it—cause the boy always seemed around close somehow and we expected a lot of nights to see him runnin' up the path to supper." His voice was shaking so he could hardly speak and he turned again to the door, his grey eyes contracted.

"That's my land out there," he said, stretching out his arm, "my land, by God—— It's all I got in the world—and ever wanted." He dashed his sleeve across his face, and his tone changed as he turned slowly and faced Samuel. "But I suppose it's got to go when they want it—it's got to go."

Samuel had to talk. He felt that in a minute more he would lose his head. So he began, as level-voiced as he could—in the sort of tone he saved for disagreeable duties.

"It's business, Mr. McIntyre," he said; "it's inside the law. Perhaps we couldn't have bought out two or three of you at any price, but most of you did have a price. Progress demands some things——"

Never had he felt so inadequate, and it was with the greatest relief that he heard hoof-beats a few hundred yards away.

But at his words the grief in McIntyre's eyes had changed to fury.

"You and your dirty gang of crooks!" he cried. "Not one of you has got an honest love for anything on God's earth! You're a herd of money-swine!"

Samuel rose and McIntyre took a step toward him.

"You long-winded dude. You got our land—take that for Peter Carhart!"

He swung from the shoulder quick as lightning and down went Samuel in a heap. Dimly he heard steps in the doorway and knew that someone was holding McIntyre, but there was no need. The rancher had sunk down in his chair, and dropped his head in his hands.

Samuel's brain was whirring. He realized that the fourth fist had hit him, and a great flood of emotion cried out that the law that had inexorably ruled his life was in motion again. In a half-daze he got up and strode from the room.

The next ten minutes were perhaps the hardest of his life. People talk of the courage of convictions, but in actual life a man's duty to his family may make a rigid course seem a selfish indulgence of his own righteousness. Samuel thought mostly of his family, yet he never really wavered. That jolt had brought him to.

When he came back in the room there were a lot of worried faces waiting for him, but he didn't waste any time explaining.

"Gentlemen," he said, "Mr. McIntyre has been kind enough to convince me that in this matter you are absolutely right, and the Peter Carhart interests absolutely wrong. As far as I am concerned you can keep your ranches to the rest of your days."

He pushed his way through an astounded gathering, and within a half-hour he had sent two telegrams that staggered the operator into complete unfitness for business; one was to Hamil in San Antonio; one was to Peter Carhart in New York.

Samuel didn't sleep much that night. He knew that for the first time in his business career he had made a dismal, miserable failure. But some instinct in him, stronger than will, deeper than training, had forced him to do what would probably end his ambitions and his happiness. But it was done and it never occurred to him that he could have acted otherwise.

Next morning two telegrams were waiting for him. The first was from Hamil. It contained three words:

"*You blamed idiot!*"

The second was from New York:

"*Deal off come to New York immediately Carhart.*"

Within a week things had happened. Hamil quarrelled furiously and violently defended his scheme. He was summoned to New York, and spent a bad half-hour on the carpet in Peter Carhart's office. He broke with the Carhart interests in July, and in August Samuel Meredith, at thirty-five years old, was, to all intents, made Carhart's partner. The fourth fist had done its work.

I suppose that there's a caddish streak in every man that runs crosswise across his character and disposition and general outlook. With some men it's secret and we never know it's there until they strike us in the dark one night. But Samuel's showed when it was in action, and the sight of it made people see red. He was rather lucky in that, because every time his little devil came up it met a reception that sent it scurrying down below in a sickly, feeble condition. It was the same devil, the same streak that made him order Gilly's friends off the bed, that made him go inside Marjorie's house.

If you could run your hand along Samuel Meredith's jaw you'd feel a lump. He admits he's never been sure which fist left it there, but he wouldn't lose it for anything. He says there's no cad like an old cad, and that sometimes just before making a decision, it's a great help to stroke his chin. The reporters call it a nervous characteristic, but it's not that. It's so he can feel again the gorgeous clarity, the lightning sanity of those four fists.

ADDITIONAL STORIES

September 1919–April 1922

BABES IN THE WOODS

She paused at the top of the staircase. The emotions of divers on spring-boards, leading ladies on opening nights and lumpy, be-striped young men on the day of the Big Game crowded through her. She felt as if she should have descended to a burst of drums or to a discordant blend of gems from "Thaïs" and "Carmen." She had never been so worried about her appearance, she had never been so satisfied with it. She had been sixteen years old for six months.

"Isabelle!" called Elaine, her cousin, from the doorway of the dressing-room.

"I'm ready." She caught a slight lump of nervousness in her throat.

"I've had to send back to the house for another pair of slippers—it'll be just a minute."

Isabelle started toward the dressing-room for a last peek at a mirror, but something decided her to stand there and gaze down the stairs. They curved tantalizingly and she could just catch a glimpse of two pairs of masculine feet in the hall below.

Pump-shod in uniform black they gave no hint of identity, but eagerly she wondered if one pair were attached to Stephen Palms. This young man, as yet unmet, had taken up a considerable part of her day—the first day of her arrival.

Going up in a machine from the station Elaine had volunteered, amid a rain of questions and comment, revelation and exaggeration——

"You remember Stephen Palms; well he is simply mad to see you again. He's stayed over a day from college and he's coming tonight. He's heard *so* much about you—"

It had pleased her to know this. It put them on more equal terms although she was accustomed to stage her own romances with or without a send-off.

But following her delighted tremble of anticipation came a sinking sensation which made her ask:

"How do you mean he's heard about me? What sort of things?"

Elaine smiled—she felt more or less in the capacity of a show-woman with her more exotic cousin.

"He knows you're good-looking and all that." She paused—"I guess he knows you've been kissed."

Isabelle had shuddered a bit under the fur robe. She was accustomed to be followed by this, but it never failed to arouse in her the same feeling of resentment; yet—in a strange town it was an advantage.

She was a "speed," was she? Well, let them find out! She wasn't quite old enough to be sorry nor nearly old enough to be glad.

Out of the window Isabelle watched the high-piled snow glide by in the frosty morning. It was ever so much colder here than in Baltimore, she had not remembered; the glass of the side door was iced and the windows were shirred with snow in the corners.

Her mind played still with one subject: Did *he* dress like that boy there who walked so calmly down what was evidently a bustling business street, in moccasins and winter-carnival costume? How very *western!* Of course he wasn't that way; he went to college, was a freshman or something.

Really she had no distinct idea of him. A two year back picture had not impressed her except by the big eyes, which he had probably grown up to by now.

However, in the last two weeks, when her Christmas visit to Elaine had been decided on, he had assumed the proportions of a worthy adversary. Children, the most astute of matchmakers, plot and plan quickly, and Elaine had cleverly played a correspondence sonata to Isabelle's excitable temperament. Isabelle was, and had been for some time, capable of very strong, if very transient emotions.

They drew up at a white-stone building, set back from the snowy street. Mrs. Hollis greeted her warmly and her various younger cousins were produced from the corners where they skulked politely. Isabelle met them quite tactfully. At her best she allied all with whom she came in contact, except older girls and some women. All the impressions that she made were conscious. The half dozen girls she renewed acquaintance with that morning were all rather impressed—and as much by her direct personality as by her reputation.

Stephen Palms was an open subject of conversation. Evidently he was a bit light of love. He was neither popular nor unpopular. Every girl there seemed to have had an affair with him at some time or other but no one volunteered any really useful information. He was going to "fall for her"....

Elaine had issued that statement to her young set and they were retailing it back to Elaine as fast as they set eyes on Isabelle. Isabelle resolved that if necessary she would force herself to like him—she owed it to Elaine—even though she were terribly disappointed. Elaine had painted him in such glowing colors—he was good-looking, had a "line" and was properly inconstant.

In fact he summed up all the romance that her age and environment led her to desire. Were those his dancing shoes that "shimmied" tentatively around the soft rug below?

All impressions and in fact all ideas were terribly kaleidoscopic to Isabelle. She had that curious mixture of the social and artistic temperaments, found so often in two classes, society girls and actresses. Her education, or rather her sophistication, had been absorbed from the boys who had dangled from her favor, her tact was instinctive and her capacity for love affairs was limited only by the number of boys she met. Flirt smiled from her large black-brown eyes and figured in her intense physical magnetism.

So she waited at the head of the stairs at the country club that evening while slippers were fetched. Just as she was getting impatient Elaine came out of the dressing-room beaming with her accustomed good nature and high spirits, and together they descended the broad stairs while the nervous searchlight of Isabelle's mind flashed on two ideas. She was glad she had high color tonight and she wondered if he danced well.

Downstairs, in the club's great room, the girls she had met in the afternoon surrounded her for a moment looking unbelievably changed by the soft yellow light; then she heard Elaine's voice repeating a cycle of names and she found herself bowing to a sextet of black and white and terribly stiff figures.

The name Palms figured somewhere, but she did not place him at first. A confused and very juvenile moment of awkward backings and bumpings, and all found themselves arranged talking to the persons they least desired to.

Isabelle maneuvered herself and Duncan Collard, a freshman from Harvard with whom she had once played hopscotch, to a seat on the stairs. A reference, supposedly humorous, to the past was all she needed.

What Isabelle could do socially with one idea was remarkable. First she repeated it rapturously in an enthusiastic contralto with a trace of a Southern accent; then she held it off at a distance and smiled at it—her wonderful smile; then she delivered it in variations and played a sort of mental catch with it, all this in the nominal form of dialogue.

Duncan was fascinated and totally unconscious that this was being done not for him but for the eyes that glistened under the shining, carefully watered hair, a little to her left. As an actor even in the fullest flush of his own conscious magnetism gets a lasting impression of most of the people in the front row, so Isabelle sized up Stephen Palms. First, he was light, and from her feeling of disappointment, she knew that she had expected him to be dark and of pencil slenderness. For the rest a faint flush, and a straight romantic profile, the effect set off by a close-fitting dress suit and a silk ruffled shirt of the kind that women still delight in on men, but men were just beginning to get tired of.

Stephen was just quietly smiling.

"Don't *you* think so?" she said suddenly, turning to him innocent eyed.

He nodded and smiled—an expectant, waiting smile.

Then there was a stir and Elaine led the way over to their table.

Stephen struggled to her side and whispered:

"You're my dinner partner—Isabelle."

Isabelle gasped—this was rather right in line. But really, she felt as if a good speech had been taken from the star and given to a minor character—she mustn't lose the leadership a bit. The dinner table glittered with laughter at the confusion of getting places and then curious eyes were turned on her, sitting near the head.

She was enjoying this immensely, and Duncan Collard was so engrossed with the added sparkle of her rising color that he forgot to pull out Elaine's chair and fell into a dim confusion. Stephen was on the other side, full of confidence and vanity, looking at her most consciously. He began directly and so did Duncan.

"I've heard a lot about you since you wore braids——"

"Wasn't it funny this afternoon——"

Both stopped.

Isabelle turned to Stephen shyly.

Her face was always enough answer for anyone, but she decided to speak.

"How—who from?"

"From everybody—for all the years since you've been away."

She blushed appropriately.

On her right Duncan was hors-de-combat already although he hadn't quite realized it.

"I'll tell you what I remembered about you all these years," Stephen continued.

She leaned slightly toward him and looked modestly at the celery before her.

Duncan sighed—he knew Stephen and the situations that Stephen was born to handle. He turned to Elaine and asked her if she was going away to school next year.

II

Isabelle and Stephen were distinctly not innocent, nor were they otherwise. Moreover, amateur standing had very little value in the game they were beginning—they were each playing a part that they might play for years. They had both started with good looks and excitable temperaments and the rest was the result of certain accessible popular novels, and dressing-room conversation culled from a slightly older set.

When Isabelle's eyes, wide and innocent, proclaimed the ingenue most, Stephen was proportionately less deceived. He waited for the mask to drop off but at the same time he did not question her right to wear it.

She, on her part, was not impressed by his studied air of blasé sophistication. She had lived in a larger city and had slightly an advantage in range. But she accepted his pose. It was one of a dozen little conventions of this kind of affair. He was aware that he was getting this particular favor now because she had been coached.

He knew that he stood for merely the best thing in sight, and that he would have to improve his opportunity before he lost his advantage.

So they proceeded, with an infinite guile that would have horrified the parents of both.

After the half dozen little dinners were over the dance began.

Everything went smoothly—boys cut in on Isabelle every few feet and then squabbled in the corners with: "You might let me get more than an *inch!*" and "She didn't like it either—she told me so next time I cut in."

It was true—she told everyone so, and gave every hand a parting pressure that said, "You know that your dances are *making* my evening."

But time passed, two hours of it, and the less subtle beaux had better learned to focus their pseudo-passionate glances elsewhere, for eleven o'clock found Isabelle and Stephen sitting on a leather lounge in a little den off the reading room. She was conscious that they were a handsome pair and seemed to belong distinctly on this leather lounge while lesser lights fluttered and chattered downstairs. Boys who passed the door looked in enviously—girls who passed only laughed and frowned, and grew wise within themselves.

They had now reached a very definite stage. They had traded ages and accounts of their lives since they had met last. She had listened to much that she had heard before. He was a freshman at college and was on his class hockey team. He had learned that some of the boys she went with in Baltimore were "terrible speeds" and came to parties intoxicated—most of them were twenty or so, and drove alluring Stutzes. A good half of them seemed to have flunked out of various boarding schools and colleges but some of them bore sporting names that made him look at her admiringly.

As a matter of fact, Isabelle's closer acquaintance with the colleges was chiefly through older cousins. She had bowing acquaintances with a lot of young men who thought she was "a pretty kid" and "worth keeping an eye on." But Isabelle strung the names into a fabrication of gaiety that would have dazzled a Viennese nobleman. Such is the power of young contralto voices on leather sofas.

I have said that they had reached a very definite stage—nay more, a very critical stage. Stephen had stayed over a day to see her and his train left at twelve-eighteen that night. His trunk and suitcase awaited him at the station and his watch was already beginning to hang heavy in his pocket.

"Isabelle," he said suddenly, "I want to tell you something."

They had been talking lightly about "that funny look in her eyes," and on the relative attractions of dancing and sitting out, and Isabelle knew from the change in his manner exactly what was coming—indeed she had been wondering how soon it would come.

Stephen reached above their heads and turned out the electric light, so they were in the dark except for the glow from the red lamps that fell through the door from the reading room. Then he began:

"I don't know—I don't know whether or not you know what you—what I'm going to say. Lordy, Isabelle—this sounds like a line, but it isn't."

"I know," said Isabelle softly.

"We may never meet again like this—I have darned hard luck sometimes."

He was leaning away from her on the other arm of the lounge, but she could see his black eyes plainly in the dark.

"You'll see me again—silly." There was just the slightest emphasis on the last word—so that it became almost a term of endearment.

He continued a bit huskily:

"I've fallen for a lot of people—girls—and I guess you have too—boys, I mean—but honestly you——" He broke off suddenly and leaned forward, chin on his hands, a favorite and studied gesture. "Oh what's the use? You'll go your way and I suppose I'll go mine."

Silence for a moment. Isabelle was quite stirred—she wound her handkerchief into a tight ball and by the faint light that streamed over her, dropped it deliberately on the floor. Their hands touched for an instant but neither spoke. Silences were becoming more frequent and more delicious. Outside another stray couple had come up and were experimenting on the piano in the next room. After the usual preliminary of "chopsticks," one of them started "Babes in the Woods" and a light tenor carried the words into the den—

"Give me your hand,
I'll understand,
We're off to slumberland."

Isabelle hummed it softly and trembled as she felt Stephen's hand close over hers.

"Isabelle," he whispered, "you know I'm mad about you. You *do* give a darn about me."

"Yes."

"How much do you care—do you like anyone better?"

"No." He could scarcely hear her, although he bent so near that he felt her breath against his cheek.

"Isabelle, I'm going back to college for six long months and why shouldn't we—if I could only just have one thing to remember you by——"

"Close the door."

Her voice had just stirred so that he half-wondered whether she had spoken at all.

As he swung the door softly shut, the music seemed quivering just outside.

"Moonlight is bright,
Kiss me good-night."

What a wonderful song, she thought—everything was wonderful tonight, most of all this romantic scene in the den with their hands clinging and the inevitable looming charmingly close.

The future vista of her life seemed an unending succession of scenes like this, under moonlight and pale starlight, and in the backs of warm limousines and in low cosy roadsters stopped under sheltering trees—only the boy might change, and this one was so nice.

"Isabelle!"

His whisper blended in the music and they seemed to float nearer together.

Her breath came faster.

"Can't I kiss you, Isabelle?"

Lips half-parted, she turned her head to him in the dark.

Suddenly the ring of voices, the sound of running footsteps surged toward them.

Like a flash Stephen reached up and turned on the light and when the door opened and three boys, the wrathy and dance-craving Duncan among them, rushed in, he was turning over the magazines on the table, while she sat without moving, serene and unembarrassed, and even greeted them with a welcoming smile. But her heart was beating wildly and she felt somehow as if she had been deprived.

It was evidently over. There was a clamor for a dance, there was a glance that passed between them, on his side despair, on hers regret, and then the evening went on, with the reassured beaux and the eternal cutting in.

At quarter to twelve Stephen shook hands with her gravely, in a small crowd assembled to wish him good-speed.

For an instant he lost his poise and she felt slightly unnecessary, when a satirical voice from a concealed wit on the edge of the company cried:

"Take her outside, Stephen."

As he took her hand he pressed it a little and she returned the pressure as she had done to twenty hands that evening—that was all.

At two o'clock, back at Hollis', Elaine asked her if she and Stephen had had a "time" in the den. Isabelle turned to her quietly. In her eyes was the light of the idealist, the inviolate dreamer of Joan-like dreams.

"No!" she answered. "I don't do that sort of thing anymore—he asked me to, but I said 'No.'"

As she crept into bed she wondered what he'd say in his special delivery tomorrow. He had such a good-looking mouth—would she ever——?

"Fourteen angels were watching o'er them," sang Elaine sleepily from the next room.

"Damn!" muttered Isabelle as she explored the cold sheets cautiously, "Damn!"

THE DEBUTANTE

(*A One–Act Play*)

SCENE I

A large and dainty bedroom in the Connage house—a girl's room; pink walls and curtains and a pink bedspread on a cream-colored bed. Pink and cream are the motifs of the room, but the only article of furniture in full view is a luxurious dressing table with a glass top and a three-sided mirror. On the walls we have an expensive print of "Cherry Ripe," a few polite dogs by Landseer, and the "King of the Black Isles" by Maxfield Parrish.

Great disorder consisting of the following items: (1) *seven or eight empty cardboard boxes, with tissue-paper tongues hanging panting from their mouths;* (2) *an assortment of street dresses mingled with their sisters of the evening, all upon the table, all evidently new;* (3) *a roll of tulle, which has lost its dignity and wound itself tortuously around everything in sight; and* (4) *upon the two small chairs, a collection of lingerie that beggars description. One would enjoy seeing the bill called forth by the finery displayed and one is possessed by a desire to see the princess for whose benefit—Look! There's someone!—Disappointment! This is only a maid looking for something—she lifts a heap from a chair—Not there; another heap, the dressing table, the chiffonier drawers. She brings to light several beautiful chemises and an amazing pajama, but this does not satisfy her—she goes out.*

An indistinguishable mumble from the next room.

Now, we are getting warm. This is Mrs. Connage, ample, dignified, rouged to the dowager point and quite worn out. Her lips move significantly as she looks for it. Her search is less thorough than the maid's, but there is a touch of fury in it that quite makes up for its sketchiness. She stumbles on the tulle and her "damn" is quite audible. She retires, empty-handed.

More chatter outside and a girl's voice, a very spoiled voice, says: "Of all the stupid people——"

After a pause a third seeker enters, not she of the spoiled voice but a younger edition. This is Cecelia Connage, sixteen, pretty, shrewd and constitutionally good-humored. She is dressed for the evening in a gown the obvious simplicity of which probably bores her. She goes to the nearest pile, selects a small pink garment and holds it up appraisingly.

CECELIA:

Pink?

ROSALIND:

Yes!

CECELIA:

Very snappy?

ROSALIND:

Yes!

CECELIA:

I've got it!

(*She sees herself in the mirror of the dressing table and commences to tickle-toe on the carpet.*)

ROSALIND:

(*Outside.*) What are you doing—trying it on?

(*Cecelia ceases and goes out, carrying the garment at the right shoulder. From the other door, enters Alec Connage, about twenty-three, healthy and quite sure of the cut of his dress clothes. He comes to the center of the room and in a huge voice shouts:*)

Mamma!

(*There is a chorus of protest from next door and encouraged he starts toward it, but is repelled by another chorus.*)

ALEC:

So *that's* where you all are! Amory Blaine is here.

CECELIA:

(*Quickly.*) Take him downstairs.

ALEC:

Oh he *is* downstairs.

MRS. CONNAGE:

Well, you can show him where his room is. Tell him I'm sorry that I can't meet him now.

ALEC:

He's heard a lot about you all. I wish you'd hurry. Father's telling him all about the war and he's restless. He's sort of temperamental.

(*This last suffices to draw Cecelia into the room.*)

CECELIA:

(*Seating herself high upon lingerie.*) How do you mean temperamental?

ALEC:

Oh, he writes stuff.

CECELIA:

Does he play the piano?

ALEC:

I don't know. He's sort of ghostly, too—makes you scared to death sometimes—you know, all that artistic business.

CECELIA:

(*Speculatively.*) Drink?

ALEC:

Yes—nothing queer about him.

CECELIA:

Money?

ALEC:

Good Lord—ask him. No, I don't think so. Still he was at Princeton when I was at New Haven. He must have some.

MRS. CONNAGE:

(*Enter Mrs. Connage.*) Alec, of course we're glad to have any friend of yours, but you must admit this is an inconvenient time, and he'll be a little neglected. This is Rosalind's week you see. When a girl comes out she needs *all* the attention.

ROSALIND:

(*Outside.*) Well, then prove it by coming here and hooking me.

(*Exit Mrs. Connage.*)

ALEC:

Rosalind hasn't changed a bit.

CECELIA:

(*In a lower tone.*) She's awfully spoiled.

ALEC:

Well, she'll meet her match tonight.

CECELIA:

Who—Mr. Amory Blaine?

(*Alec nods.*)

Well Rosalind has still to meet the man she can't outdistance. Honestly, Alec, she treats men terribly. She abuses them and cuts them and breaks dates with them and yawns in their faces—and they come back for more.

ALEC:

They love it.

CECELIA:

They hate it. She's a—she's a sort of vampire, I think—and she can make girls do what she wants usually—only she hates girls.

ALEC:

Personality runs in our family.

CECELIA:

(*Resignedly.*) I guess it ran out before it got to me.

ALEC:

Does Rosalind behave herself?

CECELIA:

Not particularly well. Oh, she's average—smokes sometimes, drinks punch, frequently kissed—Oh, yes—common knowledge—one of the effects of the war you know.

(*Emerges—Mrs. Connage.*)

MRS. CONNAGE:

Rosalind's almost finished and I can go down and meet your friend.

(*Exeunt Alec and his mother.*)

ROSALIND:

(*Outside.*) Oh, Mother——

CECELIA:

Mother's gone down.

(*Rosalind enters, dressed—except for her flowing hair. Rosalind is unquestionably beautiful. A radiant skin with two spots of vanishing color, and a face with one of those eternal mouths, which only one out of every fifty beauties possesses. It is sensual, slightly, but small and beautifully shaped. If Rosalind had less intelligence her "spoiled" expression might be called a pout, but she seems to have sprung into growth without that immaturity that "pout" suggests. She is wonderfully built, one notices immediately, slender and athletic, yet lacking underdevelopment. Her voice, scarcely musical, has the ghost of an alto quality and is full of vivid instant personality.*)

ROSALIND:

Honestly there are only two costumes in the world I really enjoy being in—(*combing her hair at the dressing table*) a hoop skirt dress with pantaloons or a bathing suit. I'm quite charming in both of them.

CECELIA:

Are you glad you're coming out?

ROSALIND:

Delighted.

CECELIA:

(*Cynically.*) So you can get married and live on Long Island with the *fast younger married set?* You want life to be a chain of flirtation with a man for every link.

ROSALIND:

Want it to be one!—You mean I've *found* it one.

CECELIA:

Ha!

ROSALIND:

Cecelia, darling, you don't know what a trial it is to be—like me—I've got to keep my face like steel in the street to keep men from winking at me. If I laugh hard from a front row at the theatre, the comedian plays to me for the rest of the evening. If I drop my voice, my eyes, my handkerchief at a dance my partner calls me up on the phone every day for a week.

CECELIA:

It must be an awful strain.

ROSALIND:

The unfortunate part is that the only men who interest me at all are the totally ineligible ones. Ah—if I were poor, I'd go on the stage. That's where my type belongs.

CECELIA:

Yes, you might as well get paid for the amount of acting you do.

ROSALIND:

Sometimes when I've felt particularly radiant I've thought—why should this be wasted on one man—?

CECELIA:

Often when you're particularly sulky, I've wondered why it should all be wasted on just one family.

(*Getting up.*) I think I'll go down and meet Mr. Amory Blaine. I like temperamental men.

ROSALIND:

My dear girl there aren't any. Men don't know how to be really angry or really happy—and the ones that do go to pieces.

CECELIA:

Well I'm glad I don't have all your worries, I'm engaged.

ROSALIND:

(*With a scornful smile.*) Engaged? Why you little lunatic. If mother heard you talking like that she'd send you off to boarding school where you belong.

CECELIA:

You won't tell her though, because I know things I could tell—and you're too selfish.

ROSALIND:

(*A little annoyed.*) Run along little girl!—Who are you engaged to, the iceman?—the man that keeps the candy store?

CECELIA:

Cheap wit—good-bye, darling, I'll see you later.

ROSALIND:

Oh be *sure* and do that—you're *such* a help.

(*Exit Cecelia. Rosalind finishes her hair and rises, humming. She goes up to the mirror and starts to dance in front of it, on the soft carpet. She watches not her feet, but her eyes—never casually but always intently, even when she smiles.*)

(*The door suddenly opens and then slams behind a good-looking young man, with a straight, romantic profile, who sees her and melts to instant confusion.*)

HE:

Oh I'm sorry, I thought——

SHE:

(*Smiling radiantly.*) Oh, you're Amory Blaine, aren't you?

HE:

(*Regarding her closely.*) And you're Rosalind?

SHE:

I'm going to call you Amory—oh, come in—it's all right —Mother'll be right in—(*under her breath*) unfortunately.

HE:

(*Gazing around.*) This is sort of a new wrinkle for me.

SHE:

This is No Man's Land.

HE:

This is where you—you——(*embarrassment.*)

SHE:

Yes—all those things.

(*She crosses to the bureau.*) See, here's my rouge—eye pencils.

HE:

I didn't know you were that way.

SHE:

What did you expect?

HE:

I thought you'd be sort of—sort of—sexless; you know, swim and play golf.

SHE:

Oh I do—but not in business hours.

HE:

Business?

SHE:

Six to two—strictly.

HE:

I'd like to have some stock in the corporation.

SHE:

Oh it's not a corporation—it's just "Rosalind, Unlimited." Fifty-one shares, name, good will and everything goes at $25,000 a year.

HE:

(*Disapprovingly.*) Sort of a chilly proposition.

SHE:

Well, Amory, you don't mind—do you? When I meet a man that doesn't bore me to death after two weeks, perhaps it'll be different.

HE:

Odd, you have the same point of view on men that I have on women.

SHE:

I'm not really feminine, you know—in my mind.

HE:

(*Interested.*) Go on.

SHE:

No, you—you go on—you've made me talk about myself. That's against the rules.

HE:

Rules?

SHE:

My own rules—but you—oh, Amory, I hear you're brilliant. The family expects so much of you.

HE:

How encouraging.

SHE:

Alec said you'd taught him to think. Did you? I don't believe anyone could.

HE:

No. I'm really quite dull.

(*He evidently doesn't intend this to be taken quite seriously.*)

SHE:

Liar.

HE:

I'm—I'm religious—I'm literary. I've—I've even written poems.

SHE:

Vers libre—splendid. (*She declaims.*)

Trees are green,
The birds are singing in the trees,
The girl sips her poison
The bird flies away; the girl dies.

HE:

(*Laughing.*) No, not that kind.

SHE:

(*Suddenly.*) I like you.

HE:

Don't.

SHE:

Modest too——

HE:

I'm afraid of you. I'm always afraid of a girl—until I've kissed her.

SHE:

(*Emphatically.*) My dear boy, the war is over.

HE:

So I'll always be afraid of you.

SHE:

(*Rather sadly.*) I suppose you will.

(*A slight pause on both their parts.*)

HE:

(*After due consideration.*) Listen. This is a frightful thing to ask.

SHE:

(*Knowing what's coming.*) After five minutes.

HE:

But will you—kiss me?—Or are you afraid?

SHE:

I'm never afraid—but your reasons are so poor.

HE:

Rosalind, I really *want* to kiss you.

SHE:

So do I.

(*They kiss—definitely and thoroughly.*)

HE:

(*After a breathless second.*) Well, your curiosity is satisfied.

SHE:

Is yours?

HE:

No, it's only aroused.

(*He looks it.*)

SHE:

(*Dreamily.*) I've kissed dozens of men, I suppose I'll kiss dozens more.

HE:

(*Abstractedly.*) Yes, I suppose you could—like that.

SHE:

Most people like the way I kiss.

HE:

(*Remembering himself.*) Good Lord, yes. Kiss me once more, Rosalind.

SHE:

No—my curiosity is generally satisfied at one.

HE:

(*Discouraged.*) Is that a rule?

SHE:

I make rules to fit the cases.

HE:

You and I are somewhat alike–except that I'm years older in experience.

SHE:

How old are you?

HE:

Twenty-three. You?

SHE:

Nineteen—just.

HE:

I suppose you're the product of a fashionable school.

SHE:

No—I'm fairly raw material. I was expelled from Spence —I've forgotten why.

HE:

What's your general trend?

SHE:

Oh, I'm bright, quite selfish, emotional when aroused, fond of admiration——

HE:

(*Suddenly.*) I don't want to fall in love with you——

SHE:

(*Raising her eyebrows.*) Nobody asked you to.

HE:

(*Continuing calmly*)—But I probably will. I love your mouth.

SHE:

Hush—please don't fall in love with my mouth—hair, eyes, shoulders, slippers—but not my mouth. Everybody falls in love with my mouth.

HE:

It's quite beautiful.

SHE:

It's too small.

HE:

No it isn't—let's see.

(*He kisses her again with the same thoroughness.*)

SHE:

(*Rather moved.*) Say something sweet.

HE:

(*Frightened.*) Lord help me.

SHE:

(*Drawing away.*) Well, don't—if it's so hard.

HE:

Shall we pretend? So soon?

SHE:

We haven't the same standards of time as other people.

HE:

Already it's—other people.

SHE:

Let's pretend.

HE:

No—I can't—it's sentiment.

SHE:

You're not sentimental?

HE:

No, I'm romantic—a sentimental person thinks things will last—a romantic person hopes against hope that they won't. Sentiment is emotional.

SHE:

And you're not? (*With her eyes half-closed.*) You probably flatter yourself that that's a superior attitude.

HE:

Well—Oh Rosalind, Rosalind, don't argue—kiss me again.

SHE:

(*Quite chilly now.*) No—I have no desire to kiss you.

HE:

(*Openly taken aback.*) You wanted to kiss me a minute ago.

SHE:

This is now.

HE:

I'd better go.

SHE:

I suppose so.

(*He goes toward the door.*)

SHE:

Oh!

(*He turns.*)

SHE:

(*Laughing.*) Score—Home Team, 100—Opponents, Zero.

(*He starts back.*)
(*Quickly.*) Rain—no game!
(*He goes out.*)
(*She goes quickly to the chiffonier, takes out a cigarette case and hides it in the side drawer of a desk. Her mother enters—notebook in hand.*)

MRS. CONNAGE:

Good—I've been wanting to speak to you alone before we go downstairs.

ROSALIND:

Heavens, you frighten me.

MRS. CONNAGE:

Rosalind, you've been a very expensive proposition.

ROSALIND:

(*Resignedly.*) Yes.

MRS. CONNAGE:

And you know your father hasn't what he once had.

ROSALIND:

(*Making a wry face.*) Oh please don't talk about money.

MRS. CONNAGE:

You can't do anything without it. This is our last year in this house—and unless things change, Cecelia won't have the advantages you've had.

ROSALIND:

(*Impatiently.*) Well—what is it?

MRS. CONNAGE:

So I ask you to please mind me in several things I've put down in my notebook. The first one is: Don't disappear with young men. There may be a time when it's valuable, but at present I want you on the dance floor where I can find you. There are certain men I want to have you meet and I don't like finding you in some corner of the conservatory exchanging silliness with anyone—or listening to it.

ROSALIND:

(*Sarcastically.*) Yes, listening to it *is* better.

MRS. CONNAGE:

And don't waste a lot of time with the college set—little boys nineteen and twenty years old. I don't mind a prom or a football game, but staying away from advantageous parties to eat in little cafés downtown with Tom, Dick and Harry——

ROSALIND:

(*Offering her code, which is by the way quite as high as her mother's.*)

Mother, it's done—one can't run everything now the way one did in the early nineties.

MRS. CONNAGE:

(*Paying no attention.*) There are several bachelor friends of your father's that I want you to meet tonight—youngish men.

ROSALIND:

(*Nodding wisely.*) About forty-five?

MRS. CONNAGE:

(*Sharply.*) Why not?

ROSALIND:

Oh, *quite* all right—they know life and are so adorably tired looking—(*shakes her head*) but they *will* dance.

MRS. CONNAGE:

I haven't met Mr. Blaine—but I don't think you'll care for him. He doesn't sound like a money maker.

ROSALIND:

Mother, I never *think* about money.

MRS. CONNAGE:

You never keep it long enough to think about it.

ROSALIND:

(*Sighs.*) Yes, I suppose someday I'll marry a ton of it—out of sheer boredom.

MRS. CONNAGE:

(*Referring to notebook.*) I had a wire from Hartford. Dawson Ryder is coming up. Now there's a young man I like, and he's floating in money. It seems to me that since you seem tired of Howard Gillespie, you might give Mr. Ryder some encouragement. This is the third time he's been up in a month.

ROSALIND:

How did you know I was tired of Howard Gillespie?

MRS. CONNAGE:

The poor boy looks so miserable every time he comes.

ROSALIND:

That was one of those romantic, pre-battle affairs. They're all wrong.

MRS. CONNAGE:

(*Her say said.*) At any rate make us proud of you tonight.

ROSALIND:

Don't you think I'm beautiful?

MRS. CONNAGE:

You know you are.

(*From downstairs is heard the shriek of a violin being tuned, the rattle of a drum. Mrs. Connage turns quickly to her daughter.*)

MRS. CONNAGE:

Come.

ROSALIND:

One minute.

(*Her mother leaves. Rosalind goes to the glass, where she gazes at herself with great satisfaction. She kisses her hand and touches her mirrored mouth with it. Then she turns out the lights and leaves the room.*)

(*Silence for a moment. A few chords from the piano, the discreet message of faint drums, the rustle of new silk, all blend on the staircase outside and drift in through the partly opened door. Bundled figures pass in the lighted hall. The laughter heard below becomes doubled and multiplied. Then someone comes in from the side, switches on the lights and closes the door. It is Cecelia. She goes to the chiffonier, looks in the drawers, hesitates—then to the desk whence she takes the cigarette case and selects one. She lights it and puffing and blowing walks toward the mirror.*)

CECELIA:

(*In tremendously sophisticated accents.*) Oh, yes, coming out is *such* a farce nowadays you know. One really plays around *so* much before one is seventeen, that it's positively anti-climax.

(*Shaking hands with a visionary, middle-aged nobleman.*)

Yes, your grace—I b'lieve I've heard my sister speak of you. Have a puff—they're very good. They're—they're Coronas. You don't smoke? What a pity! The King doesn't allow it I suppose. Yes, I'll dance.

(*So she dances around the room to a tune from downstairs. Her arms outstretched to an imaginary partner. The cigarette waving in her hand. Darkness comes quickly down and the lights stay low until*——)

SCENE II

Draperies cut off the stage to a corner of a den downstairs, filled by a very comfortable leather lounge. A small light is on each side above and in the middle; over the couch hangs a painting of a very old, very dignified gentleman, period 1860. Outside the music is heard in a fox trot.

Rosalind is seated on the lounge and on her left is Howard Gillespie, a shallow youth of about twenty-four. He is obviously very unhappy and she quite bored.

GILLESPIE:

(*Feebly.*) What do you mean I've changed. I feel the same toward you.

ROSALIND:

But you don't look the same to me.

GILLESPIE:

Three weeks ago you used to say that you liked me because I was so blasé, so indifferent—I still am.

ROSALIND:

But not about me. I used to like you because you had brown eyes and thin legs.

GILLESPIE:

(*Helplessly.*) They're still thin and brown.

ROSALIND:

I used to think you were never jealous. Now you follow me with your eyes wherever I go.

GILLESPIE:

I love you.

ROSALIND:

(*Coldly.*) I know it.

GILLESPIE:

And you haven't kissed me for two weeks. I had an idea that after a girl was kissed she was—was—won.

ROSALIND:

Those days are over. I have to be won all over again every time you see me.

GILLESPIE:

Are you serious?

ROSALIND:

About as usual. There used to be two kinds of kisses: First when girls were kissed and deserted, second when they were engaged. Now there's a third kind where the man is kissed and deserted. If Mr. Jones of the nineties bragged he'd kissed a girl everyone knew he was through with her. If Mr. Jones of 1919 brags the same, everyone knows it's because he can't kiss her any more. Given a decent start any girl can beat a man nowadays.

GILLESPIE:

Then why do you play with men?

ROSALIND:

(*Learning forward confidentially.*) For that first moment, when he's interested. There *is* a moment—Oh, just before the first kiss, a whispered word—something that makes it worth while.

GILLESPIE:

And then?

ROSALIND:

Then after that you make him talk about himself. Pretty soon he thinks of nothing but being alone with you.—He sulks, he won't fight, he doesn't want to play—Victory.

(*Enter Dawson Ryder, twenty-six, handsome, rather cold, wealthy, faithful to his own, a bore perhaps, but steady and sure of success.*)

RYDER:

I believe this is my dance, Rosalind.

ROSALIND:

Very well, Dawson. Mr. Ryder this is Mr. Gillespie. (*They shake hands and Gillespie leaves tremendously downcast.*)

RYDER:

Your party is certainly a success.

ROSALIND:

Is it—I haven't seen it lately. I'm weary—Do you mind sitting out?

RYDER:

Mind—I'm delighted. You know I loathe this "rushing" idea. See a girl yesterday, today, tomorrow.

ROSALIND:

Dawson!

RYDER:

What?

ROSALIND:

I wonder if you know you love me.

RYDER:

(*Startled.*) What—Oh—I say, you're remarkable.

ROSALIND:

Because you know I'm an awful proposition. Anyone who marries me would have his hands full. I'm mean—mighty mean.

RYDER:

Oh, I wouldn't say that.

ROSALIND:

Oh yes I am—especially to the people nearest to me.

(*She rises.*)

Come, let's go. I have changed my mind and I want to dance. Mother is probably having a fit.

(*They start out.*)

Does one shimmy in Hartford?
(*Exeunt.*)
(*Enter Alec and Cecelia.*)

CECELIA:

Just my luck to get my own brother for an intermission.

ALEC:

(*Gloomily.*) I'll go if you want me to.

CECELIA:

Good heavens no—who would I begin the next dance with?

(*Sighs.*)

There's no color in a dance since the French officers went back.

ALEC:

I hope Amory doesn't fall in love with Rosalind.

CECELIA:

Why, I had an idea you wanted him to.

ALEC:

I did, but since seeing these girls—I don't know. I'm awfully attached to Amory. He's sensitive and I don't want him to break his heart over somebody who doesn't care about him.

CECELIA:

He's very good-looking.

ALEC:

She won't marry him, but a girl doesn't have to marry a man to break his heart.

CECELIA:

What does it? I wish I knew the secret.

ALEC:

Why, you cold-blooded little kitty. It's lucky for some that the Lord gave you a pug nose.

(*Enter Mrs. Connage.*)

MRS. CONNAGE:

Where on earth is Rosalind?

ALEC:

(*Brilliantly.*) Of course you've come to the best people to find out. She'd naturally be with us.

MRS. CONNAGE:

Her father has marshalled eight bachelor millionaires to meet her.

ALEC:

You might form a squad and march through the halls.

MRS. CONNAGE:

I'm perfectly serious—for all I know she may be at the Cocoanut Grove with some football player on the night of her debut. You look left and I'll——

ALEC:

(*Flippantly.*) Hadn't you better send the butler through the cellar?

MRS. CONNAGE:

(*Perfectly serious.*) Oh, you don't think she'd be there!

CECELIA:

He's only joking, Mother.

ALEC:

Mother had a picture of her tapping a keg of beer with some high hurdler.

MRS. CONNAGE:

Let's look right away.

(*They go out. Enter Rosalind with Gillespie.*)

GILLESPIE:

Rosalind—Once more I ask you. Don't you care a blessed thing about me?

(*Enter Amory.*)

AMORY:

My dance.

ROSALIND:

Mr. Gillespie, this is Mr. Blaine.

GILLESPIE:

I've met Mr. Blaine. From Dayton, aren't you?

AMORY:

Yes.

GILLESPIE:

(*Desperately.*) I've been there. It's rather awful.

AMORY:

(*Spicily.*) I don't know. I always felt that I'd rather be provincial hot-tamale than soup without seasoning.

GILLESPIE:

What!

AMORY:

Oh, no offense.

(*Gillespie bows and leaves.*)

ROSALIND:

He's too much *people*.

AMORY:

I was in love with a *people* once.

ROSALIND:

So?

AMORY:

Oh yes, some fool—nothing at all to her except what I read into her.

ROSALIND:

What happened?

AMORY:

Finally I convinced her that she was smarter than I was—then she threw me over. Said I was impractical you know.

ROSALIND:

What do you mean, impractical?

AMORY:

Oh—drive a car, but can't change a tire.

ROSALIND:

What are you going to do?

AMORY:

Write—I'm going to start here in New York.

ROSALIND:

Greenwich Village.

AMORY:

Good heavens no—I said write—not drink.

ROSALIND:

I like business men. Clever men are usually so homely.

AMORY:

I feel as if I'd known you ages.

ROSALIND:

Oh, are you going to commence the "pyramid" story?

AMORY:

No—I was going to make it French. I was Louis 14th and you were one of my—my——(*Changing his tone.*) Suppose—we fell in love.

ROSALIND:

I've suggested pretending.

AMORY:

If we did it would be very big.

ROSALIND:

Why?

AMORY:

Because selfish people are in a way terribly capable of great loves.

ROSALIND:

Pretend. (*Turning her lips up. Very deliberately they kiss.*)

AMORY:

I can't say sweet things.—But you are beautiful.

ROSALIND:

Not that.

AMORY:

What then?

ROSALIND:

(*Sadly.*) Oh, nothing—only I want sentiment, real sentiment—and I never find it.

AMORY:

I never find anything else in the world—and I loathe it.

ROSALIND:

It's so hard to find a male to gratify one's artistic taste.

(*Someone has opened a door and the music of a waltz surges into the room. Rosalind rises.*)

ROSALIND:

Listen! they're playing "Kiss Me Again." (*He looks at her.*)

AMORY:

Well?

ROSALIND:

Well?

AMORY:

(*Softly—the battle lost.*) I love you.

ROSALIND:

I love you. (*They kiss.*)

AMORY:

Oh God, what have I done?

ROSALIND:

Nothing. Oh, don't talk. Kiss me again.

AMORY:

I don't know why or how, but I love you—from the moment I saw you.

ROSALIND:

Me too—I—I—want to belong to you. (*Her brother strolls in, starts and then in a loud voice says,* "Oh, excuse me," *and goes.*)

ROSALIND:

(*Her lips scarcely stirring.*) Don't let me go—I don't care who knows.

AMORY:

Say it.

ROSALIND:

I love you. (*They part.*)

ROSALIND:

Oh—I am very youthful, thank God—and rather beautiful, thank God—and happy, thank God, thank God—(*She pauses and then in an odd burst of frankness adds:*) Poor Amory! (*He kisses her again.*)

CURTAIN.

MYRA MEETS HIS FAMILY

Probably every boy who has attended an Eastern college in the last ten years has met Myra half a dozen times, for the Myras live on the Eastern colleges, as kittens live on warm milk. When Myra is young, seventeen or so, they call her a "wonderful kid"; in her prime—say, at nineteen—she is tendered the subtle compliment of being referred to by her name alone; and after that she is a "prom-trotter" or "the famous coast-to-coast Myra."

You can see her practically any winter afternoon if you stroll through the Biltmore lobby. She will be standing in a group of sophomores just in from Princeton or New Haven, trying to decide whether to dance away the mellow hours at the Club de Vingt or the Plaza Rose Room. Afterward one of the sophomores will take her to the theatre and ask her down to the February prom—and then dive for a taxi to catch the last train back to college.

Invariably she has a somnolent mother sharing a suite with her on one of the floors above.

When Myra is about twenty-four she thinks over all the nice boys she might have married at one time or other, sighs a little and does the best she can. But no remarks, please! She has given her youth to you; she has blown fragrantly through many ballrooms to the tender tribute of many eyes; she has roused strange surges of romance in a hundred pagan young breasts; and who shall say she hasn't counted?

The particular Myra whom this story concerns will have to have a paragraph of history. I will get it over with as swiftly as possible.

When she was sixteen she lived in a big house in Cleveland and attended Derby School in Connecticut, and it was while she was still there that she started going to prep-school dances and college proms. She decided to spend the war at Smith College, but in January of her freshman year falling violently in love with a young infantry officer she failed all her midyear examinations and retired to Cleveland in disgrace. The young infantry officer arrived about a week later.

Just as she had about decided that she didn't love him after all he was ordered abroad, and in a great revival of sentiment she rushed down to the port of embarkation with her mother to bid him good-bye. She wrote him daily for two months, and then weekly for two months, and then once more. This last letter he never got, for a machine-gun bullet ripped through his head one rainy July morning. Perhaps this was just as well, for the letter informed him that it had all been a mistake, and that something told her they would never be happy together, and so on.

The "something" wore boots and silver wings and was tall and dark. Myra was quite sure that it was the real thing at last, but as an engine went through his chest at Kelly Field in mid-August she never had a chance to find out.

Instead she came East again, a little slimmer, with a becoming pallor and new shadows under her eyes, and throughout armistice year she left the ends of cigarettes all over New York on little china trays marked "Midnight Frolic" and "Cocoanut Grove" and "Palais Royal." She was twenty-one now, and Cleveland people said that her mother ought to take her back home—that New York was spoiling her.

You will have to do your best with that. The story should have started long ago.

It was an afternoon in September when she broke a theatre date in order to have tea with young Mrs. Arthur Elkins, once her roommate at school.

"I wish," began Myra as they sat down exquisitely, "that I'd been a señorita or a mademoiselle or something. Good grief! What is there to do over here once you're out, except marry and retire!"

Lilah Elkins had seen this form of ennui before.

"Nothing," she replied coolly; "do it."

"I can't seem to get interested, Lilah," said Myra, bending forward earnestly. "I've played round so much that even while I'm kissing the man I just wonder how soon I'll get tired of him. I never get carried away like I used to."

"How old are you, Myra?"

"Twenty-one last spring."

"Well," said Lilah complacently, "take it from me, don't get married unless you're absolutely through playing round. It means giving up an awful lot, you know."

"Through! I'm sick and tired of my whole pointless existence. Funny, Lilah, but I do feel ancient. Up at New Haven last spring men danced with me that seemed like little boys and once I overheard a girl say in the dressing room, 'There's Myra Harper! She's been coming up here for eight years.' Of course she was about three years off, but it did give me the calendar blues."

"You and I went to our first prom when we were sixteen, five years ago."

"Heavens!" sighed Myra. "And now some men are afraid of me. Isn't that odd? Some of the nicest boys. One man dropped me like a hotcake after coming down from Morristown for three straight week-ends. Some kind friend told him I was husband hunting this year, and he was afraid of getting in too deep."

"Well, you are husband hunting, aren't you?"

"I suppose so—after a fashion." Myra paused and looked about her rather cautiously. "Have you ever met Knowleton Whitney? You know what a wiz he is on looks, and his father's worth a fortune, they say. Well, I noticed that the first time he met me he started when he heard my name and fought shy—and, Lilah darling, I'm not so ancient and homely as all that, am I?"

"You certainly are not!" laughed Lilah. "And here's my advice: Pick out the best thing in sight—the man who has all the mental, physical, social and financial qualities you want, and then go after him hammer and tongs—the way we used to. After you've got him don't say to yourself 'Well, he can't sing like Billy,' or 'I wish he played better golf.' You can't have everything. Shut your eyes and turn off your sense of humor, and then after you're married it'll be very different and you'll be mighty glad."

"Yes," said Myra absently; "I've had that advice before."

"Drifting into romance is easy when you're eighteen," continued Lilah emphatically; "but after five years of it your capacity for it simply burns out."

"I've had such nice times," sighed Myra, "and such sweet men. To tell you the truth I have decided to go after someone."

"Who?"

"Knowleton Whitney. Believe me, I may be a bit blasé, but I can still get any man I want."

"You really want him?"

"Yes—as much as I'll ever want anyone. He's smart as a whip, and shy—rather sweetly shy—and they say his family have the best-looking place in Westchester County."

Lilah sipped the last of her tea and glanced at her wrist watch.

"I've got to tear, dear."

They rose together and, sauntering out on Park Avenue, hailed taxi-cabs.

"I'm awfully glad, Myra; and I know you'll be glad too."

Myra skipped a little pool of water and, reaching her taxi, balanced on the running board like a ballet dancer.

"Bye, Lilah. See you soon."

"Good-bye, Myra. Good luck!"

And knowing Myra as she did, Lilah felt that her last remark was distinctly superfluous.

II

That was essentially the reason that one Friday night six weeks later Knowleton Whitney paid a taxi bill of seven dollars and ten cents and with a mixture of emotions paused beside Myra on the Biltmore steps.

The outer surface of his mind was deliriously happy, but just below that was a slowly hardening fright at what he had done. He, protected since his freshman year at Harvard from the snares of fascinating fortune hunters, dragged away from several sweet young things by the acquiescent nape of his neck, had taken advantage of his family's absence in the West to become so enmeshed in the toils that it was hard to say which was toils and which was he.

The afternoon had been like a dream: November twilight along Fifth Avenue after the matinée, and he and Myra looking out at the swarming crowds from the romantic privacy of a hansom cab—quaint device—then tea at the Ritz and her white hand gleaming on the arm of a chair beside him; and suddenly quick broken words. After that had come the trip to the jeweler's and a mad dinner in some little Italian restaurant where he had written "Do you?" on the back of the bill of fare and pushed it over for her to add the ever-miraculous "You know I do!" And now at the day's end they paused on the Biltmore steps.

"Say it," breathed Myra close to his ear.

He said it. Ah, Myra, how many ghosts must have flitted across your memory then!

"You've made me so happy, dear," she said softly.

"No—you've made me happy. Don't you know—Myra——"

"I know."

"For good?"

"For good. I've got this, you see." And she raised the diamond solitaire to her lips. She knew how to do things, did Myra.

"Good-night."

"Good-night. Good-night."

Like a gossamer fairy in shimmering rose she ran up the wide stairs and her cheeks were glowing wildly as she rang the elevator bell.

At the end of a fortnight she got a telegram from him saying that his family had returned from the West and expected her up in Westchester County for a week's visit. Myra wired her train time, bought three new evening dresses and packed her trunk.

It was a cool November evening when she arrived, and stepping from the train in the late twilight she shivered slightly and looked eagerly round for Knowleton. The station platform swarmed for a moment with men returning from the city; there was a shouting medley of wives and chauffeurs, and a great snorting of automobiles as they backed and turned and slid away. Then before she realized it the platform was quite deserted and not a single one of the luxurious cars remained. Knowleton must have expected her on another train.

With an almost inaudible "Damn!" she started toward the Elizabethan station to telephone, when suddenly she was accosted by a very dirty, dilapidated man who touched his ancient cap to her and addressed her in a cracked, querulous voice.

"You Miss Harper?"

"Yes," she confessed, rather startled. Was this unmentionable person by any wild chance the chauffeur?

"The chauffeur's sick," he continued in a high whine. "I'm his son."

Myra gasped.

"You mean Mr. Whitney's chauffeur?"

"Yes; he only keeps just one since the war. Great on economizin'—regelar Hoover." He stamped his feet nervously and smacked enormous gauntlets together. "Well, no use waitin' here gabbin' in the cold. Le's have your grip."

Too amazed for words and not a little dismayed, Myra followed her guide to the edge of the platform, where she looked in vain for a car. But she was not left to wonder long, for the person led her steps to a battered old flivver, wherein was deposited her grip.

"Big car's broke," he explained. "Have to use this or walk."

He opened the front door for her and nodded.

"Step in."

"I b'lieve I'll sit in back if you don't mind."

"Surest thing you know," he cackled, opening the back door. "I thought the trunk bumpin' round back there might make you nervous."

"What trunk?"

"Yourn."

"Oh, didn't Mr. Whitney—can't you make two trips?"

He shook his head obstinately.

"Wouldn't allow it. Not since the war. Up to rich people to set 'n example; that's what Mr. Whitney says. Le's have your check, please."

As he disappeared Myra tried in vain to conjure up a picture of the chauffeur if this was his son. After a mysterious argument with the station agent he returned, gasping violently, with the trunk on his back. He deposited it in the rear seat and climbed up in front beside her.

It was quite dark when they swerved out of the road and up a long dusky driveway to the Whitney place, whence lighted windows flung great blots of cheerful, yellow light over the gravel and grass and trees. Even now she could see that it was very beautiful, that its blurred outline was Georgian Colonial and that great shadowy garden parks were flung out at both sides. The car plumped to a full stop before a square stone doorway and the chauffeur's son climbed out after her and pushed open the outer door.

"Just go right in," he cackled; and as she passed the threshold she heard him softly shut the door, closing out himself and the dark.

Myra looked round her. She was in a large somber hall paneled in old English oak and lit by dim shaded lights clinging like luminous yellow turtles at intervals along the wall. Ahead of her was a broad staircase and on both sides there were several doors, but there was no sight or sound of life, and an intense stillness seemed to rise ceaselessly from the deep crimson carpet.

She must have waited there a full minute before she began to have that unmistakable sense of someone looking at her. She forced herself to turn casually round.

A sallow little man, bald and clean shaven, trimly dressed in a frock coat and white spats, was standing a few yards away regarding her quizzically. He must have been fifty at the least, but even before he moved she had noticed a curious alertness about him—something in his pose which promised that it had been instantaneously assumed and would be instantaneously changed in a moment. His tiny hands and feet and the odd twist to his eyebrows gave him a faintly elfish expression, and she had one of those vague transient convictions that she had seen him before, many years ago.

For a minute they stared at each other in silence and then she flushed slightly and discovered a desire to swallow.

"I suppose you're Mr. Whitney." She smiled faintly and advanced a step toward him. "I'm Myra Harper."

For an instant longer he remained silent and motionless, and it flashed across Myra that he might be deaf; then suddenly he jerked into spirited life exactly like a mechanical toy started by the pressure of a button.

"Why, of course—why, naturally. I know—ah!" he exclaimed excitedly in a high-pitched elfin voice. Then raising himself on his toes in a sort of attenuated ecstasy of enthusiasm and smiling a wizened smile, he minced toward her across the dark carpet.

She blushed appropriately.

"That's awfully nice of ——"

"Ah!" he went on. "You must be tired; a rickety, cindery, ghastly trip, I know. Tired and hungry and thirsty, no doubt, no doubt!" He looked round him indignantly. "The servants are frightfully inefficient in this house!"

Myra did not know what to say to this, so she made no answer. After an instant's abstraction Mr. Whitney crossed over with his furious energy and pressed a button; then almost as if he were dancing he was by her side again, making thin, disparaging gestures with his hands.

"A little minute," he assured her, "sixty seconds, scarcely more. Here!"

He rushed suddenly to the wall and with some effort lifted a great carved Louis Fourteenth chair and set it down carefully in the geometrical center of the carpet.

"Sit down—won't you? Sit down! I'll go get you something. Sixty seconds at the outside."

She demurred faintly, but he kept on repeating "Sit down!" in such an aggrieved yet hopeful tone that Myra sat down. Instantly her host disappeared.

She sat there for five minutes and a feeling of oppression fell over her. Of all the receptions she had ever received this was decidedly the oddest—for though she had read somewhere that Ludlow Whitney was considered one of the most eccentric figures in the financial world, to find a sallow, elfin little man who, when he walked, danced was rather a blow to her sense of form. Had he gone to get Knowleton! She revolved her thumbs in interminable concentric circles.

Then she started nervously at a quick cough at her elbow. It was Mr. Whitney again. In one hand he held a glass of milk and in the other a blue kitchen bowl full of those hard cubical crackers used in soup.

"Hungry from your trip!" he exclaimed compassionately. "Poor girl, poor little girl, starving!" He brought out this last word with such emphasis that some of the milk plopped gently over the side of the glass.

Myra took the refreshments submissively. She was not hungry, but it had taken him ten minutes to get them so it seemed ungracious to refuse. She sipped gingerly at the milk and ate a cracker, wondering vaguely what to say. Mr. Whitney, however, solved the problem for her by disappearing again—this time by way of the wide stairs—four steps at a hop—the back of his bald head gleaming oddly for a moment in the half dark.

Minutes passed. Myra was torn between resentment and bewilderment that she should be sitting on a high comfortless chair in the middle of this big hall munching crackers. By what code was a visiting fiancée ever thus received!

Her heart gave a jump of relief as she heard a familiar whistle on the stairs. It was Knowleton at last, and when he came in sight he gasped with astonishment.

"Myra!"

She carefully placed the bowl and glass on the carpet and rose, smiling.

"Why," he exclaimed, "they didn't tell me you were here!"

"Your father—welcomed me."

"Lordy! He must have gone upstairs and forgotten all about it. Did he insist on your eating this stuff? Why didn't you just tell him you didn't want any?"

"Why—I don't know."

"You mustn't mind Father, dear. He's forgetful and a little unconventional in some ways, but you'll get used to him."

He pressed a button and a butler appeared.

"Show Miss Harper to her room and have her bag carried up—and her trunk if it isn't there already." He turned to Myra. "Dear, I'm awfully sorry I didn't know you were here. How long have you been waiting?"

"Oh, only a few minutes."

It had been twenty at the least, but she saw no advantage in stressing it. Nevertheless it had given her an oddly uncomfortable feeling.

Half an hour later as she was hooking the last eye on her dinner dress there was a knock on the door.

"It's Knowleton, Myra; if you're about ready we'll go in and see Mother for a minute before dinner."

She threw a final approving glance at her reflection in the mirror and turning out the light joined him in the hall. He led her down a central passage which crossed to the other wing of the house, and stopping before a closed door he pushed it open and ushered Myra into the weirdest room upon which her young eyes had ever rested.

It was a large luxurious boudoir, paneled, like the lower hall, in dark English oak and bathed by several lamps in a mellow orange glow that blurred its every outline into misty amber. In a great armchair piled high with cushions and draped with a curiously figured cloth of silk reclined a very sturdy old lady with bright white hair, heavy features, and an air about her of having been there for many years. She lay somnolently against the cushions, her eyes half-closed, her great bust rising and falling under her black negligee.

But it was something else that made the room remarkable, and Myra's eyes scarcely rested on the woman, so engrossed was she in another feature of her surroundings. On the carpet, on the chairs and sofas, on the great canopied bed and on the soft Angora rug in front of the fire sat and sprawled and slept a great army of white poodle dogs. There must have been almost two dozen of them, with curly hair twisting in front of their wistful eyes and wide yellow bows flaunting from their necks. As Myra and Knowleton entered a stir went over the dogs; they raised one-and-twenty cold black noses in the air and from one-and-twenty little throats went up a great clatter of staccato barks until the room was filled with such an uproar that Myra stepped back in alarm.

But at the din the somnolent fat lady's eyes trembled open and in a low husky voice that was in itself oddly like a bark she snapped out: "Hush that racket!" and the clatter instantly ceased. The two or three poodles round the fire turned their silky eyes on each other reproachfully, and lying down with little sighs faded out on the white Angora rug; the tousled ball on the lady's lap dug his nose into the crook of an elbow and went back to sleep, and except for the patches of white wool scattered about the room Myra would have thought it all a dream.

"Mother," said Knowleton after an instant's pause, "this is Myra."

From the lady's lips flooded one low husky word: "Myra?"

"She's visiting us, I told you."

Mrs. Whitney raised a large arm and passed her hand across her forehead wearily.

"Child!" she said—and Myra started, for again the voice was like a low sort of growl— "you want to marry my son Knowleton?"

Myra felt that this was putting the tonneau before the radiator, but she nodded. "Yes, Mrs. Whitney."

"How old are you?" This very suddenly.

"I'm twenty-one, Mrs. Whitney."

"Ah—and you're from Cleveland?"

This was in what was surely a series of articulate barks.

"Yes, Mrs. Whitney."

"Ah——"

Myra was not certain whether this last ejaculation was conversation or merely a groan, so she did not answer.

"You'll excuse me if I don't appear downstairs," continued Mrs. Whitney; "but when we're in the East I seldom leave this room and my dear little doggies."

Myra nodded and a conventional health question was trembling on her lips when she caught Knowleton's warning glance and checked it.

"Well," said Mrs. Whitney with an air of finality, "you seem like a very nice girl. Come in again."

"Good-night, Mother," said Knowleton.

"'Night!" barked Mrs. Whitney drowsily, and her eyes sealed gradually up as her head receded back again into the cushions.

Knowleton held open the door and Myra feeling a bit blank left the room. As they walked down the corridor she heard a burst of furious sound behind them; the noise of the closing door had again roused the poodle dogs.

When they went downstairs they found Mr. Whitney already seated at the dinner table.

"Utterly charming, completely delightful!" he exclaimed, beaming nervously. "One big family, and you the jewel of it, my dear."

Myra smiled, Knowleton frowned and Mr. Whitney tittered.

"It's been lonely here," he continued; "desolate, with only us three. We expect you to bring sunlight and warmth, the peculiar radiance and efflorescence of youth. It will be quite delightful. Do you sing?"

"Why—I have. I mean, I do, some."

He clapped his hands enthusiastically.

"Splendid! Magnificent! What do you sing? Opera? Ballads? Popular music?"

"Well, mostly popular music."

"Good; personally I prefer popular music. By the way, there's a dance tonight."

"Father," demanded Knowleton sulkily, "did you go and invite a crowd here?"

"I had Monroe call up a few people—just some of the neighbors," he explained to Myra. "We're all very friendly hereabouts; give informal things continually. Oh, it's quite delightful."

Myra caught Knowleton's eye and gave him a sympathetic glance. It was obvious that he had wanted to be alone with her this first evening and was quite put out.

"I want them to meet Myra," continued his father. "I want them to know this delightful jewel we've added to our little household."

"Father," said Knowleton suddenly, "eventually of course Myra and I will want to live here with you and Mother, but for the first two or three years I think an apartment in New York would be more the thing for us."

Crash! Mr. Whitney had raked across the tablecloth with his fingers and swept his silver to a jangling heap on the floor.

"Nonsense!" he cried furiously, pointing a tiny finger at his son. "Don't talk that utter nonsense! You'll live here, do you understand me? Here! What's a home without children?"

"But, Father——"

In his excitement Mr. Whitney rose and a faint unnatural color crept into his sallow face.

"Silence!" he shrieked. "If you expect one bit of help from me you can have it under my roof—nowhere else! Is that clear? As for you, my exquisite young lady," he continued, turning his wavering finger on Myra, "you'd better understand that the best thing you can do is to decide to settle down right here. This is my home, and I mean to keep it so!"

He stood then for a moment on his tiptoes, bending furiously indignant glances first on one, then on the other, and then suddenly he turned and skipped from the room.

"Well," gasped Myra, turning to Knowleton in amazement, "what do you know about that!"

III

Some hours later she crept into bed in a great state of restless discontent. One thing she knew—she was not going to live in this house. Knowleton would have to make his father see reason to the extent of giving them an apartment in the city. The sallow little man made her nervous; she was sure Mrs. Whitney's dogs would haunt her dreams; and there was a general casualness in the chauffeur, the butler, the maids and even the guests she had met that night, that did not in the least coincide with her ideas on the conduct of a big estate.

She had lain there an hour perhaps when she was startled from a slow reverie by a sharp cry which seemed to proceed from the adjoining room. She sat up in bed and listened, and in a minute it was repeated. It sounded exactly like the plaint of a weary child stopped summarily by the placing of a hand over its mouth. In the dark silence her bewilderment shaded gradually off into uneasiness. She waited for the cry to recur, but straining her ears she heard only the intense crowded stillness of three o'clock. She wondered where Knowleton slept, remembered that his bedroom was over in the other wing just beyond his mother's. She was alone over here—or was she?

With a little gasp she slid down into bed again and lay listening. Not since childhood had she been afraid of the dark, but the unforeseen presence of someone next door startled her and sent her imagination racing through a host of mystery stories that at one time or another had whiled away a long afternoon.

She heard the clock strike four and found she was very tired. A curtain drifted slowly down in front of her imagination, and changing her position she fell suddenly to sleep.

Next morning, walking with Knowleton under starry frosted bushes in one of the bare gardens, she grew quite light-hearted and wondered at her depression of the night before. Probably all families seemed odd when one visited them for the first time in such an intimate capacity. Yet her determination that she and Knowleton were going to live elsewhere than with the white dogs and the jumpy little man was not abated. And if the nearby Westchester County society was typified by the chilly crowd she had met at the dance——

"The family," said Knowleton, "must seem rather unusual. I've been brought up in an odd atmosphere, I suppose, but Mother is really quite normal outside of her penchant for poodles in great quantities, and father in spite of his eccentricities seems to hold a secure position in Wall Street."

"Knowleton," she demanded suddenly, "who lives in the room next door to me?"

Did he start and flush slightly—or was that her imagination?

"Because," she went on deliberately, "I'm almost sure I heard someone crying in there during the night. It sounded like a child, Knowleton."

"There's no one in there," he said decidedly. "It was either your imagination or something you ate. Or possibly one of the maids was sick."

Seeming to dismiss the matter without effort he changed the subject.

The day passed quickly. At lunch Mr. Whitney seemed to have forgotten his temper of the previous night; he was as nervously enthusiastic as ever; and watching him Myra again had that impression that she had seen him somewhere before. She and Knowleton paid another visit to Mrs. Whitney—and again the poodles stirred uneasily and set up a barking, to be summarily silenced by the harsh throaty voice. The conversation was short and of inquisitional flavor. It was terminated as before by the lady's drowsy eyelids and a pæan of farewell from the dogs.

In the evening she found that Mr. Whitney had insisted on organizing an informal neighborhood vaudeville. A stage had been erected in the ballroom and Myra sat beside Knowleton in the front row and watched proceedings curiously. Two slim and haughty ladies sang, a man performed some ancient card tricks, a girl gave impersonations, and then to Myra's astonishment Mr. Whitney appeared and did a rather effective buck-and-wing dance. There was something inexpressibly weird in the motion of the well-known financier flitting solemnly back and forth across the stage on his tiny feet. Yet he danced well, with an effortless grace and an unexpected suppleness, and he was rewarded with a storm of applause.

In the half-dark the lady on her left suddenly spoke to her.

"Mr. Whitney is passing the word along that he wants to see you behind the scenes."

Puzzled, Myra rose and ascended the side flight of stairs that led to the raised platform. Her host was waiting for her anxiously.

"Ah," he chuckled, "splendid!"

He held out his hand, and wonderingly she took it. Before she realized his intention he had half led, half drawn her out onto the stage. The spotlight's glare bathed them, and the ripple of conversation washing the audience ceased. The faces before her were pallid splotches on the gloom and she felt her ears burning as she waited for Mr. Whitney to speak.

"Ladies and gentlemen," he began, "most of you know Miss Myra Harper. You had the honor of meeting her last night. She is a delicious girl, I assure you. I am in a position to know. She intends to become the wife of my son."

He paused and nodded and began clapping his hands. The audience immediately took up the clapping and Myra stood there in motionless horror, overcome by the most violent confusion of her life.

The piping voice went on: "Miss Harper is not only beautiful but talented. Last night she confided to me that she sang. I asked whether she preferred the opera, the ballad or the popular song, and she confessed that her taste ran to the latter. Miss Harper will now favor us with a popular song."

And then Myra was standing alone on the stage, rigid with embarrassment. She fancied that on the faces in front of her she saw critical expectation, boredom, ironic disapproval. Surely this was the height of bad form—to drop a guest unprepared into such a situation.

In the first hush she considered a word or two explaining that Mr. Whitney had been under a misapprehension—then anger came to her assistance. She tossed her head and those in front saw her lips close together sharply.

Advancing to the platform's edge she said succinctly to the orchestra leader: "Have you got 'Wave That Wishbone'?"

"Lemme see. Yes, we got it."

"All right. Let's go!"

She hurriedly reviewed the words, which she had learned quite by accident at a dull house party the previous summer. It was perhaps not the song she would have chosen for her first public appearance, but it would have to do. She smiled radiantly, nodded at the orchestra leader and began the verse in a light clear alto.

As she sang a spirit of ironic humor slowly took possession of her—a desire to give them all a run for their money. And she did. She injected an East Side snarl into every word of slang; she ragged; she shimmied; she did a tickle-toe step she had learned once in an amateur musical comedy; and in a burst of inspiration finished up in an Al Jolson position, on her knees with her arms stretched out to her audience in syncopated appeal.

Then she rose, bowed and left the stage.

For an instant there was silence, the silence of a cold tomb; then perhaps half a dozen hands joined in a faint, perfunctory applause that in a second had died completely away.

"Heavens!" thought Myra. "Was it as bad as all that? Or did I shock 'em?"

Mr. Whitney, however, seemed delighted. He was waiting for her in the wings and seizing her hand shook it enthusiastically.

"Quite wonderful!" he chuckled. "You are a delightful little actress—and you'll be a valuable addition to our little plays. Would you like to give an encore?"

"No!" said Myra shortly, and turned away.

In a shadowy corner she waited until the crowd had filed out, with an angry unwillingness to face them immediately after their rejection of her effort.

When the ballroom was quite empty she walked slowly up the stairs, and there she came upon Knowleton and Mr. Whitney alone in the dark hall, evidently engaged in a heated argument.

They ceased when she appeared and looked toward her eagerly.

"Myra," said Mr. Whitney, "Knowleton wants to talk to you."

"Father," said Knowleton intensely, "I ask you——"

"Silence!" cried his father, his voice ascending testily. "You'll do your duty—now."

Knowleton cast one more appealing glance at him, but Mr. Whitney only shook his head excitedly and, turning, disappeared phantomlike up the stairs.

Knowleton stood silent a moment and finally with a look of dogged determination took her hand and led her toward a room that opened off the hall at the back. The yellow light fell through the door after them and she found herself in a dark wide chamber where she could just distinguish on the walls great square shapes which she took to be frames. Knowleton pressed a button, and immediately forty portraits sprang into life—old gallants from colonial days, ladies with floppity Gainsborough hats, fat women with ruffs and placid clasped hands.

She turned to Knowleton inquiringly, but he led her forward to a row of pictures on the side.

"Myra," he said slowly and painfully, "there's something I have to tell you. These"—he indicated the pictures with his hand—"are family portraits."

There were seven of them, three men and three women, all of them of the period just before the Civil War. The one in the middle, however, was hidden by crimson velvet curtains.

"Ironic as it may seem," continued Knowleton steadily, "that frame contains a picture of my great-grandmother."

Reaching out, he pulled a little silken cord and the curtains parted, to expose a portrait of a lady dressed as a European but with the unmistakable features of a Chinese.

"My great-grandfather, you see, was an Australian tea importer. He met his future wife in Hong-Kong."

Myra's brain was whirling. She had a sudden vision of Mr. Whitney's yellowish face, peculiar eyebrows and tiny hands and feet—she remembered ghastly tales she had heard of reversions to type—of Chinese babies—and then with a final surge of horror she thought of that sudden hushed cry in the night. She gasped, her knees seemed to crumple up and she sank slowly to the floor.

In a second Knowleton's arms were round her.

"Dearest, dearest!" he cried. "I shouldn't have told you! I shouldn't have told you!"

As he said this Myra knew definitely and unmistakably that she could never marry him, and when she realized it she cast at him a wild pitiful look, and for the first time in her life fainted dead away.

IV

When she next recovered full consciousness she was in bed. She imagined a maid had undressed her, for on turning up the reading lamp she saw that her clothes had been neatly put away. For a minute she lay there, listening idly while the hall clock struck two, and then her overwrought nerves jumped in terror as she heard again that child's cry from the room next door. The morning seemed suddenly infinitely far away. There was some shadowy secret near her—her feverish imagination pictured a Chinese child brought up there in the half-dark.

In a quick panic she crept into a negligee and, throwing open the door, slipped down the corridor toward Knowleton's room. It was very dark in the other wing, but when she pushed open his door she could see by the faint hall light that his bed was empty and had not been slept in. Her terror increased. What could take him out at this hour of the night? She started for Mrs. Whitney's room, but at the thought of the dogs and her bare ankles she gave a little discouraged cry and passed by the door.

Then she suddenly heard the sound of Knowleton's voice issuing from a faint crack of light far down the corridor, and with a glow of joy she fled toward it. When she was within a foot of the door she found she could see through the crack—and after one glance all thought of entering left her.

Before an open fire, his head bowed in an attitude of great dejection, stood Knowleton, and in the corner, feet perched on the table, sat Mr. Whitney in his shirt sleeves, very quiet and calm, and pulling contentedly on a huge black pipe. Seated on the table was a part of Mrs. Whitney—that is, Mrs. Whitney without any hair. Out of the familiar great bust projected Mrs. Whitney's head, but she was bald; on her cheeks was the faint stubble of a beard, and in her mouth was a large black cigar, which she was puffing with obvious enjoyment.

"A thousand," groaned Knowleton as if in answer to a question. "Say twenty-five hundred and you'll be nearer the truth. I got a bill from the Graham Kennels today for those poodle dogs. They're soaking me two hundred and saying that they've got to have 'em back tomorrow."

"Well," said Mrs. Whitney in a low barytone voice, "send 'em back. We're through with 'em."

"That's a mere item," continued Knowleton glumly. "Including your salary, and Appleton's here, and that fellow who did the chauffeur, and seventy supes for two nights, and an orchestra—that's nearly twelve hundred, and then there's the rent on the costumes and that darn Chinese portrait and the bribes to the servants. Lord! There'll probably be bills for one thing or another coming in for the next month."

"Well, then," said Appleton, "for pity's sake pull yourself together and carry it through to the end. Take my word for it, that girl will be out of the house by twelve noon."

Knowleton sank into a chair and covered his face with his hands.

"Oh——"

"Brace up! It's all over. I thought for a minute there in the hall that you were going to balk at that Chinese business."

"It was the vaudeville that knocked the spots out of me," groaned Knowleton. "It was about the meanest trick ever pulled on any girl, and she was so darned game about it!"

"She had to be," said Mrs. Whitney cynically.

"Oh, Kelly, if you could have seen the girl look at me tonight just before she fainted in front of that picture. Lord, I believe she loves me! Oh, if you could have seen her!"

Outside Myra flushed crimson. She leaned closer to the door, biting her lip until she could taste the faintly bitter savor of blood.

"If there was anything I could do now," continued Knowleton—"anything in the world that would smooth it over I believe I'd do it."

Kelly crossed ponderously over, his bald shiny head ludicrous above his feminine negligee, and put his hand on Knowleton's shoulder.

"See here, my boy—your trouble is just nerves. Look at it this way: You undertook somep'n to get yourself out of an awful mess. It's a cinch the girl was after your money—now you've beat her at her own game an' saved yourself an unhappy marriage and your family a lot of suffering. Ain't that so, Appleton?"

"Absolutely!" said Appleton emphatically. "Go through with it."

"Well," said Knowleton with a dismal attempt to be righteous, "if she really loved me she wouldn't have let it all affect her this much. She's not marrying my family."

Appleton laughed.

"I thought we'd tried to make it pretty obvious that she is."

"Oh, shut up!" cried Knowleton miserably.

Myra saw Appleton wink at Kelly.

"'At's right," he said; "she's shown she was after your money. Well, now then, there's no reason for not going through with it. See here. On one side you've proved she didn't love you and you're rid of her and free as air. She'll creep away and never say a word about it—and your family never the wiser. On the other side twenty-five hundred thrown to the bow-wows, miserable marriage, girl sure to hate you as soon as she finds out, and your family all broken up and probably disownin' you for marryin' her. One big mess, I'll tell the world."

"You're right," admitted Knowleton gloomily. "You're right, I suppose—but oh, the look in that girl's face! She's probably in there now lying awake, listening to the Chinese baby——"

Appleton rose and yawned.

"Well——" he began.

But Myra waited to hear no more. Pulling her silk kimono close about her she sped like lightning down the soft corridor, to dive headlong and breathless into her room.

"My heavens!" she cried, clenching her hands in the darkness. "My heavens!"

V

Just before dawn Myra drowsed into a jumbled dream that seemed to act on through interminable hours. She awoke about seven and lay listlessly with one blue-veined arm hanging over the side of the bed. She who had danced in the dawn at many proms was very tired.

A clock outside her door struck the hour, and with her nervous start something seemed to collapse within her—she turned over and began to weep furiously into her pillow, her tangled hair spreading like a dark aura round her head. To her, Myra Harper, had been done this cheap vulgar trick by a man she had thought shy and kind.

Lacking the courage to come to her and tell her the truth he had gone into the highways and hired men to frighten her.

Between her fevered broken sobs she tried in vain to comprehend the workings of a mind which could have conceived this in all its subtlety. Her pride refused to let her think of it as a deliberate plan of Knowleton's. It was probably an idea fostered by this little actor Appleton or by the fat Kelly with his horrible poodles. But it was all unspeakable—unthinkable. It gave her an intense sense of shame.

But when she emerged from her room at eight o'clock and, disdaining breakfast, walked into the garden she was a very self-possessed young beauty, with dry cool eyes only faintly shadowed. The ground was firm and frosty with the promise of winter, and she found grey sky and dull air vaguely comforting and one with her mood. It was a day for thinking and she needed to think.

And then turning a corner suddenly she saw Knowleton seated on a stone bench, his head in his hands, in an attitude of profound dejection. He wore his clothes of the night before and it was quite evident that he had not been to bed.

He did not hear her until she was quite close to him, and then as a dry twig snapped under her heel he looked up wearily. She saw that the night had played havoc with him—his face was deathly pale and his eyes were pink and puffed and tired. He jumped up with a look that was very like dread.

"Good morning," said Myra quietly.

"Sit down," he began nervously. "Sit down; I want to talk to you! I've got to talk to you."

Myra nodded and taking a seat beside him on the bench clasped her knees with her hands and half closed her eyes.

"Myra, for heaven's sake have pity on me!"

She turned wondering eyes on him.

"What do you mean?"

He groaned.

"Myra, I've done a ghastly thing—to you, to me, to us. I haven't a word to say in favor of myself—I've been just rotten. I think it was a sort of madness that came over me."

"You'll have to give me a clue to what you're talking about."

"Myra—Myra"—like all large bodies his confession seemed difficult to imbue with momentum—"Myra—Mr. Whitney is not my father."

"You mean you were adopted?"

"No; I mean—Ludlow Whitney is my father, but this man you've met isn't Ludlow Whitney."

"I know," said Myra coolly. "He's Warren Appleton, the actor."

Knowleton leaped to his feet.

"How on earth——"

"Oh," lied Myra easily, "I recognized him the first night. I saw him five years ago in 'The Swiss Grapefruit.'"

At this Knowleton seemed to collapse utterly. He sank down limply onto the bench.

"You knew?"

"Of course! How could I help it? It simply made me wonder what it was all about."

With a great effort he tried to pull himself together.

"I'm going to tell you the whole story, Myra."

"I'm all ears."

"Well, it starts with my mother—my real one, not the woman with those idiotic dogs; she's an invalid and I'm her only child. Her one idea in life has always been for me to make a fitting match, and her idea of a fitting match centers round social position in England. Her greatest disappointment was that I wasn't a girl so I could marry a title; instead she wanted to drag me to England—marry me off to the sister of an earl or the daughter of a duke. Why, before she'd let me stay up here alone this fall she made me promise I wouldn't go to see any girl more than twice. And then I met you."

He paused for a second and continued earnestly: "You were the first girl in my life whom I ever thought of marrying. You intoxicated me, Myra. It was just as though you were making me love you by some invisible force."

"I was," murmured Myra.

"Well, that first intoxication lasted a week, and then one day a letter came from mother saying she was bringing home some wonderful English girl, Lady Helena Something-or-Other. And the same day a man told me that he'd heard I'd been caught by the most famous husband hunter in New York. Well, between these two things I went half-crazy. I came into town to see you and call it off—got as far as the Biltmore entrance and didn't dare. I started wandering down Fifth Avenue like a wild man, and then I met Kelly. I told him the whole story—and within an hour we'd hatched up this ghastly plan. It was his plan—all the details. His histrionic instinct got the better of him and he had me thinking it was the kindest way out."

"Finish," commanded Myra crisply.

"Well, it went splendidly, we thought. Everything—the station meeting, the dinner scene, the scream in the night, the vaudeville—though I thought that was a little too much until—until—— Oh, Myra, when you fainted under that picture and I held you there in my arms, helpless as a baby, I knew I loved you. I was sorry then, Myra."

There was a long pause while she sat motionless, her hands still clasping her knees—then he burst out with a wild plea of passionate sincerity.

"Myra!" he cried. "If by any possible chance you can bring yourself to forgive and forget I'll marry you when you say, let my family go to the devil, and love you all my life."

For a long while she considered, and Knowleton rose and began pacing nervously up and down the aisle of bare bushes, his hands in his pockets, his tired eyes pathetic now, and full of dull appeal. And then she came to a decision.

"You're perfectly sure?" she asked calmly.

"Yes."

"Very well, I'll marry you today."

With her words the atmosphere cleared and his troubles seemed to fall from him like a ragged cloak. An Indian summer sun drifted out from behind the grey clouds and the dry bushes rustled gently in the breeze.

"It was a bad mistake," she continued, "but if you're sure you love me now, that's the main thing. We'll go to town this morning, get a license, and I'll call up my cousin, who's a minister in the First Presbyterian Church. We can go West tonight."

"Myra!" he cried jubilantly. "You're a marvel and I'm not fit to tie your shoe strings. I'm going to make up to you for this, darling girl."

And taking her supple body in his arms he covered her face with kisses.

The next two hours passed in a whirl. Myra went to the telephone and called her cousin, and then rushed upstairs to pack. When she came down a shining roadster was waiting miraculously in the drive and by ten o'clock they were bowling happily toward the city.

They stopped for a few minutes at the City Hall and again at the jeweler's, and then they were in the house of the Reverend Walter Gregory on 69th Street, where a sanctimonious gentleman with twinkling eyes and a slight stutter received them cordially and urged them to a breakfast of bacon and eggs before the ceremony.

On the way to the station they stopped only long enough to wire Knowleton's father, and then they were sitting in their compartment on the Broadway Limited.

"Darn!" exclaimed Myra. "I forgot my bag. Left it at Cousin Walter's in the excitement."

"Never mind. We can get a whole new outfit in Chicago."

She glanced at her wrist watch.

"I've got time to telephone him to send it on."

She rose.

"Don't be long, dear."

She leaned down and kissed his forehead.

"You know I couldn't. Two minutes, honey."

Outside Myra ran swiftly along the platform and up the steel stairs to the great waiting room, where a man met her—a twinkly-eyed man with a slight stutter.

"How d-did it go, M-myra?"

"Fine! Oh, Walter, you were splendid! I almost wish you'd join the ministry so you could officiate when I do get married."

"Well—I r-rehearsed for half an hour after I g-got your telephone call."

"Wish we'd had more time. I'd have had him lease an apartment and buy furniture."

"H'm," chuckled Walter. "Wonder how far he'll go on his honeymoon."

"Oh, he'll think I'm on the train till he gets to Elizabeth." She shook her little fist at the great contour of the marble dome. "Oh, he's getting off too easy—far too easy!"

"I haven't f-figured out what the f-fellow did to you, M-myra."

"You never will, I hope."

They had reached the side drive and he hailed her a taxi-cab.

"You're an angel!" beamed Myra. "And I can't thank you enough."

"Well, anytime I can be of use t-to you—— By the way, what are you going to do with all the rings?"

Myra looked laughingly at her hand.

"That's the question," she said. "I may send them to Lady Helena Something-or-Other—and—well, I've always had a strong penchant for souvenirs. Tell the driver 'Biltmore,' Walter."

THE SMILERS

I

We all have that exasperated moment!

There are times when you almost tell the harmless old lady next door what you really think of her face—that it ought to be on a night-nurse in a house for the blind; when you'd like to ask the man you've been waiting ten minutes for if he isn't all overheated from racing the postman down the block; when you nearly say to the waiter that if they deducted a cent from the bill for every degree the soup was below tepid the hotel would owe you half a dollar; when—and this is the infallible earmark of true exasperation—a smile affects you as an oil-baron's undershirt affects a cow's husband.

But the moment passes. Scars may remain on your dog or your collar or your telephone receiver, but your soul has slid gently back into its place between the lower edge of your heart and the upper edge of your stomach, and all is at peace.

But the imp who turns on the shower-bath of exasperation apparently made it so hot one time in Sylvester Stockton's early youth that he never dared dash in and turn it off—in consequence no first old man in an amateur production of a Victorian comedy was ever more pricked and prodded by the daily phenomena of life than was Sylvester at thirty.

Accusing eyes behind spectacles—suggestion of a stiff neck—this will have to do for his description, since he is not the hero of this story. He is the plot. He is the factor that makes it one story instead of three stories. He makes remarks at the beginning and end.

The late afternoon sun was loitering pleasantly along Fifth Avenue when Sylvester, who had just come out of that hideous public library where he had been consulting some ghastly book, told his impossible chauffeur (it is true that I am following his movements through his own spectacles) that he wouldn't need his stupid, incompetent

services any longer. Swinging his cane (which he found too short) in his left hand (which he should have cut off long ago since it was constantly offending him), he began walking slowly down the Avenue.

When Sylvester walked at night he frequently glanced behind and on both sides to see if anyone was sneaking up on him. This had become a constant mannerism. For this reason he was unable to pretend that he didn't see Betty Tearle sitting in her machine in front of Tiffany's.

Back in his early twenties he had been in love with Betty Tearle. But he had depressed her. He had misanthropically dissected every meal, motor trip and musical comedy that they attended together, and on the few occasions when she had tried to be especially nice to him—from a mother's point of view he had been rather desirable—he had suspected hidden motives and fallen into a deeper gloom than ever. Then one day she told him that she would go mad if he ever again parked his pessimism in her sun-parlor.

And ever since then she had seemed to be smiling—uselessly, insultingly, charmingly smiling.

"Hello, Sylvo," she called.

"Why—how do Betty." He wished she wouldn't call him Sylvo—it sounded like a—like a darn monkey or something.

"How goes it?" she asked cheerfully. "Not very well, I suppose."

"Oh, yes," he answered stiffly, "I manage."

"Taking in the happy crowd?"

"Heavens, yes." He looked around him. "Betty, why are they happy? What are they smiling at? What do they find to smile at?"

Betty flashed at him a glance of radiant amusement.

"The women may smile because they have pretty teeth, Sylvo."

"You smile," continued Sylvester cynically, "because you're comfortably married and have two children. You imagine you're happy, so you suppose everyone else is."

Betty nodded.

"You may have hit it, Sylvo——" The chauffeur glanced around and she nodded at him. "Good-bye."

Sylvo watched with a pang of envy which turned suddenly to exasperation as he saw she had turned and smiled at him once

more. Then her car was out of sight in the traffic, and with a voluminous sigh he galvanized his cane into life and continued his stroll.

At the next corner he stopped in at a cigar store and there he ran into Waldron Crosby. Back in the days when Sylvester had been a prize pigeon in the eyes of debutantes he had also been a game partridge from the point of view of promoters. Crosby, then a young bond salesman, had given him much safe and sane advice and saved him many dollars. Sylvester liked Crosby as much as he could like anyone. Most people did like Crosby.

"Hello, you old bag of 'nerves,'" cried Crosby genially, "come and have a big gloom-dispelling Corona."

Sylvester regarded the cases anxiously. He knew he wasn't going to like what he bought.

"Still out at Larchmont, Waldron?" he asked.

"Right-o."

"How's your wife?"

"Never better."

"Well," said Sylvester suspiciously, "you brokers always look as if you're smiling at something up your sleeve. It must be a hilarious profession."

Crosby considered.

"Well," he admitted, "it varies—like the moon and the price of soft drinks—but it has its moments."

"Waldron," said Sylvester earnestly, "you're a friend of mine—please do me the favor of not smiling when I leave you. It seems like a—like a mockery."

A broad grin suffused Crosby's countenance.

"Why, you crabbed old son-of-a-gun!"

But Sylvester with an irate grunt had turned on his heel and disappeared.

He strolled on. The sun finished its promenade and began calling in the few stray beams it had left among the westward streets. The Avenue darkened with black bees from the department stores; the traffic swelled into an interlaced jam; the busses were packed four deep like platforms above the thick crowd; but Sylvester, to whom the daily shift and change of the city was a matter only of sordid

monotony, walked on, taking only quick sideward glances through his frowning spectacles.

He reached his hotel and was elevated to his four-room suite on the twelfth floor.

"If I dine downstairs," he thought, "the orchestra will play either 'Smile, Smile, Smile' or 'The Smiles that You Gave to Me.' But then if I go to the Club I'll meet all the cheerful people I know, and if I go somewhere else where there's no music, I won't get anything fit to eat."

He decided to have dinner in his rooms.

An hour later, after disparaging some broth, a squab and a salad, he tossed fifty cents to the room waiter, and then held up his hand warningly.

"Just oblige me by not smiling when you say thanks?"

He was too late. The waiter had grinned.

"Now, will you please tell me," asked Sylvester peevishly, "what on earth you have to smile about?"

The waiter considered. Not being a reader of the magazines he was not sure what was characteristic of waiters, yet he supposed something characteristic was expected of him.

"Well, Mister," he answered, glancing at the ceiling with all the ingenuousness he could muster in his narrow, sallow countenance, "it's just something my face does when it sees four bits comin'."

Sylvester waved him away.

"Waiters are happy because they've never had anything better," he thought. "They haven't enough imagination to want anything."

At nine o'clock from sheer boredom he sought his expressionless bed.

II

As Sylvester left the cigar store, Waldron Crosby followed him out, and turning off Fifth Avenue down a cross street entered a brokerage office. A plump man with nervous hands rose and hailed him.

"Hello, Waldron."

"Hello, Potter—I just dropped in to hear the worst."

The plump man frowned.

"We've just got the news," he said.

"Well, what is it. Another drop?"

"Closed at seventy-eight. Sorry, old boy."

"Whew!"

"Hit pretty hard?"

"Cleaned out!"

The plump man shook his head, indicating that life was too much for him, and turned away.

Crosby sat there for a moment without moving. Then he rose, walked into Potter's private office and picked up the phone.

"Gi'me Larchmont 838."

In a moment he had his connection.

"Mrs. Crosby there?"

A man's voice answered him.

"Yes; this you, Crosby? This is Doctor Shipman."

"Dr. Shipman?" Crosby's voice showed sudden anxiety.

"Yes—I've been trying to reach you all afternoon. The situation's changed and we expect the child tonight."

"Tonight?"

"Yes. Everything's O.K. But you'd better come right out."

"I will. Good-bye."

He hung up the receiver and started out the door, but paused as an idea struck him. He returned, and this time called a Manhattan number.

"Hello, Donny, this is Crosby."

"Hello, there, old boy. You just caught me; I was going——"

"Say, Donny, I want a job right away, quick."

"For whom?"

"For me."

"Why, what's the——"

"Never mind. Tell you later. Got one for me?"

"Why, Waldron, there's not a blessed thing here except a clerkship. Perhaps next——"

"What salary goes with the clerkship?"

"Forty—say forty-five a week."

"I've got you. I start tomorrow."

"All right. But say, old man——"

"Sorry, Donny, but I've got to run."

Crosby hurried from the brokerage office with a wave and a smile at Potter. In the street he took out a handful of small change and after surveying it critically hailed a taxi.

"Grand Central—quick!" he told the driver.

III

At six o'clock Betty Tearle signed the letter, put it into an envelope and wrote her husband's name upon it. She went into his room and after a moment's hesitation set a black cushion on the bed and laid the white letter on it so that it could not fail to attract his attention when he came in. Then with a quick glance around the room she walked into the hall and upstairs to the nursery.

"Clare," she called softly.

"Oh, Mummy!" Clare left her doll's house and scurried to her mother.

"Where's Billy, Clare?"

Billy appeared eagerly from under the bed.

"Got anything for me?" he inquired politely.

His mother's laugh ended in a little catch and she caught both her children to her and kissed them passionately. She found that she was crying quietly and their flushed little faces seemed cool against the sudden fever racing through her blood.

"Take care of Clare—always—Billy darling——"

Billy was puzzled and rather awed.

"You're crying," he accused gravely.

"I know—I know I am——"

Clare gave a few tentative sniffles, hesitated, and then clung to her mother in a storm of weeping.

"I d-don't feel good, Mummy—I don't feel good."

Betty soothed her quietly.

"We won't cry any more, Clare dear—either of us."

But as she rose to leave the room her glance at Billy bore a mute appeal, too vain, she knew, to be registered on his childish consciousness.

Half an hour later as she carried her traveling bag to a taxi-cab at the door she raised her hand to her face in mute admission that a veil served no longer to hide her from the world.

"But I've chosen," she thought dully.

As the car turned the corner she wept again, resisting a temptation to give up and go back.

"Oh, my God!" she whispered. "What am I doing? What have I done? What have I done?"

IV

When Jerry, the sallow, narrow-faced waiter, left Sylvester's rooms he reported to the head-waiter, and then checked out for the day.

He took the subway south and alighting at Williams Street walked a few blocks and entered a billiard parlor.

An hour later he emerged with a cigarette drooping from his bloodless lips, and stood on the sidewalk as if hesitating before making a decision. He set off eastward.

As he reached a certain corner his gait suddenly increased and then quite as suddenly slackened. He seemed to want to pass by, yet some magnetic attraction was apparently exerted on him, for with a sudden face-about he turned in at the door of a cheap restaurant—half-cabaret, half chop-suey parlor—where a miscellaneous assortment gathered nightly.

Jerry found his way to a table situated in the darkest and most obscure corner. Seating himself with a contempt for his surroundings that betokened familiarity rather than superiority he ordered a glass of claret.

The evening had begun. A fat woman at the piano was expelling the last jauntiness from a hackneyed fox-trot, and a lean, dispirited male was assisting her with lean, dispirited notes from a violin. The attention of the patrons was directed at a dancer wearing soiled stockings and done largely in peroxide and rouge who was about

to step upon a small platform, meanwhile exchanging pleasantries with a fat, eager person at the table beside her who was trying to capture her hand.

Over in the corner Jerry watched the two by the platform and, as he gazed, the ceiling seemed to fade out, the walls growing into tall buildings and the platform becoming the top of a Fifth Avenue bus on a breezy spring night three years ago. The fat, eager person disappeared, the short skirt of the dancer rolled down and the rouge faded from her cheeks—and he was beside her again in an old delirious ride, with the lights blinking kindly at them from the tall buildings beside and the voices of the street merging into a pleasant somnolent murmur around them.

"Jerry," said the girl on top of the bus, "I've said that when you were gettin' seventy-five I'd take a chance with you. But, Jerry, I can't wait forever."

Jerry watched several street numbers sail by before he answered.

"I don't know what's the matter," he said helplessly, "they won't raise me. If I can locate a new job——"

"You better hurry, Jerry," said the girl; "I'm gettin' sick of just livin' along. If I can't get married I got a couple of chances to work in a cabaret—get on the stage maybe."

"You keep out of that," said Jerry quickly. "There ain't no need, if you just wait about another month or two."

"I can't wait forever, Jerry," repeated the girl. "I'm tired of stayin' poor alone."

"It won't be so long," said Jerry clenching his free hand. "I can make it somewhere, if you'll just wait."

But the bus was fading out and the ceiling was taking shape and the murmur of the April streets was fading into the rasping whine of the violin—for that was all three years before and now he was sitting here.

The girl glanced up on the platform and exchanged a metallic impersonal smile with the dispirited violinist, and Jerry shrank farther back in his corner watching her with burning intensity.

"Your hands belong to anybody that wants them now," he cried silently and bitterly. "I wasn't man enough to keep you out of that—not man enough, by God, by God!"

But the girl by the door still toyed with the fat man's clutching fingers as she waited for her time to dance.

V

Sylvester Stockton tossed restlessly upon his bed. The room, big as it was, smothered him, and a breeze drifting in and bearing with it a rift of moon seemed laden only with the cares of the world he would have to face next day.

"They don't understand," he thought. "They don't see, as I do, the underlying misery of the whole damn thing. They're hollow optimists. They smile because they think they're always going to be happy.

"Oh, well," he mused drowsily, "I'll run up to Rye tomorrow and endure more smiles and more heat. That's all life is—just smiles and heat, smiles and heat."

THE POPULAR GIRL

Along about half past ten every Saturday night Yanci Bowman eluded her partner by some graceful subterfuge and from the dancing floor went to a point of vantage overlooking the country-club bar. When she saw her father she would either beckon to him, if he chanced to be looking in her direction, or else she would dispatch a waiter to call attention to her impendent presence. If it were no later than half past ten—that is, if he had had no more than an hour of synthetic gin rickeys—he would get up from his chair and suffer himself to be persuaded into the ballroom.

"Ballroom," for want of a better word. It was that room, filled by day with wicker furniture, which was always connotated in the phrase "Let's go in and dance." It was referred to as "inside" or "downstairs." It was that nameless chamber wherein occur the principal transactions of all the country clubs in America.

Yanci knew that if she could keep her father there for an hour, talking, watching her dance, or even on rare occasions dancing himself, she could safely release him at the end of that time. In the period that would elapse before midnight ended the dance, he could scarcely become sufficiently stimulated to annoy anyone.

All this entailed considerable exertion on Yanci's part, and it was less for her father's sake than for her own that she went through with it. Several rather unpleasant experiences were scattered through this past summer. One night when she had been detained by the impassioned and impossible-to-interrupt speech of a young man from Chicago her father had appeared swaying gently in the ballroom doorway; in his ruddy handsome face two faded blue eyes were squinted half-shut as he tried to focus them on the dancers, and he was obviously preparing to offer himself to the first dowager who caught his eye. He was ludicrously injured when Yanci insisted upon an immediate withdrawal.

After that night Yanci went through her Fabian maneuver to the minute.

Yanci and her father were the handsomest two people in the Middle Western city where they lived. Tom Bowman's complexion was hearty from twenty years spent in the service of good whisky and bad golf. He kept an office downtown, where he was thought to transact some vague real-estate business; but in point of fact his chief concern in life was the exhibition of a handsome profile and an easy well-bred manner at the country club, where he had spent the greater part of the ten years that had elapsed since his wife's death.

Yanci was twenty, with a vague die-away manner which was partly the setting for her languid disposition and partly the effect of a visit she had paid to some Eastern relatives at an impressionable age. She was intelligent, in a flitting way, romantic under the moon and unable to decide whether to marry for sentiment or for comfort, the latter of these two abstractions being well enough personified by one of the most ardent among her admirers. Meanwhile she kept house, not without efficiency, for her father, and tried in a placid unruffled tempo to regulate his constant tippling to the sober side of inebriety.

She admired her father. She admired him for his fine appearance and for his charming manner. He had never quite lost the air of having been a popular Bones man at Yale. This charm of his was a standard by which her susceptible temperament unconsciously judged the men she knew. Nevertheless, father and daughter were far from that sentimental family relationship which is a stock plant in fiction, but in life usually exists in the mind of only the older party to it. Yanci Bowman had decided to leave her home by marriage within the year. She was heartily bored.

Scott Kimberly, who saw her for the first time this November evening at the country club, agreed with the lady whose house guest he was that Yanci was an exquisite little beauty. With a sort of conscious sensuality surprising in such a young man—Scott was only twenty-five—he avoided an introduction that he might watch her undisturbed for a fanciful hour, and sip the pleasure or the disillusion of her conversation at the drowsy end of the evening.

"She never got over the disappointment of not meeting the Prince of Wales when he was in this country," remarked Mrs. Orrin Rogers, following his gaze. "She said so, anyhow; whether she was serious or not I don't know. I hear that she has her walls simply plastered with pictures of him."

"Who?" asked Scott suddenly.

"Why, the Prince of Wales."

"Who has plaster pictures of him?"

"Why, Yanci Bowman, the girl you said you thought was so pretty."

"After a certain degree of prettiness, one pretty girl is as pretty as another," said Scott argumentatively.

"Yes, I suppose so."

Mrs. Rogers' voice drifted off on an indefinite note. She had never in her life compassed a generality until it had fallen familiarly on her ear from constant repetition.

"Let's talk her over," Scott suggested.

With a mock reproachful smile Mrs. Rogers lent herself agreeably to slander. An encore was just beginning. The orchestra trickled a light overflow of music into the pleasant green-latticed room and the two score couples who for the evening comprised the local younger set moved placidly into time with its beat. Only a few apathetic stags gathered one by one in the doorways, and to a close observer it was apparent that the scene did not attain the gayety which was its aspiration. These girls and men had known each other from childhood; and though there were marriages incipient upon the floor tonight, they were marriages of environment, of resignation, or even of boredom.

Their trappings lacked the sparkle of the seventeen-year-old affairs that took place through the short and radiant holidays. On such occasions as this, thought Scott as his eyes still sought casually for Yanci, occurred the matings of the left-overs, the plainer, the duller, the poorer of the social world; matings actuated by the same urge toward perhaps a more glamorous destiny, yet, for all that, less beautiful and less young. Scott himself was feeling very old.

But there was one face in the crowd to which his generalization did not apply. When his eyes found Yanci Bowman among the dancers he felt much younger. She was the incarnation of all in which the dance failed—graceful youth, arrogant, languid freshness and beauty that was sad and perishable as a memory in a dream. Her partner, a young man with one of those fresh red complexions ribbed with white streaks, as though he had been slapped on a cold day, did not appear to be holding her interest, and her glance fell here and there upon a group, a face, a garment, with a far-away and oblivious melancholy.

"Dark-blue eyes," said Scott to Mrs. Rogers. "I don't know that they mean anything except that they're beautiful, but that nose and upper lip and chin are certainly aristocratic—if there is any such thing," he added apologetically.

"Oh, she's very aristocratic," agreed Mrs. Rogers. "Her grandfather was a senator or governor or something in one of the Southern states. Her father's very aristocratic-looking too. Oh, yes, they're very aristocratic; they're aristocratic people."

"She looks lazy."

Scott was watching the yellow gown drift and submerge among the dancers.

"She doesn't like to move. It's a wonder she dances so well. Is she engaged? Who is the man who keeps cutting in on her, the one who tucks his tie under his collar so rakishly and affects the remarkable slanting pockets?"

He was annoyed at the young man's persistence, and his sarcasm lacked the ring of detachment.

"Oh, that's"—Mrs. Rogers bent forward, the tip of her tongue just visible between her lips—"that's the O'Rourke boy. He's quite devoted, I believe."

"I believe," Scott said suddenly, "that I'll get you to introduce me if she's near when the music stops."

They arose and stood looking for Yanci—Mrs. Rogers, small, stoutening, nervous, and Scott Kimberly, her husband's cousin, dark and just below medium height. Scott was an orphan with half a million of his own, and he was in this city for no more reason than that he had missed a train. They looked for several minutes, and in vain. Yanci, in her yellow dress, no longer moved with slow loveliness among the dancers.

The clock stood at half past ten.

II

"Good evening," her father was saying to her at that moment in syllables faintly slurred. "This seems to be getting to be a habit."

They were standing near a side stairs, and over his shoulder through a glass door Yanci could see a party of half a dozen men sitting in familiar joviality about a round table.

"Don't you want to come out and watch for awhile?" she suggested, smiling and affecting a casualness she did not feel.

"Not tonight, thanks."

Her father's dignity was a bit too emphasized to be convincing.

"Just come out and take a look," she urged him. "Everybody's here, and I want to ask you what you think of somebody."

This was not so good, but it was the best that occurred to her.

"I doubt very strongly if I'd find anything to interest me out there," said Tom Bowman emphatically. "I observe that f'some insane reason I'm always taken out and aged on the wood for half an hour as though I was irresponsible."

"I only ask you to stay a little while."

"Very considerate, I'm sure. But tonight I happ'n be interested in a discussion that's taking place in here."

"Come on, Father."

Yanci put her arm through his ingratiatingly; but he released it by the simple expedient of raising his own arm and letting hers drop.

"I'm afraid not."

"I'll tell you," she suggested lightly, concealing her annoyance at this unusually protracted argument, "you come in and look, just once, and then if it bores you you can go right back."

He shook his head.

"No thanks."

Then without another word he turned suddenly and reentered the bar. Yanci went back to the ballroom. She glanced easily at the stag line as she passed, and making a quick selection murmured to a man near her, "Dance with me, will you, Carty? I've lost my partner."

"Glad to," answered Carty truthfully.

"Awfully sweet of you."

"Sweet of me? Of you, you mean."

She looked up at him absently. She was furiously annoyed at her father. Next morning at breakfast she would radiate a consuming chill, but for tonight she could only wait, hoping that if the worst happened he would at least remain in the bar until the dance was over.

Mrs. Rogers, who lived next door to the Bowmans, appeared suddenly at her elbow with a strange young man.

"Yanci," Mrs. Rogers was saying with a social smile. "I want to introduce Mr. Kimberly. Mr. Kimberly's spending the week-end with us, and I particularly wanted him to meet you."

"How perfectly slick!" drawled Yanci with lazy formality.

Mr. Kimberly suggested to Miss Bowman that they dance, to which proposal Miss Bowman dispassionately acquiesced. They mingled their arms in the gesture prevalent and stepped into time with the beat of the drum. Simultaneously it seemed to Scott that the room and the couples who danced up and down upon it converted themselves into a background behind her. The commonplace lamps, the rhythm of the music playing some paraphrase of a paraphrase, the faces of many girls, pretty, undistinguished or absurd, assumed a certain solidity as though they had grouped themselves in a retinue for Yanci's languid eyes and dancing feet.

"I've been watching you," said Scott simply. "You look rather bored this evening."

"Do I?" Her dark-blue eyes exposed a borderland of fragile iris as they opened in a delicate burlesque of interest. "How perfectly kill-ing!" she added.

Scott laughed. She had used the exaggerated phrase without smiling, indeed without any attempt to give it verisimilitude. He had heard the adjectives of the year—"hectic," "marvelous" and "slick"—delivered casually, but never before without the faintest meaning. In this lackadaisical young beauty it was inexpressibly charming.

The dance ended. Yanci and Scott strolled toward a lounge set against the wall, but before they could take possession there was a shriek of laughter and a brawny damsel dragging an embarrassed boy in her wake skidded by them and plumped down upon it.

"How rude!" observed Yanci.

"I suppose it's her privilege."

"A girl with ankles like that has no privileges."

They seated themselves uncomfortably on two stiff chairs.

"Where do you come from?" she asked of Scott with polite disinterest.

"New York."

This having transpired, Yanci deigned to fix her eyes on him for the best part of ten seconds.

"Who was the gentleman with the invisible tie," Scott asked rudely, in order to make her look at him again, "who was giving you such a rush? I found it impossible to keep my eyes off him. Is his personality as diverting as his haberdashery?"

"I don't know," she drawled; "I've only been engaged to him for a week."

"My Lord!" exclaimed Scott, perspiring suddenly under his eyes. "I beg your pardon. I didn't——"

"I was only joking," she interrupted with a sighing laugh. "I thought I'd see what you'd say to that."

Then they both laughed, and Yanci continued, "I'm not engaged to anyone. I'm too horribly unpopular." Still the same key, her languorous voice humorously contradicting the content of her remark. "No one'll ever marry me."

"How pathetic!"

"Really," she murmured; "because I have to have compliments all the time, in order to live, and no one thinks I'm attractive anymore, so no one ever gives them to me."

Seldom had Scott been so amused.

"Why, you beautiful child," he cried, "I'll bet you never hear anything else from morning till night!"

"Oh, yes I do," she responded, obviously pleased. "I never get compliments unless I fish for them."

"Everything's the same," she was thinking as she gazed around her in a peculiar mood of pessimism. Same boys sober and same boys tight; same old women sitting by the walls—and one or two girls sitting with them who were dancing this time last year.

Yanci had reached the stage where these country-club dances seemed little more than a display of sheer idiocy. From being an enchanted carnival where jeweled and immaculate maidens rouged to the pinkest propriety displayed themselves to strange and fascinating men, the picture had faded to a medium-sized hall where was an almost indecent display of unclothed motives and obvious failures. So much for several years! And the dance had changed scarcely by a ruffle in the fashions or a new flip in a figure of speech.

Yanci was ready to be married.

Meanwhile the dozen remarks rushing to Scott Kimberly's lips were interrupted by the apologetic appearance of Mrs. Rogers.

"Yanci," the older woman was saying, "the chauffeur's just telephoned to say that the car's broken down. I wonder if you and your father have room for us going home. If it's the slightest inconvenience don't hesitate to tell——"

"I know he'll be terribly glad to. He's got loads of room, because I came out with someone else."

She was wondering if her father would be presentable at twelve.

He could always drive at any rate—and, besides, people who asked for a lift could take what they got.

"That'll be lovely. Thank you so much," said Mrs. Rogers.

Then, as she had just passed the kittenish late thirties when women still think they are *persona grata* with the young and entered upon the early forties when their children convey to them tactfully that they no longer are, Mrs. Rogers obliterated herself from the scene. At that moment the music started and the unfortunate young man with white streaks in his red complexion appeared in front of Yanci.

Just before the end of the next dance Scott Kimberly cut in on her again.

"I've come back," he began, "to tell you how beautiful you are."

"I'm not, really," she answered. "And, besides, you tell everyone that."

The music gathered gusto for its finale, and they sat down upon the comfortable lounge.

"I've told no one that for three years," said Scott.

There was no reason why he should have made it three years, yet somehow it sounded convincing to both of them. Her curiosity was stirred. She began finding out about him. She put him to a lazy questionnaire which began with his relationship to the Rogerses and ended, he knew not by what steps, with a detailed description of his apartment in New York.

"I want to live in New York," she told him; "on Park Avenue, in one of those beautiful white buildings that have twelve big rooms in each apartment and cost a fortune to rent."

"That's what I'd want, too, if I were married. Park Avenue—it's one of the most beautiful streets in the world, I think, perhaps chiefly because it hasn't any leprous park trying to give it an artificial suburbanity."

"Whatever that is," agreed Yanci. "Anyway, Father and I go to New York about three times a year. We always go to the Ritz."

This was not precisely true. Once a year she generally pried her father from his placid and not unbeneficent existence that she might spend a week lolling by the Fifth Avenue shop windows, lunching or having tea with some former school friend from Farmover, and occasionally going to dinner and the theatre with boys who came up from Yale or Princeton for the occasion. These had been pleasant adventures—not one but was filled to the brim with colorful hours—dancing at Montmartre, dining at the Ritz, with some movie star or supereminent society woman at the next table, or else dreaming of what she might buy at Hempel's or Waxe's or Thrumble's if her father's income had but one additional naught on the happy side of the decimal. She adored New York with a great impersonal affection—adored it as only a Middle Western or Southern girl can. In its gaudy bazaars she felt her soul transported with turbulent delight, for to her eyes it held nothing ugly, nothing sordid, nothing plain.

She had stayed once at the Ritz—once only. The Manhattan, where they usually registered, had been torn down. She knew that she could never induce her father to afford the Ritz again.

After a moment she borrowed a pencil and paper and scribbled a notification "To Mr. Bowman in the grill" that he was expected to drive Mrs. Rogers and her guest home, "by request"—this last underlined. She hoped that he would be able to do so with dignity. This note she sent by a waiter to her father. Before the next dance began it was returned to her with a scrawled O.K. and her father's initials.

The remainder of the evening passed quickly. Scott Kimberly cut in on her as often as time permitted, giving her those comforting assurances of her enduring beauty which not without a whimsical pathos she craved. He laughed at her also, and she was not so sure that she liked that. In common with all vague people, she was unaware that she was vague. She did not entirely comprehend when Scott Kimberly told her that her personality would endure long after she was too old to care whether it endured or not.

She liked best to talk about New York, and each of their interrupted conversations gave her a picture or a memory of the metropolis on which she speculated as she looked over the shoulder of Jerry O'Rourke or Carty Braden or some other beau, to whom, as to all of them, she was comfortably anesthetic. At midnight she sent another note to her father, saying that Mrs. Rogers and Mrs. Rogers' guest would meet him immediately on the porch by the main driveway. Then, hoping for the best, she walked out into the starry night and was assisted by Jerry O'Rourke into his roadster.

III

"Good night, Yanci." With her late escort she was standing on the curbstone in front of the rented stucco house where she lived. Mr. O'Rourke was attempting to put significance into his lingering rendition of her name. For weeks he had been straining to boost their relations almost forcibly onto a sentimental plane; but Yanci, with her vague impassivity, which was a defense against almost anything, had brought to naught his efforts. Jerry O'Rourke was an old story. His family had money; but he—he worked in a brokerage house along with most of the rest of his young generation. He sold bonds—bonds were now the thing; real estate was once the thing—in the days of the boom; then automobiles were the thing. Bonds were the thing now. Young men sold them who had nothing else to go into.

"Don't bother to come up, please." Then as he put his car into gear, "Call me up soon!"

A minute later he turned the corner of the moonlit street and disappeared, his cut-out resounding voluminously through the night as it declared that the rest of two dozen weary inhabitants was of no concern to his gay meanderings.

Yanci sat down thoughtfully upon the porch steps. She had no key and must wait for her father's arrival. Five minutes later a roadster turned into the street, and approaching with an exaggerated caution stopped in front of the Rogers' large house next door. Relieved, Yanci arose and strolled slowly down the walk. The door of the car had swung open and Mrs. Rogers, assisted by Scott Kimberly, had alighted safely upon the sidewalk; but to Yanci's surprise Scott Kimberly, after escorting Mrs. Rogers to her steps, returned to the car. Yanci was close enough to notice that he took the driver's seat. As he drew up at the Bowmans' curbstone Yanci saw that her father was occupying the far corner, fighting with ludicrous dignity against a sleep that had come upon him. She groaned. The fatal last hour had done its work—Tom Bowman was once more *hors de combat.*

"Hello," cried Yanci as she reached the curb.

"Yanci," muttered her parent, simulating, unsuccessfully, a brisk welcome. His lips were curved in an ingratiating grin.

"Your father wasn't feeling quite fit, so he let me drive home," explained Scott cheerfully as he got himself out and came up to her.

"Nice little car. Had it long?"

Yanci laughed, but without humor.

"Is he paralyzed?"

"Is who paralyze'?" demanded the figure in the car with an offended sigh.

Scott was standing by the car.

"Can I help you out, sir?"

"I c'n get out. I c'n get out," insisted Mr. Bowman. "Just step a li'l' out my way. Someone must have given me some stremely bad wisk'."

"You mean a lot of people must have given you some," retorted Yanci in cold unsympathy.

Mr. Bowman reached the curb with astonishing ease; but this was a deceitful success, for almost immediately he clutched at a handle of air perceptible only to himself, and was saved by Scott's quickly proffered arm. Followed by the two men, Yanci walked toward the house in a furor of embarrassment. Would the young man think that such scenes went on every night? It was chiefly her own presence that made it humiliating for Yanci. Had her father been carried to bed by two butlers each evening she might even have been proud of the fact that he could afford such dissipation; but to have it thought that she assisted, that she was burdened with the worry and the care! And finally she was annoyed with Scott Kimberly for being there, and for his officiousness in helping to bring her father into the house.

Reaching the low porch of tapestry brick, Yanci searched in Tom Bowman's vest for the key and unlocked the front door. A minute later the master of the house was deposited in an easy-chair.

"Thanks very much," he said, recovering for a moment. "Sit down. Like a drink? Yanci, get some crackers and cheese, if there's any, won't you, dear?"

At the unconscious coolness of this Scott and Yanci laughed.

"It's your bedtime, Father," she said, her anger struggling with diplomacy.

"Give me my guitar," he suggested, "and I'll play you tune."

Except on such occasions as this, he had not touched his guitar for twenty years. Yanci turned to Scott.

"He'll be fine now. Thanks a lot. He'll fall asleep in a minute and when I wake him he'll go to bed like a lamb."

"Well——"

They strolled together out the door.

"Sleepy?" he asked.

"No, not a bit."

"Then perhaps you'd better let me stay here with you a few minutes until you see if he's all right. Mrs. Rogers gave me a key so I can get in without disturbing her."

"It's quite all right," protested Yanci. "I don't mind a bit, and he won't be any trouble. He must have taken a glass too much, and this whisky we have out here—you know! This has happened once before—last year," she added.

Her words satisfied her; as an explanation it seemed to have a convincing ring.

"Can I sit down for a moment, anyway?" They sat side by side upon a wicker porch settee.

"I'm thinking of staying over a few days," Scott said.

"How lovely!" Her voice had resumed its die-away note.

"Cousin Pete Rogers wasn't well today, but tomorrow he's going duck shooting, and he wants me to go with him."

"Oh, how thrill-ing! I've always been mad to go, and Father's always promised to take me, but he never has."

"We're going to be gone about three days, and then I thought I'd come back here and stay over the next week-end——" He broke off suddenly and bent forward in a listening attitude.

"Now what on earth is that?"

The sounds of music were proceeding brokenly from the room they had lately left—a ragged chord on a guitar and half a dozen feeble starts.

"It's father!" cried Yanci.

And now a voice drifted out to them, drunken and murmurous, taking the long notes with attempted melancholy:

Sing a song of cities,
Ridin' on a rail,
A niggah's ne'er so happy
As when he's out-a jail.

"How terrible!" exclaimed Yanci. "He'll wake up everybody in the block."

The chorus ended, the guitar jangled again, then gave out a last harsh spang! and was still. A moment later these disturbances were followed by a low but quite definite snore. Mr. Bowman, having indulged his musical proclivity, had dropped off to sleep.

"Let's go to ride," suggested Yanci impatiently. "This is too hectic for me."

Scott arose with alacrity and they walked down to the car.

"Where'll we go?" she wondered.

"I don't care."

"We might go up half a block to Crest Avenue—that's our show street—and then ride out to the river boulevard."

IV

As they turned into Crest Avenue the new cathedral, immense and unfinished, in imitation of a cathedral left unfinished by accident in some little Flemish town, squatted just across the way like a plump white bulldog on its haunches. The ghosts of four moonlit apostles looked down at them wanly from wall niches still littered with the white, dusty trash of the builders. The cathedral inaugurated Crest Avenue. After it came the great brownstone mass built by R. R. Comerford, the flour king, followed by a half mile of pretentious stone houses put up in the gloomy 90's. These were adorned with monstrous driveways and porte-cochères which had once echoed to the hoofs of good horses and with huge circular windows that corseted the second stories.

The continuity of these mausoleums was broken by a small park, a triangle of grass where Nathan Hale stood ten feet tall with his hands bound behind his back by stone cord and stared over a great bluff at the slow Mississippi. Crest Avenue ran along the bluff, but neither faced it nor seemed aware of it, for all the houses fronted inward toward the street. Beyond the first half mile it became newer, essayed ventures in terraced lawns, in concoctions of stucco or in granite mansions which imitated through a variety of gradual refinements the marble contours of the Petit Trianon. The houses of this phase rushed by the roadster for a succession of minutes; then the way turned and the car was headed directly into the moonlight which swept toward it like the lamp of some gigantic motorcycle far up the avenue.

Past the low Corinthian lines of the Christian Science Temple, past a block of dark frame horrors, a deserted row of grim red brick—an unfortunate experiment of the late 90's—then new houses again, bright-red brick now, with trimmings of white, black iron fences and hedges binding flowery lawns. These swept by, faded, passed, enjoying their moment of grandeur; then waiting there in the moonlight to be outmoded as had the frame, cupolaed mansions of lower town and the brownstone piles of older Crest Avenue in their turn.

The roofs lowered suddenly, the lots narrowed, the houses shrank up in size and shaded off into bungalows. These held the street for the last mile, to the bend in the river which terminated the prideful avenue at the statue of Chelsea Arbuthnot. Arbuthnot was the first governor—and almost the last of Anglo-Saxon blood.

All the way thus far Yanci had not spoken, absorbed still in the annoyance of the evening, yet soothed somehow by the fresh air of Northern November that rushed by them. She must take her fur coat out of storage next day, she thought.

"Where are we now?"

As they slowed down Scott looked up curiously at the pompous stone figure, clear in the crisp moonlight, with one hand on a book and the forefinger of the other pointing, as though with reproachful symbolism, directly at some construction work going on in the street.

"This is the end of Crest Avenue," said Yanci, turning to him. "This is our show street."

"A museum of American architectural failures."

"What?"

"Nothing," he murmured.

"I should have explained it to you. I forgot. We can go along the river boulevard if you'd like—or are you tired?"

Scott assured her that he was not tired—not in the least.

Entering the boulevard, the cement road twisted under darkling trees.

"The Mississippi—how little it means to you now!" said Scott suddenly.

"What?" Yanci looked around. "Oh, the river."

"I guess it was once pretty important to your ancestors up here."

"My ancestors weren't up here then," said Yanci with some dignity. "My ancestors were from Maryland. My father came out here when he left Yale."

"Oh!" Scott was politely impressed.

"My mother was from here. My father came out here from Baltimore because of his health."

"Oh!"

"Of course we belong here now, I suppose"—this with faint condescension—"as much as anywhere else."

"Of course."

"Except that I want to live in the East and I can't persuade Father to," she finished.

It was after one o'clock and the boulevard was almost deserted. Occasionally two yellow disks would top a rise ahead of them and take shape as a late-returning automobile. Except for that they were alone in a continual rushing dark. The moon had gone down.

"Next time the road goes near the river let's stop and watch it," he suggested.

Yanci smiled inwardly. This remark was obviously what one boy of her acquaintance had named an international petting cue, by which was meant a suggestion that aimed to create naturally a situation for a kiss. She considered the matter. As yet the man had made no particular impression on her. He was good-looking, apparently well-to-do and from New York. She had begun to like him during the dance, increasingly as the evening had drawn to a close; then the incident of her father's appalling arrival had thrown cold water upon this tentative warmth; and now—it was November, and the night was cold. Still——

"All right," she agreed suddenly.

The road divided; she swerved around and brought the car to a stop in an open place high above the river.

"Well?" she demanded in the deep quiet that followed the shutting off of the engine.

"Thanks."

"Are you satisfied here?"

"Almost. Not quite."

"Why not?"

"I'll tell you in a minute," he answered. "Why is your name Yanci?"

"It's a family name."

"It's very pretty." He repeated it several times caressingly. "Yanci—it has all the grace of Nancy, and yet it isn't prim."

"What's your name?" she inquired.

"Scott."

"Scott what?"

"Kimberly. Didn't you know?"

"I wasn't sure. Mrs. Rogers introduced you in such a mumble."

There was a slight pause.

"Yanci," he repeated; "beautiful Yanci, with her dark-blue eyes and her lazy soul. Do you know why I'm not quite satisfied, Yanci?"

"Why?"

Imperceptibly she had moved her face nearer until as she waited for an answer with her lips faintly apart he knew that in asking she had granted.

Without haste he bent his head forward and touched her lips.

He sighed, and both of them felt a sort of relief—relief from the embarrassment of playing up to what conventions of this sort of thing remained.

"Thanks," he said as he had when she first stopped the car.

"Now are you satisfied?"

Her blue eyes regarded him unsmilingly in the darkness.

"After a fashion; of course, you can never say—definitely."

Again he bent toward her, but she stooped and started the motor. It was late and Yanci was beginning to be tired. What purpose there was in the experiment was accomplished. He had had what he asked. If he liked it he would want more, and that put her one move ahead in the game which she felt she was beginning.

"I'm hungry," she complained. "Let's go down and eat."

"Very well," he acquiesced sadly. "Just when I was so enjoying—the Mississippi."

"Do you think I'm beautiful?" she inquired almost plaintively as they backed out.

"What an absurd question!"

"But I like to hear people say so."

"I was just about to—when you started the engine."

Downtown in a deserted all-night lunch room they ate bacon and eggs. She was pale as ivory now. The night had drawn the lazy vitality and languid color out of her face. She encouraged him to talk to her of New York until he was beginning every sentence with, "Well, now, let's see——"

The repast over, they drove home. Scott helped her put the car in the little garage, and just outside the front door she lent him her lips again for the faint brush of a kiss. Then she went in.

The long living room which ran the width of the small stucco house was reddened by a dying fire which had been high when Yanci left and now was faded to a steady undancing glow. She took a log from the fire box and threw it on the embers, then started as a voice came out of the half-darkness at the other end of the room.

"Back so soon?"

It was her father's voice, not yet quite sober, but alert and intelligent.

"Yes. Went riding," she answered shortly, sitting down in a wicker chair before the fire. "Then went down and had something to eat."

"Oh!"

Her father left his place and moved to a chair nearer the fire, where he stretched himself out with a sigh. Glancing at him from the corner of her eye, for she was going to show an appropriate coldness, Yanci was fascinated by his complete recovery of dignity in the space of two hours. His greying hair was scarcely rumpled; his handsome face was ruddy as ever. Only his eyes, crisscrossed with tiny red lines, were evidence of his late dissipation.

"Have a good time?"

"Why should you care?" she answered rudely.

"Why shouldn't I?"

"You didn't seem to care earlier in the evening. I asked you to take two people home for me, and you weren't able to drive your own car."

"The deuce I wasn't!" he protested. "I could have driven in—in a race in an arana, areaena. That Mrs. Rogers insisted that her young admirer should drive, so what could I do?"

"That isn't her young admirer," retorted Yanci crisply. There was no drawl in her voice now. "She's as old as you are. That's her niece—I mean her nephew."

"Excuse me!"

"I think you owe me an apology." She found suddenly that she bore him no resentment. She was rather sorry for him, and it occurred to her that in asking him to take Mrs. Rogers home she had somehow imposed on his liberty. Nevertheless, discipline was necessary—there would be other Saturday nights. "Don't you?" she concluded.

"I apologize, Yanci."

"Very well, I accept your apology," she answered stiffly.

"What's more, I'll make it up to you."

Her blue eyes contracted. She hoped—she hardly dared to hope that he might take her to New York.

"Let's see," he said. "November, isn't it? What date?"

"The twenty-third."

"Well, I'll tell you what I'll do." He knocked the tips of his fingers together tentatively. "I'll give you a present. I've been meaning to let you have a trip all fall, but business has been bad." She almost smiled—as though business was of any consequence in his life. "But then you need a trip. I'll make you a present of it."

He rose again, and crossing over to his desk sat down.

"I've got a little money in a New York bank that's been lying there quite a while," he said as he fumbled in a drawer for a check book. "I've been intending to close out the account. Let—me—see. There's just——" His pen scratched. "Where the devil's the blotter? Uh!"

He came back to the fire and a pink oblong paper fluttered into her lap.

"Why, Father!"

It was a check for three hundred dollars.

"But can you afford this?" she demanded.

"It's all right," he reassured her, nodding. "That can be a Christmas present, too, and you'll probably need a dress or a hat or something before you go."

"Why," she began uncertainly, "I hardly know whether I ought to take this much or not! I've got two hundred of my own downtown, you know. Are you sure——"

"Oh, yes!" He waved his hand with magnificent carelessness. "You need a holiday. You've been talking about New York, and I want you to go down there. Tell some of your friends at Yale and the other colleges and they'll ask you to the prom or something. That'll be nice. You'll have a good time."

He sat down abruptly in his chair and gave vent to a long sigh. Yanci folded up the check and tucked it into the low bosom of her dress.

"Well," she drawled softly with a return to her usual manner, "you're a perfect lamb to be so sweet about it, but I don't want to be horribly extravagant."

Her father did not answer. He gave another little sigh and relaxed sleepily into his chair.

"Of course I do want to go," went on Yanci.

Still her father was silent. She wondered if he were asleep.

"Are you asleep?" she demanded, cheerfully now. She bent toward him; then she stood up and looked at him.

"Father," she said uncertainly.

Her father remained motionless; the ruddy color had melted suddenly out of his face.

"Father!"

It occurred to her—and at the thought she grew cold, and a brassière of iron clutched at her breast—that she was alone in the room. After a frantic instant she said to herself that her father was dead.

V

Yanci judged herself with inevitable gentleness—judged herself very much as a mother might judge a wild, spoiled child. She was not hard-minded, nor did she live by any ordered and considered philosophy of her own. To such a catastrophe as the death of her father her immediate reaction was a hysterical self-pity. The first three days were something of a nightmare; but sentimental civilization, being as infallible as Nature in healing the wounds of its more fortunate children, had inspired a certain Mrs. Oral, whom Yanci had always loathed, with a passionate interest in all such crises. To all intents and purposes Mrs. Oral buried Tom Bowman. The morning after his death Yanci had wired her maternal aunt in Chicago, but as yet that undemonstrative and well-to-do lady had sent no answer.

All day long, for four days, Yanci sat in her room upstairs, hearing steps come and go on the porch, and it merely increased her nervousness that the doorbell had been disconnected. This by order of Mrs. Oral! Doorbells were always disconnected! After the burial of the dead the strain relaxed. Yanci, dressed in her new black, regarded herself in the pier glass, and then wept because she seemed to herself very sad and beautiful. She went downstairs and tried to read a moving-picture magazine, hoping that she would not be alone in the house when the winter dark came down just after four.

This afternoon Mrs. Oral had said *carpe diem* to the maid, and Yanci was just starting for the kitchen to see whether she had yet gone when the reconnected bell rang suddenly through the house. Yanci started. She waited a minute, then went to the door. It was Scott Kimberly.

"I was just going to inquire for you," he said.

"Oh! I'm much better, thank you," she responded with the quiet dignity that seemed suited to her role.

They stood there in the hall awkwardly, each reconstructing the half-facetious, half-sentimental occasion on which they had last met. It seemed such an irreverent prelude to such a somber disaster. There was no common ground for them now, no gap that could be bridged by a slight reference to their mutual past, and there was no foundation on which he could adequately pretend to share her sorrow.

"Won't you come in?" she said, biting her lip nervously. He followed her to the sitting room and sat beside her on the lounge. In another minute, simply because he was there and alive and friendly, she was crying on his shoulder.

"There, there!" he said, putting his arm behind her and patting her shoulder idiotically. "There, there, there!"

He was wise enough to attribute no ulterior significance to her action. She was overstrained with grief and loneliness and sentiment; almost any shoulder would have done as well. For all the biological thrill to either of them he might have been a hundred years old. In a minute she sat up.

"I beg your pardon," she murmured brokenly. "But it's—it's so dismal in this house today."

"I know just how you feel, Yanci."

"Did I—did I—get—tears on your coat?"

In tribute to the tenseness of the incident they both laughed hysterically, and with the laughter she momentarily recovered her propriety.

"I don't know why I should have chosen you to collapse on," she wailed. "I really don't just go round doing it in-indiscriminately on anyone who comes in."

"I consider it a—a compliment," he responded soberly, "and I can understand the state you're in." Then, after a pause, "Have you any plans?"

She shook her head.

"Va-vague ones," she muttered between little gasps. "I tho-ought I'd go down and stay with my aunt in Chicago awhile."

"I should think that'd be best—much the best thing." Then, because he could think of nothing else to say, he added, "Yes, very much the best thing."

"What are you doing—here in town?" she inquired, taking in her breath in minute gasps and dabbing at her eyes with a handkerchief.

"Oh, I'm here with—with the Rogerses. I've been here."

"Hunting?"

"No, I've just been here."

He did not tell her that he had stayed over on her account. She might think it fresh.

"I see," she said. She didn't see.

"I want to know if there's any possible thing I can do for you, Yanci. Perhaps go downtown for you, or do some errands—anything. Maybe you'd like to bundle up and get a bit of air. I could take you out to drive in your car some night, and no one would see you."

He clipped his last word short as the inadvertency of this suggestion dawned on him. They stared at each other with horror in their eyes.

"Oh, no, thank you!" she cried. "I really don't want to drive."

To his relief the outer door opened and an elderly lady came in. It was Mrs. Oral. Scott rose immediately and moved backward toward the door.

"If you're sure there isn't anything I can do——"

Yanci introduced him to Mrs. Oral; then leaving the elder woman by the fire walked with him to the door. An idea had suddenly occurred to her.

"Wait a minute."

She ran up the front stairs and returned immediately with a slip of pink paper in her hand.

"Here's something I wish you'd do," she said. "Take this to the First National Bank and have it cashed for me. You can leave the money here for me any time."

Scott took out his wallet and opened it.

"Suppose I cash it for you now," he suggested.

"Oh, there's no hurry."

"But I may as well." He drew out three new one-hundred-dollar bills and gave them to her.

"That's awfully sweet of you," said Yanci.

"Not at all. May I come in and see you next time I come West?"

"I wish you would."

"Then I will. I'm going East tonight."

The door shut him out into the snowy dusk and Yanci returned to Mrs. Oral. Mrs. Oral had come to discuss plans.

"And now, my dear, just what do you plan to do? We ought to have some plan to go by, and I thought I'd find out if you had any definite plan in your mind."

Yanci tried to think. She seemed to herself to be horribly alone in the world.

"I haven't heard from my aunt. I wired her again this morning. She may be in Florida."

"In that case you'd go there?"

"I suppose so."

"Would you close this house?"

"I suppose so."

Mrs. Oral glanced around with placid practicality. It occurred to her that if Yanci gave the house up she might like it for herself.

"And now," she continued, "do you know where you stand financially?"

"All right, I guess," answered Yanci indifferently. And then with a rush of sentiment, "There was enough for t-two; there ought to be enough for o-one."

"I didn't mean that," said Mrs. Oral. "I mean, do you know the details?"

"No."

"Well, I thought you didn't know the details. And I thought you ought to know all the details—have a detailed account of what and where your money is. So I called up Mr. Haedge, who knew your father very well personally, to come up this afternoon and glance through his papers. He was going to stop in your father's bank, too, by the way, and get all the details there. I don't believe your father left any will."

Details! Details! Details!

"Thank you," said Yanci. "That'll be—nice."

Mrs. Oral gave three or four vigorous nods that were like heavy periods. Then she got up.

"And now if Hilma's gone out I'll make you some tea. Would you like some tea?"

"Sort of."

"All right, I'll make you some ni-ice tea."

Tea! Tea! Tea!

Mr. Haedge, who came from one of the best Swedish families in town, arrived to see Yanci at five o'clock. He greeted her funereally; said that he had been several times to inquire for her; had organized the pallbearers and would now find out how she stood in no time. Did she have any idea whether or not there was a will? No? Well, there probably wasn't one.

There was one. He found it almost at once in Mr. Bowman's desk—but he worked there until eleven o'clock that night before he found much else. Next morning he arrived at eight, went down to the bank at ten, then to a certain brokerage firm, and came back to Yanci's house at noon. He had known Tom Bowman for some years, but he was utterly astounded when he discovered the condition in which that handsome gallant had left his affairs.

He consulted Mrs. Oral, and that afternoon he informed a frightened Yanci in measured language that she was practically penniless. In the midst of the conversation a telegram from Chicago told her that her aunt had sailed the week previous for a trip through the Orient and was not expected back until late spring.

The beautiful Yanci, so profuse, so debonair, so careless with her gorgeous adjectives, had no adjectives for this calamity. She crept upstairs like a hurt child and sat before a mirror, brushing her luxurious hair to comfort herself. One hundred and fifty strokes she gave it, as it said in the treatment, and then a hundred and fifty more—she was too distraught to stop the nervous motion. She brushed it until her arm ached, then she changed arms and went on brushing.

The maid found her next morning, asleep, sprawled across the toilet things on the dresser in a room that was heavy and sweet with the scent of spilled perfume.

VI

To be precise, as Mr. Haedge was to a depressing degree, Tom Bowman left a bank balance that was more than ample—that is to say, more than ample to supply the post-mortem requirements of his own person. There was also twenty years' worth of furniture, a temperamental roadster with asthmatic cylinders and two one-thousand-dollar bonds of a chain of jewelry stores which yielded 7.5 per cent interest. Unfortunately these were not known in the bond market.

When the car and the furniture had been sold and the stucco bungalow sublet, Yanci contemplated her resources with dismay. She had a bank balance of almost a thousand dollars. If she invested this she would increase her total income to about fifteen dollars a month. This, as Mrs. Oral cheerfully observed, would pay for the boarding-house room she had taken for Yanci as long as Yanci lived. Yanci was so encouraged by this news that she burst into tears.

So she acted as any beautiful girl would have acted in this emergency. With rare decision she told Mr. Haedge that she would leave her thousand dollars in a checking account, and then she walked out of his office and across the street to a beauty parlor to have her hair waved. This raised her morale astonishingly. Indeed, she moved that very day out of the boarding house and into a small room at the best hotel in town. If she must sink into poverty she would at least do so in the grand manner.

Sewed into the lining of her best mourning hat were the three new one-hundred-dollar bills, her father's last present. What she expected of them, why she kept them in such a way, she did not know, unless perhaps because they had come to her under cheerful auspices and might through some gayety inherent in their crisp and virgin paper buy happier things than solitary meals and narrow hotel beds. They were hope and youth and luck and beauty; they began, somehow, to stand for all the things she had lost in that November night when Tom Bowman, having led her recklessly into space, had plunged off himself, leaving her to find the way back alone.

Yanci remained at the Hiawatha Hotel for three months, and she found that after the first visits of condolence her friends had happier things to do with their time than to spend it in her company. Jerry O'Rourke came to see her one day with a wild Celtic look in his eyes, and demanded that she marry him immediately. When she asked for time to consider he walked out in a rage. She heard later that he had been offered a position in Chicago and had left the same night.

She considered, frightened and uncertain. She had heard of people sinking out of place, out of life. Her father had once told her of a man in his class at college who had become a worker around saloons, polishing brass rails for the price of a can of beer; and she knew also that there were girls in this city with whose mothers her own mother had played as a little girl, but who were poor now and had grown common; who worked in stores and had married into the proletariat. But that such a fate should threaten her—how absurd! Why, she knew everyone! She had been invited everywhere; her great-grandfather had been governor of one of the Southern states!

She had written to her aunt in India and again in China, receiving no answer. She concluded that her aunt's itinerary had changed, and this was confirmed when a post card arrived from Honolulu which showed no knowledge of Tom Bowman's death, but announced that she was going with a party to the east coast of Africa. This was a last straw. The languorous and lackadaisical Yanci was on her own at last.

"Why not go to work for awhile?" suggested Mr. Haedge with some irritation. "Lots of nice girls do nowadays, just for something to occupy themselves with. There's Elsie Prendergast, who does society news on the 'Bulletin,' and that Semple girl——"

"I can't," said Yanci shortly with a glitter of tears in her eyes. "I'm going East in February."

"East? Oh, you're going to visit someone?"

She nodded.

"Yes, I'm going to visit," she lied, "so it'd hardly be worth while to go to work." She could have wept, but she managed a haughty look. "I'd like to try reporting sometime, though, just for the fun of it."

"Yes, it's quite a lot of fun," agreed Mr. Haedge with some irony. "Still, I suppose there's no hurry about it. You must have plenty of that thousand dollars left."

"Oh, plenty!"

There were a few hundred, she knew.

"Well, then I suppose a good rest, a change of scene would be the best thing for you."

"Yes," answered Yanci. Her lips were trembling and she rose, scarcely able to control herself. Mr. Haedge seemed so impersonally cold. "That's why I'm going. A good rest is what I need."

"I think you're wise."

What Mr. Haedge would have thought had he seen the dozen drafts she wrote that night of a certain letter is problematical. Here are two of the earlier ones. The bracketed words are proposed substitutions:

Dear Scott: Not having seen you since that day I was such a silly ass and wept on your coat, I thought I'd write and tell you that I'm coming East pretty soon and would like you to have lunch [dinner] with me or something. I have been living in a room [suite] at the Hiawatha Hotel, intending to meet my aunt, with whom I am going to live [stay], and who is coming back from China this month [spring]. Meanwhile I have a lot of invitations to visit, etc., in the East, and I thought I would do it now. So I'd like to see you——

This draft ended here and went into the wastebasket. After an hour's work she produced the following:

My dear Mr. Kimberly: I have often [sometimes] wondered how you've been since I saw you. I am coming East next month before going to visit my aunt in Chicago, and you must come and see me. I have been going out very little, but my physician advises me that I need a change, so I expect to shock the proprieties by some very gay visits in the East——

Finally in despondent abandon she wrote a simple note without explanation or subterfuge, tore it up and went to bed. Next morning she identified it in the wastebasket, decided it was the best one after all and sent him a fair copy. It ran:

Dear Scott: Just a line to tell you I will be at the Ritz-Carlton Hotel from February seventh, probably for ten days. If you'll phone me some rainy afternoon I'll invite you to tea.

Sincerely,
YANCI BOWMAN.

VII

Yanci was going to the Ritz for no more reason than that she had once told Scott Kimberly that she always went there. When she reached New York—a cold New York, a strangely menacing New York, quite different from the gay city of theatres and hotel-corridor rendezvous that she had known—there was exactly two hundred dollars in her purse.

It had taken a large part of her bank account to live, and she had at last broken into her sacred three hundred dollars to substitute pretty and delicate quarter-mourning clothes for the heavy black she had laid away.

Walking into the hotel at the moment when its exquisitely dressed patrons were assembling for luncheon, it drained at her confidence to appear bored and at ease. Surely the clerks at the desk knew the contents of her pocketbook. She fancied even that the bell boys were snickering at the foreign labels she had steamed from an old trunk of her father's and pasted on her suitcase. This last thought horrified her. Perhaps the very hotels and steamers so grandly named had long since been out of commission!

As she stood drumming her fingers on the desk she was wondering whether if she were refused admittance she could muster a casual smile and stroll out coolly enough to deceive two richly dressed women standing near. It had not taken long for the confidence of twenty years to evaporate. Three months without security had made an ineffaceable mark on Yanci's soul.

"Twenty-four sixty-two," said the clerk callously.

Her heart settled back into place as she followed the bell-boy to the elevator, meanwhile casting a nonchalant glance at the two fashionable women as she passed them. Were their skirts long or short?—longer, she noticed.

She wondered how much the skirt of her new walking suit could be let out.

At luncheon her spirits soared. The head-waiter bowed to her. The light rattle of conversation, the subdued hum of the music soothed her. She ordered supreme of melon, eggs Susette and an artichoke, and signed her room number to the check with scarcely a glance at it as it lay beside her plate. Up in her room, with the telephone directory open on the bed before her, she tried to locate her scattered metropolitan acquaintances. Yet even as the phone numbers, with their supercilious tags, Plaza, Circle and Rhinelander, stared out at her, she could feel a cold wind blow at her unstable confidence. These girls, acquaintances of school, of a summer, of a house party, even of a week-end at a college prom—what claim or attraction could she, poor and friendless, exercise over them? They had their loves, their dates, their week's gayety planned in advance. They would almost resent her inconvenient memory.

Nevertheless, she called four girls. One of them was out, one at Palm Beach, one in California. The only one to whom she talked said in a hearty voice that she was in bed with grippe, but would phone Yanci as soon as she felt well enough to go out. Then Yanci gave up the girls. She would have to create the illusion of a good time in some other manner. The illusion must be created—that was part of her plan.

She looked at her watch and found that it was three o'clock. Scott Kimberly should have phoned before this, or at least left some word. Still, he was probably busy—at a club, she thought vaguely, or else buying some neckties. He would probably call at four.

Yanci was well aware that she must work quickly. She had figured to a nicety that one hundred and fifty dollars carefully expended would carry her through two weeks, no more. The idea of failure, the fear that at the end of that time she would be friendless and penniless had not begun to bother her.

It was not the first time that for amusement, for a coveted invitation or for curiosity she had deliberately set out to capture a man; but it was the first time she had laid her plans with necessity and desperation pressing in on her.

One of her strongest cards had always been her background, the impression she gave that she was popular and desired and happy. This she must create now, and apparently out of nothing. Scott must somehow be brought to think that a fair portion of New York was at her feet.

At four she went over to Park Avenue, where the sun was out walking and the February day was fresh and odorous of spring and the high apartments of her desire lined the street with radiant whiteness. Here she would live on a gay schedule of pleasure. In these smart not-to-be-entered-without-a-card women's shops she would spend the morning hours acquiring and acquiring, ceaselessly and without thought of expense; in these restaurants she would lunch at noon in company with other fashionable women, orchid-adorned always, and perhaps bearing an absurdly dwarfed Pomeranian in her sleek arms.

In the summer—well, she would go to Tuxedo, perhaps to an immaculate house perched high on a fashionable eminence, where she would emerge to visit a world of teas and balls, of horse shows and polo. Between the halves of the polo game the players would cluster around her in their white suits and helmets, admiringly, and when she swept away, bound for some new delight, she would be followed by the eyes of many envious but intimidated women.

Every other summer they would, of course, go abroad. She began to plan a typical year, distributing a few months here and a few months there until she—and Scott Kimberly, by implication—would become the very auguries of the season, shifting with the slightest stirring of the social barometer from rusticity to urbanity, from palm to pine.

She had two weeks, no more, in which to attain to this position. In an ecstasy of determined emotion she lifted up her head toward the tallest of the tall white apartments.

"It will be too marvelous!" she said to herself.

For almost the first time in her life her words were not too exaggerated to express the wonder shining in her eyes.

VIII

About five o'clock she hurried back to the hotel, demanding feverishly at the desk if there had been a telephone message for her. To her profound disappointment there was nothing. A minute after she had entered her room the phone rang.

"This is Scott Kimberly."

At the words a call to battle echoed in her heart.

"Oh, how do you do?"

Her tone implied that she had almost forgotten him. It was not frigid—it was merely casual.

As she answered the inevitable question as to the hour when she had arrived, a warm glow spread over her. Now that, from a personification of all the riches and pleasure she craved, he had materialized as merely a male voice over the telephone, her confidence became strengthened. Male voices were male voices. They could be managed; they could be made to intone syllables of which the minds behind them had no approval. Male voices could be made sad or tender or despairing at her will. She rejoiced. The soft clay was ready to her hand.

"Won't you take dinner with me tonight?" Scott was suggesting.

"Why"—perhaps not, she thought; let him think of her tonight—"I don't believe I'll be able to," she said. "I've got an engagement for dinner and the theatre. I'm terribly sorry."

Her voice did not sound sorry—it sounded polite. Then as though a happy thought had occurred to her as to a time and place where she could work him into her list of dates, "I'll tell you: Why don't you come around here this afternoon and have tea with me?"

He would be there immediately. He had been playing squash and as soon as he took a plunge he would arrive. Yanci hung up the phone and turned with a quiet efficiency to the mirror, too tense to smile.

She regarded her lustrous eyes and dusky hair in critical approval. Then she took a lavender tea gown from her trunk and began to dress.

She let him wait seven minutes in the lobby before she appeared; then she approached him with a friendly, lazy smile.

"How do you do?" she murmured. "It's marvelous to see you again. How are you?" And, with a long sigh, "I'm frightfully tired. I've been on the go ever since I got here this morning; shopping and then tearing off to luncheon and a matinée. I've bought everything I saw. I don't know how I'm going to pay for it all."

She remembered vividly that when they had first met she had told him, without expecting to be believed, how unpopular she was. She could not risk such a remark now, even in jest. He must think that she had been on the go every minute of the day.

They took a table and were served with olive sandwiches and tea. He was so good-looking, she thought, and marvelously dressed. His grey eyes regarded her with interest from under immaculate ash-blond hair. She wondered how he passed his days, how he liked her costume, what he was thinking of at that moment.

"How long will you be here?" he asked.

"Well, two weeks, off and on. I'm going down to Princeton for the February prom and then up to a house party in Westchester County for a few days. Are you shocked at me for going out so soon? Father would have wanted me to, you know. He was very modern in all his ideas."

She had debated this remark on the train. She was not going to a house party. She was not invited to the Princeton prom. Such things, nevertheless, were necessary to create the illusion. That was everything—the illusion.

"And then," she continued, smiling, "two of my old beaus are in town, which makes it nice for me."

She saw Scott blink and she knew that he appreciated the significance of this.

"What are your plans for this winter?" he demanded. "Are you going back West?"

"No. You see, my aunt returns from India this week. She's going to open her Florida house, and we'll stay there until the middle of

March. Then we'll come up to Hot Springs and we may go to Europe for the summer."

This was all the sheerest fiction. Her first letter to her aunt, which had given the bare details of Tom Bowman's death, had at last reached its destination. Her aunt had replied with a note of conventional sympathy and the announcement that she would be back in America within two years if she didn't decide to live in Italy.

"But you'll let me see something of you while you're here," urged Scott, after attending to this impressive program. "If you can't take dinner with me tonight, how about Wednesday—that's the day after tomorrow?"

"Wednesday? Let's see." Yanci's brow was knit with imitation thought. "I think I have a date for Wednesday, but I don't know for certain. How about phoning me tomorrow, and I'll let you know? Because I want to go with you, only I think I've made an engagement."

"Very well, I'll phone you."

"Do—about ten."

"Try to be able to—then or any time."

"I'll tell you—if I can't go to dinner with you Wednesday I can go to lunch surely."

"All right," he agreed. "And we'll go to a matinée."

They danced several times. Never by word or sign did Yanci betray more than the most cursory interest in him until just at the end, when she offered him her hand to say good-bye.

"Good-bye, Scott."

For just the fraction of a second—not long enough for him to be sure it had happened at all, but just enough so that he would be reminded, however faintly, of that night on the Mississippi boulevard—she looked into his eyes. Then she turned quickly and hurried away.

She took her dinner in a little tea room around the corner. It was an economical dinner which cost a dollar and a half. There was no date concerned in it at all, and no man except an elderly person in spats who tried to speak to her as she came out the door.

IX

Sitting alone in one of the magnificent moving-picture theatres—a luxury which she thought she could afford—Yanci watched Mae Murray swirl through splendidly imagined vistas, and meanwhile considered the progress of the first day. In retrospect it was a distinct success. She had given the correct impression both as to her material prosperity and as to her attitude toward Scott himself. It seemed best to avoid evening dates. Let him have the evenings to himself, to think of her, to imagine her with other men, even to spend a few lonely hours in his apartment, considering how much more cheerful it might be if—— Let time and absence work for her.

Engrossed for awhile in the moving picture, she calculated the cost of the apartment in which its heroine endured her movie wrongs. She admired its slender Italian table, occupying only one side of the large dining room and flanked by a long bench which gave it an air of medieval luxury. She rejoiced in the beauty of Mae Murray's clothes and furs, her gorgeous hats, her short-seeming French shoes. Then after a moment her mind returned to her own drama; she wondered if Scott were already engaged, and her heart dipped at the thought. Yet it was unlikely. He had been too quick to phone her on her arrival, too lavish with his time, too responsive that afternoon.

After the picture she returned to the Ritz, where she slept deeply and happily for almost the first time in three months. The atmosphere around her no longer seemed cold. Even the floor clerk had smiled kindly and admiringly when Yanci asked for her key.

Next morning at ten Scott phoned. Yanci, who had been up for hours, pretended to be drowsy from her dissipation of the night before.

No, she could not take dinner with him on Wednesday. She was terribly sorry; she had an engagement, as she had feared. But she could have luncheon and go to a matinée if he would get her back in time for tea.

She spent the day roving the streets. On top of a bus, though not on the front seat, where Scott might possibly spy her, she sailed out Riverside Drive and back along Fifth Avenue just at the winter twilight, and her feeling for New York and its gorgeous splendors deepened and redoubled. Here she must live and be rich, be nodded to by the traffic policemen at the corners as she sat in her limousine—with a small dog—and here she must stroll on Sunday to and from a stylish church, with Scott, handsome in his cutaway and tall hat, walking devotedly at her side.

At luncheon on Wednesday she described for Scott's benefit a fanciful two days. She told of a motoring trip up the Hudson and gave him her opinion of two plays she had seen with—it was implied—adoring gentlemen beside her. She had read up very carefully on the plays in the morning paper and chosen two concerning which she could garner the most information.

"Oh," he said in dismay, "you've seen 'Dulcy'? I have two seats for it—but you won't want to go again."

"Oh, no, I don't mind," she protested truthfully. "You see, we went late, and anyway I adored it."

But he wouldn't hear of her sitting through it again—besides, he had seen it himself. It was a play Yanci was mad to see, but she was compelled to watch him while he exchanged the tickets for others, and for the poor seats available at the last moment. The game seemed difficult at times.

"By the way," he said afterwards as they drove back to the hotel in a taxi, "you'll be going down to the Princeton prom tomorrow, won't you?"

She started. She had not realized that it would be so soon or that he would know of it.

"Yes," she answered coolly. "I'm going down tomorrow afternoon."

"On the 2:20, I suppose," Scott commented. And then, "Are you going to meet the boy who's taking you down—at Princeton?"

For an instant she was off her guard.

"Yes, he'll meet the train."

"Then I'll take you to the station," proposed Scott. "There'll be a crowd, and you may have trouble getting a porter."

She could think of nothing to say, no valid objection to make. She wished she had said that she was going by automobile, but she could conceive of no graceful and plausible way of amending her first admission.

"That's mighty sweet of you."

"You'll be at the Ritz when you come back?"

"Oh, yes," she answered. "I'm going to keep my rooms."

Her bedroom was the smallest and least expensive in the hotel.

She concluded to let him put her on the train for Princeton; in fact, she saw no alternative. Next day as she packed her suitcase after luncheon the situation had taken such hold of her imagination that she filled it with the very things she would have chosen had she really been going to the prom. Her intention was to get out at the first stop and take the train back to New York.

Scott called for her at half past one and they took a taxi to the Pennsylvania Station. The train was crowded as he had expected, but he found her a seat and stowed her grip in the rack overhead.

"I'll call you Friday to see how you've behaved," he said.

"All right. I'll be good."

Their eyes met and in an instant, with an inexplicable, only half-conscious rush of emotion, they were in perfect communion. When Yanci came back, the glance seemed to say, ah, then——

A voice startled her ear:

"Why, Yanci!"

Yanci looked around. To her horror she recognized a girl named Ellen Harley, one of those to whom she had phoned upon her arrival.

"Well, Yanci Bowman! You're the last person I ever expected to see. How are you?"

Yanci introduced Scott. Her heart was beating violently.

"Are you coming to the prom? How perfectly slick!" cried Ellen. "Can I sit here with you? I've been wanting to see you. Who are you going with?"

"No one you know."

"Maybe I do."

Her words, falling like sharp claws on Yanci's sensitive soul, were interrupted by an unintelligible outburst from the conductor. Scott bowed to Ellen, cast at Yanci one level glance and then hurried off.

The train started. As Ellen arranged her grip and threw off her fur coat Yanci looked around her. The car was gay with girls whose excited chatter filled the damp, rubbery air like smoke. Here and there sat a chaperon, a mass of decaying rock in a field of flowers, predicting with a mute and somber fatality the end of all gayety and all youth. How many times had Yanci herself been one of such a crowd, careless and happy, dreaming of the men she would meet, of the battered hacks waiting at the station, the snow-covered campus, the big open fires in the clubhouses, and the imported orchestra beating out defiant melody against the approach of morning.

And now—she was an intruder, uninvited, undesired. As at the Ritz on the day of her arrival, she felt that at any instant her mask would be torn from her and she would be exposed as a pretender to the gaze of all the car.

"Tell me everything!" Ellen was saying. "Tell me what you've been doing. I didn't see you at any of the football games last fall."

This was by way of letting Yanci know that she had attended them herself.

The conductor was bellowing from the rear of the car, "Manhattan Transfer next stop!"

Yanci's cheeks burned with shame. She wondered what she had best do—meditating a confession, deciding against it, answering Ellen's chatter in frightened monosyllables—then, as with an ominous thunder of brakes the speed of the train began to slacken, she sprang on a despairing impulse to her feet.

"My heavens!" she cried. "I've forgotten my shoes! I've got to go back and get them."

Ellen reacted to this with annoying efficiency.

"I'll take your suitcase," she said quickly, "and you can call for it. I'll be at the Charter Club."

"No!" Yanci almost shrieked. "It's got my dress in it!"

Ignoring the lack of logic in her own remark, she swung the suitcase off the rack with what seemed to her a superhuman effort and went reeling down the aisle, stared at curiously by the arrogant eyes of many girls. When she reached the platform just as the train came to a stop she felt weak and shaken. She stood on the hard cement which marks the quaint old village of Manhattan Transfer and tears were streaming down her cheeks as she watched the unfeeling cars speed off to Princeton with their burden of happy youth.

After half an hour's wait Yanci got on a train and returned to New York. In thirty minutes she had lost the confidence that a week had gained for her. She came back to her little room and lay down quietly upon the bed.

X

By Friday Yanci's spirits had partly recovered from their chill depression. Scott's voice over the telephone in mid-morning was like a tonic, and she told him of the delights of Princeton with convincing enthusiasm, drawing vicariously upon a prom she had attended there two years before. He was anxious to see her, he said. Would she come to dinner and the theatre that night? Yanci considered, greatly tempted. Dinner—she had been economizing on meals, and a gorgeous dinner in some extravagant show place followed by a musical comedy appealed to her starved fancy, indeed; but instinct told her that the time was not yet right. Let him wait. Let him dream a little more, a little longer.

"I'm too tired, Scott," she said with an air of extreme frankness; "that's the whole truth of the matter. I've been out every night since I've been here, and I'm really half-dead. I'll rest up on this house party over the weekend and then I'll go to dinner with you any day you want me."

There was a minute's silence while she held the phone expectantly.

"Lot of resting up you'll do on a house party," he replied; "and, anyway, next week is so far off. I'm awfully anxious to see you, Yanci."

"So am I, Scott."

She allowed the faintest caress to linger on his name. When she had hung up she felt happy again. Despite her humiliation on the train her plan had been a success. The illusion was still intact; it was nearly complete. And in three meetings and half a dozen telephone calls she had managed to create a tenser atmosphere between them than if he had seen her constantly in the moods and avowals and beguilements of an out-and-out flirtation.

When Monday came she paid her first week's hotel bill. The size of it did not alarm her—she was prepared for that—but the shock of seeing so much money go, of realizing that there remained only one hundred and twenty dollars of her father's present, gave her a peculiar sinking sensation in the pit of her stomach. She decided to bring guile to bear immediately, to tantalize Scott by a carefully planned incident, and then at the end of the week to show him simply and definitely that she loved him.

As a decoy for Scott's tantalization she located by telephone a certain Jimmy Long, a handsome boy with whom she had played as a little girl and who had recently come to New York to work. Jimmy Long was deftly maneuvered into asking her to go to a matinée with him on Wednesday afternoon. He was to meet her in the lobby at two.

On Wednesday she lunched with Scott. His eyes followed her every motion, and knowing this she felt a great rush of tenderness toward him. Desiring at first only what he represented, she had begun half-unconsciously to desire him also. Nevertheless, she did not permit herself the slightest relaxation on that account. The time was too short and the odds too great. That she was beginning to love him only fortified her resolve.

"Where are you going this afternoon?" he demanded.

"To a matinée—with an annoying man."

"Why is he annoying?"

"Because he wants me to marry him and I don't believe I want to."

There was just the faintest emphasis on the word "believe." The implication was that she was not sure—that is, not quite.

"Don't marry him."

"I won't—probably."

"Yanci," he said in a low voice, "do you remember a night on that boulevard——"

She changed the subject. It was noon and the room was full of sunlight. It was not quite the place, the time. When he spoke she must have every aspect of the situation in control. He must say only what she wanted said; nothing else would do.

"It's five minutes to two," she told him, looking at her wrist watch. "We'd better go. I've got to keep my date."

"Do you want to go?"

"No," she answered simply.

This seemed to satisfy him, and they walked out to the lobby. Then Yanci caught sight of a man waiting there, obviously ill at ease and dressed as no habitué of the Ritz ever was. The man was Jimmy Long, not long since a favored beau of his Western city. And now—his hat was green, actually! His coat, seasons old, was quite evidently the product of a well-known ready-made concern. His shoes, long and narrow, turned up at the toes. From head to foot everything that could possibly be wrong about him was wrong. He was embarrassed by instinct only, unconscious of his *gaucherie*, an obscene specter, a Nemesis, a horror.

"Hello, Yanci!" he cried, starting toward her with evident relief.

With a heroic effort Yanci turned to Scott, trying to hold his glance to herself. In the very act of turning she noticed the impeccability of Scott's coat, his tie.

"Thanks for luncheon," she said with a radiant smile. "See you tomorrow."

Then she dived rather than ran for Jimmy Long, disposed of his outstretched hand and bundled him bumping through the revolving door with only a quick "Let's hurry!" to appease his somewhat sulky astonishment.

The incident worried her. She consoled herself by remembering that Scott had had only a momentary glance at the man, and that he had probably been looking at her anyhow. Nevertheless, she was horrified, and it is to be doubted whether Jimmy Long enjoyed her company enough to compensate him for the cut-price, twentieth-row tickets he had obtained at Black's Drug Store.

But if Jimmy as a decoy had proved a lamentable failure, an occurrence of Thursday offered her considerable satisfaction and paid tribute to her quickness of mind. She had invented an engagement for luncheon, and Scott was going to meet her at two o'clock to take her to the Hippodrome. She lunched alone somewhat imprudently in the Ritz dining room and sauntered out almost side by side with a good-looking young man who had been at the table next to her.

She expected to meet Scott in the outer lobby, but as she reached the entrance to the restaurant she saw him standing not far away.

On a lightning impulse she turned to the good-looking man abreast of her, bowed sweetly and said in an audible, friendly voice, "Well, I'll see you later."

Then before he could even register astonishment she faced about quickly and joined Scott.

"Who was that?" he asked, frowning.

"Isn't he darling-looking?"

"If you like that sort of looks."

Scott's tone implied that the gentleman referred to was effete and overdressed. Yanci laughed, impersonally admiring the skillfulness of her ruse.

It was in preparation for that all-important Saturday night that on Thursday she went into a shop on 42nd Street to buy some long gloves. She made her purchase and handed the clerk a fifty-dollar bill so that her lightened pocketbook would feel heavier with the change she could put in. To her surprise the clerk tendered her the package and a twenty-five-cent piece.

"Is there anything else?"

"The rest of my change."

"You've got it. You gave me five dollars. Four-seventy-five for the gloves leaves twenty-five cents."

"I gave you fifty dollars."

"You must be mistaken."

Yanci searched her purse.

"I gave you fifty!" she repeated frantically.

"No, ma'am, I saw it myself."

They glared at each other in hot irritation. A cash girl was called to testify, then the floor-manager; a small crowd gathered.

"Why, I'm perfectly sure!" cried Yanci, two angry tears trembling in her eyes. "I'm positive!"

The floor-manager was sorry, but the lady really must have left it at home. There was no fifty-dollar bill in the cash drawer. The bottom was creaking out of Yanci's rickety world.

"If you'll leave your address," said the floor manager, "I'll let you know if anything turns up."

"Oh, you damn fools!" cried Yanci, losing control. "I'll get the police!"

And weeping like a child she left the shop. Outside, helplessness overpowered her. How could she prove anything? It was after six and the store was closing even as she left it. Whichever employee had the fifty-dollar bill would be on her way home now before the police could arrive, and why should the New York police believe her, or even give her fair play?

In despair she returned to the Ritz, where she searched through her trunk for the bill with hopeless and mechanical gestures. It was not there. She had known it would not be there. She gathered every penny together and found that she had fifty-one dollars and thirty cents. Telephoning the office, she asked that her bill be made out up to the following noon—she was too dispirited to think of leaving before then.

She waited in her room, not daring even to send for ice water. Then the phone rang and she heard the room clerk's voice, cheerful and metallic.

"Miss Bowman?"

"Yes."

"Your bill, including tonight, is ex-act-ly fifty-one twenty."

"Fifty-one twenty?" Her voice was trembling.

"Yes, ma'am."

"Thank you very much."

Breathless, she sat there beside the telephone, too frightened now to cry. She had ten cents left in the world!

XI

Friday. She had scarcely slept. There were dark rings under her eyes, and even a hot bath followed by a cold one failed to arouse her from a despairing lethargy. She had never fully realized what it would mean to be without money in New York; her determination and vitality seemed to have vanished at last with her fifty-dollar bill. There was no help for it now—she must attain her desire today or never.

She was to meet Scott at the Plaza for tea. She wondered—was it her imagination, or had his manner been consciously cool the afternoon before? For the first time in several days she had needed to make no effort to keep the conversation from growing sentimental. Suppose he had decided that it must come to nothing—that she was too extravagant, too frivolous. A hundred eventualities presented themselves to her during the morning—a dreary morning, broken only by her purchase of a ten-cent bun at a grocery store.

It was her first food in twenty hours, but she self-consciously pretended to the grocer to be having an amusing and facetious time in buying one bun. She even asked to see his grapes, but told him, after looking at them appraisingly—and hungrily—that she didn't think she'd buy any. They didn't look ripe to her, she said. The store was full of prosperous women who, with thumb and first finger joined and held high in front of them, were inspecting food. Yanci would have liked to ask one of them for a bunch of grapes. Instead she went up to her room in the hotel and ate her bun.

When four o'clock came she found that she was thinking more about the sandwiches she would have for tea than of what else must occur there, and as she walked slowly up Fifth Avenue toward the Plaza she felt a sudden faintness which she took several deep breaths of air to overcome. She wondered vaguely where the bread line was. That was where people in her condition should go—but where was it? How did one find out? She imagined fantastically that it was in the phone book under *B*, or perhaps under *N*, for New York Bread Line.

She reached the Plaza. Scott's figure, as he stood waiting for her in the crowded lobby, was a personification of solidity and hope.

"Let's hurry!" she cried with a tortured smile. "I feel rather punk and I want some tea."

She ate a club sandwich, some chocolate ice cream and six tea biscuits. She could have eaten much more, but she dared not. The eventuality of her hunger having been disposed of, she must turn at bay now and face this business of life, represented by the handsome young man who sat opposite watching her with some emotion whose import she could not determine just behind his level eyes.

But the words, the glance, subtle, pervasive and sweet, that she had planned, failed somehow to come.

"Oh, Scott," she said in a low voice, "I'm so tired."

"Tired of what?" he asked coolly.

"Of—everything."

There was a silence.

"I'm afraid," she said uncertainly—"I'm afraid I won't be able to keep that date with you tomorrow."

There was no pretense in her voice now. The emotion was apparent in the waver of each word, without intention or control.

"I'm going away."

"Are you? Where?"

His tone showed a strong interest, but she winced as she saw that that was all.

"My aunt's come back. She wants me to join her in Florida right away."

"Isn't this rather unexpected?"

"Yes."

"You'll be coming back soon?" he said after a moment.

"I don't think so. I think we'll go to Europe from—from New Orleans."

"Oh!"

Again there was a pause. It lengthened. In the shadow of a moment it would become awkward, she knew. She had lost—well? Yet, she would go on to the end.

"Will you miss me?"

"Yes."

One word. She caught his eyes, wondered for a moment if she saw more there than that kindly interest; then she dropped her own again.

"I like it—here at the Plaza," she heard herself saying.

They spoke of things like that. Afterwards she could never remember what they said. They spoke—even of the tea, of the thaw that was ended and the cold coming down outside. She was sick at heart and she seemed to herself very old. She rose at last.

"I've got to tear," she said. "I'm going out to dinner."

To the last she would keep on—the illusion, that was the important thing. To hold her proud lies inviolate—there was only a moment now. They walked toward the door.

"Put me in a taxi," she said quietly. "I don't feel equal to walking."

He helped her in. They shook hands.

"Good-bye, Scott," she said.

"Good-bye, Yanci," he answered slowly.

"You've been awfully nice to me. I'll always remember what a good time you helped to give me this two weeks."

"The pleasure was mine. Shall I tell the driver the Ritz?"

"No. Just tell him to drive out Fifth. I'll tap on the glass when I want him to stop."

Out Fifth! He would think, perhaps, that she was dining on Fifth. What an appropriate finish that would be! She wondered if he were impressed. She could not see his face clearly, because the air was dark with the snow and her own eyes were blurred by tears.

"Good-bye," he said simply.

He seemed to realize that any pretense of sorrow on his part would be transparent. She knew that he did not want her.

The door slammed, the car started, skidding in the snowy street.

Yanci leaned back dismally in the corner. Try as she might, she could not see where she had failed or what it was that had changed his attitude toward her. For the first time in her life she had ostensibly offered herself to a man—and he had not wanted her. The precariousness of her position paled beside the tragedy of her defeat.

She let the car go on—the cold air was what she needed, of course. Ten minutes had slipped away drearily before she realized that she had not a penny with which to pay the driver.

"It doesn't matter," she thought. "They'll just send me to jail, and that's a place to sleep."

She began thinking of the taxi driver.

"He'll be mad when he finds out, poor man. Maybe he's very poor, and he'll have to pay the fare himself." With a vague sentimentality she began to cry.

"Poor taxi man," she was saying half aloud. "Oh, people have such a hard time—such a hard time!"

She rapped on the window and when the car drew up at a curb she got out. She was at the end of Fifth Avenue and it was dark and cold.

"Send for the police!" she cried in a quick low voice. "I haven't any money!"

The taxi man scowled down at her.

"Then what'd you get in for?"

She had not noticed that another car had stopped about twenty-five feet behind them. She heard running footsteps in the snow and then a voice at her elbow.

"It's all right," someone was saying to the taxi man. "I've got it right here."

A bill was passed up. Yanci slumped sideways against Scott's overcoat.

Scott knew—he knew because he had gone to Princeton to surprise her, because the stranger she had spoken to in the Ritz had been his best friend, because the check of her father's for three hundred dollars had been returned to him marked "No funds." Scott knew—he had known for days.

But he said nothing; only stood there holding her with one arm as her taxi drove away.

"Oh, it's you," said Yanci faintly. "Lucky you came along. I left my purse back at the Ritz, like an awful fool. I do such ridiculous things——"

Scott laughed with some enjoyment. There was a light snow falling, and lest she should slip in the damp he picked her up and carried her back toward his waiting taxi.

"Such ridiculous things," she repeated.

"Go to the Ritz first," he said to the driver. "I want to get a trunk."

TWO FOR A CENT

When the rain was over the sky became yellow in the west and the air was cool. Close to the street, which was of red dirt and lined with cheap bungalows dating from 1910, a little boy was riding a big bicycle along the sidewalk. His plan afforded a monotonous fascination. He rode each time for about a hundred yards, fell off, turned the bicycle around so that it adjoined a stone step and getting on again, not without toil or heat, retraced his course. At one end this was bounded by a colored girl of fourteen holding an anemic baby, and at the other by a scarred, ill-nourished kitten, squatting dismally on the curb. These four were the only souls in sight.

The little boy had accomplished an indefinite number of trips oblivious alike to the melancholy advances of the kitten at one end and to the admiring vacuousness of the colored girl at the other when he swerved dangerously to avoid a man who had turned the corner into the street and recovered his balance only after a moment of exaggerated panic.

But if the incident was a matter of gravity to the boy, it attracted scarcely an instant's notice from the newcomer, who turned suddenly from the sidewalk and stared with obvious and peculiar interest at the house before which he was standing. It was the oldest house in the street, built with clapboards and a shingled roof. It was a *house*—in the barest sense of the word: the sort of house that a child would draw on a blackboard. It was of a period, but of no design, and its exterior had obviously been made only as a decent cloak for what was within. It antedated the stucco bungalows by about thirty years and except for the bungalows, which were reproducing their species with prodigious avidity as though by some monstrous affiliation with the guinea-pig, it was the most common type of house in the country. For thirty years such dwellings had satisfied the canons of the middle class; they had satisfied its financial canons by being cheap, they had satisfied its aesthetic canons by being hideous. It was a house built by a race whose more energetic complement hoped either to move up or move on, and it was the more remarkable that its instability had survived so many summers and retained its pristine hideousness and discomfort so obviously unimpaired.

The man was about as old as the house, that is to say, about forty-five. But unlike the house, he was neither hideous nor cheap. His clothes were too good to have been made outside of a metropolis—moreover, they were so good that it was impossible to tell in which metropolis they were made. His name was Abercrombie and the most important event of his life had taken place in the house before which he was standing. He had been born there.

It was one of the last places in the world where he should have been born. He had thought so within a very few years after the event and he thought so now—an ugly home in a third-rate Southern town where his father had owned a partnership in a grocery store. Since then Abercrombie had played golf with the President of the United States and sat between two duchesses at dinner. He had been bored with the President, he had been bored and not a little embarrassed with the duchesses—nevertheless, the two incidents had pleased him and still sat softly upon his naive vanity. It delighted him that he had gone far.

He had looked fixedly at the house for several minutes before he perceived that no one lived there. Where the shutters were not closed it was because there were no shutters to be closed and in these vacancies, blind vacuous expanses of grey window looked unseeingly down at him. The grass had grown wantonly long in the yard and faint green mustaches were sprouting facetiously in the wide cracks of the walk. But it was evident that the property had been recently occupied for upon the porch lay half a dozen newspapers rolled into cylinders for quick delivery and as yet turned only to a faint resentful yellow.

They were not nearly so yellow as the sky when Abercrombie walked up on the porch and sat down upon an immemorial bench, for the sky was every shade of yellow, the color of tan, the color of gold, the color of peaches. Across the street and beyond a vacant lot rose a rampart of vivid red brick houses and it seemed to Abercrombie that the picture they rounded out was beautiful—the warm earthy brick and the sky fresh after the rain, changing and grey as a dream. All his life when he had wanted to rest his mind he had called up into it the image those two things had made for him when the air was clear just at this hour. So Abercrombie sat there thinking about his young days.

Ten minutes later another man turned the corner of the street, a different sort of man, both in the texture of his clothes and the texture of his soul. He was forty-six years old and he was a shabby drudge, married to a woman, who, as a girl, had known better days. This latter fact, in the republic, may be set down in the red italics of misery.

His name was Hemmick—Henry W. or George D. or John F.—the stock that produced him had had little imagination left to waste either upon his name or his design. He was a clerk in a factory which made ice for the long Southern summer. He was responsible to the man who owned the patent for canning ice, who, in his turn was responsible only to God. Never in his life had Henry W. Hemmick discovered a new way to advertise canned ice nor had it transpired that by taking a diligent correspondence course in ice canning he had secretly been preparing himself for a partnership. Never had he rushed home to his wife, crying: "You can have that servant now, Nell, I have been made General Superintendent." You will have to take him as you take Abercrombie, for what he is and will always be. This is a story of the dead years.

When the second man reached the house he turned in and began to mount the tipsy steps, noticed Abercrombie, the stranger, with a tired surprise, and nodded to him.

"Good evening," he said.

Abercrombie voiced his agreement with the sentiment.

"Cool"—The newcomer covered his forefinger with his handkerchief and sent the swatched digit on a complete circuit of his collar band. "Have you rented this?" he asked.

"No, indeed, I'm just—resting. Sorry if I've intruded—I saw the house was vacant——"

"Oh, you're not intruding!" said Hemmick hastily. "I don't reckon anybody *could* intrude in this old barn. I got out two months ago. They're not ever goin' to rent it any more. I got a little girl about this high—" he held his hand parallel to the ground and at an indeterminate distance "—and she's mighty fond of an old doll that got left here when we moved. Began hollerin' for me to come over and look it up."

"You used to live here?" inquired Abercrombie with interest.

"Lived here eighteen years. Came here'n I was married, raised four children in this house. Yes, *sir*. I know this old fellow." He struck the door-post with the flat of his hand. "I know every leak in her roof and every loose board in her old floor."

Abercrombie had been good to look at for so many years that he knew if he kept a certain attentive expression on his face his companion would continue to talk—indefinitely.

"You from up North?" inquired Hemmick politely, choosing with habituated precision the one spot where the anemic wooden railing would support his weight. "I thought so," he resumed at Abercrombie's nod. "Don't take long to tell a Yankee."

"I'm from New York."

"So?" The man shook his head with inappropriate gravity. "Never have got up there, myself. Started to go a couple of times, before I was married, but never did get to go."

He made a second excursion with his finger and handkerchief and then, as though having come suddenly to a cordial decision, he replaced the handkerchief in one of his bumpy pockets and extended the hand toward his companion.

"My name's Hemmick."

"Glad to know you." Abercrombie took the hand without rising. "Abercrombie's mine."

"I'm mighty glad to know you, Mr. Abercrombie."

Then for a moment they both hesitated, their two faces assumed oddly similar expressions, their eyebrows drew together, their eyes looked far away. Each was straining to force into activity some minute cell long sealed and forgotten in his brain. Each made a little noise in his throat, looked away, looked back, laughed. Abercrombie spoke first.

"We've met."

"I know," agreed Hemmick, "but whereabouts? That's what's got me. You from New York you say?"

"Yes, but I was born and raised in this town. Lived in this house till I left here when I was about seventeen. As a matter of fact, I remember you—you were a couple of years older."

Again Hemmick considered.

"Well," he said vaguely, "I sort of remember, too. I *begin* to remember—I got your name all right and I guess maybe it was your daddy had this house before I rented it. But all I can recollect about you is, that there was a boy named Abercrombie and he went away."

In a few moments they were talking easily. It amused them both to have come from the same house—amused Abercrombie especially, for he was a vain man, rather absorbed, that evening, in his own early poverty. Though he was not given to immature impulses he found it necessary somehow to make it clear in a few sentences that five years after he had gone away from the house and the town he had been able to send for his father and mother to join him in New York.

Hemmick listened with that exaggerated attention which men who have not prospered generally render to men who have. He would have continued to listen had Abercrombie become more expansive, for he was beginning faintly to associate him with an Abercrombie who had figured in the newspapers for several years at the head of shipping boards and financial committees. But Abercrombie, after a moment, made the conversation less personal.

"I didn't realize you had so much heat here, I guess I've forgotten a lot in twenty-five years."

"Why, this is a *cool* day," boasted Hemmick, "this is *cool.* I was just sort of overheated from walking when I came up."

"It's too hot," insisted Abercrombie with a restless movement; then he added abruptly, "I don't like it here. It means nothing to me—nothing—I've wondered if I did, you know, that's why I came down. And I've decided.

"You see," he continued hesitantly, "up to recently the North was still full of professional Southerners, some real, some by sentiment, but all given to flowery monologues on the beauty of their old family plantations and all jumping up and howling when the band played 'Dixie.' You know what I mean,"—he turned to Hemmick,— "it got to be a sort of a national joke. Oh, I was in the game, too, I suppose, I used to stand up and perspire and cheer, and I've given young men positions for no particular reason except that they claimed to come from South Carolina or Virginia—" again he broke off and became suddenly abrupt—"but I'm through, I've been here six hours and I'm through!"

"Too hot for you?" inquired Hemmick, with mild surprise.

"Yes! I've felt the heat and I've seen the men—those two or three dozen loafers standing in front of the stores on Jackson Street—in thatched straw hats,"—then he added, with a touch of humor, "they're what my son calls 'slash-pocket, belted-back boys.' Do you know the ones I mean?"

"Jelly-beans," Hemmick nodded gravely, "we call 'em Jelly-beans. No-account lot of boys all right. They got signs up in front of most of the stores asking 'em not to stand there."

"They ought to!" asserted Abercrombie, with a touch of irascibility. "That's my picture of the South now, you know—a skinny, dark-haired young man with a gun on his hip and a stomach full of corn liquor or Dope Dola, leaning up against a drug store waiting for the next lynching."

Hemmick objected, though with apology in his voice.

"You got to remember, Mr. Abercrombie, that we haven't had the money down here since the war——"

Abercrombie waved this impatiently aside.

"Oh, I've heard all that," he said, "and I'm tired of it. And I've heard the South lambasted till I'm tired of that, too. It's not taking France and Germany fifty years to get on their feet, and their war made your war look like a little fracas up an alley. And it's not your fault and it's not anybody's fault. It's just that this is too damn hot to be a white man's country and it always will be. I'd like to see 'em pack two or three of these states full of darkies and drop 'em out of the Union."

Hemmick nodded, thoughtfully, though without thought. He had never thought; for over twenty years he had seldom ever held opinions, save the opinions of the local press or of some majority made articulate through passion. There was a certain luxury in thinking that he had never been able to afford. When cases were set before him he either accepted them outright, if they were comprehensible to him, or rejected them if they required a modicum of concentration. Yet he was not a stupid man. He was poor and busy and tired and there were no ideas at large in his community, even had he been capable of grasping them. The idea that he did not think would have been equally incomprehensible to him. He was a closed book, half-full of badly printed, uncorrelated trash.

Just now, his reaction to Abercrombie's assertion was exceedingly simple. Since the remarks proceeded from a man who was a Southerner by birth, who was successful—moreover, who was confident and decisive and persuasive and suave—he was inclined to accept them without suspicion or resentment.

He took one of Abercrombie's cigars and pulling on it, still with a stern imitation of profundity upon his tired face, watched the color glide out of the sky and the grey veils come down. The little boy and his bicycle, the baby, the nursemaid, the forlorn kitten, all had departed. In the stucco bungalows pianos gave out hot weary notes that inspired the crickets to competitive sound, and squeaky graphophones filled in the intervals with patches of whining ragtime until the impression was created that each living room in the street opened directly out into the darkness.

"What *I* want to find out," Abercrombie was saying with a frown, "is why I didn't have sense enough to *know* that this was a worthless town. It was entirely an accident that I left here, an utterly blind chance, and as it happened, the very train that took me away was full of luck for me. The man I sat beside gave me my start in life." His tone became resentful. "But I thought this was all right. I'd have stayed except that I'd gotten into a scrape down at the High School—I got expelled and my daddy told me he didn't want me at home any more. Why didn't I know the place wasn't any good? Why didn't I *see?*"

"Well, you'd probably never known anything better?" suggested Hemmick mildly.

"That wasn't any excuse," insisted Abercrombie. "If I'd been any good I'd have known. As a matter of fact—as—a—matter—of—fact," he repeated slowly, "I think that at heart I was the sort of boy who'd have lived and died here happily and never known there was anything better." He turned to Hemmick with a look almost of distress. "It worries me to think that my—that what's happened to me can be ascribed to chance. But that's the sort of boy I think I was. I didn't start off with the Dick Whittington idea—I started off by accident."

After this confession, he stared out into the twilight with a dejected expression that Hemmick could not understand. It was impossible for the latter to share any sense of the importance of such a distinction—in fact from a man of Abercrombie's position it struck him as unnecessarily trivial. Still, he felt that some manifestation of acquiescence was only polite.

"Well," he offered, "it's just that some boys get the bee to get up and go North and some boys don't. I happened to have the bee to go North. But I didn't. That's the difference between you and me."

Abercrombie turned to him intently.

"You did?" he asked, with unexpected interest, "you wanted to get out?"

"At one time." At Abercrombie's eagerness Hemmick began to attach a new importance to the subject. "At one time," he repeated, as though the singleness of the occasion was a thing he had often mused upon.

"How old were you?"

"Oh—'bout twenty."

"What put it into your head?"

"Well, let me see—" Hemmick considered. "—I don't know whether I remember sure enough but it seems to me that when I was down to the University—I was there two years—one of the professors told me that a smart boy ought to go North. He said, business wasn't going to amount to much down here for the next fifty years. And I guessed he was right. My father died about then, so I got a job as runner in the bank here, and I didn't have much interest in anything except saving up enough money to go North. I was bound I'd go."

"Why didn't you? Why didn't you?" insisted Abercrombie in an aggrieved tone.

"Well," Hemmick hesitated. "Well, I right near did but—things didn't work out and I didn't get to go. It was a funny sort of business. It all started about the smallest thing you can think of. It all started about a penny."

"A penny?"

"That's what did it—one little penny. That's why I didn't go 'way from here and all, like I intended."

"Tell me about it, man!" exclaimed his companion. He looked at his watch impatiently. "I'd like to hear the story."

Hemmick sat for a moment, distorting his mouth around the cigar.

"Well, to begin with," he said, at length, "I'm going to ask you if you remember a thing that happened here about twenty-five years ago. A fellow named Hoyt, the cashier of the Cotton National Bank, disappeared one night with about thirty thousand dollars in cash. Say, man, they didn't talk about anything else down here at the time. The whole town was shaken up about it, and I reckin' you can imagine the disturbance it caused down at all the banks and especially at the Cotton National."

"I remember."

"Well, they caught him, and they got most of the money back, and by and by the excitement died down, except in the bank where the thing had happened. Down there it seemed as if they'd never get used to it. Mr. Deems, the First Vice President, who'd always been pretty kind and decent, got to be a changed man. He was suspicious of the clerks, the tellers, the janitor, the watchman, most of the officers, and yes, by Golly, I guess he got so he kept an eye on the President himself.

"I don't mean he was just watchful—he was downright hipped on the subject. He'd come up and ask you funny questions when you were going about your business. He'd walk into the teller's cage on tiptoe and watch him without saying anything. If there was any mistake of any kind in the bookkeeping, he'd not only fire a clerk or so, but he'd raise such a riot that he made you want to push him into a vault and slam the door on him.

"He was just about running the bank then, and he'd affected the other officers, and—oh, you can imagine the havoc a thing like that could work on any sort of an organization. Everybody was so nervous that they made mistakes whether they were careful or not. Clerks were staying downtown until eleven at night trying to account for a lost nickel. It was a thin year, anyhow, and everything financial was pretty rickety, so one thing worked on another until the crowd of us were as near craziness as anybody can be and carry on the banking business at all.

"I was a runner—and all through the heat of one Godforsaken summer I ran. I ran and I got mighty little money for it, and that was the time I hated that bank and this town, and all I wanted was to get out and go North. I was getting ten dollars a week, and I'd decided that when I'd saved fifty out of it I was going down to the depot and buy me a ticket to Cincinnati. I had an uncle in the banking business there, and he said he'd give me an opportunity with him. But he never offered to pay my way, and I guess he thought if I was worth having I'd manage to get up there by myself. Well, maybe I wasn't worth having because, anyhow, I never did.

"One morning on the hottest day of the hottest July I ever knew—and you know what that means down here—I left the bank to call on a man named Harlan and collect some money that'd come due on a note. Harlan had the cash waiting for me all right, and when I counted it I found it amounted to three hundred dollars and eighty-six cents, the change being in brand new coin that Harlan had drawn from another bank that morning. I put the three one-hundred-dollar bills in my wallet and the change in my vest pocket, signed a receipt and left. I was going straight back to the bank.

"Outside the heat was terrible. It was enough to make you dizzy, and I hadn't been feeling right for a couple of days, so, while I waited in the shade for a street car, I was congratulating myself that in a month or so I'd be out of this and up where it was some cooler. And then as I stood there it occurred to me all of a sudden that outside of the money which I'd just collected, which, of course, I couldn't touch, I didn't have a cent in my pocket. I'd have to walk back to the bank, and it was about fifteen blocks away. You see, on the night before, I'd found that my change came to just a dollar, and I'd traded it for a bill at the corner store and added it to the roll in the bottom of my trunk. So there was no help for it—I took off my coat and I stuck my handkerchief into my collar and struck off through the suffocating heat for the bank.

"Fifteen blocks—you can imagine what that was like, and I was sick when I started. From away up by Juniper Street—you remember where that is; the new Mieger Hospital's there now—all the way down to Jackson. After about six blocks I began to stop and rest whenever I found a patch of shade wide enough to hold me, and as I got pretty near I could just keep going by thinking of the big glass of iced tea my mother'd have waiting beside my plate at lunch. But after that I began getting too sick to even want the iced tea—I wanted to get rid of that money and then lie down and die.

"When I was still about two blocks away from the bank I put my hand into my watch pocket and pulled out that change; was sort of jingling it in my hand; making myself believe that I was so close that it was convenient to have it ready. I happened to glance into my hand, and all of a sudden I stopped up short and reached down quick into my watch pocket. The pocket was empty. There was a little hole in the bottom, and my hand held only a half dollar, a quarter and a dime. I had lost one cent.

"Well, sir, I can't tell you, I can't express to you the feeling of discouragement that this gave me. One penny, mind you—but think: just the week before a runner had lost his job because he was a little bit shy twice. It was only carelessness; but there you were! They were all in a panic that they might get fired themselves, and the best thing to do was to fire someone else—first.

"So you can see that it was up to me to appear with that penny.

"Where I got the energy to care as much about it as I did is more than I can understand. I was sick and hot and weak as a kitten, but it never occurred to me that I could do anything except find or replace that penny, and immediately I began casting about for a way to do it. I looked into a couple of stores, hoping I'd see someone I knew, but while there were a few fellows loafing in front, just as you saw them today, there wasn't one that I felt like going up to and saying: 'Here! You got a penny?' I thought of a couple of offices where I could have gotten it without much trouble, but they were some distance off, and besides being pretty dizzy, I hated to go out of my route when I was carrying bank money, because it looked kind of strange.

"So what should I do but commence walking back along the street toward the Union Depot where I last remembered having the penny. It was a brand new penny, and I thought maybe I'd see it shining where it dropped. So I kept walking, looking pretty carefully at the sidewalk and thinking what I'd better do. I laughed a little, because I felt sort of silly for worrying about a penny, but I didn't enjoy laughing, and it really didn't seem silly to me at all.

"Well, by and by I got back to the Union Depot without having either seen the old penny or having thought what was the best way to get another. I hated to go all the way home, 'cause we lived a long distance out; but what else was I to do? So I found a piece of shade close to the depot, and stood there considering, thinking first one thing and then another, and not getting anywhere at all. One little penny, just *one*—something almost any man in sight would have given me; something even the nigger baggage-smashers were jingling around in their pockets. . . . I must have stood there about five minutes. I remember there was a line of about a dozen men in front of an army recruiting station they'd just opened, and a couple of them began to yell: 'Join the Army!' at me. That woke me up, and I moved on back toward the bank, getting worried now, getting mixed up and sicker and sicker and knowing a million ways to find a penny and not one that seemed convenient or right. I was exaggerating the importance of losing it, and I was exaggerating the difficulty of finding another, but you just have to believe that it seemed about as important to me just then as though it were a hundred dollars.

"Then I saw a couple of men talking in front of Moody's soda place, and recognized one of them—Mr. Burling—who'd been a friend of my father's. That was a relief, I can tell you. Before I knew it I was chattering to him so quick that he couldn't follow what I was getting at.

"'Now,' he said, 'you know I'm a little deaf and can't understand when you talk that fast! What is it you want, Henry? Tell me from the beginning.'

"'Have you got any change with you?' I asked him just as loud as I dared. 'I just want——' Then I stopped short; a man a few feet away had turned around and was looking at us. It was Mr. Deems, the first Vice-President of the Cotton National Bank."

Hemmick paused, and it was still light enough for Abercrombie to see that he was shaking his head to and fro in a puzzled way.

When he spoke his voice held a quality of pained surprise, a quality that it might have carried over twenty years.

"I never *could* understand what it was that came over me then. I must have been sort of crazy with the heat—that's all I can decide. Instead of just saying, 'Howdy' to Mr. Deems, in a natural way, and telling Mr. Burling I wanted to borrow a nickel for tobacco, because I'd left my purse at home, I turned away quick as a flash and began walking up the street at a great rate, feeling like a criminal who had come near being caught.

"Before I'd gone a block I was sorry. I could almost hear the conversation that must've been taking place between those two men:

"'What do you reckon's the matter with that young man?' Mr. Burling would say without meaning any harm. 'Came up to me all excited and wanted to know if I had any money, and then he saw you and rushed away like he was crazy.'

"And I could almost see Mr. Deems' big eyes get narrow with suspicion and watch him twist up his trousers and come strolling along after me. I was in a real panic now, and no mistake. Suddenly I saw a one-horse surrey going by, and recognized Bill Kennedy, a friend of mine, driving it. I yelled at him, but he didn't hear me. Then I yelled again, but he didn't pay any attention, so I started after him at a run, swaying from side to side, I guess, like I was drunk, and calling his name every few minutes. He looked around once, but he didn't see me; he kept right on going and turned out of sight at the next corner. I stopped then because I was too weak to go any farther. I was just about to sit down on the curb and rest when I looked around, and the first thing I saw was Mr. Deems walking after me as fast as he could come. There wasn't any of my imagination about it this time—the look in his eyes showed he wanted to know what was the matter with *me!*

"Well, that's about all I remember clearly until about twenty minutes later, when I was at home trying to unlock my trunk with fingers that were trembling like a tuning fork. Before I could get it open, Mr. Deems and a policeman came in. I began talking all at once about not being a thief and trying to tell them what had happened, but I guess I was sort of hysterical, and the more I said the worse matters were. When I managed to get the story out it seemed sort of crazy, even to me—and it was true—it was true, true as I've told you—every word!—that one penny that I lost somewhere down by the station——" Hemmick broke off and began laughing grotesquely—as though the excitement that had come over him as he finished his tale was a weakness of which he was ashamed. When he resumed it was with an affectation of nonchalance.

"I'm not going into the details of what happened because nothing much did—at least not on the scale you judge events by up North. It cost me my job, and I changed a good name for a bad one. Somebody tattled and somebody lied, and the impression got around that I'd lost a lot of the bank's money and had been tryin' to cover it up.

"I had an awful time getting a job after that. Finally I got a statement out of the bank that contradicted the wildest of the stories that had started, but the people who were still interested said it was just because the bank didn't want any fuss or scandal—and the rest had forgotten: that is they'd forgotten what had happened, but they remembered that somehow I just wasn't a young fellow to be trusted——"

Hemmick paused and laughed again, still without enjoyment, but bitterly, uncomprehendingly, and with a profound helplessness.

"So, you see, that's why I didn't go to Cincinnati," he said slowly; "my mother was alive then, and this was a pretty bad blow to her. She had an idea—one of those old-fashioned Southern ideas that stick in people's heads down here—that somehow I ought to stay here in town and prove myself honest. She had it on her mind, and she wouldn't hear of my going. She said that the day I went'd be day she'd die. So I sort of had to stay till I'd got back my—my reputation."

"How long did that take?" asked Abercrombie quietly.

"About—ten years."

"Oh——"

"Ten years," repeated Hemmick, staring out into the gathering darkness. "This is a little town you see: I say ten years because it was about ten years when the last reference to it came to my ears. But I was married long before that; had a kid. Cincinnati was out of my mind by that time."

"Of course," agreed Abercrombie.

They were both silent for a moment—then Hemmick added apologetically:

"That was sort of a long story, and I don't know if it could have interested you much. But you asked me——"

"It *did* interest me," answered Abercrombie politely. "It interested me tremendously. It interested me much more than I thought it would."

It occurred to Hemmick that he himself had never realized what a curious, rounded tale it was. He saw dimly now that what had seemed to him only a fragment, a grotesque interlude, was really significant, complete. It was an interesting story; it was the story upon which turned the failure of his life. Abercrombie's voice broke in upon his thoughts.

"You see, it's so different from my story," Abercrombie was saying. "It was an accident that you stayed—and it was an accident that I went away. You deserve more actual—actual credit, if there is such a thing in the world, for your intention of getting out and getting on. You see, I'd more or less gone wrong at seventeen. I was—well, what you call a Jelly-bean. All I wanted was to take it easy through life—and one day I just happened to see a sign up above my head that had on it: 'Special rate to Atlanta, three dollars and forty-two cents.' So I took out my change and counted it——"

Hemmick nodded. Still absorbed in his own story, he had forgotten the importance, the comparative magnificence of Abercrombie. Then suddenly he found himself listening sharply:

"I had just three dollars and forty-one cents in my pocket. But, you see, I was standing in line with a lot of other young fellows down by the Union Depot about to enlist in the army for three years. And I saw that extra penny on the walk not three feet away. I saw it because it was brand new and shining in the sun like gold."

The Georgia night had settled over the street, and as the blue drew down upon the dust the outlines of the two men had become less distinct, so that it was not easy for anyone who passed along the walk to tell that one of these men was of the few and the other of no importance. All the detail was gone—Abercrombie's fine gold wrist watch, his collar, that he ordered by the dozen from London, the dignity that sat upon him in his chair—all faded and were engulfed with Hemmick's awkward suit and preposterous humped shoes into that pervasive depth of night that, like death, made nothing matter, nothing differentiate, nothing remain. And a little later on a passerby saw only the two glowing disks about the size of a penny that marked the rise and fall of their cigars.

RECORD OF VARIANTS

The lists below record the editorial decisions amongst the variant readings, substantive and accidental, in the significant witnesses for each of Fitzgerald's stories. In the case of *Flappers and Philosophers*, these are the serial text and the text of the Scribners 1920 first edition, first printing. Also included in the lists are independent emendations by the editor. The first reading in each entry is that printed in the Cambridge text. It is followed by a bracket, then by a siglum indicating the text from which the reading is drawn. There is a dividing semicolon, followed by a record of the variant reading(s) in other form(s) of the text. The following sigla and symbols are employed:

~	the same word
¶	new paragraph
‸	space or the absence of punctuation or paragraphing
ed	an independent editorial emendation
A1	first printing of Scribners 1920
A4	fourth printing of Scribners 1920
ser	serial text of the story
B	*Bits of Paradise*
P	*The Price Was High*
MS	Early partial holograph of "Babes in the Woods"
TS	Sheets from *Smart Set* carbon typescript of "The Debutante" incorporated into the MS of *This Side of Paradise*
trsh	Tearsheets of "Two for a Cent"
BSS	*The Best Short Stories of 1922*, ed. O'Brien

Substantives

"The Offshore Pirate"

6.1	mechanically . . . distance,] A1; mechanically‸ ser
6.12	you?" ¶ The lemon . . . scornfully.] A1; you?" ser

6.26	No.] A1; No. It's too low. ser
7.7	to so much as] A1; so much as to ser
8.11	woman, Mimi] A1; Mimi ser
8.25	show a little intelligence] A1; have ~ ~sense ser
8.27	Don't you suppose I] A1; I ser
8.28	know by this time] A1; know ser
10.5	deck] ser; desk A1
14.8	detraction] A1; distraction ser
15.30	inevitably] A1; always ser
15.37	children—nice white children] A1; children‸ ser
16.2	poh] A1; po' ser
21.4	all."] A1; ~." ¶ Ardita thought for a moment. ¶ "I'll name it," she said. "It'll be the Isle of Illusion." ¶ "Or of Disillusion," murmured Carlyle. ¶ "Disillusion, if more people know about it than Babe seems to think." ser
21.16	hanged] ed; hung ser, A1
21.24	me] A1; I ser
22.20	had had] A1; had ser
23.20	sculptor up at Rye] A1; sculptor ser
24.1	Two years] A1; One year ser
24.29	a fancy-dress party] A1; fancy-dress parties ser
25.29	splash] ser; slash A1
26.26	her young perfection] A1; the young life within her ser
27.20	naïf] A1; untutored ser
27.31	she said] A1; said Ardita ser
27.33	musical instruments] A1; instruments ser
29.20	round] ser; around A1
32.18	resistance, for two] A1; ~. ¶ Two ser
33.28	with a] A1; with a—a ser
34.2	He] A1; Her uncle ser
34.26	passed across] A1; came over ser
35.22	"Perhaps . . . illustration.] A1; ¶ And Ardita being a girl of some perspicacity had not difficulty guessing the other. ser

"The Ice Palace"

36.11	Ford] A1; flivver ser
37.13	lie] ser; lay A1
37.22	somewhat] A1; rather ser

37.24	had] A1; ~ what was locally called ser
38.4	niggery street] A1; street ser
38.6	Ford] A1; flivver ser
38.21	question] A1; ~ to ask a girl ser
38.23	summer] A1; summah ser
38.29	offer] A1; offah ser
38.30	support] A1; suppawt ser
38.32	Yankee," he persisted.] A1; ~." ser
39.37	sort] A1; sawt ser
40.23	for] A1; faw ser
40.32	she] A1; Sally Carrol ser
41.27	alice] A1; bright ser
43.2	sort] A1; sawt ser
43.21	I] A1; it ser
43.34	sleep. She] A1; ~. ¶ Sally Carrol ser
44.7	whose every branch was] A1; with each branch ser
48.25	French] A1; seventeenth-century French ser
50.5	haunting] A1; hauntin' ser
53.16	Mobile] A1; Birmingham ser
53.30	brimming with] A1; full of ser
55.35	was] ser; were A1
56.35	they entered they] A1; it ~ it ser
57.23	mitten] A1; glove ser
60.16	Ford] A1; flivver ser

"Head and Shoulders"

62.18	Pall Malls] A1; cigarettes ser
62.23	appreciate the significance] A1; synchronize the sources ser
63.21	The] A1; Why, the ser
64.21	Juliet] ed; Juliette ser, A1
64.32	snore] A1; snooze ser
70.35	Nabiscos] ed; biscuits ser, Nabiscoes A1
76.24	magazine] ser; magazines A1
79.30	four] A1; three ser
81.18	a] A1; the ser
85.12	celebrities. I've . . . me. M'sieur] A1; celebrities. M'sieur ser
85.14	Laurier!" exclaimed Horace.] A1; Laurier!" ser

"The Cut-Glass Bowl"

87.10	from the] A1; from ser
105.7	with black . . . with blue] A1; with blue ser
106.7	panorama] A4; panoply ser, A1
106.20	up] A1; up to ser

"Bernice Bobs Her Hair"

110.4	"crazy about her."] A1; ‸wildly in love with her.‸ ser
110.5	feeling] A1; feelings ser
110.18	dopeless] A1; hopeless ser
117.13	railroad ticket] A1; ticket ser
124.13	before Marjorie dug it out of her trunk—] A1; before— ser
127.29	Good] A1; Swell ser
130.8	the cleaners] A1; Derry's shop ser
130.9	dress] A1; hat ser

"Benediction"

135.5	damn] A1; blamed ser
135.19	through eastern] A1; through ser
138.4	around. I] A1; around because I ser
144.20	There . . . eyes.] A1; Lois felt the rims of her eyes growing suddenly red. ser
148.37	knew then that I wanted more] A1; knew I wanted more then ser
149.7	then. I wanted the] A1; than I wanted—the ser

"Dalyrimple Goes Wrong"

151.16	luck triumphant or sentiment rampant] A1; luck or sentiment ser
151.26	blah!] A1; bad ser
154.14	stank] A1; reeked ser
154.19	grey] ed; gray A1; coloured ser
154.27	Hell] A1; Slush ser
158.18	principles] A1; principals ser

"The Four Fists"

175.6 laughingly apologetic] A1; laughing ser
176.18 great deal] A1; lot ser
176.23 her best friend] A1; big brother ser
176.26 her best friend] A1; big brother ser
179.6 selfishness.] A1; ~. It made him sick to think of it, and feeling sick with one's self is not bad medicine in a world that is primarily cynical. ser
180.12 answered Carhart] A1; he answered ser
180.29 San Felipe] A1; Tumlo ser
183.21 long-winded dude] A1; starchy, arguin' snake ser
183.24 Dimly he] A1; He ser
183.24 doorway] A1; door ser
183.30 got up and strode] A1; strode ser
184.19 *blamed*] A1; *insane* ser

"Babes in the Woods"

191.34 up terribly] MS; terrible ser
194.15 learned] MS; learn ser

"The Debutante"

198.2 (*A One-Act Play*)] ser; Omitted TS
199.19 *at*] ser; *on* TS
203.18 skirt] ser; shirt TS
205.18 *finishes*] ed; *finished* TS, ser
207.16 view on men] ser; view TS
213.4 sentiment] TS; sentimental ser
217.29 *puffing*] ser; *then puffing* TS
221.5 loathe] ed; loath TS, ser
225.11 some] ser; with some TS
228.24 CURTAIN.] ser; Omitted TS

"Myra Meets His Family"

229.13 Rose] ed; Red ser, P
Fitzgerald evidently misremembered the name; dinner dances were held at the Plaza Rose Room.
233.21 telegram] ser; telegraph P

"The Smilers"

Note: No substantive emendations have been made in the *Smart Set* text.

"The Popular Girl"

Note: This story appeared in two parts in the *Post*; the division was between sections V and VI.

263.4	to a] B; to ser
269.14	eyes. "I] ed; ~. ¶ "~ ser, B
272.30	now the] ser; the new B

"Two for a Cent"

309.6	fell off] trsh; dismounted ser
314.29	It's . . . Union."] ser Omitted P
323.32	Georgia] BSS; Alabama ser

Accidentals

"The Offshore Pirate"

5.13	spoiled‸] A1; ~, ser
5.23	width,] A1; ~‸ ser
5.28	long‸] A1; ~, ser
7.16	‸way] ser; '~ A1
8.3	tire‸] ser; ~, A1
8.28	that?] A1; ~. ser
8.34	‸way] ser; 'way A1
9.18	"Carrots . . . bellows."] A1; ‸*Carrots . . . bellows*.‸ ser The song verses that follow in the story are given the same typographical treatment.
10.33	brunet] ser; brunette A1
11.30	and‸ wheeling about‸] A1; ~, ~ ~, ser
11.37	hours,] A1; ~‸ ser
12.2	passed,] A1; ~‸ ser
12.3	vacated‸] A1; ~, ser

12.5 brass‸] ser; ~, A1
12.6 book‸] ser; ~, A1
12.27 walk,] A1; ~‸ ser
13.31 Ardita‸] ser; ~, A1
14.12 egotists—] A1; ~; ser
14.16 her,] A1; ~‸ ser
14.22 man, . . . contrary,] A1; ~‸ . . . ~‸ ser
15.22 awning‸] ser; ~, A1
15.23 artichokes‸] ser; ~, A1
16.6 country‸] ser; ~, A1
16.24 pianist,] A1; ~‸ ser
16.34 greenroom‸] ser; ~, A1
17.1 money and time,] A1; ~, ~ ~‸ ser
18.25 Angels,] A1; ~‸ ser
18.27 delight‸] ser; ~, A1
19.12 present‸] ser; ~, A1
19.33 toward, . . . from,] A1; ~‸ . . . ~‸ ser
20.6 swim‸] ser; ~, A1
20.23 contagious‸] ser; ~, A1
20.28 sand,] A1; ~; ser
20.31 flat‸] ser; ~, A1
20.31 and‸ . . . vegetation‸] A1; ~, . . . ~, ser
21.5 boulders] A1; bowlders ser
21.23 wharfs] A1; wharves ser
21.33 India.] A1; ~! ser
23.8 edge‸] A1; ~, ser
23.26 and, . . . rock,] A1; ~‸ . . . ~‸ ser
23.28 wide,] A1; ~‸ ser
24.30 York‸] ser; ~, A1
25.9 life‸] ser; ~, A1
25.15 déclassé] A1; *déclassée* ser
25.31 plowing] ser; ploughing A1
26.12 high‸] ser; ~, A1
26.31 air‸] ser; ~, A1
27.2 ax] ser; axe A1
27.4 suit‸] ser; ~, A1
27.13 long‸] ser; ~, A1
27.20 imagination‸] ser; ~, A1
27.23 island‸] ser; ~, A1
27.26 breed‸] A1; ~, ser

27.33	instruments‸] ser; ~, A1
28.5	kidnapped] A1; kidnaped ser
29.9	left‸] ser; ~, A1
29.9	worshipped] A1; worshiped ser
29.16	hair‸] ser; ~, A1
30.26	voice‸] ser; ~, A1
32.1	lusterless] ser; lustreless A1
32.16	settees‸] ser; ~, A1
32.21	up‸] ser; ~, A1
32.23	round‸] ser; ~, A1
32.32	pretty,] A1; ~‸ ser
33.5	breathless‸] ser; ~, A1
33.9	one‸] ser; ~, A1
34.35	disbelief‸] ser; ~, A1

"The Ice Palace"

36.2	jar,] A1; ~‸ ser
36.6	sun‸] ser; ~, A1
36.8	Georgia—] ser; ~, A1
36.14	part‸] ser; ~, A1
37.11	nose‸] ser; ~, A1
37.21	lean‸] ser; ~, A1
37.25	gasoline] ser; gasolene A1
37.26	town,] A1; ~‸ ser
37.34	something,] A1; ~‸ ser
37.35	golf, . . . billiards,] A1; ~‸ . . . ~‸ ser
38.4	gracious‸] ser; ~, A1
38.4	girls,] A1; ~‸ ser
38.9	prosperous‸] ser; ~, A1
39.23	failures, . . . sad,] A1; ~‸ . . . ~‸ ser
40.11	door‸] ser; ~, A1
40.15	earth‸ . . . toil‸] ser; ~, . . . ~, A1
40.18	comforting‸] ser; ~, A1
40.27	broad‸] ser; ~, A1
41.4	paused‸ irresolute‸] ser; ~, ~, A1
41.10	moldy] ser; mouldy A1
41.21	"‸Margery Lee,‸"] A1; "'~ ~,'" ser
41.21	"‸1844–1873.] A1; "' ~–~'. ser
41.30	wide‸] ser; ~, A1

42.12	endless‸] ser; ~, A1
42.17	it‸] ser; ~, A1
42.22	unimportant‸ evidently‸] A1; ~, ~, ser
43.18	sleigh-riding‸] ser; ~, A1
44.15	"Then . . . go,"] A1; ‸*Then . . . go*,‸ ser
	Lyrics and verses of poetry in the remainder of the story are given the same typographical treatment.
45.1	exclamations, and perfunctory‸] A1; ~‸ ~ ~, ser
45.2	dears] A1; dear's ser
45.2	Myra,] A1; ~‸ ser
45.11	egg‸] ser; ~, A1
45.12	breathless‸] A1; ~, ser
45.14	library,] A1; ~‸ ser
45.21	home‸ . . . books‸] ser; ~, . . . ~, A1
45.22	great-uncles‸] ser; ~, A1
46.2	family‸] ser; ~, A1
46.6	father‸] ser; ~, A1
46.11	‸‸For] A1; ¶ "For ser
47.1	expect‸] ser; ~, A1
47.10	party‸] ser; ~, A1
47.18	states] ser; States A1
47.37	dinner‸] ser; ~, A1
48.10	eyes‸] ser; ~, A1
48.14	formal‸] ser; ~, A1
48.15	her‸] A1; ~, ser
49.27	narrow‸] ser; ~, A1
51.1	tangled‸] A1; ~, ser
51.9	fancy,] A1; ~‸ ser
51.19	center] ser; centre A1
51.26	tedious‸] A1; ~, ser
52.19	‸And] A1; ¶ ~ ser
52.21	held‸] ser; ~, A1
53.5	criticized] ser; criticised A1
53.8	saw,] A1; ~‸ ser
53.13	Haven‸] ser; ~, A1
53.15	carpetbagger‸] ser; ~, A1
53.28	nodded‸] A1; ~, ser
53.33	Harry, . . . wrong,] A1; ~‸ . . . ~‸ ser
54.4	Dixie‸] A1; ~, ser
54.6	forward‸] A1; ~, ser

54.22	wind‸] ser; ~, A1
55.6	melting‸] ser; ~, A1
55.12	eyelashes‸] ser; ~, A1
55.14	line‸] ser; ~, A1
55.34	Patton‸] ser; ~, A1
56.8	this] A1; This ser
57.8	thunder‸] ser; ~, A1
57.18	chant‸] ser; ~, A1
57.23	gauntlet] ser; gantlet A1
57.24	ice‸] ser; ~, A1
57.27	room‸] A1; ~, ser
58.5	long‸] ser; ~, A1
58.7	flat‸] ser; ~, A1
58.10	Red Sea] A1; red sea ser
58.17	out‸] ser; ~, A1
58.18	small‸ frightened cry‸] ser; ~, ~ ~, A1
58.23	smokeless‸] ser; ~, A1
58.27	furious‸] ser; ~, A1
59.2	body‸] ser; ~, A1
59.15	young‸ white brow‸ and wide‸ welcoming eyes‸] ser; ~, ~ ~, ~ ~, ~ ~, A1
59.28	her‸] ser; ~, A1
59.28	cheek—] A1; ~, ser
60.8	day-long] ed; ~‸~ ser, A1
60.13	arm‸] ser; ~, A1
60.22	'Tain't] A1; 'Taint ser
60.23	enough!] A1; ~, ser

"Head and Shoulders"

61.5	Geometry‸] ser; ~, A1
61.19	armistice] A1; Armistice ser
62.1	him‸] ser; ~, A1
62.10	James!] ed; ~‸ ser, A1
62.20	Sheffield‸] ser; ~, A1
62.23	Frenchman‸ Laurier‸] A1; ~, ~, ser
63.12	Two ("Oh . . . dancing!"),] A1; ~ —‸ "~ . . . ~!"‸— ser
64.23	leap‸] ser; ~, A1
66.1	then, . . . mind,] A1; ~‸ . . . ~‸ ser
66.19	professors‸] ser; ~, A1

68.7 banister:] A1; ~, ser
68.18 flight‸] ser; ~, A1
68.26 near,] A1; ~‸ ser
68.29 real‸] ser; ~, A1
68.35 James!] ed; ~‸ ser, A1
69.13 "DEAR OMAR . . . MEADOW."] A1; ‸*Dear Omar* . . . ~.‸ ser
70.8 Hm] A1; H'm ser
The same spelling choice is made throughout the story.
70.10 pause:] A1; ~ — ser
71.3 Divinerries'‸] ser; ~, A1
71.6 Marvelous] ser; Marvellous A1
71.7 newspaper‸] ser; ~, A1
71.9 letter‸] ser; ~, A1
71.22 signaled] ser; signalled A1
72.14 couch‸] ser; ~, A1
72.21 Marcia‸] ser; ~, A1
73.6 hurriedly‸] ser; ~, A1
73.27 "Uptown . . . moon."] A1; ‸*Uptown* . . . *moon*.‸ ser
The remaining lyrics in the story are given the same typographical treatment.
73.32 criticizing] ser; criticising A1
74.7 you'll‸] A1; ~—— ser
74.15 another‸] ser; ~, A1
74.21 rather‸ stifled] A1; ~-|~ ser
74.24 ‸The] A1; ¶ The ser
77.16 Manhattan‸] ser; ~, A1
77.21 factotum‸] ser; ~, A1
77.25 energy‸] ser; ~, A1
77.30 lipped‸ . . . man‸] ser; ~, . . . ~, A1
77.37 today‸] ser; ~, A1
80.6 course‸] A1; ~, ser
80.15 wonder, . . . humor,] A1; ~‸ . . . ~‸ ser
80.19 lit‸] ser; ~, A1
80.25 over‸] ser; ~, A1
80.34 parabolas,] A1; ~‸ ser
80.37 low‸] ser; ~, A1
81.8 Hippodrome,] A1; ~‸ ser
81.26 indeed,] A1; ~‸ ser
81.30 white‸] ser; ~, A1

82.5	Wendell‸] A1; ~, ser
82.11	pillow‸] ser; ~, A1
82.18	happy‸] ser; ~, A1
82.25	closed‸] ser; ~, A1
83.16	grammar‸] ser; ~, A1
84.3	Magazine,] A1; ~‸ ser
84.4	installment] ser; instalment A1
	The same spelling choice is made at 84.15.
84.20	County‸] ser; ~, A1
84.21	garage,] A1; ~‸ ser
84.22	study‸] ser; ~, A1
84.24	abated‸] ser; ~, A1
85.8	Jordan‸] ser; ~, A1
85.16	Madame] A1; madame ser
85.16	Madame‸] ser; ~, A1
85.33	qualities‸] ser; ~, A1
86.1	reading‸] ser; ~, A1

"The Cut-Glass Bowl"

87.3	bronze age‸] ser; ~ ~, A1
87.19	fractures,] A1; ~‸ ser
89.8	herself,] A1; ~‸ ser
90.6	till] A1; 'til ser
94.1	Hilda‸ and,] ser; ~, ~‸ A1
99.15	'fore] A1; 'for ser
101.33	room‸ and,] ser; ~, ~‸ A1
103.8	upstairs,] A1; ~‸ ser
105.16	since,] A1; ~‸ ser

"Bernice Bobs Her Hair"

108.19	dangerous‸] ser; ~, A1
108.21	But‸] ser; ~, A1
109.6	*la*-de-*da*-*da* dum-*dum*] A1; *la*-de-*da*-dadum-*dum* ser
109.26	looked‸] ser; ~, A1
109.33	parties‸] ser; ~, A1
109.34	Williams‸] ser; ~, A1
113.14	in,] A1; ~‸ ser

113.18 qualities,] ser; ~. A1
113.34 sharply,] ed; ~‸ ser, A1
117.7 marvelously] ser; marvellously A1
117.27 ‘Little Women’] A1; ‸~ ~‸ ser
118.19 farther] A1; further ser
118.27 persisting,] A1; ~‸ ser
120.16 you,] A1; ~‸ ser
121.7 beauty‸] ser; ~, A1
121.30 chair‸] ser; ~, A1
126.11 mirror,] A1; ~‸ ser
128.25 nonsense,] ed; ~—ser, A1
128.29 bench,] A1; ~‸ ser
130.29 ‘The . . . Generation’] A1; ‸~ . . . ~‸ ser
131.25 negligée] A1; negligee ser
132.10 clenching] ser; clinching A1
132.14 drawerfuls] stet
Strictly correct usage would require “drawersful,” but the narrator is telling the story in a colloquial voice. It seems best not to emend.
132.17 traveling] ser; travelling A1
132.20 it and] ser; ~, ~ A1
133.8 blonde] ed; blond ser, A1

“Benediction”

135.9 “*Arrived* . . . “Lois.”] A1; ‸~ . . . ‸*LOIS*.~ ser
135.9 *Arrived* . . . *Love*] ser; Arrived . . . Love A1
136.2 front, . . . half-hour,] ed; ~‸ . . . ~‸ ser, A1
136.13 blond] A1; blonde ser
136.35 traveling] ser; travelling A1
137.2 still, . . . here,] A1; ~‸ . . . ~‸ ser
137.37 Keith] ed; Kieth ser, A1
This spelling change is made throughout the story. See the introduction to the present volume, p. xxvii.
138.3 rector‸] A1; ~, ser
138.35 farther] A1; further ser
139.11 brother?] A1; ~. ser
140.12 He] A1; he ser
140.17 some‸time,] A1; sometime‸ ser

140.18	traveler] ser; traveller A1
140.32	lately?] A1; ~. ser
141.11	deal,] A1; ~‸ ser
141.33	sweet, . . . me,] A1; ~‸ . . . ~‸ ser
142.14	course‸] A1; ~, ser
142.18	nodded. "Some] ed; ~. ¶ "~ ser, A1
144.13	monk,] A1; ~‸ ser
144.28	‸*O . . . Hostia*‸] ser; "~ . . . ~" A1
144.30	left,] A1; ~‸ ser
144.32	profiles‸] ed; ~, ser, A1
144.34	eyes?] A1; ~. ser
144.34	slightly:] A1; ~, ser
145.8	fidgeted‸] ser; ~, A1
145.11	laugh,] A1; ~‸ ser
145.13	it?] A1; ~. ser
145.17	straight,] A1; ~‸ ser
146.2	finally,] A1; ~‸ ser
147.17	instance,] A1; ~‸ ser
148.9	pietà] A1; pieta ser
149.15	cheeks,] A1; ~‸ ser
149.25	pietà] A1; pieta ser
150.11	"*This* . . . LOIS."] A1; ‸~ . . . ‸*Lois*.‸ ser
150.11	*This . . . Italy*.] ser; This . . . Italy. A1

"Dalyrimple Goes Wrong"

151.20	state] ser; State A1
151.21	Sirs‸] ser; ~, A1
152.1	state] ser; State A1
152.10	state university] ser; State University A1
152.11	son's] A1; sons's ser
152.23	How do, Bryan.] ser; how ~, ~? A1
152.35	awhile‸] ser; ~, A1
152.37	talking‸] ser; ~, A1
153.5	university] A1; University ser
153.11	continued—"about] A1; ~"— ~ ser
154.7	morning‸] ser; ~, A1
154.15	billiards‸] ser; ~, A1
154.17	ties‸] ser; ~, A1

154.20	moral‸] ser; ~, A1
154.20	anemia] ser; anæmia A1
155.10	morning‸] ser; ~, A1
155.10	it,] ser; ~‸ A1
155.13	week‸] A1; ~, ser
155.25	sleep‸] ser; ~, A1
156.1	Why‸—] A1; ~,— ser
157.9	chaotically] ed; chaoicly ser; chaoticly A1
157.25	out‸] A1; ~, ser
157.27	rain,] A1; ~‸ ser
157.35	East] A1; east ser
158.31	heredity-and-environment] A1; ~ — ~ — ~ ser
158.33	Macy,] A1; ~‸ ser
159.7	coat‸] ser; ~, A1
159.19	lamp-post] ser; ~, A1
159.27	grunt‸] ser; ~, A1
159.31	you] A1; You ser
159.36	mask,] A1; ~‸ ser
160.2	however‸] A1; ~, ser
160.23	color] A1; colour ser
160.23	honor] A1; honour ser
160.24	completely?] ed; ~‸ ser, A1
161.10	*The . . . clock*!] ser; The . . . clock! A1
162.3	supple,] A1; ~‸ ser
162.9	pocket-flash‸] ser; ~, A1
162.12	plans,] A1; ~‸ ser
162.15	intuition‸] ser; ~, A1
162.33	afterwards] ser; afterward A1
164.13	clue . . . clue] ser; clew . . . clew A1
164.18	him,] A1; ~‸ ser
164.18	three,] A1; ~‸ ser
164.21	Coleman,] A1; ~‸ ser
164.24	Fourth] A1; fourth ser
164.24	July,] A1; ~‸ ser
164.29	unarmored] A1; unarmoured ser
165.18	hadn't,] A1; ~ ser
165.29	eyes‸] ser; ~, A1
165.33	optimism‸] ser; ~, A1
166.1	sir,] ed; sir? ser, A1

166.8	beginning,] A1; ~‸ ser
166.14	shoulder,] A1; ~‸ ser
166.24	place,] A1; ~‸ ser
166.24	you,] A1; ~‸ ser
166.29	but] ser; But A1
167.17	through,] A1; ~‸ ser
167.30	Fraser,] A1; ~‸ ser
168.3	clenched] ed; clinched ser, A1
168.4	portières] A1; portiéres ser

"The Four Fists"

169.12	clenching] ed; clinching ser, A1
169.27	biased] ser; biassed A1
173.7	clenched] ed; clinched ser, A1
174.9	educated‸] ser; ~, A1
176.17	ultra-sensitive, super-critical] ser; ultrasensitive, supercritical A1
180.13	first . . . first] ser; 1st . . . 1st A1
182.35	close‸ somehow‸] ser; ~, ~, A1
184.19	*You . . . idiot!*] ser; You . . . idiot! A1
184.21	*Deal . . . Carhart.*] ser; Deal . . . Carhart. A1

"Babes in the Woods"

189.3	nights‸] MS; ~, ser
189.4	Game‸] MS; ~, ser
189.28	terms‸] MS; ~, ser
191.4	other‸] MS; ~, ser
191.8	resolved‸ . . . necessary‸] MS; ~, . . . ~, ser
191.12	fact‸] MS; ~, ser
191.15	impressions‸ . . . ideas‸] MS; ~, . . . ~, ser
191.21	large‸] MS; ~, ser
191.30	club's] ed; Club's ser, MS
191.31	moment‸] MS; ~, ser
192.6	First‸] MS; ~, ser
192.12	done‸ . . . him‸] MS; ~, . . . ~, ser
192.18	rest‸ . . . flush,] MS; ~, . . . ~‸ ser
192.29	really,] MS; ~‸ ser
193.10	right‸] MS; ~, ser

193.24	temperaments‸] MS; ~, ser
193.27	ingenue] MS; ingénue ser
193.29	off‸] MS; ~, ser
194.29	colleges‸] MS; ~, ser
195.10	indeed‸] MS; ~, ser
195.26	have‸] MS; ~, ser
195.29	Oh‸] MS; ~, ser
195.33	instant‸] MS; ~, ser
196.7	me.] MS; ~? ser
196.27	low‸] MS; ~, ser

"The Debutante"

Note: Several conventions of typographical styling are adopted from the *Smart Set* text: the centering of characters' names in the dialogue; the setting of these names in capitals and small capitals; italic type for stage directions; capitalization of the first word in parenthetical stage directions; a period at the end of such directions; no new line or indentation for dialogue that follows such directions; roman opening and closing parentheses around such directions.

198.1	DEBUTANTE] ed; DÉBUTANTÉ ser, [no title] TS
198.3	SCENE I ¶ *A*] ed; ¶ *Scene I—A* TS, ser
198.27	it] TS; *it* ser
198.32	people——"] ed; ~"— ser, TS
199.10	*Very*] ser; Very TS
199.21	*twenty-three*] ser; 23 TS
199.23	*shouts*:] ser; ~‸ TS
200.2	*that's*] ser; that's TS
200.6	*is*] ser; is TS
203.11	*immediately*,] ser; ~‸ TS
203.13	*voice*, . . . *musical*,] ser; ~‸ . . . ~‸ TS
203.21	out?] ser; ~. TS
203.26	*fast . . . set*?] ser; fast . . . set? TS
203.27	flirtation‸] TS; ~, ser
203.29	*Want . . . found*] ser; Want . . . found TS
203.29	You] TS; you ser
204.28	girl‸] TS; ~, ser
205.17	*sure . . . such*] ser; sure . . . such TS

207.6	Unlimited."] ser; ~". TS
207.8	$25,000‸] ser; ~. TS
208.23	away; the] ser; ~, | The TS
209.25	*want*] ser; want TS
212.16	sweet.] TS; ~! ser
215.18	cafés] ser; cafes TS
216.4	*quite*] ser; quite TS
216.5	*will*] ser; will TS
217.7	beautiful?] ed; ~. TS, ser
218.3	*such . . . so*] ser; such . . . so TS
219.3	blasé] ser; blase TS
220.10	Oh,] ser; ~‸ TS
220.19	*handsome*,] ser; ~‸ TS
220.23	dance,] ser; ~‸ TS
220.25	well,] ser; ~‸ TS
221.20	Oh,] ser; ~‸ TS
221.22	Oh‸] TS; ~, ser
221.24	Come,] ser; ~‸ TS
222.1	shimmy] ser; Shimmee TS
222.19	did,] ser; ~‸ TS
223.27	joking,] ser; ~‸ TS
224.25	What!] TS; ~? ser
225.5	*people . . . people*] ser; people . . . people TS
225.11	her‸] TS; ~, ser
225.16	impractical‸] TS; ~, ser
225.18	mean,] ser; ~‸ TS
226.20	Why?] ser; ~. TS
226.25	Pretend. (*Turning . . . up*. *Very . . . kiss*.)] ed; (*Turning . . . up*‸) Pretend. (*Very . . . kiss*). ser, TS
227.2	things.—] TS; ~.‸ ser
227.6	then?] ser; ~. TS
227.17	Listen!] TS; ~, ser
228.2	Oh‸] TS; ~, ser
228.10	Oh . . . me] ed; *Oh . . . me* TS, ser
228.11	me,] ser; ~‸ TS

"Myra Meets His Family"

229.30	year‸ . . . officer‸] ser; ~, . . . ~, P
230.17	Cocoanut] ed; Coconut ser, P

The New York nightclub of this period was the Cocoanut Grove; the night spot of the 1950s and 1960s was the Coconut Grove.

231.1 me,] P; ~‸ ser
250.12 clue] ed; clew ser, P

"The Smilers"

255.17 sun-parlor] ed; ~-parlour ser, P
256.26 favor] ed; favour ser, P
260.16 parlor] ed; parlour ser, P
261.26 hand.] ed; ~, ser, P

"The Popular Girl"

263.19 dance,] ed; ~‸ ser, B
266.14 states] ed; States ser, B
267.29 No‸] B; ~, ser
267.30 reentered] B; reëntered ser
272.5 which‸ . . . pathos‸] ser; ~, . . . ~, B
272.15 anesthetic] ed; anæsthetic ser, B
277.12 symbolism,] ser; ~‸ B
280.31 him,] ser; ~‸ B
282.29 upstairs,] ser; ~‸ B
283.5 maid,] ser; ~‸ B
285.32 indifferently. And] ed; ~; and ser, B
288.26 states] ed; States ser, B
293.15 arrived,] ed; ~‸ ser, B
297.28 commented. And] ed; ~; and ser, B
304.5 employee] B; employe ser

"Two for a Cent"

314.38 outright,] ser; ~‸ P
315.1 him,] ed; ~‸ ser, P
317.4 man!] ed; ~, ser, P
318.19 one-hundred-dollar] P; ~‸~‸~ ser
323.11 interlude,] ed; ~‸ ser, P

Compounds

Compound adjectives and verbs beginning with "half," "high," "self," and "well" have been regularized to hyphenated forms. Compounds beginning with "over" have been regularized to one word. Two-color compound adjectives (blue-and-white, grey-green) have been hyphenated, as have compound adjectives in which the word designating color is second in order (dark-blue). When the color word is first in an adjectival usage (blue satin, crimson velvet), the compound is printed as two words. Three-word heights (five feet four) and times of day (half past five) are unhyphenated; money (Four-seventy-five) is hyphenated.

The following common compound words have been regularized to Fitzgerald's preferred forms, determined from the same or similar compounds in his surviving holographs: anybody, anymore, anyone, anything, any‸time, anyway, anywhere, awhile, barber‸shop (noun), bedroom (noun and adj.), boarding‸house, boarding‸school, bookkeeper, country‸club (noun), country-club (adj.), cut‸glass (noun), cut-glass (adj.), dining‸room (noun), dining-room (adj.), dinner‸table, doorbell, doorway, downstairs, downtown, dressing‸room (noun), dressing-room (adj.), everybody, everyone, everything, everywhere, far-away (adj.), football, fox-trot, good-bye, good-looking, good-morning, good-night, grey-haired, half‸a‸dozen, half‸an‸hour, halfway, highball, middle-aged, moonlight, moonlit, notebook, post‸card, punch-bowl, ragtime, rowboat, sideboard, sidewalk, somebody, someday, someone, street-car, taxi-cab, tiptoe, today, tomorrow, tonight, toothbrush, upstairs, week-end, worth‸while, wrist‸watch.

The following compound-word readings, which appear in fewer instances, have also been made to conform to the same or similar compounds in Fitzgerald's manuscripts: a‸priori (160.32), age-old (40.15), all-important (121.6, 303.14), all-night (279.28), all-winter (81.8), anti-climax (218.5), arc-lights (18.5), aristocratic-looking (266.14), arm‸in‸arm (136.21), armchair (62.33, 75.2), ash-blond (294.17), back‸drop (73.30), ballroom (108.10, 229.21), band‸leader (17.13), barb-wire (adj.) (120.11), bargain counter (62.2), barn-door (noun) (165.29, 167.14), bathing‸suit (23.15, 27.4), be-striped (189.3), bed-rail (100.32), bedclothes (43.34, 82.26), bedside (132.33), bell-boy (29.9, 169.24, 291.5), best-known (125.13), best-liked (172.1), better-looking (175.34), big-timber (adj.) (69.15, 69.21), black-and-white (preceding noun) (43.13), blackbirds (74.20), blindfold (verb) (128.23), blood-poisoning (100.15, 100.18, 101.32,

102.9, 102.15), blood-shot (102.3), bluejackets (32.19), board‸bill (159.5), bookcases (105.4, 105.19), bookkeeping (317.28), bootblacks (129.3), bow-wows (248.24), boxing‸lessons (119.7), brand‸new (318.18), brass‸band (61.18), breakfast-food (adj.) (20.5), breakfast‸table (116.26), bric-à-brac (93.18), brigadier‸general (17.12), broad-browed (169.17), brother-in-law (99.1), burlesque‸shows (154.15), byplay (62.37, 108.22), cabin‸boy (21.14), cable-car (175.3, 175.24), candlesticks (87.14), canteen‸singer (64.21), carpetbagger (53.15), cart-wheel (110.1, 161.7), cast-off (160.14), cave-dwellers (155.17), cement-walled (155.20), check‸book (281.13), checker-board (136.4), china-closet (87.14), chorus‸man (16.32), cigarette‸case (155.24), class‸ring (163.16), clean‸shaven (235.15), clear-cut (62.24), clear-headed (77.25), close-fitting (192.19), clubman (8.15), clubroom (108.10), coal-black (11.16), cobblestone (173.18), coffee‸trader (21.15), cold-blooded (223.4), come-back (126.36), common‸sense (noun) (159.2, 167.34), companionway (5.26, 7.21, 11.32, 33.37, 34.25), corn‸flake (115.33), corncob (40.11), corn-colored (37.12), cotton‸fields (40.13), country‸houses (55.3), coworkers (77.27), cream-colored (131.25, 198.5), crosswise (27.21, 184.29), crystal-clear (20.16), curling-iron (131.3, 131.29), cut-out (273.2), cut-price (302.29), daredevil (adj.) (164.25), darling-looking (303.9), day-long (60.8), daytime (noun) (16.31), dead-white (177.31), death‸dance (29.32), death-rattle (36.19), deckhouse (18.34), deep-set (165.29), delicate-looking (143.29), demi-monde (7.8), die-away (264.12, 275.4), dime-novel (adj.) (173.13), dinner-coat (adj.) (109.16), dinner-dance (46.36, 121.2), dinner-glasses (87.7, 87.19), dinner-party (47.10), dirt‸road (158.13), divorce‸court (178.6), door-post (312.8), double‸irons (10.28), down-turning (92.16), downcast (118.28), dream‸boat (14.35), dressmaker (97.15, 175.13), dried-up (75.31), driftwood (14.11), dumb-bells (78.11), dusty-grey (41.10), electric-light (adj.) (123.21), elevator‸man (72.24), empty-handed (198.30), eyebrows (119.17, 119.23, 136.31), eye-holes (159.15), eyelashes (55.12), face-about (125.33, 260.23), fairyland (43.17), fairylike (109.37), fancy-dress (adj.) (24.29), fanfare (151.14), farmhouse (44.8), ferry-boat (174.23), field‸glasses (31.8, 32.4, 155.25), fiery‸red (70.1), fine-particled (54.22), finger-bowls (87.7), fingernail (adj.) (11.7), firearms (178.6), fireplace (45.16), first-class (151.7), five‸inches‸square (159.8), flashlight (adj.) (57.16), floor-manager (303.33), floor-walker (153.9), flower-faced (69.5), flower-filled (37.32), flower-strewn (55.1), flying-ring (adj.) (85.30), foot-falls (159.23), footlights (70.33), foot-steps (5.25, 159.20, 159.34), foreground (172.31), four‸months' (84.27), four-and-a-half-day (adj.) (76.27), four-in-hands (154.18), full-featured (173.13), full-length

(173.18), full-throated (56.26), fur-bundled (44.26), gas-jet (176.19), gate-post (149.22), get-away (19.9), gloom-dispelling (256.12), gold-plated (163.15), golden-green (41.3), golf‸course (108.3), good-humored (198.35), good-speed (197.13), graveyard (50.9), great-grandfather (245.31, 288.26), great-grandmother (245.27), great-uncles (45.22), green-latticed (265.20), greenroom (16.34), grey-mackinawed (56.30), grocery‸bills (152.13), grocery‸house (152.20), grocery men (93.19), guerilla‸warfare (160.21), half‸a‸billion (162.26), half‸a‸mile (5.7), half‸a‸million (266.32), half‸after‸midnight (112.31), half‸chop-suey (260.24), hallway (53.29), hammer blows (145.31), hand‸grenade (115.26), handwritings (110.12), hangdog (53.8), hard-minded (282.18), harebrained (34.7), headquarters (adj.) (17.12, 17.15), headstone (41.19, 54.33), head-waiter (260.14, 291.11), healthy-looking (52.18), heavy-eyed (172.21), heavy-looking (11.20), heredity-and-environment (158.31), hiding‸place (19.5, 20.24), highbrow (67.8), hold-up (160.8, 160.8), hollow-cheeked (137.6), home‸town (noun) (151.23), home-town (adj.) (113.14), hoof-beats (183.15), hoop-skirt (41.27, 59.16), horse-car (172.16), hot-tamale (224.23), hotel-corridor (290.16), house-guest (151.28), house-parties (109.33), how-things-turn-out (106.13), ice-bound (58.22), ice‸cream (noun) (16.37, 138.29, 144.17), ice-cream (adj.) (87.7), ice-like (105.27), icy-cold (44.30), ill‸at‸ease (302.6), ill-dressed (53.8), immature-looking (77.30), innermost (165.5), innocent‸eyed (192.23), iron-grey (51.8), jackknife (adj.) (24.21), Jazz-bound (69.4), jazz-nourished (111.23), jewelry‸stores (28.37), kettledrums (54.10), kidnapped (28.5), knock-out (noun) (43.20), lame-duck (adj.) (114.14), lamp-post (159.19, 161.15), lantern-hung (109.18), large-mouthed (164.7), last-a-century (135.27), lead-smeared (82.28), left-overs (265.32), lemon‸juice (12.8), less‸biased (169.27), level-voiced (183.9), life-size (148.9), long-winded (183.21), lookout (78.22), loophole (181.4), love‸affairs (103.13), love‸letter (81.24), loving cup (166.10), low-moaning (38.12), lukewarm (147.33), lunch‸room (160.6, 279.28), machine-gun (adj. and noun) (31.24, 162.17), madcap (27.14), Madonna-like (129.31), mantelpieces (104.18), many-colored (106.27), meet-my-friend (adj.) (71.1), mid-January (43.15), mid-Victorian (152.12), midair (24.20), middle‸classes (154.21), middle-sized (87.18), midfloor (109.9), midsummer (40.30), milk‸toast (71.6), misty-eyed (14.28), money-swine (183.19), moonshine (14.30), moving-picture (50.19, 283.2), much-abused (85.35), music‸room (88.29, 101.4, 104.17), mutton-chop (176.19), narrow-faced (260.13), near-sighted (61.23), nearby (242.4), neckties (172.27, 174.7), new-found (59.25), newsboy (61.13), newspaper‸reporters (151.22), nice-looking

(49.1), nickname (51.27), night-nurse (254.5), no‸one (172.1), noncommittal (117.7), nose‸ring (30.13), nurse-girl's (164.17), nut‸farm (10.20), oil-baron's (254.12), oil‸paintings (45.22), onto (243.13), orchestra-circle (108.27), out-and-out (300.33), outlook (184.29), packing‸room (156.30), pale‸lilac (154.18), pale‸yellow (59.24), panic-stricken (35.1), pantry-door (91.17), parent-arranged (113.1), parlor‸maid (125.24), partly‸opened (113.32), party‸ticket (167.8), passer-by (186.00, 324.5), pearl-grey (preceding noun) (20.32), phone‸book (305.25), phonograph‸record (63.33), pieface (170.7), pigtail (132.37), pin-tray (87.16), ping-pong (119.30), pink-jerseyed (79.23), pink-shaded (74.20), place-card (121.4), plate‸glass (noun) (78.21), plate-glass (adj.) (128.17), pleasant-looking (169.16), pleasure-dome (56.13), pocket-flash (162.9), pocketbook (290.26, 303.17), police‸station (164.1), policeman (161.24), porthole (27.3), postman (104.11), post-mortem (287.12), pre-battle (217.2), present-day (adj.) (153.18), prizefighter (25.14), prizefights (25.15), prom-trotter (229.7), pump-and-slipper (110.2), Pump-shod (189.18), puppylike (125.5), quarter‸of‸a‸mile (161.13), quarter-back (10.34), quarter-mourning (290.21), reading‸room (195.13), ready-made (302.10), real-estate (264.7), reception‸room (143.27), re-echoed (91.13), resting‸places (160.19), rice‸planter (67.20), ring-box (163.21), road-street (36.6), room‸clerk's (304.17), room‸waiter (257.12), roommate (169.28, 170.15, 171.17), rose-littered (37.12), runaway (adj.) (33.28), Saturday-afternoon (adj.) (62.2), Saturday-night (adj.) (108.11), sawdust (10.11), school‸pet (169.29), schoolboy (155.15), screen‸door (129.8), searchlight (191.27), seat-back (40.6), second-line (64.19), semicircle (148.10), semicruel (108.26), semidark (109.17), send-off (189.30), sewing-basket (93.29), sheepskin (55.36), shirt-sleeves (174.12), shock-absorber (127.25, 161.30), shopping‸bag (133.6), short-seeming (296.17), show‸place (300.13), shower-bath (254.17), showwoman (190.2), side‸by‸side (31.13, 126.21, 302.36), side-line (119.37), side-track (noun) (141.21), sister-in-law (49.36, 51.12), sitting‸room (84.33), skirmish‸line (55.14), slate-pencil (145.7), sleigh-riding (noun) (43.18), slot-machine (adj.) (66.37), small-mouthed (164.7), small-town (adj.) (53.9), snapshots (137.11, 148.23), sneak-thief (182.3), snow-covered (299.5), snowdrift (51.2), snow-filled (55.31), snowflakes (54.25), snowman (46.29), snow-shoeing (51.3), snow-shoes (43.19, 56.31), soft-leather (adj.) (57.5), soft-voiced (38.4), son-in-law (165.25), sound-proof (84.22), soup‸plates (121.8), spellbound (10.15), sporting‸sheet (160.10), spring-boards (189.3), stage‸fright (73.13), stained-glass (144.26), staircase (189.2), standby (164.17), star-bound

(14.35), steam-yacht (5.9), steering-gear (36.17), stick-pins (163.1), store‸detective (155.6), store‸rooms (157.32), street‸corner (52.22), street‸lights (77.33), stub-pencils (136.30), stuck-up (170.4), subalterns (180.4), sugar-dish (87.18), sugar-market (174.13), summer‸dresses (132.14), summer‸time (108.16), sunbonnet (37.12), sundown (73.28), sun-flooded (18.20), sunflowers (77.11), sunlight (36.2, 60.7), sun-parlor (255.17), sunshine (51.3, 136.27, 137.18), super-critical (176.17), supper‸room (70.38), sure-fire (20.24), swan-like (26.25), tea‸room (32.30, 70.35, 295.33), tear-stained (94.7), tear-wet (149.16), telegraph‸booth (149.30), telegraph‸desk (134.3), telegraph‸pole (44.20), thank‸you (noun) (156.16, 168.15), thank-you (adj.) (71.8, 87.6), tight-lipped (77.30), time-clock (154.7, 155.7), time-honored (69.2), to-do (60.9), toboggan‸ride (50.31), tombstones (59.19), too-often-mentioned (128.23), torchlight (adj.) (43.19), tortoise-shell (adj.) (129.13), tough-minded (136.24), trolley‸car (44.22), turning‸point (57.35), twentieth-row (302.29), two‸score (265.21), two‸weeks' (adj.) (76.28, 79.36), two-by-four (111.10, 111.11, 125.9), ultra-sensitive (176.17), under‸way (13.20), underdevelopment (203.12), undersized (169.29), undertone (14.33, 122.7), underwent (165.1), uptown (73.27, 73.35), vegetable‸gardens (135.31), wallpaper (77.11), watchchain (99.23), waterfront (noun) (21.23), water-tap (105.20), wave‸tip (5.6, 5.6), weak-chinned (156.29), weary-looking (81.27), well‸known (after verb) (108.15), what-ch-call-em (67.9), wherever (182.17), whole-hearted (34.3), wide-eyed (129.3), wild-grown (40.13), wind-shaken (adj.) (109.28), window‸pane (181.2), window‸seat (60.14), window-sill (36.22), windshield (39.9), wine-glasses (87.7, 87.18), workman (173.16, 173.37, 179.4), yellow-haired (5.11), you-all (39.3, 39.21), zigzagged (123.7), zigzagging (12.31, 19.7, 23.00).

Hyphenated Compounds

The compound words in the table below are hyphenated at the ends of lines in the Cambridge text. The hyphens should be preserved when quoting these words. All other compound words hyphenated at the ends of lines should be quoted as a single word.

10.33 quarter-back; 20.16 crystal-clear; 52.18 healthy-looking; 58.22 ice-bound; 62.24 clear-cut; 63.18 street-car; 67.26 week-end; 71.8 thank-you; 87.6 punch-bowls; 103.10 half-laugh; 113.4 home-town;

114.14 lame-duck; 123.21 electric-light; 126.36 come-back; 137.6 hollow-cheeked; 157.8 half-forgotten; 162.9 pocket-flash; 169.16 pleasant-looking; 175.34 better-looking; 189.3 be-striped; 191.10 good-looking; 202.1 out-distance; 205.23 *good-looking*; 232.6 best-looking; 249.22 self-possessed; 254.5 night-nurse; 290.16 hotel-corridor; 294.17 ash-blond; 298.16 half-conscious; 302.29 twentieth-row.

EXPLANATORY NOTES

Annotated below are references to persons, places, literary and dramatic works, public figures, movie and cabaret stars, and New York nightspots of the period. Fitzgerald today commands an international audience; U.S. and British readers should know that some references glossed here will be familiar to them but not to readers from other cultures. Unannotated references in the texts are unidentified or have been judged not to require explanation.

"The Offshore Pirate"

5.11 "The Revolt of the Angels"

Ardita is reading the urbane satirical fantasy by Anatole France (pseud. for Jacques Anatole François Thibault), first published in translation in the United States in 1914. In the fantasy, an angel named Arcade reads so widely in the field of science that he loses his faith in God. Together with thousands of other young angels, he plots to overthrow the Kingdom of Heaven, though at the last moment he desists. France's satire—critical of religious, governmental, and financial institutions, as well as conventional sexual mores—would appeal to Ardita. The critic H. L. Mencken reviewed *The Revolt of the Angels* in *Smart Set*, January 1915, calling it the "most delightful piece of fooling that I have seen in many a long day, a book of waggery and gusto all compact." See the explanatory note at 189.6.

12.8 Stonewall Jackson claimed that lemon juice cleared his head.

This common piece of apocrypha about the Confederate general originated in Richard Taylor's colorful memoir *Destruction and Reconstruction: Personal Experiences of the Late War* (1879), in which Jackson is pictured as habitually sucking on lemons. "Where Jackson got his lemons 'no fellow could find out,'" writes Taylor, "but he was rarely without one" (p. 50).

12.38 Sing Sing

The New York state penitentiary at Ossining, where the worst of the state's criminals were incarcerated and where executions were carried out.

13.9 the Winter Garden and the Midnight Frolic

The Winter Garden, owned by Louis Minsky, was located at Broadway and 50th Street in New York City. It was a mildly risqué place: its shows included burlesque acts, often attacked by John S. Sumner of the New York Society for the Suppression of Vice. The Midnight Frolic, operated by the theatrical impresario Florenz Ziegfeld, was a roof garden atop the New Amsterdam Theater at 214 West 42d Street. Showgirls from Ziegfeld's *Follies* starred in the cabaret there. The Midnight Frolic is mentioned in "Myra Meets His Family," 230.17 of this edition.

15.36 Belle Pope Calhoun

The name suggests the mixture of southern, northern, and African American cultures found in the border state of Tennessee, and probably in the music that Belle plays. John Pope (1822–1892), a Union general, commanded the Army of Virginia at Second Manassas; John C. Calhoun (1752–1850) was a South Carolina statesman and ardent secessionist; "Belle" suggests the conventional southern belle.

16.5 ragtime

This musical style, African American in its origins, was popular in the late nineteenth and early twentieth centuries in the United States. Ragtime was composed (not improvised) and was usually played on the piano. A melodic line was syncopated over a four-beat march-style bass; sometimes a violin carried the melody.

16.7 Orpheum circuit

The major vaudeville circuit for the Midwest and West Coast, with origins dating to 1887. The Orpheum operated theaters in Wisconsin, Missouri, Iowa, Indiana, Illinois, California, Oregon, and other states; as a teenager, Fitzgerald went to the Orpheum Theater in his home town of St. Paul. For a photograph of that theater, ca. 1905, see David Page and John Koblas,

F. Scott Fitzgerald in Minnesota: Toward the Summit (St. Cloud, Minn.: North Star Press, 1996): 2.

16.34 the chatter of the greenroom

The greenroom, so called because its walls are often painted a soft green, is an anteroom in a concert hall or theater. Performers talk and relax in the greenroom before going on stage and meet friends and admirers there afterwards.

17.11 Plattsburg

A large World War I training center for army officers and enlisted men was located in Plattsburg, New York. Many recruits from Princeton passed through this camp.

21.12 Callao

The major port of Peru, eighteen miles southwest of Lima, and the last Spanish-held position in South America (until 1826). By 1920 it was an industrial center and a stopping-off point for ships that had rounded Cape Horn.

23.18 from Biddeford Pool to St. Augustine

Popular East Coast resorts of the time. Biddeford Pool, in southwest Maine, was among the northernmost vacation spots in the country; St. Augustine, in northeast Florida, was one of the southernmost.

26.8 I don't want to sound like Pollyanna

Ardita refers to the novel *Pollyanna* (1913) by Eleanor H. Porter (1868–1920) in which the heroine, a young girl beset by adversities, plays the "Glad Game" and always looks on the bright side. Pollyanna's name is synonymous with fatuous optimism and idealism—hence Ardita's disclaimer.

"The Ice Palace"

37.26 Georgia Tech

The Georgia Institute of Technology in Atlanta, chartered in 1885, was important in the industrialization of the New South after the Civil War.

The emphasis at Georgia Tech was on mechanical engineering, agriculture, and commerce, not the liberal arts. The founding of Georgia Tech was a sign that the South's agrarian economy was giving way to new commercialism and urbanization—underlying issues in "The Ice Palace."

38.23 Asheville

A fashionable resort in the western mountains of North Carolina, frequented by such wealthy northerners as John D. Rockefeller, Henry Ford, and Theodore Roosevelt. George Washington Vanderbilt, grandson of the railroad tycoon Cornelius Vanderbilt, built the Biltmore Estate near Asheville in the late 1880s. One learns later in the story (p. 48) that Asheville is as far north as Sally Carroll has ever traveled. Fitzgerald lived there during the 1930s at the Grove Park Inn.

44.15 Then blow, ye winds, heigho!

Sally Carroll sings the refrain from the faux sea chantey "A Capital Ship" by Charles E. Carryl (1841–1920).

48.17 Carmen from the South . . . Dangerous Dan McGrew

The first allusion is to the passionate heroine of Bizet's *Carmen*, set in Seville, in the south of Spain. Dangerous Dan McGrew is the main character in Robert W. Service's "The Shooting of Dan McGrew" from *Song of a Sourdough* (1907), retitled *The Spell of the Yukon* (1915): "Back of the bar, in a solo game, sat Dangerous Dan McGrew, / And watching his luck was his light-o'-love, the lady that's known as Lou." Service is mentioned again at 154.15, in "Dalyrimple Goes Wrong."

49.24 Ever read any Ibsen?

The Norwegian poet and playwright Henrik Ibsen (1828–1906) was known for several then-controversial plays, including *A Doll's House* (1879) and *Hedda Gabler* (1890), both of which examine the roles of women in modern society. Later in the story, Roger Patton finds Sally Carroll reading Ibsen's *Peer Gynt* (1867), a mock-heroic verse fantasy about a Norse folk figure.

52.3 the Serbia in the case

The "Serbia," in this odd-sounding usage, would be the cause of the quarrel. The reference is to the group of seven young Serbian nationalists who murdered the Archduke Francis Ferdinand and his wife, Sophie, in the Bosnian town of Sarajevo on 28 June 1914, an act that triggered the outbreak of World War I.

55.21 the ice palace

The first ice palaces were built in eighteenth-century Russia; the fascination with these structures reached its peak during the late nineteenth and early twentieth centuries in Montreal, Quebec, Ottawa, and St. Paul. The palaces were elaborate feats of engineering—civic projects meant to draw visitors during winter festivals. The palaces in St. Paul were illuminated after dark for fireworks and mock castle stormings. Contests in toboggan sliding, ice skating, showshoeing, curling, and blanket tossing were also staged. Large ice palaces were built in St. Paul from 1886 to 1890; another ice palace was erected in 1896, the year of Fitzgerald's birth; then the practice lapsed until 1916 and 1917, when small "ice forts," which he probably saw, were erected (see Illustrations 1 and 2). In an account published in *The Editor* 53 (Second July Number, 1920): 121–122 (Appendix 2 of this edition), Fitzgerald wrote about the genesis of his story; the idea, he said, came from his mother's recollections of an ice palace built in St. Paul during the 1880s. This palace was probably the structure of 1888, the only one that had a maze at its center. See chapter 4 of Fred Anderes and Ann Agranoff, *Ice Palaces* (New York: Abbeville Press, 1983), and Lloyd C. Hackl, *"Still Home to Me": F. Scott Fitzgerald and St. Paul, Minnesota, An Illustrated Biography* (Cambridge, Minn.: Adventure Publications, 1996): 53–54.

56.8 this Canuck

A mildly derogatory term for a French-Canadian. A. C. and J. H. Hutchison, both Canadians, had in fact been brought down from Montreal to St. Paul to design and build the ice palace of 1886.

56.10 two lines from "Kubla Khan"

The lines here are the last two of the second section of Coleridge's "Kubla Khan" (1798, 1816). The ominous imagery suggests what Sally Carroll's reaction to the ice palace will be.

56.21 "Hail, Hail, the Gang's All Here!"

This 1917 song by D. A. Esrom (pseud. for Theodore A. Morse) was popular in the United States during World War I; it is sung to the tune of "Come, Friends, Who Plough the Sea" from the Gilbert and Sullivan operetta *The Pirates of Penzance* (1879/1880).

57.1 the Wacouta Club

This club, formed in November 1885, claimed to be the earliest-established of the St. Paul winter sports clubs. It was named for Wakute, a chief of the Dakota Indians who counseled peace during the Sioux uprising of 1862. Other prestigious clubs (which included both men and women members) were the Nushka and Windsor.

"Head and Shoulders"

61.6 "Over There"

This famous song, by the Broadway performer and singer George M. Cohan (1878–1942), became identified with U.S. involvement in World War I. Cohan composed it on 8 April 1917 after hearing Woodrow Wilson's declaration of war against Germany. By the time of the armistice the song had sold over two million copies in sheet music. Twenty-five years later Cohan was awarded the Congressional Medal of Honor for having composed "Over There" and "You're a Grand Old Flag."

61.9 Château-Thierry

The opening engagement of the Aisne Offensive by German forces (27 May–4 June 1918) took place at Château-Thierry. The Germans were met and defeated in this French village on 31 May by advance troops of the U.S. Third Division. The Germans then moved toward Vaux and Belleau Wood, but by 4 June their drive had been halted by the U.S. Second Division. These victories were reported with much exuberance by the U.S. press. The linking of Château-Thierry with the songs by George M. Cohan a few lines above is appropriate.

61.12 New Realists

There was no formal movement called New Realism during the 1920s, but "realism" in philosophy generally asserts the existence of universal entities, of material objects existing independently of their perception, and of the objects of scientific enquiry existing independently of the enquiry. The form of perceptual realism dominant during this period was "Representative Realism," which argued for a causal chain between object and percept. For someone with Horace's pragmatic turn of mind this would have been an attractive stance.

61.19 the false armistice

On 7 November 1918, Roy W. Howard, the head of United Press International in Europe, transmitted a report that an armistice had been signed between Germany and the Allied powers. The news touched off carnival-like celebrations in many U.S. cities and towns; some of these became violent, with rioting and vandalism, when Howard's report turned out to be erroneous. The true armistice was called for 11:00 A.M. on 11 November 1918: the eleventh hour of the eleventh day of the eleventh month (see Matthew 20:1–16). Fighting in some sectors went on until the very hour of the cease-fire.

62.10 "Home James!" opened at the Shubert

Broadway dramas and musicals were often given out-of-town tryouts at the Shubert Theatre in New Haven. Fitzgerald is mixing references here, however: "Home James!" was the title of the 1917 Varsity Show at Columbia University, performed at the Hotel Astor on the nights of 28–31 March. The production marked a debut for Oscar Hammerstein II, who wrote book and lyrics with his friend Herman Axelrod; favorable reviews appeared in the *New York Times* and the *New York Herald* on the 29th.

Fitzgerald was finishing his last full year at Princeton that spring; probably he went to "Home James!" with some of his Triangle Club friends. Ormond V. Gould, a member of Triangle whom Fitzgerald knew, was "loaned out" to play the part of Lucius Vodka in the production. Hammerstein himself played the maître d'hôtel, Armand Dubonnett.

In March 1917 Fitzgerald, who had collaborated on book and lyrics for three Triangle productions, would have seen Hammerstein as a friendly rival. By the time he wrote "Head and Shoulders," both he and Hammerstein were rising talents in New York, though in different fields. Fitzgerald might have hoped that Hammerstein would see the reference in the story and be amused by it. Hammerstein's children Alice and William, however, do not remember meeting the Fitzgeralds, nor does any family member possess a copy of *Flappers and Philosophers* inscribed by Fitzgerald to Hammerstein (letter of 7 November 1997).

The lyrics and sheet music for "Home James!" survive in the manuscript collections at the University Archives and Columbiana Library, Columbia University. There is no indication that the players (all males, as in the Triangle shows) performed the Shimmy, which was not yet a dance craze, but "Home James!" did include a burlesque Hawaiian hula in grass skirts, followed by a ragtime chorus. For the Shimmy, see the explanatory note at 144.11-12.

62.11 a song about the Blundering Blimp

Fitzgerald is alluding to one of his own lyrics, sung by the character Julie in the one-act play "Porcelain and Pink" (*Smart Set*, January 1920). The last four lines of the lyric read as follows: "Never skimp (it's too late) / Learn to limp (*vi-brate!*) / As you blunder blindly, kindly through / The blinking, winking Blimp!" (p. 77). A different lyric was substituted for the appearance of the play in *Tales of the Jazz Age* (1922), Fitzgerald's second collection of short fiction.

62.18 five thousand Pall Malls

Pall Mall, an expensive English-blend cigarette marketed by the American Tobacco Company, was aimed at women who wanted to project a sophisticated air.

62.20 a senior in Sheffield

Horace's cousin goes to Sheffield Scientific School at Yale. This undergraduate college offered a three-year Bachelor of Philosophy degree, with no requirement for Latin or Greek—as there was in the regular Yale B.A. program. Sheffield, or "Sheff," was considered academically below the salt.

63.9 One chair he called Berkeley, the other he called Hume

George Berkeley (1685–1753) was an Anglo-Irish bishop and scientist known for his Empiricist philosophy; for Berkeley all things other than the spiritual existed only insofar as they were perceived by the senses. The Scottish philosopher, historian, and economist David Hume (1711–1776) is remembered for his philosophical skepticism; Hume restricted knowledge to the experience of ideas and denied the possibility of verifying their truth. The two figures are often taught together in introductory courses in philosophy.

63.13 Omar Khayyam

English translations of 101 of the epigrammatic quatrains of this Persian poet and astronomer (d. 1123) were published in 1859 by Edward FitzGerald (1809–1883) as *The Rubaiyat of Omar Khayyam*. The poems, many with sensual imagery, treat matters of religion, destiny, and ethics. FitzGerald's graceful translations influenced the fin de siècle poets and were popular in England and the United States until well into the twentieth century.

64.6 the ten-twenty-thirty

Slang for a repertory company on the small-time circuit; their tickets were priced at ten, twenty, and thirty cents.

64.19-20 the Floradora Sextette

Floradora was a popular 1899 British musical comedy that premiered on Broadway in 1900 (the year in which Marcia was born). At the high point of the show, the Floradora Sextette, six buxom young women wearing high-collared, frilly dresses and elaborate picture hats, promenaded on stage with six swains in cutaways, the group singing the hit song "Tell Me Pretty Maiden." Women in the sextette, known as "Floradora girls," often had later successes in the theater or married millionaires. The Floradora girls epitomized female beauty at the turn of the century; by 1920 they had given way to the more boyish, "fast" new women of the postwar era, such as Marcia.

64.21 Mrs. Sol Smith's Juliet

Sol Smith (1801–1869), a famous theater manager and actor, ran a traveling company in the U.S. West and South during the 1830s and 1840s. He starred in many roles, from low comedy to Shakespeare, and also wrote humorous sketches for William Trotter Porter's *New York Spirit of the Times*. His second wife, the actress Elizabeth Pugsley, sometimes played Juliet to his Romeo. Marcia would have to be very old indeed to have played Juliet's nurse in a Sol Smith production, and even older to have been a "canteen singer during the War of 1812."

66.16 Uncle Remus

A reference to dialect folk tales and fables adapted by Joel Chandler Harris (1848–1908) from the African American vernacular and published in several collections during the 1880s and 1890s. The best known of these stories are in *Uncle Remus, His Songs and His Sayings* (1880). The tales, narrated by a black man called Uncle Remus, were often read to young children.

67.22 'The Bohemian Girl'

This rousing, action-filled English melodramatic opera, by Michael William Balfe, opened in the United States in 1844 and remained popular for many years. In the show a young girl was kidnapped by gypsies; its best-known song was "I Dreamt That I Dwelt in Marble Halls." Fitzgerald, living in New York in the spring of 1919, might have seen the revival at the Park Theatre, reviewed in the *New York Times* for 4 March 1919. Horace's stiffish comment ("I enjoyed it—to some extent.") suggests something about his personality at this point in the story.

69.2 jokes in the Hammerstein tradition

Light humor from the Broadway shows of the Hammerstein family. Oscar Hammerstein (d. 1919) was a German American opera impresario who built the Harlem Opera House (1888) and the Manhattan Opera House (1906). His son Arthur (1876–1955) was a producer and theater manager whose New York productions in 1920 included *Jimmie*, *Always You*, and *Tickle Me*. William Hammerstein (1878–1914) was manager of the Victoria Theatre; his son Oscar Hammerstein II (1895–1960), glossed in the note for 62.10 earlier, was just beginning his career as a librettist in 1919 and 1920; he wrote the musical plays for the three titles just mentioned.

69.14 the Taft Grill

There was a Hotel Taft in New Haven during this period; its bar and grill could be entered from Chapel Street. But Fitzgerald might have been mixing cities here: a better-known Taft Grill was one of the two dining rooms at the Hotel Taft, Seventh Avenue at 50th Street in New York City. This Taft Grill featured a dance orchestra in the evenings. See the introduction, xxvi–xxvii.

69.15 big-timber guide

Slang for someone who is stupid or oafish.

71.3-4 Divinerries'...Palais Royal

This is Gloria's mispronunciation of Devinière's, a popular cabaret and lobster palace in the theater district. The Palais Royal was a classy establishment at 1590 Broadway, two floors above the Moulin Rouge, a basement night club. Patrons of the Palais Royal wore evening clothes; the floor shows featured chorines in expensive costumes: "It's women and clothes," said *Variety*. "Why try to make it anything else?" (4 October 1918). Both cabarets featured orchestras, dancing, and faux Parisian decor; the bandleader Paul Whiteman made his New York debut at the Palais Royal.

71.5 Peter Boyce Wendell, the columnist

Fitzgerald might have had in mind Franklin P. Adams, known as F. P. A., whose column "The Conning Tower" appeared in the *New York Tribune*. Adams sometimes reported on New York nightlife; he also wrote about current literature and had been one of the sharpest critics of the misspellings in *This Side of Paradise* (see the Cambridge edition: xxxvi and Appendix 3).

71.7 vaudeville

Vaudeville reached its heyday in the United States between 1900 and 1925. The typical show was a series of short acts, most of them musical or comedic, though some might involve trained animals or acrobats. Vaudeville performers toured on a nationwide circuit and usually played two shows a day. Several famous Broadway performers (Lillian Russell, George M. Cohan, and Eva Tanguay, for example) began their careers in vaudeville.

74.8 ushers with St. Vitus dance

St. Vitus' dance, a type of the neurological disease called chorea, brings on uncontrollable shaking; sufferers during the Middle Ages went to the chapels of St. Vitus, who was thought to have curative powers.

76.28 a flat in Harlem

This section of New York City, next to the Harlem River in the Bronx, was a suburb for well-to-do whites during the late nineteenth century. By the time Horace and Marcia moved there it was the best-known African American community in the United States, famous for its nightlife and jazz clubs. Although most of its residents were black, some young white couples, attracted by low rents, lived there.

78.28 Pepys' Diary

Samuel Pepys (1633–1703) was an English public servant best known for his *Diary*, which he kept in shorthand between 1660 and 1669. Parts of the diary were deciphered and published in 1825; later and fuller editions followed. Pepys' diary offers a vivid picture of life in London during the period.

78.33 *Mens sana in corpore sano*

Part of the line "*Orandum est ut sit mens sana in corpore sano*," from Juvenal, *Satires* 10.356; usually translated as "One should pray for a healthy mind in a healthy body."

79.5 the fourth proposition of Euclid

If certain elements in a figure are given, the other elements are also given—a principle that Horace might have applied to his gymnastics.

79.14 *quod erat demonstrandum*

The *q.e.d.* for a Euclidian proof, meaning "which was to be demonstrated." The phrase is a Medieval or Renaissance Latin translation of Euclid's *hoti edei deikhthai*, used to conclude his proofs.

81.8 Hippodrome

The gaudily decorated Hippodrome, patterned after the indoor circuses of Europe, occupied the city block on the east side of Sixth Avenue between 43d and 44th Streets. Performances included colossal special effects and elaborate scenery and tableaux. A huge water tank, for aquatic feats, stood in front of the stage. The Hippodrome presented auto races, baseball games, flying dirigibles, earthquakes, and animal acts (usually featuring one or more elephants). It is also mentioned in "The Popular Girl," 302.35 of this edition.

84.20 Westchester County

Many private estates for the wealthy were located in Westchester County, on the east bank of the Hudson River north of New York City. But there were some modest dwellings as well, such as the bungalow taken by Horace and Marcia.

"The Cut-Glass Bowl"

87.10 Back Bay

The most fashionable residential section of Boston, developed during the Civil War and in the late years of the nineteenth century. The Back Bay is known for its broad avenues, handsome row houses, and large mansions.

96.25 an extreme Empire gown

Empire fashions were worn originally by the Empress Josephine during the First Empire, 1804–1814. An Empire gown resembled a floor-length chemise; it was belted beneath the bosom, with long or short sleeves, and in its extreme form had low décolletage. Mrs. Ahearn's dress would have been inappropriate for this occasion.

103.6 how many clubs were out

In bridge one keeps track of how many cards in the trump suit have been played and how many are still "out." Evylyn, distracted, has not done so.

"Bernice Bobs Her Hair"

108.31 Hill School

A large, academically rigorous boys' prep school at Pottstown, Pennsylvania, established in 1851.

109.35 Hiram Johnson or Ty Cobb

Johnson (1866–1945), a U.S. senator for twenty-eight years, was known to Fitzgerald's generation as a staunch isolationist. He opposed the Treaty of Versailles and helped to keep the United States from joining the League of Nations. Cobb (1886–1961), nicknamed the "Georgia Peach," was a famous professional baseball player, remembered today for his hitting and base stealing.

110.13 Eau Claire

Eau Claire, Wisconsin, an industrialized city on the Chippewa River, is ninety miles east of St. Paul. Eau Claire was at the center of the pine-logging business in Wisconsin from 1850 to 1900; it was a rough-and-tumble frontier town of sawmills, lumberjacks, and river rats. By the time of Fitzgerald's story the city was a center for rubber-tire manufacture and food processing. Social life for Bernice in Eau Claire would have been much less sophisticated than the goings-on in St. Paul—which is the setting for "Bernice Bobs Her Hair," though Fitzgerald does not mention the city by name.

110.18 sorta dopeless

Slang for uninformed, not among the initiated. "Dope" means inside information.

113.15-16 the warm milk prepared by Annie Fellows Johnston

Johnston wrote sentimental books for young people and was best known for *Mary Ware, the Little Colonel's Chum* (1908), a story of the trials and victories of a good-hearted girl in an exclusive girls' school. Amory Blaine reads *Mary Ware* in *This Side of Paradise* (Cambridge edition, 23.22).

115.1 as though Arizona were the place for her

Mrs. Harvey thinks that Roberta looks tubercular; Arizona, with its dry air, was the site of sanitariums for consumptives.

117.27 "Oh, please don't quote 'Little Women'!"

Marjorie is talking about Louisa May Alcott's *Little Women* (1869), de rigueur reading for girls of her mother's generation, who often modeled themselves after one or another of the March sisters—Meg, Jo, Beth, or Amy—in the novel.

121.6 the all-important left

Etiquette dictated that a young woman's dinner partner was the man seated to her left. Most of the mealtime conversation was supposed to be directed at this partner; it was a great advantage to have a socially polished man to one's left at table.

122.10 Marjorie had culled this from Oscar Wilde

Lord Illingworth to Gerald, in Act III of *A Woman of No Importance* (1893): "To get into the best society, nowadays, one has either to feed people, amuse people, or shock people—that is all!"

127.29 a summer bobbing party

Otis is punning on the bobsledding party, often called a bobbing party—a winter amusement for midwestern youths during Fitzgerald's boyhood. Myra St. Claire invites Amory to a bobbing party in *This Side of Paradise* (Cambridge edition, p. 15).

"Benediction"

136.11 Cardinal Mercier

Desiré Joseph Mercier (1851–1926) founded the Institut Supérieur de Philosophie in 1889 at Louvain in Belgium; he worked to restore the philosophy of St. Thomas Aquinas to the church and to harmonize Thomist teachings with modern science. For him philosophy was a rational pursuit distinct from theology; he established an early laboratory of experimental psychology at his institute. He was made a cardinal in 1907.

139.26 Farmington

Miss Porter's School in Farmington, Connecticut, established in 1844 and by 1920 one of the most prestigious girls' prep schools in the United States. See Nancy Davis and Barbara Donahue, *Miss Porter's School, A History* (Farmington, Conn.: Miss Porter's School, 1992).

140.23 Jesuit College in Philadelphia

Probably St. Joseph's College, a Jesuit institution founded near Independence Hall in 1851. Scholastic disputations in Latin were still given there until World War I.

144.11-12 shimmys . . . maxixe

The Shimmy, also called the Shimmy Shake, was a dance of African American origin, popularized by the singer Gilda Gray ("I'm shaking my shimmy, that's what I'm doing."). Mae West also did a version in her cabaret act. Women did the Shimmy in tasseled or fringed dresses; they shook their shoulders and upper bodies while holding their heads and hips still. The Maxixe, also known as the Brazilian Tango, was performed in New York cabarets before World War I by professional dancing teams. The dancers performed the steps, then taught them to the patrons. Other new dances included the Hesitation Waltz, the Apache Dance, the Military Glide, and the Cinq-á-Sept. These dances helped bring about a symbolic revolution in social dancing, with each couple performing individual steps, apart from the group, rather than moving in unison—as with the classic waltz or fox-trot.

144.23 Benediction

In the paraliturgical service of Benediction, the Sacred Host is venerated by the people. The priest exposes the host (the "central spot of white" in line 144.25) in a monstrance—a vessel sometimes decorated with jewels. The hymn *O Salutaris Hostia* is sung, and incense is burned after the act of veneration.

144.26 St. Francis Xavier

One of the seven original Jesuits who took vows at Montmartre in 1534, this priest was among the greatest of Catholic missionaries. He preached, taught, and made converts in the East Indies, along the Malay Peninsula, and in Ceylon, Japan, and India. Canonized in 1622, he is remembered for his selflessness and humility.

147.21 He says Christ was a great socialist

Howard has been reading Archibald McCowan's didactic novel *Christ, the Socialist* (1894), which argues that socialism, especially the variety in Edward Bellamy's *Looking Backward* (1888), is the political application of Christian principles.

"Dalyrimple Goes Wrong"

151.15 a Lewis gun

This weapon, carried by U.S. troops during the war, was a one-man air-cooled automatic gun identifiable by its circular cartridge drum.

151.18-19 General Pershing and Sergeant York

John J. "Black Jack" Pershing (1860–1948) was chief commander of U.S. troops in Europe during World War I; Sergeant Alvin Cullum York (1887–1964) was a war hero, decorated for bravery at Chatel-Cheherz.

154.15 Robert Service

The author of "The Shooting of Dan McGrew," glossed at 48.17 of this edition.

154.26 a piker organization

A "piker" is someone who gambles or speculates in a cautious, niggardly way.

160.10-12 Doctor Crane's crop of seasoned bromides . . . Mutt and Jeff

Syndicated columns of the Methodist minister Frank Crane (1861–1928) were carried in many newspapers of the time and were much admired by the plain folk. The columns, each around four hundred words, were didactic, inspirational, and sentimental. T. Cholmondeley Frink, in Sinclair Lewis's *Babbitt* (1922), is a popular syndicated poet of this variety. Mutt and Jeff were popular figures in a newspaper comic strip of the time.

161.10 "*The moon is down—I have not heard the clock!*"

Spoken by Fleance to Banquo in *Macbeth* II.i.2. The king is murdered in the next scene.

"The Four Fists"

169.23 Phillips Andover Academy

The prestigious Phillips Academy in Andover, Massachusetts (est. 1780), was the oldest boys' prep school in the country. It was called Phillips Academy or "Andover" to differentiate it from Phillips Exeter Academy in Exeter, New Hampshire (est. 1781), which is sometimes referred to as "Exeter."

172.5 tandems and coaches and tallyhos

These were horse-drawn vehicles for the well-to-do: the tandem was a dog-cart, meant to be driven with a tandem team and usually elaborate in its appointments; the coach was a large vehicle drawn by a team of four or six horses; the tallyho was a four-in-hand coach, used for transportation within cities.

176.12 *congé*

A signal for departure or dismissal, from the French.

176.27 hansom

A hansom cab, named for its inventor, Joseph Hansom, was a two-wheeled vehicle with a body hung close to the ground, giving easy access for passengers. In later designs the driver sat on a high seat mounted in the rear.

179.29 in the Adiron——

Samuel is trying to mention the Adirondack Mountains in northeastern New York, a popular spot for outdoor vacations.

180.29 San Felipe, New Mexico

This town, established in 1822, was the headquarters for Stephen F. Austin's colony. Austin used the Texas Rangers for the first time in San Felipe to defend the town against the Mexicans; later, in 1835, plans for the Texas Revolution were drawn up there. San Felipe brings to mind the pioneering spirit of the Texas frontier; it is the right place for Samuel to meet McIntyre in the scene that follows. In the serial text the town was given the fictitious name Tumlo.

"Babes in the Woods"

189.6 "Thaïs"

Massenet's opera *Thaïs*, based on a tale by Anatole France, had opened at the Metropolitan in February 1917, with Geraldine Farrar as the title character. Thaïs meets Damiel, a monk of the desert, and enters a convent, renouncing her allegiance to Venus. France's *The Revolt of the Angels* is glossed in "The Offshore Pirate," at 5.11 of the explanatory notes.

191.28 She was glad she had high color tonight

Isabelle would have been thought too young in the 1910s to wear cosmetics; naturally high facial color was therefore a considerable advantage for her.

192.29 Isabelle gasped

Our heroine is surprised because Stephen has called her by her first name. Proper etiquette required that he call her Miss Borgé (her last name in *This Side of Paradise*) and she call him Mr. Palms until they were better acquainted. Stephen has dispensed with these formalities.

194.28 alluring Stutzes

Isabelle's admirers drive the Stutz Bearcat, an expensive two-seater sports car popular during the first two decades of the century. The Stutz was a true sports vehicle, with no protection from the weather and little space for luggage.

195.36 "Babes in the Woods"

The lyrics in the paragraphs that follow, and the title of the story as well, are taken from "Babes in the Wood," a brother-and-sister duet written by Jerome Kern and Schuyler Greene for *Very Good Eddie*, a 1915 Broadway musical. Fitzgerald has changed the title slightly.

"The Debutante"

198.9-10 *Landseer... Maxfield Parrish*

Sir Edwin Henry Landseer (1802–1873) was a British artist known for his paintings of animals. His sentimental images of dogs were much admired; Queen Victoria commissioned him to paint her pets. Maxfield Parrish (1870–1966), a pupil of the painter Howard Pyle, was a poster artist and book illustrator whose works were popular with girls of Rosalind's social set.

207.12 Well, Amory, you don't mind—do you?

Rosalind is impatient with rules that dictate modes of address. Like Stephen in "Babes in the Woods," she is immediately moving to first names (see the note at 192.29). Young men were usually the ones who tried to move past these formalities, but Rosalind is taking the initiative here.

211.15 I was expelled from Spence

The Spence School for Girls, a fashionable and exclusive prep school of around three hundred students, was then located at 30 West 55th Street in New York City. From a 1918 guide to U.S. preparatory schools: "The resident pupils come from wealthy families of all sections, who appreciate the social and academic advantages of the associations the school offers."

218.8 they're Coronas

Coronas, like Pall Malls, were cigarettes aimed at a sophisticated market; women often smoked them. When "The Debutante" was first published, it was still thought improper for a woman of Cecelia's class to smoke in public. These cigarettes should not be confused with the cigars mentioned in "The Smilers," 256.12 of this edition.

222.12 no color . . . since the French officers went back

French officers stationed in New York during the war attended dances and other formal functions in their red and blue dress uniforms, providing contrast to the standard black-and-white evening dress of the American men.

223.19 Cocoanut Grove

A nightclub in New York City, glossed in "Myra Meets His Family" at 230.17.

226.12 I was Louis 14th and you were one of my—my——

The word Stephen does not utter is "mistresses." The wife of Louis XIV was Marie-Thérèse of Austria, but he had a long succession of mistresses, one of whom was the Marquise de Montespan.

227.17 "Kiss Me Again"

This song by Victor Herbert was originally the last part of a long piece for the lead soprano in *Mlle. Modiste*, a musical of the period. Issued separately in 1915, "Kiss Me Again" became the signature song of Fritzi Scheff—a cabaret star who sang often at the Palais Royal and who married the Hollywood cowboy star Bronco Billy Anderson.

"Myra Meets His Family"

229.10 the Biltmore lobby

The lobby of the large and elegant Biltmore Hotel, Madison and 43d, just across from Grand Central Station, was a popular place for rendezvous. The Cascades, a restaurant on its nineteenth floor, featured a twenty-eight-foot waterfall; the hotel also had the finest Turkish baths in the city.

229.11 New Haven

Fitzgerald is referring to Yale University in New Haven, Connecticut.

229.12-13 Club de Vingt or the Plaza Rose Room

The Club de Vingt, at 42 East 58th Street, was a respectable establishment where young women (usually chaperoned) came to dance with their escorts. The Rose Room at the Plaza Hotel was an elaborately decorated dining room, often the site of elegant dinner dances.

229.27 Derby School in Connecticut

Fitzgerald was probably thinking of Derby Academy in Derby, Vermont, a coeducational school established in 1840.

229.29 Smith College

A women's college of high reputation in Northampton, Massachusetts, chartered in 1871. Smith was one of the "Seven Sisters," a group of exclusive women's colleges in the Northeast, comparable to the colleges and universities of the Ivy League.

230.12 Kelly Field

Kelly Field, a major U.S. training camp for aviation recruits during World War I, was constructed in 1917. The installation was located just south of San Antonio, Texas.

230.17 "Midnight Frolic" and "Cocoanut Grove" and "Palais Royal"

The Midnight Frolic is glossed at 13.9 of this edition, the Palais Royal at 71.3-4. The Cocoanut Grove (not to be confused with the Coconut Grove, a Manhattan nightclub of a later era) was a high-priced roof garden above the Century Theater, established in 1917 by Morris Gest and famous for its glittering floor shows.

234.8 regelar Hoover

The driver means that Mr. Whitney is tight-fisted. The reference is to Herbert Hoover (1874–1964), elected as the thirty-first president of the United States in 1928, but at this point known to readers for managing the Food Administration during World War I. Hoover encouraged voluntary conservation, asking restaurants and householders to observe meatless and wheatless days. During the war the word "Hooverize" meant to save or economize.

234.14 flivver

Slang for a small, cheap automobile. The derivation of the term is unknown.

239.3 putting the tonneau before the radiator

In early automobiles, the tonneau was an enclosed passenger compartment in the rear. The radiator in most cars is in the front. Fitzgerald is substituting automobile terms in the expression "putting the cart before the horse."

244.14 East Side snarl

Myra is using a tough accent from the Lower East Side of Manhattan, where working-class immigrants lived.

244.14-15 she ragged . . . shimmied . . . tickle-toe

The Rag, the Shimmy, and the Tickle-Toe were all popular dances of the time, seen in the theater district cafes and on Broadway.

244.17 an Al Jolson position

Jolson (1886–1950) began in vaudeville in 1901 and rose to fame on Broadway. Appearing as a blackface character known as "Gus," he danced and sang popular songs or sentimental ballads. His best-known tunes were "Swanee," "Toot, Toot, Tootsie," and "California, Here I Come." Jolson often finished his performances on one or both knees, with arms outstretched to the audience, the pose that Myra strikes here.

245.16 floppity Gainsborough hats

A reference to the work of the English painter Thomas Gainsborough (1727–1788), several of whose best-known portraits (those of the Countess Howe and of Mrs. Sarah Siddons, for example) are of women wearing large-brimmed straw hats adorned with flowers or drooping feathers.

247.17 supes

Slang for actors with small, nonspeaking parts in movies or stage shows; a shortened form of "supernumeraries."

252.25 Broadway Limited

This luxury express train went into operation in 1902; it ran between New York, Philadelphia, and Chicago. The Broadway Limited left Penn Station every afternoon at three o'clock, passed through Philadelphia to take on passengers, then headed west to Chicago, a trip altogether of some 908 miles.

253.11 the marble dome

A reference to the high marble vaulted arches of the old Penn Station waiting room; the walls were decorated with murals by Jules Guerin.

"The Smilers"

255.2 his left hand

Matthew 5:30: "And if thy right hand offend thee, cut it off, and cast it from thee."

255.9 Tiffany's

Tiffany and Co., the famous jewelry store, was founded in 1837; during this period it was located at Fifth Avenue and 37th Street. The facade was adorned then (as it is today) by a bronze figure of Atlas with a clock on his shoulders.

256.12 Corona

A brand name for a Cuban cigar of the time; the word also describes a type of cigar, between five and six inches long, with a rounded head and cut foot.

256.15 Larchmont

A suburb for the well-to-do, in southern Westchester County on the Long Island Sound, a little over three miles northeast of New York City. Larchmont was fashionable: cinema and stage stars such as Mary Pickford, Douglas Fairbanks, and the Barrymores had summer houses there. Andrew Carnegie, J. P. Morgan, and several of the Vanderbilts kept steam yachts at the Larchmont Yacht Club.

257.6 'Smile, Smile, Smile' or 'The Smiles that You Gave to Me'

The first song is likely "Pack Up Your Troubles in Your Old Kit Bag and Smile, Smile, Smile" (1915), lyrics by George Asaf, music by Felix Powell, featured in the musicals *Her Soldier Boy* and *Dancin'*. The second tune is probably the top hit of 1917, "Smiles," with lyrics by J. Will Callahan and music by Lee G. Roberts, performed on Broadway in *The Passing Show of 1918*.

259.7 Grand Central

A reference to Grand Central Station at Park Avenue and East 42d Street, one of the two major railroad passenger terminals in the city. See the note at 298.12.

262.12 Rye

Rye is a suburban residential town, northeast of New York City near the Connecticut border, and a few miles east of Scarsdale.

"The Popular Girl"

264.1 Fabian

Using a strategy of harassment and avoidance of battle; so named for Quintus Fabius Maximus, the third-century B.C. Roman general who employed such tactics to frustrate Hannibal in the Second Punic War.

264.24 a popular Bones man at Yale

As an undergraduate at Yale, Tom Bowman had been tapped for Skull and Bones, the most prestigious of the secret senior societies there. One remained a "Bones man" for life.

265.1 not meeting the Prince of Wales

Edward VIII (1894–1972), Prince of Wales from 1911 to 1936, made a tour of Canada and the United States in the summer and autumn of 1919. A small, blond, handsome man, he was then regarded as the world's most eligible bachelor; many young women vied to be introduced to him. In New York he was given a ticker-tape parade and attended the Ziegfeld Follies. He (or rather his image) is used as a plot device in Fitzgerald's story "Rags Martin-Jones and the Pr-nce of W-les" (1924).

271.12 the Ritz

The Ritz-Carlton Hotel, one of the most elegant hostelries in New York City, and known especially for its Palm Room, was then at Madison and 46th. The hotel is mentioned also in "Myra Meets His Family," 232.34 of this edition, and in "The Diamond as Big as the Ritz" (1922).

271.16 Farmover

Perhaps an oblique reference to Farmington, as Miss Porter's School was often called; see the annotation at 139.26.

271.20 dancing at Montmartre

Montmartre, at Broadway and 50th in the shadow of the Winter Garden (13.9), was an upscale nightspot with no cabaret—only an orchestra and dance floor. The club was established in 1916 by Paul Salvin and Jim Thompson—also the proprietors of the Moulin Rouge and the Palais Royal (see 71.3-4).

271.29 The Manhattan

This moderately priced and not terribly fashionable hotel occupied an entire block between 42d and 43d Streets, diagonally across from the more ornate

Biltmore, which stood at Madison and 43d. Its lobby featured painted murals; its most popular restaurant was the Palm Court. The hotel was renovated in 1915 but by 1922, the date of publication for "The Popular Girl," it had been torn down.

273.2 his cut-out resounding

Many sports cars of the period were rigged with cut-out switches; the driver could pull a lever and let the engine exhaust bypass the muffler. This produced a loud, irritating racket.

275.36 Crest Avenue—that's our show street ...

"The Popular Girl" is set in a fictional version of St. Paul, though Fitzgerald does not mention the city by name. In this long passage, Scott and Yanci travel down Summit Avenue, ending their drive at the Mississippi River. The "new cathedral" at 276.2 corresponds to the Roman Catholic Cathedral of St. Paul, erected between 1906 and 1915; the "ghosts of four moonlit apostles" are among the statues of Christ and the twelve apostles above the Summit Avenue entrance to the church. At 276.8, the "great brownstone mass built by R. R. Comerford, the flour king," is the mansion of the railroad baron James J. Hill, built at 240 Summit in the late 1880s, with thirty-two rooms, a ballroom, and a two-story art gallery. Nathan Hale Park, at 276.15, is a triangular block of land at the intersection of Summit and Portland Avenues, about two blocks west of the Hill mansion; the statue Fitzgerald describes was put there in 1907 by the Daughters of the American Revolution. The Christian Science Temple in the next paragraph stands at the northeast corner of Grotto Street; it is low and square, with Corinthian-style columns across its facade. Chelsea Arbuthnot is apparently fictitious; the first governor of Minnesota was Henry Hastings Sibley.

276.22 the marble contours of the Petit Trianon

A reference to the graceful country house erected by Louis XV, at the suggestion of Mme de Pompadour, in the park of Versailles. The Petit Trianon, designed by Jacques-Ange Gabriel, was begun in 1762 and completed in 1768. The walls are of a cream-colored limestone; the surrounding gardens are laid out in a style known as Anglo-Chinese.

291.18 Plaza, Circle and Rhinelander

Telephone exchanges for some of the most fashionable residential sections of New York City. Phone numbers of the period (e.g., PL2345) began with the first two letters of the exchange. Yanci, searching through the directory for the names of her New York friends, can tell approximately where they live by their exchanges.

292.22 Tuxedo

Yanci is dreaming of Tuxedo Park, a prestigious gated enclave some forty miles outside New York in Orange County, near the New Jersey border. Tuxedo Park was created in 1886 by Pierre Lorrillard, scion of the wealthy tobacco family; most of its residents were millionaires; many maintained strings of polo ponies. The black dinner jacket known as a tuxedo was worn first by denizens of Tuxedo Park, and takes it name from the community.

295.1 Hot Springs

A reference to The Homestead, a fashionable resort at Hot Springs in the mountains of Virginia, known especially for its golf courses and mineral baths.

296.3 Mae Murray

This glamorous dancer and movie actress (1889–1965) was called "The Girl with Bee-Stung Lips." She became famous during the late 'teens as a dancer in New York cafes and ballrooms; often she headlined at the Sans Souci, a cabaret on 42d Street, and she appeared in Irving Berlin's first hit, *Watch Your Step* (1914). Mae Murray later became a movie star at Universal Pictures, commanding a weekly salary of $10,000 and appearing in films with Rudolph Valentino.

296.25 when Yanci asked for her key

At first-class urban hotels of the period, one left one's room key with a clerk, stationed on each floor, when away from the hotel.

297.12 'Dulcy'

Scott has tickets for *Dulcy: A Comedy in Three Acts*, by George S. Kaufman and Marc Connelly. The play was running at the Frazee Theatre; Alexander Woollcott had called it "an urbane satirical comedy of American authorship" in the *New York Times* for 17 August 1921. Dulcy (Dulcinea) was played by Lynn Fontanne.

298.12 Pennsylvania Station

Pennsylvania Station, completed in 1911, was the last work of the architect Charles Follen McKim, who modeled the structure on the Baths of Caracalla. Penn Station (as it was called) and Grand Central Station were the two main railway terminals in the city; Penn Station covered two blocks bounded by 33d Street, Seventh Avenue, 31st Street, and Eighth Avenue. The structure was demolished in 1965.

299.17-18 Manhattan Transfer

Manhattan Transfer was an interchange station in the New Jersey Meadowlands; Fitzgerald is being ironic, six paragraphs along, when he calls the spot a "quaint old village." Passengers coming into the city caught trains heading under the Hudson to Penn Station; outward-bound passengers boarded trains to Jersey City.

299.28 I'll be at the Charter Club

Social life at Princeton revolved around the undergraduate eating clubs, which hosted dance weekends. The clubs maintained dining establishments and had much influence on student dress and behavior. Charter Club was organized in 1901 and occupied various quarters until the fall of 1914, when its new building on Prospect Street was finished. During the war years, however, this clubhouse was closed because most of the members of Charter were away in military service. The few remaining members enjoyed privileges at Cottage Club, where Fitzgerald was a member. Ellen does not mean that she will be staying at Charter Club (she would stay at a private residence in Princeton), but that she can be contacted via Charter.

305.1 Plaza

One of the most fashionable hotels in the city, at Fifth Avenue and 59th Street. Afternoon tea dances, known as *thé dansant*, were held in the Plaza Grill; dinner dances were given in the Rose Room.

"Two for a Cent"

311.15 the patent for canning ice

During this period, artificial ice was made by filling metal cans with distilled water and suspending them in chilled brine. The "raw-water can system," invented around 1910, produced clear ice at low cost; ownership of the patent to such a process would have been valuable. Ice was delivered in blocks to most middle-class homes, where it was used in iceboxes.

314.19 Dope Dola

Slang for the soft drink Coca-Cola, known as "dope" because it contained trace elements of cocaine. Drugstore soda fountains were called "dope shops."

315.18 graphophones

The graphophone, one of Alexander Graham Bell's inventions, played music recorded on wax-covered cylinders; the sounds emerged from a large horn.

316.2 the Dick Whittington idea

Richard "Dick" Whittington (d. 1423) was three times Lord Mayor of London. According to popular legend he came to the city as a poor country lad, determined to rise; by good fortune he sold his cat, an excellent mouser, to the King of Morocco for a fabulous sum. Dick began in business with this money, grew wealthy, married his master's daughter, and was knighted.

ILLUSTRATIONS

1. The St. Paul ice palace of 1886. Fitzgerald based the structure in his story on accounts and newspaper sketches of the early ice palaces in the city.

2. The St. Paul "ice fort" of 1917, which Fitzgerald likely saw. By Fitzgerald's time the practice of erecting huge ice palaces had lapsed. These smaller structures were efforts to keep the tradition alive.

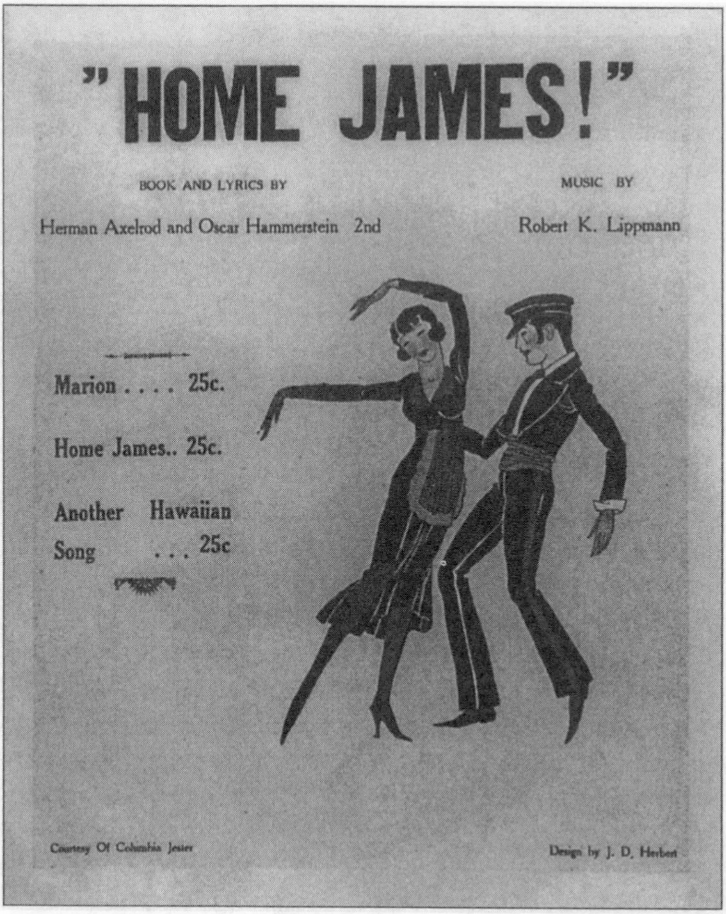

3. Sheet music for "Home James!"—the 1917 Varsity Show at Columbia University, with book and lyrics by Herman Axelrod and Oscar Hammerstein II. The production is mentioned by title in "Head and Shoulders." Butler Library, Columbia University.

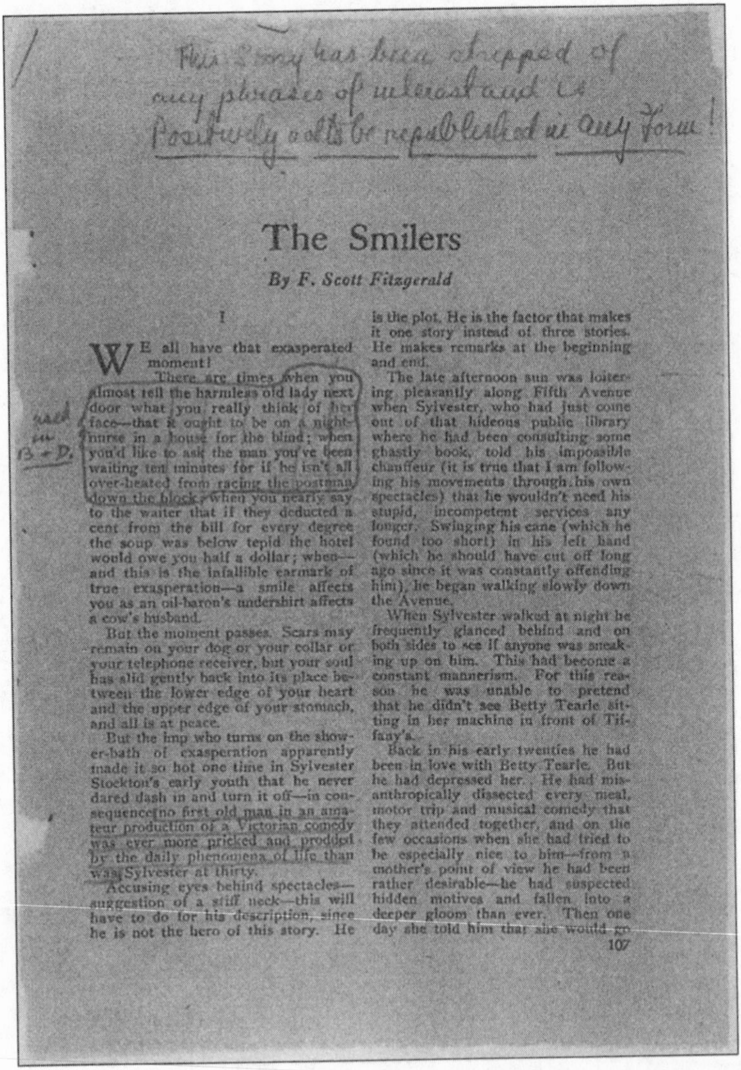

This story has been stripped of any phrases of interest and is Positively not to be republished in any Form!

The Smilers

By F. Scott Fitzgerald

I

WE all have that exasperated moment!

There are times when you almost tell the harmless old lady next door what you really think of her face—that it ought to be on a night-nurse in a house for the blind; when you'd like to ask the man you've been waiting ten minutes for if he isn't all over-heated from racing the postman down the block; when you nearly say to the waiter that if they deducted a cent from the bill for every degree the soup was below tepid the hotel would owe you half a dollar; when—and this is the infallible earmark of true exasperation—a smile affects you as an oil-baron's undershirt affects a cow's husband.

used in B + D.

But the moment passes. Scars may remain on your dog or your collar or your telephone receiver, but your soul has slid gently back into its place between the lower edge of your heart and the upper edge of your stomach, and all is at peace.

But the imp who turns on the shower-bath of exasperation apparently made it so hot one time in Sylvester Stockton's early youth that he never dared dash in and turn it off—in consequence no first old man in an amateur production of a Victorian comedy was ever more pricked and prodded by the daily phenomena of life than was Sylvester at thirty.

Accusing eyes behind spectacles—suggestion of a stiff neck—this will have to do for his description, since he is not the hero of this story. He is the plot. He is the factor that makes it one story instead of three stories. He makes remarks at the beginning and end.

The late afternoon sun was loitering pleasantly along Fifth Avenue when Sylvester, who had just come out of that hideous public library where he had been consulting some ghastly book, told his impossible chauffeur (it is true that I am following his movements through his own spectacles) that he wouldn't need his stupid, incompetent services any longer. Swinging his cane (which he found too short) in his left hand (which he should have cut off long ago since it was constantly offending him), he began walking slowly down the Avenue.

When Sylvester walked at night he frequently glanced behind and on both sides to see if anyone was sneaking up on him. This had become a constant mannerism. For this reason he was unable to pretend that he didn't see Betty Tearle sitting in her machine in front of Tiffany's.

Back in his early twenties he had been in love with Betty Tearle. But he had depressed her. He had misanthropically dissected every meal, motor trip and musical comedy that they attended together, and on the few occasions when she had tried to be especially nice to him—from a mother's point of view he had been rather desirable—he had suspected hidden motives and fallen into a deeper gloom than ever. Then one day she told him that she would go

107

4. The initial page of Fitzgerald's tearsheets for "The Smilers" (*Smart Set*, June 1920), bearing his annotations. Papers of F. Scott Fitzgerald, Princeton University Library.

APPENDIX 1

GENESIS OF "BERNICE BOBS HER HAIR"

Fitzgerald prepared this treatise of quasi-Chesterfieldian advice for his sister, Annabel, probably in 1915, when she was fourteen years old. The document, ten pages in holograph, survives among his papers at Princeton. These words appear at the top of the first page in Fitzgerald's mature hand: "Written by me at 19 or so | Basis of Bernice." The text was first published in *Correspondence of F. Scott Fitzgerald*, ed. Matthew J. Bruccoli and Margaret M. Duggan, with the assistance of Susan Walker (New York: Random House, 1980): 15–18. "Ginevra" in the letter is Ginevra King, Fitzgerald's first serious love and the model for many of the heroines in his early writings.

<u>The General Subject of Conversation</u>

Conversation like grace is a cultivated art. Only to the very few does it come naturally. You are as you know, not a good conversationalist and you might very naturally ask, "What do boys like to talk about?'

(1) Boys like to talk about themselves—much more than girls. A girl once, named Helen Walcott, told me (and she was the most popular debutante in Washington one winter) that as soon as she got a man talking about himself she had him cinched and harnessed—they give themself away. Here are some leading questions for a girl to use.

a) You dance so much better than you did last year.

b) How about giving me that sporty necktie when you're thru with it.

c) You've got the longest eyelashes! (This will embarrass him, but he likes it)

d) I hear you've got a "line"!

e) Well who's you're latest crush!

<u>Avoid</u>

a) When do you go back to school?

b) How long have you been home?

c) Its warm or the orchestras good or the floors good.

Also avoid any talk about relations or mutual friends. Its a sure sign you're hard up for talk if you ask Jack Allen about Harriette or Tuby about Martha. Dont be afraid of slang—use it, but be careful to use the most modern and sportiest like "line," camafluage etc. Never talk to a boy about about his school or college unless he's done something special or unless he starts the subject. In a conversation its always good to start by talking about nothing—just some fresh camafluage; but start it yourself—never let the boy start it: Dont talk about your school—no matter where you go. Never sing no matter how big the chorus.

2.

As you get a little old you'll find that boys like to talk about such things as smoking and drinking. Always be very liberal—boys hate a prig—tell them you dont object to a girl smoking but dont like cigarettes yourself. Tell them you smoke only cigars—kid them!—When you're old still you want always to have a line on the latest books plays and music. More men like that than you can imagine.

In your conversation always affect a complete frankness but really be only as frank as you wish to be. Never try to give a boy the affect that you're popular—Ginevra always starts by saying shes a poor unpopular woman without any beaux. Always pay close attention to the man. Look at him in his eyes if possible. Never effect boredom. Its terribly hard to do it gracefully Learn to be worldly. Remember in all society nine girls out of ten marry for money and nine men out of ten are fools.

Poise: Carriage: Dancing: Expression

(1) Poise depends on carriage, expression and conversation and having discussed the last and most important I'll say a few words on the other two.

(2) A girl should hold herself straight. Margaret Armstrongs slouch has lost her more attention than her lack of beauty. Even Sandy is

critiscized for stooping. When you cross a room before people nine out of ten look at you and if you're straight and self contained and have a graceful atheletic carriage most of them will remark on it. In dancing it is very important to hold yourself well and remember to dance hard. Dancers like Betty and Grace and Alice work hard. Alice is an entirely self made dancer. At sixteen she was no better than you, but she practised and tried. A dancer like Elizabeth Clarkson looses partners. You can not be lazy. You should try not to trow a bit of weight on the man and keep your mind on it enough to follow well. If you'd spent the time on dancing with me as I've often asked you instead of playing the piano youd be a good dancer. Louis Ordway taught Kit to dance the Castle walk one summer and as long as it lasted she was almost rushed at dances. And dancing counts as nothing else does.

(3) Expression that is facial expression, is one of your weakest points. A girl of your good looks and at your age ought to have almost perfect control of her face. It ought to be almost like a mask so that she'd have perfect control of any expression or impression she might wish to use.

a) A good smile and one that could be assumed at will, is an absolute necesity. You smile on one side which is absolutely wrong. Get before a mirror and practise a smile and get a good one, a "radiant smile" ought to be in the facial vocubulary of every girl. Practise it—on girls, on the family. Practise doing it when you dont feel happy and when you're bored. When youre embarrassed, when you're at a disadvantage. Thats when you'll have to use it in society and when you've practised a thing in calm, then only are you sure of it as a good weapon in tight places.

(b) A laugh isn't as important but its well to have a good one on ice. You natural one is very good, but your artificial one is bum. Next time you laugh naturally remember it and practise so you can do it any time you want. Practise anywhere.

(c) A pathetic, appealing look is one every girl ought to have. Sandra and Ginevra are specialists at this: so is Ardita, Its best done by opening the eyes wide and drooping the mouth a little, looking upward (hanging the head a little) directly into the eyes of the man you're talking to. Ginevra and Sandra use this when getting of their

"I'm so unpopular speeches and indeed they use it about half the time. Practise this.

(d) Dont bit or twist your lips—its sure death for any expression

(e) The two expressions <u>you</u> <u>have</u> <u>control</u> <u>over</u> now are no good. One is the side smile and the other is the thoughtful look with the eyes half closed.

I'm telling you this because mother and I have absolutely no control over our facial expressions and we miss it. Mothers worse than I am—you know how people take advantage of what ever mood her face is in and kid the life out of her.—Well you're young enough to get over it—tho' you're worse than I am now. The value of this practise is that whenever you're at a disadvantage you dont show it and boys hate to see a girl at a disadvantage.

<u>Practise</u> <u>Now</u>

<u>Dress and Personality.</u>

(A) No two people look alike in the same thing. but very few realize it. Shop keepers make money on the fact that the fat Mrs. Jones will buy the hat that looked well on the thin Mrs. Smith. You've got to find your type. To do so always look at girls about your <u>size</u> and <u>coloring</u> and notice what they look well in. Never buy so much as a sash without the most careful consideration <u>Study your type</u>. That is get your good points and accentuate them. For instance you have very good features—you ought to be able to wear jaunty hats and so forth.

(B) Almost all neatness is gained in man or woman by the arrangement of the hair. You have beautiful hair—you ought to be able to do something with it. Go to the best groomed girl in school and ask her and then wear it that way—Dont get tired and changed unless you're sure the new way is better. Catherine Tie is dowdy about her hair lately Dont I notice it? When Grace's hair looks well—She looks well When its unkempt it looks like the devil. Sandy and Betty always look neat and its their hair that does it.

(2)

(C) I'll line up your good points against your bad physically.

Good	Bad
Hair	Teeth only fair
Good general size	Pale complexion
Good features	Only fair figure
	Large hands and feet.

Now you see of the bad points only the last cannot be remedied. Now while slimness is a fashion you can cultivate it by exercise—Find out now from some girl. Exercise would give you a healthier skin. You should never rub cold cream into your face because you have a slight tendency to grow hairs on it. I'd find out about this from some Dr. who'd tell you what you could use in place of a skin cream.

(D) A girl should always be careful about such things as underskirt showing, long drawers showing under stockings, bad breath, mussy eyebrows (with such splendid eyebrows as yours you should brush them or wet them and train them every morning and night as I advised you to do long ago. They oughtn't to have a hair out of place.

(E) Walk and general physical grace. The point about this is that you'll be up against situations when ever you go out which will call for you to be graceful—not to be physically clumsly. Now you can only attain this by practise because it no more comes naturally to you than it does to me. Take some stylish walk you like and imitate it. A girl should have a little class. Look what a stylish walk Eleanor and Grace and Betty have and what a homely walk Marie and Alice have. Just because the first three deliberately practised every where until now its so natural to them that they cant be ungraceful—This is true about every gesture. I noticed last Saturday that your gestures are awkward and so unnatural as to seem affected. Notice the way graceful girls hold their hands and feet. How they stoop, wave, run and then try because you cant practise those things when men are around. Its too late then. They ought to be incentive then

(F) General summing up.

(1) dress scrupulously neatly and then forget your personal appearance. Every stocking should be pulled up to the last wrinkle.

(2) Dont wear things like that fussy hat that aren't becoming to you—At least buy no more. Take someone who knows with you—some one who really knows.

(3) Conform to your type no matter what looks well in the store

(4) Cultivate deliberate physical grace. You'll never have it if you dont. I'll discuss dancing in a latter letter.

(G) You see if you get any where and feel you look alright then there's one worry over and one bolt shot for self-confidence—and the person you're with, man, boy, woman, whether its Aunt Millie or Jack Allen o myself likes to feel that the person they're sponsoring is at least externally a credit.

APPENDIX 2

COMPOSITION OF "THE ICE PALACE," JULY 1920

This account, written by Fitzgerald for a feature called "Contemporary Writers and Their Work" in the periodical *The Editor*, describes the genesis and composition of "The Ice Palace." The text published below appeared in vol. 53 (Second July Number, 1920): 121–122; it was reprinted in *Correspondence*: 61–62.

The idea of "The Ice Palace" (Saturday Evening Post, May 22d), grew out of a conversation with a girl out in St. Paul, Minnesota, my home. We were riding home from a moving picture show late one November night.

"Here comes winter," she said, as a scattering of confetti-like snow blew along the street.

I thought immediately of the winters I had known there, their bleakness and dreariness and seemingly infinite length, and then we began talking about life in Sweden.

"I wonder," I said casually, "if the Swedes aren't melancholy on account of the cold—if this climate doesn't make people rather hard and chill—" and then I stopped, for I had scented a story.

I played with the idea for two weeks without writing a line. I felt I could work out a tale about some person or group of persons of Anglo-Saxon birth living for generations in a very cold climate. I already had one atmosphere detail—the first wisps of snow weaving like advance-guard ghosts up the street.

At the end of two weeks I was in Montgomery, Alabama, and while out walking with a girl I wandered into a graveyard. She told me I could never understand how she felt about the Confederate graves, and I told her I understood so well that I could put it on paper. Next day on my way back to St. Paul it came to me that it was all one story—the contrast between Alabama and Minnesota. When I reached home I had

(1) The idea of this contrast.

(2) The natural sequence of the girl visiting in the north.

(3) The idea that some phase of the cold should prey on her mind.

(4) That this phase should be an ice palace—I had had the idea of using an ice palace in a story since several months before when my mother told me about one they had in St. Paul in the eighties.

(5) A detail about snow in the vestibule of a railway train.

When I reached St. Paul I intrigued my family into telling me all they remembered about the ice palace. At the public library I found a rough sketch of it that had appeared in a newspaper of the period. Then I went carefully through my notebook for any incident or character that might do—I always do this when I am ready to start a story—but I don't believe that in this case I found anything except a conversation I had once had with a girl as to whether people were feline or canine.

Then I began. I did an atmospheric sketch of the girl's life in Alabama. This was part one. I did the graveyard scene and also used it to begin the love interest and hint at her dislike of cold. This was part two. Then I began part three which was to be her arrival in the northern city, but in the middle I grew bored with it and skipped to the beginning of the ice palace scene, a part I was wild to do. I did the scene where the couple were approaching the palace in a sleigh, and of a sudden I began to get the picture of an ice labyrinth so I left the description of the palace and turned at once to the girl lost in the labyrinth. Parts one and two had taken two days. The ice palace and labyrinth part (part five) and the last scene (part six) which brought back the Alabama motif were finished the third day. So there I had my beginning and end which are the easiest and most enjoyable for me to write, and the climax, which is the most exciting and stimulating to work out. It took me three days to do parts three and four, the least satisfactory parts of the story, and while doing them I was bored and uncertain, constantly re-writing, adding and cutting and revising—and in the end didn't care particularly for them.

That's the whole story. It unintentionally illustrates my theory that, except in a certain sort of naturalistic realism, what you enjoy writing is liable to be much better reading than what you labor over.

APPENDIX 3

ORIGINAL ENDING FOR "THE OFFSHORE PIRATE"

When Fitzgerald sent "The Offshore Pirate" (then entitled "The Proud Piracy") to Paul Revere Reynolds, his literary agent, on 27 January 1920, he called it "a very odd story" in his cover letter. Then he added: "If you think the end spoils it clip it off." Reynolds, perhaps with the concurrence of George Horace Lorimer, editor of the *Saturday Evening Post*, appears literally to have followed Fitzgerald's suggestion, scissoring the last two lines from page 37 and removing all of page 38 from the typescript of the story.

In this discarded ending one learns that Ardita's voyage with Toby Moreland was a dream, and that "Curtis Carlyle and his Six Black Buddies" was a vaudeville act seen by her maid, Félice, that spring.

The ending survives as a fragment, formerly in the papers of Harold Ober Associates, Inc., now in the Bruccoli Collection at the Thomas Cooper Library, University of South Carolina. The fragment bears revisions in a printed hand that Fitzgerald sometimes used when revising fair copies that he submitted to magazines or to publishers.

A diplomatic text of the clipped ending is given below; the pages are reproduced on the rear of the dust jacket of this edition. Canceled words appear within angle brackets; words added by Fitzgerald appear in bold type. The conclusion, with commentary, was first published by Jennifer McCabe Atkinson in "The Discarded Ending of 'The Offshore Pirate,'" *Fitzgerald/Hemingway Annual*, 1974: 47–49.

... Ardita's eyes opened slowly. It was very dark and quiet and she realized that it must be quite late. Her book had fallen from her

(38)

lap, but in her hand she still clutched the remains of a sucked lemon. She stretched herself and yawned and listened as she heard steps on the ladder and her uncle's panting as he climbed.

"Did you buy me a bathing suit, Félice?" she called.

Her maid's voice rose from the ladder.

"Ah no, ma'moselle. The store said he had no call for Ma'moselle's kind."

Mr. Farnam's head appeared, **then Mr. Farnam**, and after him Félice. He nodded at her coldly.

"You won't need a bathing suit;" he said, "we're starting north right away."

"Oh, shut up!" **suggested** <said> Ardita from sheer force of habit. She turned to her maid.

"Félice," she **demanded** <said>, "was it you who told me you'd seen a wonderful **vaudeville** act last spring called Curtis Carlyle and his Six **Black** <Brown> Buddies?"

"Yes — Ma'moselle, ah, it was truly marvelous —"

"Tell me," interrupted Ardita **eagerly**, "was Curtis Carlyle a dark-haired young man with blue eyes - very good looking?"

"Oh, no, Ma'moselle. Oh, <u>no</u>! He is small and ugly as sinning. He has grey hair and his legs they are bow-legged."

"Hm," remarked Ardita thoughtfully. "It's a darn funny world, isn't it, Felice?"

"Oh, yes," **agreed** <replied> Félice, "It's a darn funny world."

APPENDIX 4

COMPOSITION, PUBLICATION, AND EARNINGS

Composition dates and amounts earned for the stories have been taken from Fitzgerald's correspondence and from his professional ledger. Publication and price are for first U.S. serial appearances only; the fees are those paid before the literary agent's commission was deducted. Later appearances of the stories are listed in *F. Scott Fitzgerald: A Descriptive Bibliography* (rev. ed., 1987). Much of the information in this table appeared initially in Appendix A of Bryant Mangum's *A Fortune Yet: Money in the Art of F. Scott Fitzgerald's Short Stories* (New York: Garland, 1991). Abbreviations of magazine titles are as follows: *Saturday Evening Post* (SEP), *Smart Set* (SS), *Scribner's Magazine* (SM), *Metropolitan Magazine* (Metro), *Nassau Literary Magazine* (NLM).

FLAPPERS AND PHILOSOPHERS

Title	*Composed*	*Published*	*Price*
"The Offshore Pirate"	Feb. 1920	SEP, 192 (29 May 1920)	$500
"The Ice Palace"	Dec. 1919	SEP, 192 (22 May 1920)	$400
"Head and Shoulders"	Nov. 1919	SEP, 192 (21 Feb. 1920)	$400
"The Cut-Glass Bowl"	Oct. 1919	SM, 67 (May 1920)	$150
"Bernice Bobs Her Hair"	Jan. 1920	SEP, 192 (1 May 1920)	$500
"Benediction"	Oct. 1919	SS, 61 (Feb. 1920)	$ 40
"Dalyrimple Goes Wrong"	Sept. 1919	SS, 61 (Feb. 1920)	$40
"The Four Fists"	May 1919	SM, 67 (June 1920)	$150

ADDITIONAL STORIES

Title	*Composed*	*Published*	*Price*
"Babes in the Woods"	Mar. 1917	NLM, 73 (May 1917)	—
"Babes in the Woods"	Mar. 1919 (revised)	SS, 60 (Sept. 1919)	$30
"The Debutante"	Dec. 1917	NLM, 72 (Jan. 1917)	—
"The Debutante"	Apr. 1919 (revised)	SS, 60 (Nov. 1919)	$35
"Myra Meets His Family"	Dec. 1919	SEP, 192 (20 Mar. 1920)	$400
"The Smilers"	Sept. 1919	SS, 62 (June 1920)	$35
"The Popular Girl"	Nov. 1921	SEP, 194 (11 and 18 Feb. 1922)	$1,500
"Two for a Cent"	Sept. 1921	Metro, 55 (Apr. 1922)	$900